ARCHAON

EVERCHOSEN

'It seems we shall need an army,' Archaon announced. 'Fortunately for us, our gods have seen fit to furnish us with one – for it has long been in the ramblings of heretics and madmen that the greatest concentration of fighting men in the world can be found in the dread lands that are our path. We shall cross the Wastes. We shall kill the weak, conquer the strong and build an army of our own from the very best our enemies have to offer. Our banner shall bear the Ruinous Star of Chaos in all its glory. We shall best, commandeer and welcome warriors of all Dark Gods and creeds beneath the folds of its foetid fabric. It will be an army without equal. The Wastes will never know its like again, unless the gods of Chaos themselves decree so. I shall lead this army into the land of murder, where these ancient watchtowers will fall. The secrets of this Altar of Ultimate Darkness shall be mine and my host shall be sacrificed to the Ruinous Powers in its taking. This I pledge to my daemon gods – as always – with the blackness of my lost soul.'

In the same series

ARCHAON: LORD OF CHAOS
A novel by Rob Sanders

The story continues as Archaon's invasion begins in

WARHAMMER®
THE END TIMES

SIGMAR'S BLOOD
The Prequel to the End Times
Phil Kelly

THE RETURN OF NAGASH
Book One of the End Times
A novel by Josh Reynolds

THE FALL OF ALTDORF
Book Two of the End Times
A novel by Chris Wraight

THE CURSE OF KHAINE
Book Three of the End Times
A novel by Gav Thorpe

THE RISE OF THE HORNED RAT
Book Four of the End Times
A novel by Guy Haley

KINSLAYER
Book One of the Doom of Gotrek Gurnisson
A novel by David Guymer

SLAYER
Book Two of the Doom of Gotrek Gurnisson
A novel by David Guymer

DEATHBLADE
A Chronicle of Malus Darkblade
A novel by C L Werner

Visit blacklibrary.com *for more tales from the End Times, as well as many more Warhammer novels, novellas, audio dramas and Quick Reads, along with exclusive titles*

A WARHAMMER NOVEL

ARCHAON
EVERCHOSEN

Rob Sanders

BLACK LIBRARY

For TC, Jonah and Elliot – you know why…

A BLACK LIBRARY PUBLICATION

First published in Great Britain in 2014.
This edition published 2015 by
Black Library,
Games Workshop Ltd.,
Willow Road,
Nottingham, NG7 2WS, UK.

10 9 8 7 6 5 4 3 2 1

Cover by Raymond Swanland.
Map by Nuala Kinrade.

A CIP record for this book is available from the British Library.

UK ISBN: 978 1 84970 832 6
US ISBN: 978 1 84970 833 3

Printed and bound by CPI Group (UK) Ltd, Croydon, CR0 4YY

This is a dark age, a bloody age, an age of daemons and of sorcery. It is an age of battle and death, and of the world's ending. Amidst all of the fire, flame and fury it is a time, too, of mighty heroes, of bold deeds and great courage.

At the heart of the Old World sprawls the Empire, the largest and most powerful of the human realms. Known for its engineers, sorcerers, traders and soldiers, it is a land of great mountains, mighty rivers, dark forests and vast cities. And from his throne in Altdorf reigns the Emperor Karl Franz, sacred descendant of the founder of these lands, Sigmar, and wielder of his magical warhammer.

But these are far from civilised times. Across the length and breadth of the Old World, from the knightly palaces of Bretonnia to ice-bound Kislev in the far north, come rumblings of war. In the towering Worlds Edge Mountains, the orc tribes are gathering for another assault. Bandits and renegades harry the wild southern lands of the Border Princes. There are rumours of rat-things, the skaven, emerging from the sewers and swamps across the land. And from the northern wildernesses there is the ever-present threat of Chaos, of daemons and beastmen corrupted by the foul powers of the Dark Gods. As the time of battle draws ever near, the Empire needs heroes like never before.

NORTHERN LANDS UNDER THE
SHADOW OF CHAOS
North
Legendary battle
The Desolation of Galrauch
The Dreichei Bloodbath
The Dark Hunt
Yin
Manticorea
The Hung
Seagrave
Doom Crag
Cathay
Dreaded Wo
Naggaroth
Massacre at the Eyrie
Chi-An
Battle of 10,000 Blades
The Battle of Barking Dogs
Man-Chu
Weijin
Tu-Ka
Naggarond
Wei-Tu
Kuj
The Siege of the Great Bastion
The Bloody Revenge of Ulthspar
The Bane of Kzich-Lu
Hag Graef
Ghrond
Mung
The Eternal Battle
Avags
Khazags
Har Ganeth
Clar Karond
The Bloodrift
Ogdai Khan's Last Charge
The Kurgan
The Hydra Wars
The Cauldron
Aghols
The Nine Deaths of the Great Beast
Yusak
Karond Kar
The Tong War
Eastern Steppes
Arena of the Gods
Tong
Tokmars
The Mawhunt
Kvelligs
Bonespear's Last Stand
The Norscan Wars
Gharhars
Tahmaks
Hastlings
Dolgans
The Slaying of Jurgen's Wyrm
Tribeslaughter
Vargs
Bjornlings
Graelings
The Norse
Aeslings
Kul
The Trails of Hashut
Skaelings
Karak Dum
Sarls
Baersonlings
Sea of Chaos
The Fjordwar
Sea of Claws
Praag
The Invasion of the Pit
Blood River
The Dark Lands
Erengrad
The Battle of Cursed Mount
The Battle of Ten Thanes
Marienburg
The Sack of Mariengate
The Quenching of Gharakis
Worlds Edge Mountains
The Sacking of Requiel's Armada
The Empire
Silverspear's Conquest
Bonehell
Slaughter of Dark Fen
Kordi's Point
The Warpstone Wars

'Mortals are free to do as they will. The gods give them no choice.'

– *Imperial proverb*

VOLUME ONE

BORN OF BLOOD

'Smothered in the midnight
Draped in woe, sits dread itself,
Meditating misfortunes unknown.'

– Anspracher, *The Threads of Fate*

PROLOGUE

'O'er those unborn, whose ruin the light will grieve
wing'd harbingers sit to receive
and set such servants the world to cleave.'

– Fliessbach, *Tales Untold*

The Republic of Remas – Tilea
The Lands of the South
The Year of Light and Law (IC 1586)

'You shall know me by my works,' the prognosticator howled.

They knew him by his pain. The agonies erupting from his ruined face. The gasps of relief and hope – both sweet and dangerous – that escaped his broken body inbetween tortures. They called it the Cracker. An ugly name for an ugly contraption. With the victim's head braced between the unforgiving metal of a chin bar and a closing crown-cap, the two were drawn together by the slow turn of a handle screw. It had earned such a name for its effectiveness in producing confessions.

'Battista Gaspar Necrodomo,' a priestly witch hunter read from a blood-spattered scroll, 'his holy vengefulness, Solkan – God of Light and Law – has judged you witchfilth and false prophet, denying the poor and ignorant of this republic the comforts of his guidance.'

'You will know me by my works,' Necrodomo spat. His words escaped the clenched mantrap of his own jaw in a hissing rasp. Bloody lip-spittle sprayed the interrogator sitting opposite. One of the priests milling in the dungeon-darkness beyond tore a strip from his ragged grey robes.

'Grand inquisitori,' he mumbled, kissing the rag and handing it to his spiritual superior. The interrogator dabbed his speckled cheeks and the whiteness of his beard.

'Again,' the grand inquisitori said.

'No,' Necrodomo groaned, his pleadings pathetic and palsied. A priestly servant of Solkan turned the screw and fresh agonies filled the dungeon chamber. Necrodomo's screams were muffled shrieks of gargling desperation. As the turns of the screw abated, the freshly blinded seer sobbed and moaned.

'You are a charlatan,' the grand inquisitori said slowly, his voice threaded with the certainty of his age and station. He was the Avenger's high hand in these low dealings of the world. 'You are the herald of lies. You are an artist of nothings. You read the eye, the lip, the face and write false prophecy on the stars. You tell gullible widows what they want to hear, no? A sayer of soothings. Saw you this coming, prognosticator?'

'No…' Necrodomo managed through his shattered jaw.

'If you had stuck to prattlemongering,' the venerable inquisitori told him, 'you just might have escaped the attentions of the brotherhood. Though Avenger knows, your professed haruspexery would have been known to him – he who sees all and judges all. Your time would have come, Necrodomo. Necrodomo the foreteller. Necrodomo the skygazer. Necrodomo the reader of futures dark. Now to be known – if known at all – as Necrodomo the Insane. By my order.'

'No…' Necrodomo whimpered. 'Know…'

'This, however,' the grand inquisitori continued, picking up a bony fistful of pamphlets that littered the table, 'this goes beyond the pilfering of credulous coin. *The Celestine Prophecies*. *Signs and Wonders*. *Transcendentia*. *The Days of Doom to Come*. *The End Times*. This is heresy in our midst. This is demagoguery, spreading fear through the people. It is a challenge to the Republic. It is a corruption advertised and an invitation of vengeance. It is what brought us to you, Necrodomo. It is what brought you to this.'

The grand inquisitori gestured at the quill and pots of ink on the table and the thick, unmarked tome that sat before the groaning Necrodomo, its pages clean and waiting for his confession. 'Help me by helping yourself, Necrodomo. Confess your crimes to the brotherhood. Allow Solkan into your heart and I promise a death swift and clean enough to take you to his judgement. Why dally here in the meaningless filth of lies and conspiracy? Why suffer here as well as before the Lord of Light and Law? Commit your contrition to these pages and let me grant you the relief of death.'

'Forgive...' Necrodomo begged through shattered teeth.

'It is not for me to do so. Only the Avenger can grant you that. All I can grant you is an unburdened conscience and free passage. Your crimes are grievous. These bold pronouncements of coming apocalypse, printed and passed between the people. We are the light in the ignorance you sought to spread with your writings of the trembling world and the End Times you profess are to come. The world already trembles, Necrodomo. It trembles with the vengeance of Solkan the Mighty. It trembles with his judgement on the unnatural and the wicked. This is the greatest of your sins, false prophet. Fear is not your weapon to wield. It is ours. Armageddon is not yours to portend. The world is the Avenger's to destroy at a time of his choosing. If his servants fail, if the land can bear no more evil and the filth of corruption floods the–'

The oratory was shattered by a single clap. Followed by another. And another. Like the grand inquisitori, the witch hunters and priestly torturers of the chamber turned to the entrance. Stepping down from the rusted ladder that led from the trapdoor in the dungeon's ceiling, a lone priest in the hooded, ragged robes of the Avenger stood in slow applause. Sallow clouds of brimstone drifted down from the chamber above and descended about the interloper.

'How dare you interrupt the holy work of–' a priest began.

'Enough,' the interloper said, the word drenched in the sickly, mellifluous urgency of an infernal order. The final clap was louder and more insistent than the caustic applause that had preceded it. With the sound echoing about the dungeon like a thunderclap, the priests and servants of Solkan proceeded to untie the ropes about their waists and disrobe.

'What do you think you are doing?' the grand inquisitori barked at them. As he stared about in righteous incredulity, the witch hunters and interrogators crafted swift nooses from their belts. The grand inquisitori was out of his seat, his beard shaking and his eyes screwed up with rage. 'Stop this madness at once. The Avenger compels you.' He turned back to the priest standing at the ladder. Within the darkness of the interloper's hood, the inquisitori could make out the pin-prick glow of eyes ancient and burning like the embers of eternity. The inquisitori hadn't realised that he had soiled himself. A pool of urine was gathering on the filthy dungeon floor about him. 'Guards! Guards!' he roared. Above he could hear the clink of the plate, helms and halberds of the Reman Republican Guard.

The interloper looked up through the open trapdoor entrance. Something like a momentary storm passed through the chamber above, the influence of the sudden tempest felt on Necrodomo's apocalyptic pamphlets, which were blown from the table. The screams were brief. With the interloper still staring through the dungeon opening, it began to rain blood. The Republican Guard gaolers were now nothing but a cruel drizzle drifting, dripping and dribbling from the trapdoor entrance. The interloper allowed the downpour to blotch his robes to a gory crimson. As his ghastly gaze returned to the grand inquisitori, the trapdoor slammed shut and thundered with heavy chains securing the dungeon entrance.

The robed thing moved across the chamber with the dread purpose of something unreal. As it passed them the servants of Solkan dropped from stools and improvised furniture to dance a spasmodic jig from their belt-nooses and the rings set in the dungeon ceiling. The interloper drifted through the forest of hanging priests.

'Sit,' it commanded.

The grand inquisitori wailed as his knees gave way, causing him to fall back into his interrogator's throne.

The interloper moved towards the throne like an ancient evil. It pulled back its hood, revealing the full, unspeakable horror of its daemonic visage to the chamber. The robes fell like a fearful whisper from its barbed unflesh. It grew with each flagstone-pulverising step of its taloned feet, twisted bones blooming with muscle that ruptured into existence about them, lending the beast a glorious brawn and sinew. It dragged a serpentine tail, shot through with spikes, behind its infernal form, while both the daemon-crown of horns warping their way out of its head and the thumb-claws erupting from the dreadful magnificence of its wings scraped the dungeon ceiling.

Like a nightmare, it lowered its blood-curdling skull and moved up behind the interrogator's throne. Necrodomo, still clamped between the bar and crown-cap of the torture device, had no eyes with which to behold the beast. The grand inquisitori found, with his heart in the grasp of terror, cold, dark and despair that he could not move. As the daemon brought its unseen face forward, both the venerable priest and the prognosticator found their cheeks bathed in the radiance of infernal royalty. A princely power of hellish birthright; a creature of unimaginable darkness; horror incarnate.

The grand inquisitori felt the thing touch him. At once all that had remained pure and noble in the man shrivelled within his soul. Darkness blossomed within the priest. Every ill-deed committed in the service of selfish weakness and temptation grew through his being like a rampant cancer. His eyes turned to inky twilight as his face became a cadaverous mask of ghoulish anticipation. The daemon clasped the grand inquisitori's head in its claws.

'You search for darkness in wretched madmen,' the daemon prince whispered to the venerable priest – every word falling on the inquisitori with the force of a furnace, 'when you should have been searching for it within your own ranks. No matter… You are mine now and have no need for this vessel of flesh. Before I take your soul, there is something you should know, priest. A gift for the journey *you* are about to take.' The daemon leant in closer. 'Your. God. Is. A. Lie.' With that, the daemon prince crushed the grand inquisitori's skull between its claws with effortless ease.

Slashing both the headless body and the back of the throne from the seat with a swoosh of its serpent tail, the daemon prince took a seat before Necrodomo. Necrodomo the foreteller. Necrodomo the reader of futures dark. Necrodomo the Insane. The thing drummed its talons across the desk, prompting the torturous contraption known as the Cracker to rust to disintegration about the blind prisoner's head. Necrodomo pulled away immediately. The prognosticator was out of his mind with pain, but something spiritual and instinctive told him that he was in the presence of a dangerous evil. He felt fear without sight. Dread without sanity. Being contorted within the vice for so long, Necrodomo found that his legs no longer supported him. Crashing to the filthy floor he scrabbled away from the daemon prince like an animal until he felt his back against the cold stone of the dungeon wall.

'Do not fear me,' the beast told him. 'I am your saviour – as you are mine. My name, for all it matters to you, madman, is Be'lakor.' The monster allowed the 'r' of its name to hang like a forlorn echo. 'I am known by many titles: the Harbinger, the Herald and the Bearer.

To the northmen, I am the Shadowlord. In the Empire and the *civilised* lands of the south, I am the Dark Master. To you, mortal, I am simply Master.'

Necrodomo curled up in agony. He was rocking, shaking and whimpering.

'You are Necrodomo. Though your heretic name shall be whispered in the shadows, your work shall echo through eternity.'

Be'lakor looked down on the pamphlets decorating the desk. 'I am an appreciator of your work – charlatan or not. Now I wish to become facilitator. Your masterpiece is yet to be written.'

The beast laid its claw on the empty tome intended for the prognosticator's confession. Under the touch of its talons, the leather of the cover moaned and warped to a gruesome ghastliness. Its spine became as barbed bone and the bronze lock-clasps holding its pages closed melted into sets of jaws that snapped open. The cover smoked as hellfire scorched fresh lettering into the leather. As the tome writhed to stillness and Be'lakor removed his talon, the words *LIBER CAELESTIOR* afflicted the cover in the dark tongue of his Ruinous masters, accompanied by the name BATTISTA GASPAR NECRODOMO.

'We shall wield your prophecies like a weapon,' the Dark Master told him. 'We shall make history together, you and I. We shall unite the gods and harness war, famine and plague in honour of a champion of ultimate darkness. We shall craft through destiny a warrior worthy of the challenges to come. Worthy to bear the blessing of each of my Ruinous masters in equal measure and be called Everchosen of Chaos. He will be the key, as I am the keeper of the coming apocalypse. Between us, we shall herald the coming of the End Times – the doom you spoke of, my friend. Rejoice, soothsayer. They are coming. When we do… when I have no more need of your words or his deeds, I shall assume the Everchosen's flesh in true coronation – the flesh your prophecies shall exalt to the status of legend – and I shall take my rightful place as Lord of the End Times. Once more the world will be mine to plunge into darkness and ruin.'

Necrodomo groaned and shrieked. If the pain of torture hadn't driven him into the embrace of insanity, then the daemon prince's words had. He was gone – a willing host to oblivion that, like a leech, sapped him of the last of his mental strength. The prognosticator moaned insensibilities. He laughed at his agonies and shrieked at nothing. Necrodomo let go and Be'lakor let him.

'No matter,' the daemon prince said to the madman. He opened the tome to its first blank page and selecting a quill, dipped it into the ink on the table. 'I will assist you. I will transcribe. I have a name already. The name I shall bequeath my champion. The name I shall eventually take, with the body of the Everchosen I shall possess and assume. A name of your southern tongue, prognosticator, honouring both the ancient I have been and the eternity I have yet to become. We shall be known as... Archaon.'

'There comes to the Emperor's shores
one night, driven before a storm,
a gift in the guise of a child
unknowing, unknown and unsought.

'From womb to sea he is returned,
a victim of the churning surf –
to be saved by a fisherman
who sees the gift and not the curse.

'The error of the innocent –
a commoner baseborn and bred,
will never cost the land so dear
or put its people to the test.

'If murder comes more easily –
or rude compassion shows its heel,
then worlds old and new will be saved
from the coming catastrophe.

'For despite early clemency,
and the God-King's watchful gaze
The child finds its path to darkness
and returns not man but plague.'

– Necrodomo the Insane,
The Liber Caelestior (The Celestine Book of Divination)

CHAPTER I

'–Art thou some darknid thing?
Wielding accident and advantage from the shadows?
Some spirit, some fiend, some godless fury from afar, that stays the dice and winds the thread of life about its claws,
that turns blood to ice and shivers the spine,
With dark providence and blessed tragedies?
Tell me devil, what thou art.'

– Geisenberg, *Destinations*

The village of Hargendorf
Nordland Coast – The Empire
Dunkelstag, IC 2390

The north. The north. Always the north. Out of the north they came, riding the storm. The rough wool cloth of their sails knew it. The rotting timbers of their clinkered hulls knew it. The marauders knew it in their hot bones and salt-stained flesh. This was no natural tempest. A wretched squall that had slammed the northmen from their bloody course and swept them south before gales serrated like their weapons, and rain fell like pellets of frosted iron. A blessing from the north. From the Wastes. From the Powers allowed to be.

Vargs, far from home. Like fire on the water, they lived for the basest expression of their miserable existence. War – wherever it could be found, women and the favours that could be ripped from them, and the cruel laughter that could be drawn from mens' bellies in the face of calamities wrought. When not engaged in such mordant pursuits, the northmen might have remembered to eat or sleep or attend to their weapons, their vessels or the monstrous darkness to which they had pledged their lives. Their names were made up of consonants that cut the mouth and their hearts were hollow and black. Some bore the ghastly afflictions of their calling but most were ugly enough before – being grizzled of limb, scarred of flesh and ragged of beard. They cursed the elements and spat in the face of Manann, god of the seas for his free passage. They honoured their patron Powers with action. They honoured them with the wolfish howls they roared at the tumultuous skies, as their boats cut through the range of mountainous waves before them and revealed the glint of torches and lanterns. The coast of some victim nation. The darkened shore.

As the storm smashed them on, lightning seethed through the sky. The world was fit to break. The furious flashes revealed a shale beach. On the shore sat a collection of beached fishing boats, rocking in the storm. Beyond lay a fishing village. Innocent. Provocative. Vulnerable. The barbarians stood in their dripping furs and spiked armour. They could already feel the spray of hot blood across their faces. The screams and the begging that aroused them so, soothing the mind and ear. The ache of omnipotence flooded their being. Hands stain-speckled with death reached for the tools of their trade – wicked blades, slender axes and spear shafts of saturated gore. They were the storm. The sudden and sickening eruption of forces unknown upon the helpless and afeared. The stinking and smoking ruin that their progress left in its path – the northmen's advertisement to the world. They were there. They robbed. They ravaged. They murdered. And they lived.

The hovel's roof flashed white in the storm. Rain lashed the windows clean and the shrieking north wind battered the door with the insistence that it be admitted. As the oldest homestead in Hargendorf and one of the closest to the beach, the hovel bore the full fury of the coming storm. Within, a fish broth bubbled above the fire, both being attended by Viktoria Rothschild. It was cold for the time of year but storms didn't bother Viktoria. She was a fisherman's daughter and a fisherman's wife. The north winds warranted nothing more than a shawl. She had nets to mend and three young boys to tend to.

Otto pretended to be asleep in his bunk. He had never liked the Nordland storms and his father feared for the kind of fisherman he would make. His brother Dietfried, on the other hand, pushed his face to the window, feeling the drum of droplets through the glass and his nose. As thunder shook the hovel and lightning bleached the young boy's face, his mother called him away. Dietfried retreated. A little. Only Lutz seemed oblivious to the tempest, sitting with his mother by the fire. He had no intention of helping her. With a stomach like a grotto or sea cave, the boy merely waited for his broth and the salt bread that would go with it.

Viktoria sighed. Lutz's stomach was usually a good indicator of when her husband Roald was due to return. In weather like this she expected him even earlier but reasoned that the boats would need dragging further up the beach and securing in the storm. Between the claps of thunder she heard the sound of boots on shale. Roald was home. She handed bowls and wooden spoons to Lutz from the shelf.

'Set the table for your father,' Viktoria told the boy. 'Dietfried, help your brother.'

When Dietfried didn't reply, the fishwife turned on him with a face like the squall. 'Dietfried,' she carped, heading to unbar the door, her hands busy with salt bread. The boy was staring out of the window. He looked back at her, his face cast in shadows of concern by the flashing outside.

'Mother…' he began, turning back to the window.

There was shouting. Course and guttural. With bread in hand, Viktoria approached the window. Shadows passed before it in quick succession. The shadows of men in the village, but instead of nets and boat hooks and buckets, their hands glinted with the metal of blades, spear tips and axes.

Viktoria dropped the bread.

She grabbed Dietfried and went to pull him away from the window. The horror held them there, however. There was screaming now. Hedda Molinger was dead. Viktoria heard it. She had probably gone out to greet her husband, Edsel. The Rodeckers' dog was barking and then promptly stopped. Old Mother Irmgard was suddenly out in the street, the centre of a mob of kicking and stamping. Bertilda's boys Gelbert and Jorgan were straight out into the unfolding havoc but within moments were on their knees and pleading for their lives, but their entreaties went unheeded.

Viktoria couldn't quite catch her breath. She hauled Dietfried back and found both Lutz and Otto – awake and out of bed – clutching at her skirts. She looked about the hovel. They were fisherfolk and had little coin to spend on weapons like swords. She wouldn't know what to do with it even if she had one. The best they had was a wood axe but it was wedged in a log amongst the firewood piled outside the door.

She felt her heart hammer in her chest. As the shadows continued to flash by the window and she could hear the crunch of boots up the beach and into the village, she felt the hammering accelerate to a lightheaded flutter. She went to say something to her children but the words wouldn't come. A silhouette eclipsed the storm at the window. It was a man. Big in his furs and spiked armour. He wasn't running into the havoc unfolding in the centre of Hargendorf like the others. He had stayed to finish Old Mother Irmgard, while his barbarian battle-kin had surged on to pillage and slaughter children and womenfolk.

He stood still like a predator, the wind and rain whipping about him. The shape of a woman tore by, shrieking the name 'Brigette'. Through the glass, Viktoria saw it was Carla Vohssen. The marauder sprung like a trap, snatching the screaming woman by the hair and pulling her into the hovel wall. His shadow held hers there. She fought but the barbarian stood like a statue above her. Viktoria heard the slow sound of a blade escaping its scabbard. Carla Vohssen's voice was a strangled whisper. She alternated between begging and praying but the marauder silenced her with a single 'Sssshhhhhh' from behind his helmet. As the tip of his broad blade dimpled her flesh, Viktoria heard Carla fall once again to screaming and struggling. Her elbow crashed through the hovel window, allowing the storm to scream inside. Viktoria clutched her children to her and retreated further into the hovel.

Viktoria felt her children cling to her. In the distance the shrine bells were ringing. The temple. It somehow calmed Viktoria. She knew she had to act. Pushing Dietfried, Otto and Lutz to the corner of the hovel, she lifted the mound of fishing nets waiting for her attention there. There was no time for words, even ones of maternal comfort. They were all too scared. The boys instinctively understood what their mother wanted and crawled beneath, Dietfried's hand lingering on Viktoria's as she positioned the netting over them. An impact on the hovel door sent the child's hand shooting back beneath the material. Viktoria stood bolt upright.

The shadow was missing from the window. The marauder's armoured boot slammed into the door but it was barred against the storm and held. Viktoria slipped the knife she had been using to gut the fish off the table. She backed towards the fire, the stinking blade behind her. She watched. She waited.

The third impact splintered the bar in two and the smashed door was battered aside, allowing the maelstrom in. Framed in the doorway, in the flaring storm, in her nightmares, was the marauder. Rain cascaded from his furs and the urchin-like outline of his armour. Where leather, mail and plate failed to contain the northman's brawn, his flesh was tattooed and scarred. Centred about his heart and crossing one great pectoral muscle, the warrior had a rough tattoo in the shape of an eight-pointed star. Viktoria felt both drawn to and despairing of the symbol but decided that it would be the best place to bury her knife when she had the chance. The warrior's helm was horned and covered his face. Light was admitted by a number of rough puncture holes in the faceplate that, for all Viktoria knew, afflicted the marauder's hidden face also. The tempest whipped Carla's lifeblood and gore from the huge blade of the sword in the marauder's mailed fist.

He entered. Slowly. Like his knife had the girl outside. His sea-drenched boots carried him calmly across the hovel. There was no frenzied attack. Nothing like the butchery behind him as marauders moved through the village like a pack of wolves, slashing, tearing and sharing. Viktoria picked up a plate and threw it, and another, but they bounced uselessly off the marauder's chest. He kept coming. Slow. Deliberate. His blade held in casual readiness. He reached out for her but she retreated, grabbing the pot of fish broth by one burning handle and flinging it awkwardly at the warrior. As the heavy pot clattered to the floor, the boiling broth steamed off the marauder's scalded flesh and armour. If he felt pain, the warrior didn't show it.

Viktoria backed away. She felt a sob erupt from her. Futility and frustration. She was about to die and she knew it. At the sound the boys beneath the fishing net stifled their own terror, as the marauder's helm drew around to the corner of the hovel. The action turned

Viktoria's stomach to stone. She reached into the fire for a partially burning log. She would torch the northerner. His mailed fist snapped around her wrist like vice. She strained but the warrior held her there. She felt his balance change. The tip of his sword was up and resting on her stomach. He intended to skewer her like he had Carla.

And the marauder would have done, but Viktoria brought the knife from behind her back with her other hand and thrust the blade at the tattoo of the star across the monster's heart. The tip of the knife punctured the skin and slipped partly into the warrior's flesh. The marauder was no fish, however. Muscle, bone and whatever protection the unholy symbol offered barred the way to his heart. As Viktoria stood there, frozen with horror, an instant of dark connection was made between their two souls, their two bodies. Shocked and sickened, she released her grip on the weapon, and tried to pull away.

He looked down at the knife protruding from his flesh, then back at Viktoria. She thought she saw his eyes, the light of the fire penetrating the helmet and revealing the jaundiced, bloodshot peace of his gaze. He released her wrist but backhanded her away from the fire. The mailed palm took several of the fishwife's teeth and she hit the wall with an ugly, head-gashing crack. The children squealed from beneath the netting.

'Stay where you are,' Viktoria called to them. 'Mummy's all right.'

The knife clanged to the floor as the marauder swept his own weapon around, smashing the handle down and the blade tip from his flesh. He turned towards the mound of nets but Viktoria called, 'No'. She spat blood. She sobbed. 'Here. Here.'

She backed into the hovel's only other room. The bedroom. She was crying. The marauder stopped. He considered. Finally he slid his sword slowly back into its scabbard. The marauder advanced. Viktoria retreated. She cried out as the back of her legs hit the bed. She fell back into the blankets. The marauder entered. In his armour and helm he seemed to fill the tiny room. Thunder crashed. The wind moaned. The skies wept.

Viktoria lifted her back from the covers.

'No,' she wept.

The marauder brought his mail fist up to the helm and extended a finger. 'Sssshhhhhhh,' he told her.

Someone was behind him. The warrior went for his sword and turned. The boat hook smashed through the side of both his helm and skull. Roald Rothschild held him there for a moment, the fisherman's weapon keeping the marauder in place as he began to tremble and shake. Rothschild had no warrior skill. He had been fortunate in both his approach and the hook's destination. Fear had driven him on. A husband's wrath had carried him through doubt. The ungainly wickedness of his improvised weapon had done the rest. Lowering the warrior to his armoured knees, Roald shook the hook loose from the twisted metal of the helm and allowed his victim to fall. The marauder crashed onto the floor and fell into a brief fit, the insides of his head leaking out of the side of the helmet, before finally falling silent and still.

All Viktoria could see was her husband. His beard hid the grimness on his lips. Dietfried, Otto and Lutz were suddenly about his legs, crying. He put his finger to his lips and bid them be quiet before extending a hand to his wife. Viktoria took it and the family fled the hovel, heading into the storm – Roald's fishing boat waiting for them, a little way up the rain-lashed beach.

Legends are not made in this way…

The Dark Master will not be thwarted thus. What is a prophecy if not a truth promised to be? The skill is knowing where to exert force. It is true that with so many competing forces in the world, so many invested entities and powers, with so many destinies at odds, it is nigh but impossible to change the great happenings of the age – any age – directly. There is balance, except when there is not. With a lever long enough, however, I could balance it across the great mountains of the Worlds Edge and prise mighty Morrslieb from the night sky.

This world was once mine. A glorious ruin of ash and flame. It will be again. And so like the pages of a book, flicked back to read again that which was missed the first time, I bring forth my instrument of destruction. He, who is destined for Armageddon's crown. He, whose anointed flesh is destined to be my own. Archaon… will be.

Small changes can make a big difference – sometimes, all the difference.

Which is why this time the shrine bells of Hargendorf never rang.

CHAPTER I

'Every new beginning comes from some other beginning's end.'

– Senectra the Younger, *Dialogues*

The village of Hargendorf
Nordland Coast – The Empire
Mitterfruhl, IC 2391

The water was cold, as was her purpose. Viktoria Rothschild stood in the shallows. She had been crouching there for some time and her legs were numb. The waters splashed up against her knees and swollen belly and on up along the shale beach. She looked out across the bay. Beyond extended the Sea of Claws and beyond that, only the gods knew what. The sea had been good to her family. To her father. To her father's father. To herself, Roald and the boys. It was a giver of life. Dietfried, Otto and Lutz had grown strong and healthy on whatever the sea had provided for them. Roald had his boat. She sold the fish he caught. The sea *had* been good to them.

Manann's realm could be fickle, however. As well as giver it was also the taker of life. Isolde Altoff's boy Hanke had drowned off

Stukker Nook. Viktoria's cousin Gretel had been taken by a wyrm on the beaches of Lugren when Viktoria had been just a teenager. Three generations of the Lassowitz family had been lost in one night during a squall on the Hunderbank. The sea would take another that morning.

The slosh of the waves and the offshore breeze stole her grunts and exertions. She was a mother of three fine boys. She had done this before. About her the water was a murky crimson. She cried for the last few minutes. Above, dark clouds were gathering and the wind turned.

'Viktoria!'

It was Roald. He had been running up the beach calling her name. His boots took him into the shallows. 'Gods, woman, no,' he said, swirling about the bloody waters with his big hands. 'Viktoria, no.'

She turned to him and staggered. He caught her and held her for a moment. He looked out to sea while she peered back up the shale beach to the hovel. It was one of the last standing after the terrible night of slaughter nine months before. The hovel that had admitted the marauder and borne witness to the dark gift he had bestowed on Viktoria Rothschild. The gift of a child unwanted. Viktoria blinked the salt from her eyes. If only there had been a warning. If only the shrine bells had rung. If only Roald and the fishermen had returned earlier. But they hadn't and Viktoria had bought herself and her children time with her miseries.

'We shall be punished for this,' Roald told her. 'The gods will punish us.'

Viktoria held him a little longer.

'We've been punished enough,' Viktoria said bleakly, before wading out of the shallows and back up the shale. Otto and Lutz were playing outside, while Dietfried watched them from up the beach, from where he had been helping his father with the catch.

Roald Rothschild remained, the waves rising and falling about him. He looked but saw nothing. The sea had taken the child. It was one with the depths. He cast his gaze up at the haemorrhaging sky. There would be another storm. It was the season. The fisherman's lips moved silently. Roald Rothschild prayed. He prayed to Manann. He prayed to Sigmar. He prayed to any and all that were listening. Little could he know that a force dark and powerful had indeed heard his fearful prayers.

You would consign fate, crafted in flesh and blood, to the depths? The gifts of Chaos are not to be refused. They are not demanded or earned, they are visited upon mortals at the pleasure of Dark Gods and the princes of ruin.

This story cannot be untold. The will of daemons cannot be undone. It is decided. Doom lives on. Damnation endures. From the darkness of the depths to the darkness of the womb, the gift shall be returned.

And so I petition the moons and turn back the tide. The black depths reject that which has been rejected. Once more the fruit is swollen with the seed of doom. This child shall live and in doing so bring about the death of all the world. Consider this already done. Done in the name of god-thwarted Be'lakor.

CHAPTER I

Now it is the time of night,
when fears surmount their mighty sum,
and the grave gapes forth its welcome.

– Nelkenthal, *The Raven's Call*

The village of Hargendorf
Nordland
Nacht der Kranken, IC 2391

Viktoria sent Dietfried for the midwife from Schlaghugel. Gunda Schnass had brought all three of her sons successfully into the world and Viktoria would have no one else for the fourth. Although a lapsed follower of Shallya, Gunda made her offerings to the God-King at Dempster's Rock. The temple was nearer and according to Dietfried – who she had also delivered – there was little time. Gunda didn't even know Viktoria was expecting. It seemed strange after the tragedy that had befallen Hargendorf. There was so much work to do in rebuilding and managing the catch alone that another child – so soon – struck Gunda as an extra burden. Asking for Sigmar's blessing on her work and strong sons for his Empire, the midwife made her way to Hargendorf with Dietfried Rothschild walking miserably behind. She tried to prise some conversation from the boy on their journey but he would not be drawn. He had turned into a serious child, hard of face and burdened by his thoughts. The midwife expected little else from the youngling: he had been taken by the heel and dipped in tragedy head first. He had seen things no one was meant to see.

Gunda had had no reason to visit the fishing village in the past few months. The marauder attack had been swift and brutal. Hovels and boats had been put to the flame while men, women and children had been put to the sword. Gunda waddled through the ash-drowned ruins, the slaughter and decimation evident everywhere: in the torched timbers, in the stains of old blood on the cobbles, in the absence of gossip and children's laughter on the air.

She found the Rothschilds' hovel at the edge of the shale where she had left it four years before, after bringing the angel-faced Otto into the world. It was easy to find. It was one of the only buildings left standing. The Rothschilds had been fortunate that terrible night. Roald had got Viktoria and the children out and to his boat, the family taking refuge in the storm-mauled bay while the village burned on the shore. Few others had been so fortunate. Others who had survived had left, leaving the atrocities at Hargendorf behind – though as a survivor of life's myriad misfortunes herself, Gunda knew that you could walk to the other side of the Empire and never quite escape the darkness of your past. It waited for you behind the closing of each eye, to be relived each night.

She didn't bother to knock. Viktoria's suffering could be heard up the empty street. The hovel was dark and muggy. Roald stood by the fire. He was impassive, like one of the wooden statues lining the temple at Dempster's Rock. He said nothing. A pot of water boiled over a spitting fire. The children were seated at the table, tearing material into the rags Gunda would need. There was no greeting from the younglings either. Dietfried joined them. Their eyes were directed through the bedroom door, on their mother and her pain. The last time they had heard their mother scream had been nine months before, on the night of the attack. The night the marauders arrived. The night the marauder crossed the doorstep and entered their lives.

'Well, let's get started then,' Gunda said, rolling up her sleeves. She thought she should say something. In reality, Viktoria was well on her way but it was proving to be a troublesome birth. The midwife washed her hands. She told Viktoria that everything would be all right. Roald and the children just stared, as though seeing something far off. Gunda wasn't happy. Viktoria's cries were unnaturally harsh for a mother already of three. The tide came in. The sun went down. The midwife pressed on with the difficult birth. Viktoria reached out for Roald but the fisherman stayed by the fire, sending the children across the room when Gunda needed something. Viktoria's suffering went on into the night. She became weaker and more frightened and Gunda felt the woman slipping from her grasp.

The baby was born to silence. It was a strong little thing, Gunda had to admit. A boy. Few children she had brought into the world had endured such a delivery. It had fought its way through the first trial of its life and emerged bloody, bonny and full of fight. Its screams seemed to produce a reaction in the family. The children too fell to sobbing but they were not tears of joy. No thanks were offered to the gods and so it fell to Gunda to mumble a prayer to Sigmar – as she had done in his temple some hours before – acknowledging that another son of the Empire had been born.

With the child wrapped in swaddling and placed on the bed, Gunda turned her attentions back to Viktoria. She told her how brave she had been. How well she had fought to see her son into the world. That she had attended few births so difficult. She lifted water to her lips from a ladle but Viktoria would not take it. Her eyes fluttered and her head fell to one side.

'Don't do this, lassie,' Gunda said, but then the convulsions started. Viktoria was experiencing some kind of violent fit. Arms flew out and her legs kicked across the bed. 'The baby!' Gunda cried out. 'Get the baby.' Roald and the children just watched. Moving the child to the floor and away from the violence of his mother's passing, Gunda attempted to hold Viktoria down. Bracing a wound rag across her mouth like a bridle, the midwife tried to stop her biting down on her own tongue. 'Roald,' the midwife called. 'Get over here and help me.'

Putting one horrified foot in front of the other, Roald made it across the hovel and into the bedroom. The children, now descended into a sobbing mess, followed him. The four of them joined Gunda by the bed. Together they held their mother down. They felt the heat of her skin and the last of the fight within her, until finally she fell still. The children wept into the blankets. Roald bawled his grief at his wife's silence. The baby cried for attention it would not get. Gunda felt her own tears come. She backed away from the bed feeling like an intruder, knowing that the family needed this moment alone.

'I'm so sorry,' she murmured before making for the door. It seemed to take an eternity to reach it.

'Take it with you,' Roald managed, snatching a breath.

'Roald, no,' Gunda said.

'I beg you,' the fisherman cried, his sorrow cutting through him like a sword. His face was a contorted mask of unbearable woe.

'He's your son, man,' Gunda implored.

'He's not my son,' Roald barked, his anger driving his whimpers away. 'He's not my son.'

Gunda stared at them all. The inconsolable younglings. The fisherman, his shoulders broad and taut, as if under some fresh burden. Viktoria Rothschild, bloody and broken on the bed. She came to understand how tragedy might have intruded on the household that dreadful night nine months ago. How the Rothschilds might not have been as fortunate as gossip had supposed. 'Take it,' Roald hissed through his pain and gritted teeth. 'Or I will see to it that the tide will.'

The midwife nodded, picked up the child and held the swaddling to her chest. She opened the door. It was the dead of night. The sky was open and a chill breeze felt its way through the layers of her clothing.

'I'm truly sorry,' the midwife said, tears rolling down her rounded cheeks.

Gunda settled into her hood and, pulling the babe close to the warmth of her body, set off into the Nordland night.

CHAPTER II

'Thus Gerreon's blade found its way to
Pendrag's heart and love,
and the winds took its wielder north to the
realm of bear and wolf,
Sigmar followed with a sword-brother's
rage – eager to avenge fair Pendrag's blood,
He searched for dark Gereon through mount
and wood,
But vengeance turned to calling with Sigmar
crushing the Norsii beneath his boot.'

– Hollenstein, *Chronicles*

The Schlaghugel Road
Nordland
Pendragstag, IC 2391

The Schlaghugel Road was a ghoulish ribbon winding its way between the gurgling darkness that was the River Demst and the dread of Laurelorn Forest. *Road* was a charitable description for the channel-hugging pathway that couldn't decide whether it was wagon-hardened earth, moss-threaded gravel or the occasional lonely cobblestone. It was the small hours of the night and there were no merchant wagons travelling the road. Not a messenger. Not a mail coach. Not even a footpad or highwayman. Both Swift Nikolaus and 'Six-Fingered' Dirk were regular sights on the route. Killers both, Gunda Schnass would even have welcomed the company of such robbers on the Schlaghugel Road that night. The breeze hissed like a serpent through towering treetops, which drooped like closing jaws over the miserable path.

Gunda would never ordinarily have left a birth. Traditionally a midwife would remain until morning. Both mother and baby needed care, comfort and advice. The passage was safer during the day and with their wives resting, husbands were sometimes reticent about payment for the midwifery services rendered. The Rothschilds' tragedy did not allow for such luxury, however, and Gunda found herself out on the open road, late into the night with a mewling child drawing the attention of every wretched thing that haunted the edge of the forest. Gunda saw shapes moving through the brush and the glint of eyes in moonlight.

It was cold. The heavens were cloudless and the constellations hung above the forest like secret signs and indecipherable symbols. Gunda wasn't much of a reader as it was and her talents certainly didn't extend to interpreting the stars. The midwife peered up into the depths of the heavens with ignorance and suspicion. The sky didn't look good, whatever it said. It wasn't helped by the moons. Mannslieb's great disk was settled amongst the treetops, staining them a sickly yellow. Morrslieb was in the ascendant, rising high overhead, throwing its dread radiance down upon all that might walk, crawl or creep through the Laurelorn Forest.

Gunda hugged the child close to her. The boy was wet and hungry. His bawling left the midwife in no doubt of his displeasure. Although she had taken the child at Roald's insistence, she had little idea what she was to do with him. She was too old to raise him herself. She was a midwife but her husband Ambros had long passed. Her daughter was a wet nurse in Beilen and there was an orphanage in distant Dieterschafen – but neither would take the boy if they knew the circumstances of his conception. The reavers and marauders of the north were known to be polluted from their compacts with dark forces and enjoyed visiting that pollution on others.

Gunda found herself singing a low tune. Something her father had taught her as a child – *The Knight's Dalliance* – about a knight's encounter one night with a beautiful elfin stranger on the empty roads of the Laurelorn Forest. It was a deceptively cheerful tune but did not end well. Despite the comfort it gave her, Gunda allowed the song to trail off on the breeze, lest it attract the attentions of some lonely member of the elder races, whose villages were rumoured to haunt the depths of the forest hereabouts.

She heard the growls first. Low, predacious rattles from the back of blood-slick throats. As she crunched her way along the Schlaghugel Road, Gunda couldn't help looking behind her – hoping for a farmer on a cart of hay or a fellow traveller on foot. Instead she discovered dark shapes that dribbled from the shadowy treeline, like an ink blot running on parchment. Ulric's children. Wolves drawn from the forest by Morrslieb's boldness. They snapped and snarled. They skulked up behind her in a loose pack, waspish in their wasted want. Their eyes glinted with craven hunger.

Even if the child's mewling hadn't drawn their ragged ears, the pack could probably smell the baby's unwashed body. Holding the babe to her bust, Gunda snatched a rock from the road and tossed it at the beasts. The crack of the stone off the road shot through the night. The wolves kept their distance, hugging her scent along the river. Their numbers grew and the midwife's heart sank with every step. The forest fiends would soon tire of their fearful game. Their number would overcome their feral caution with baying and the baring of teeth. They would attack. Before long all Gunda could think of was the sun rising over her bone-picked corpse. Darker thoughts still were prompted by the snapping of the emboldened monstrosities at her heels. She would not die for this child. This screeching orphan. This northman's mongrel.

Morrslieb, full and furious, leered over the treetops at her. With each of the midwife's prayer-mumbling steps, however, a silhouette rose from the canopy. Framed in the moon's lurid glare was Sigmar's glorious form. Cut out of the moon's surface like a shadow, the unmistakable outline of the Heldenhammer rose to greet her. It was the temple. It was Dempster's Rock. Sigmar's statue stood proud atop the tower-dome crowning the rugged brickwork of the temple. The pitch outline of the forest broke for the tree-sparse hillocks amongst which the temple nestled. Gunda Schnass had never been so pleased to see the God-King's bronze form. As her waddling step and the roll of her ample hips took her towards the tall temple doors she felt the wolf pack fall away. She could hear the hackle and snap of their frustration. The God-King was an imposing sight, even for the mindless, savage beasts of the world. The fearful power of Sigmar's image held sway even over them.

Under the temple's great archway, Gunda found the mighty doors closed and barred. Given the hour, this did not surprise the midwife. It was not unusual to find Father Dagobert late at study but it was the dead of night, when most god-fearing folk were wisely in their beds and not in need of a priest. Unlike Gunda. Unlike the child. Huddled beneath the protective stonework of the small temple, Gunda's tired, dread-addled mind came to a conclusion. She could not care for this child. She could not ask her daughter Ada or Mistress Buttenhauser in Dieterschafen to care for it either, not knowing where he came from. What if his father came for him one day? What if the child himself harboured an unknown darkness? He was safest there, Gunda realised, under Sigmar's unflinching gaze. The God-King would see the child right. Gunda – a humble midwife – had seen him safely to Sigmar's door. She had done her best. His fate was in the God-King's hands now.

Pulling the child away from the warmth of her breast and laying the swaddling package in the nook of the arch, Gunda laid a kiss on the boy's forehead with her cracked lips.

'Gods forgive me,' the midwife told him as the child's screams intensified. Gunda did not want to be seen and with heavy heart and tears on her wrinkled cheek, she hurried away – the shame of her steps carrying her off towards Schlaghugel and the hovel she called a home.

As night wore on and the child screamed, the fell radiance of the witchmoon probed the temple archway. The great disk of Morrslieb – like a great bauble in the sky – peered from behind the temple stonework and soothed the babe with its brilliance. The child stared up in infant wonder, its eyes wide and its cries stifled. Moonlight reached through the forest also, calling to its bestial acolytes. The ill-light of the moon eclipsed Sigmar's statue, shielding the coward-hearts of forest savages from the reproach of the God-King's gaze. The treeline bled its gathering darkness and soon the hillocks of Dempster's Rock were swarming with their vicious kind, baying to the moon and drooling their intention to tear and shred. What the sordid effulgence did for their night eyes the unchanged swaddling did for their empty bellies. The forest was saturated with the baby's smell. Its tender flesh called to them.

As the most brazen and ravenous of the wolves ventured before the great doors and into the arch, they snarled and snapped their claim, streams of slobber tossing this way and that as each advancing beast attempted to secure the prize for itself. They nipped experimentally at the swaddling, dragging the babe from the archway and down the steps. Again the child's screams shattered the night, as it became the object of a tug-of-war between two great black beasts.

The first barely managed a half-yelp before its skull was smashed into the ground. The second was allowed a fleeting moment of wide-eyed panic as it released the child. The spiked metal ball that had demolished its competitor came up on a chain. It accomplished a moon-scraping orbit before coming crashing down on the wolf with equal fervour. A second smash pulverised the beast and finished it.

'Get out of here!' the weapon's wielder roared. Father Hieronymous Dagobert's vestments hung down about his waist; the hairy belly that wobbled generously with every swing of the twin-entwined chains was pale in the moonlight. He had been woken by the cries of a baby before his temple's doors and had hurriedly donned his robes and his boots. The morning star clutched in his pudgy fists was in fact the temple censer, streaming incense from the heavy ball of its spiked thurible.

'Back, beast,' Dagobert compelled the pack savages, his boots kicking teeth from the jaws of skulking scavengers and breaking the backs of the fleeing creatures. 'Back, I say! In the name of Sigmar back, or you'll get a taste of the Herald.'

Dagobert swung the spiked ball about his great body on its twin chain, the gust-fed incense within glowing like a comet through the sky.

Within moments of the priest erupting from the doors of his temple, the ravenous pack recovered. Lurkers slinked in under the Herald's arc to snap at the child, who once again had become transfixed – this time by the streaming afterglow of the priest's Herald. Beasts left the ground and snapped for Dagobert's own ample flesh. He pounded them back with bloodied fists and tight swings of the chain. A rumble built within the priest's belly that became a growl of his own as he smashed the children of the night out of the air and into the ground. With his chest rising and falling, and the Herald burning bright at its chain-end, the pack broke off. Enough of the scavengers were dead to shake loose the moon-fuelled confederacy of their number.

'Back, you beasts,' Dagobert said finally, spitting his derision down on the mashed carcasses of wolves that had incurred the wrath of Sigmar's Herald. Beside him, the baby stared up in blood-speckled wonder.

'Now who are you,' the priest put to the child, 'abroad on such an evil night?' He looked about for any sign of who had left the infant before shrugging. 'You'd best come in with me then,' he said, the kindness of his words labouring against the catching of his breath.

With the babe in one hand, held against his rounded belly, and the Herald coiled in the other, Father Dagobert made his way back towards the temple. Beneath the bronze gaze of Sigmar he nodded silently, before stomping in under the archway and kicking the great temple doors closed behind him.

CHAPTER III

'The corn is cut and the crops are reap'd.
Taal is praised and the gathering heap'd.
Thanks are given for the kindly skies,
And that fruit was not taken before it was ripe.'

– *The Reaper's Danse* (Anon)

Dempster's Rock
Nordland
Vigil der Erntezeit, IC 2399

Hieronymous Dagobert's footfalls were heavy on the scullery steps. The kitchen fire was roaring but there was nothing cooking on it. The priest was silent as he reached the basement flags.

'Father,' a voice came, just audible above the roar of the fire. It was tender with age. Young, fragile and broken. More of a devastated whisper than a voice. The word rattled off into a coughing fit, which prompted the priest to close his eyes. 'Hieronymous, is that you?'

Dagobert stood with his broad back to the child. His hand had formed a fist. He bit at his knuckle absently. His eyes were rheumy and his cheeks flushed but Lady Magdalena of the Salzenmund Hospice had assured him that it wasn't the pestilence and that he was merely overwrought in his tending to the child. She could not say the same of the boy, however. Worse, the priestess of Shallya told him that the disease was not known to her or her order and the best she could do was make him comfortable for the coming end.

'Father?'

'I'm here, my son,' Dagobert assured the young boy. He opened his misery-clutched eyes and walked to the scullery side where a pot of medicinal tea had been cooling. Ravenswort and ground Staffroot, Magdalena had told him. Something to help the suffering. If taken in quantity, something to help the sufferer slip away. 'You should take some more of your tea,' Dagobert called over the fire. 'As Lady Magdalena instructed.' He picked up the fire-burnished pot and poured the foul-smelling infusion into a wooden mug. He stopped. His hand was shaking. The misty liquid sloshed about the cup. Dagobert slammed it back down on the tabletop. 'No,' he said to himself. 'Sigmar forgive me. One more night.' Leaving the concoction, Dagobert crossed the scullery to where he had positioned the boy's bed before the fire.

'Oh, Little Diederick,' Dagobert said. The youngling looked terrible. A veritable corpse. He was shaking – his frame continually wracked by shivers that even the most furious fire failed to combat. Dagobert had called the boy Little Diederick, but for eight he had been quite tall and brawny. The pestilence, however, had wasted him to a husk. A field mouse could have lifted him from the bed. His young flesh was threaded through with a canker that opened up splits and welts that would not heal and in turn gave breed to a pox that had turned his skin to scab and scale. His fine, blond hair had fallen away and his sockets were bruised brown with corruption. The eyes within had clouded over and consigned the boy to darkness. Worst of all, a bloody and black treacle continually leaked from the corner of the youngling's mouth, proceeding from both his chest and his stomach, making it difficult for him to breathe and almost impossible for him to eat.

Despite the boy's myriad sufferings, the priest hardly ever heard him complain. He had a strength of body and mind that Dagobert both admired and dreaded. The more Little Diederick fought and the longer he endured the more he would suffer. Lady Magdalena told Dagobert that despite the boy's undeniable spirit, he was finished.

Dagobert had wept before the priestess. He had raised Little Diederick at the temple. They had not been apart for eight years and Dagobert – who had no children of his own – discovered that the boy had brought meaning to his life he had not expected. The act of charity in saving him that fateful, moonlit night and taking him in had turned into an act of love. He was both a spiritual and substitute father to the child. He had named him, for Sigmar's sake. The truth was that the tears Dagobert shed were tinged with relief as well as sorrow. It was almost over for the poor boy. A day at most, the priestess had given him. Then she had given Dagobert the tea to ease both the boy's suffering and the way to Shallya's bosom.

'Father,' Little Diederick wheezed. 'Am I dying?'

'Yes, my boy,' Dagobert answered. The words came fast and easier than he expected. 'Not long... Not long. Your trials will soon be at an end and you will be free. Do you suffer, Diederick?' Dagobert asked.

'I don't feel much,' the boy said. Dagobert nodded. Lady Magdalena's concoction had been successful in cushioning her patient from the worst of his agonies. 'I'm frightened,' the boy admitted.

Dagobert took the small, silver hammer he wore about his fat neck in reverence to his God-King – the emblem of his holy office – and draped it about the child's neck. The boy didn't even feel it.

'Don't be,' Dagobert said. 'I'm here. I'll always be here – at your side.'

The boy was still shivering, despite the fire. Dagobert sidled around the bed and lay down behind Diederick. He put his arm about the child, trying to warm him further. The pair of them lay still awhile, staring into the raging kitchen fire. Minutes passed. The boy's breathing grew increasingly laboured. Dagobert held him through a savage coughing fit that shook the delicate child until he was almost insensible.

As he rescued his breath and returned to solemn silence, Dagobert spoke.

'Diederick?'

'Yes, father.'

'Do you think you might ever find it in yourself to forgive me?' the priest asked, his voice strained with emotion.

'For what?' Little Diederick hissed, his words reedy.

'This is my fault,' Dagobert admitted. 'I don't think you caught this pestilence in the forest or from the river. I don't think a visitor to the temple brought it to us. And neither does Lady Magdalena.'

'What's wrong with me?' the child asked with a chilling directness. Dagobert turned his eyes from the blinding flicker of the fire.

'I sent you for the books,' he told the boy. 'I was distracted. I left the vault door open. I never thought that...' The priest caught himself. 'These things are all my fault.'

'I don't understand,' Diederick said, moving his head, causing more black ooze to roll from the corner of his mouth.

'The vault is a special place,' Dagobert said. 'A secure place, where I am required to keep special things.'

'Special things?' Little Diederick asked.

'Tomes. Manuscripts. Works of great age.'

'Books?'

'Yes, but not the ones I sent you for. Those would never be found in such a place. The vault contains tomes of dangerous knowledge and ideas,' Dagobert said. 'Knowledge that can hurt people. Understanding for which the world will never be ready. Each temple has a vault of such heresies stored securely beneath the holy ground of its flagstones.'

'Why do you keep such things, father?' Diederick asked, devolving once more into a horrible coughing fit. Blood, fresh and raw from the lungs appeared on the boy's lips, prompting Dagobert to wipe it away with the tails of his priestly robe. Little Diederick appeared to be in greater discomfort. Every breath was an effort.

Dagobert thought on the question as the boy grew still once more.

'In order to better protect ourselves from the enemies of Sigmar,' the priest said, 'and the God-King has many. We must know what they know. We study and translate them to know how the servants and darkness might be stopped. Sigmar entrusts such a solemn and hazardous task to a chosen few.'

'Who?' Little Diederick rasped.

'His priests,' Dagobert said. 'His templar knights. You remember meeting Sieur Kastner, yes?'

'Yes...'

'He came searching for such a tome,' Dagobert told him. 'That was why the vault was open. You have to know, Diederick, it was a mistake. I would never have exposed you to such dangers intentionally.'

'I never found the books you asked for,' Diederick said.

'But you found others,' Dagobert pressed tautly.

'Yes...'

'Did you read them?'

'I knocked over a pile,' Diederick said, his face creasing with further pain and discomfort. 'One lay open. I leant in to look. It was covered in strange symbols. I did not understand.'

'Lady Magdalena and I found the toppled books in the vault,' Dagobert said.

'Does Lady Magdalena think I got this for reading one of the dangerous books?'

'No, my child.'

'Is Sigmar angry with me,' Diederick said, bloody tears welling in the mist of his eyes, 'for reading the book?'

'No, Little Diederick,' Dagobert told the boy, 'he is not. The God-King could not be prouder of your hard work in the temple and in your studies. Lady Magdalena thinks that you might have breathed something in: some ancient pestilence or contamination. Something left there a long time ago by one of Sigmar's enemies. The God-King is not angry with you. He is angry with me. I am the one to be punished.'

Diederick began to cough. This time it took several minutes to stop. Dagobert held him, lest the fragile boy shake himself to ruin. As they lay there, before the fury of the fire they both became still and silent.

'Father?' Diederick said, his voice but a strangled sigh.

'Yes, my dear child?' Dagobert dared to answer.

'I forgive you,' the boy mouthed.

The priest read the words on his dry, blackening lips. Tears rolled down the priest's fat cheeks. He laid the child on his back. It was time.

'The God-King waits for you,' Dagobert told him.

'There is something there,' Diederick hissed. 'In the darkness.'

'It is He,' Dagobert said. 'Don't be frightened. Go to him.'

The boy's face contorted with sudden horror and disgust. 'It's not the God-King…' Diederick said. The words were still on his lips as his last breath escaped him.

The Lord of All enjoys the songs, the chanting of children at play, holding hands and dancing around. They sing of flowers, of his plagues that sweep through the land and the ashes of bodies burned. They celebrate this life of death, for he is both the cause of their suffering and he who would save them from it. He defines the times with the pain and fear he brings into mortal lives. Though they would not know it, they sing and dance to the tune of the Great Pestilence's calling.

He takes so many souls in this way. Like the harvest, they are weighed and measured. They are his tithe. His reward for the architecture of agony that is his contribution to their mortal failing.

Like the scythe, the Lord of All does not choose between the one stalk and the other. With so many souls feeding his eternal appetite for affliction and end, he will not miss the one stalk. Does the mill miss the single grain? The bread bereft of flour that dusts the floor with its forgotten bounty? The mouth the crumb that falls from the lip?

He will not miss the one soul unpromised to him. The one soul destined for more than his plague or pestilence. For this one grain re-planted will yield a reaper's harvest. A celebration of death and suffering the like of which the world has never known. He will be a scourge, a disease all of his own. A plague from which the world will never recover. And so I release this soul from its suffering and send it back so that it might be a worm in the rotting carcass of the world. And not a carcass in itself.

CHAPTER III

'The great and the good carry the same flaws as you and I.
They are just buried deeper or concealed with greater skill.
Accept this as truth. Though it is true also that such revelations are a fall from which we never truly recover.'

– Eugen Kufka, *A History of the Empire v.XII*

Holzbeck
Middenland
Jhardrung's Eve, IC 2404

Oberon.

Diederick had always liked the horse's name. It rang of nobility. The kind of muscular majesty the monstrous, black stallion projected in its every step. Diederick would know. The page had one of the horse's goliath hooves between his thighs. He held it still, placing a new shoe on the foot. He was overdue a change. As page to Sieur Kastner's squire Nils, it had been Diederick's honour to attend the templar's horse.

Placing the shoe that Diederick had had specially made by Holzbeck's only farrier to accommodate the stallion's size, he positioned the first nail. The shoeing hammer made easy work of the hoof, sending the nail out of the hoof topside, where Diederick expertly bent and twisted it secure. As he went about his work, his hammer pendant swung like a pendulum from the chain about his neck. It had been given to him by Father Dagobert upon being appointed as Sieur Kastner's page, so that Sigmar would watch over him. Grabbing the hammer he held it to stillness. The coolness of the Middenland night crept into the blacksmith's stable. Diederick felt the chill through the wool of his hood and tabard. It was a patched cast-off that had formerly belonged to Nils. Diederick had inherited both the position and the ragged uniform. With both blacksmith and farrier enjoying the night's festivities at the Three Ways Inn across the road, Diederick and Nils were alone and without the blaze of the forge to warm them.

'Nils,' Diederick said. The squire ignored him. 'You cold, Nils?'

'I am,' Nils admitted, going to work with cloth and oil at the broad, heavy blade of Sieur Kastner's greatsword *Terminus*. It was a magnificent weapon. As tall as the squire cradling it. The weapon was ostentatious only in the shameless craft of its blade and the death-dealing certainty of its cleaving edge – although you wouldn't know it to watch Sieur Kastner hack at the unliving like a woodcutter or make a bludgeoned mess of forest-infesting goblinoids. The crusader blade had been in the Kastner family for generations – an heirloom passed from father to eldest son. The guard was inset with the bejewelled modesty of the Kastner family's wealth. The blade itself was inscribed with the weapon's honourable name – earned by Sieur Kastner's great-great grandfather a hundred years before at the side of Magnus the Pious. Along its holy length it bore the crafted design of the twin-tailed comet that heralded the Heldenhammer's coming. The pommel was a simple metal orb, into which the Imperial cross was crafted, honouring the Kastner family's service in the name of Sigmar. The weapon gleamed in the lantern-light of the stable. Nils was careful not to leave the greasy marks of his fingertips on the blade. He rubbed the metal with a cloth, holding it up to the light, his study of the weapon fastidious to the point of obsession. Such imprints would lead to corrosive blemishes, the like of which the squire had suffered for previously at his master's hand. 'Just busy yourself with your work,' Nils told the page. 'The burn of honest labours will warm you to your bed tonight.'

The young Diederick raised an eyebrow. It sounded like something Sieur Kastner would say in one of his more knightly moments but coming from Nils sounded like a hustle. Since there were three more shoes to be fitted and only the filthy straw of the stable waiting for him, Diederick found the invitation a hollow one. As the page finished the first shoe and allowed the steed's great hoof to fall, he walked up the beast's silky, black flank. He patted it softly, noticing the animal flinch a little as he reached the whipping scars on his hindquarters.

'Good Oberon,' Diederick said. 'That's it, boy – just three more to go.'

The night air did little to bother Oberon. He was a Sollander. A pureblood charger from the Upper Soll Valley – although Diederick suspected that in reality he had more than a little Bretonnian Draught in him. As a knight's destrier he was tall and strong. A wall of darkness and muscle standing next to the page.

The inn door opened and the gaiety of fiddle, raucous song and empty steins slammed on tables briefly intruded on the muddy road. It was Jhardrung's Eve, the turning of one year to another. The entirety of Holzbeck had crammed itself into the Three Ways – so called because the inn sat on a well-travelled junction between the City of the White Wolf, Grimminhagen and the Old Forest Road that took the unwary through the dark and dangerous Drakwald. Diederick found himself standing at the stable door as Nils went on with his oiling of the sword.

Without his plate and shield – also waiting for Nils's efforts with cloth and oil – Sieur Kastner cut an unimpressive figure. If it hadn't been for the worn finery of his garments or the dwindling weight of his purse, he could have been trader, cleric or blacksmith. The strength and skill of a warrior's body was long hidden beneath a small mountain of fat. Chicken scraps from an earlier feast clung to grease-spots on the silk of his tent-like smock, while beer-froth sat in his greasy beard like the webs of busy spiders.

The templar clutched his prize for the night to his massive frame. One of the innkeeper's buxom daughters. The innkeeper of the Three Ways wasn't about to argue with a Knight of the Twin-Tailed Orb and might even have hoped that issue from such a union might bright him connections to the Kastner family and their estates in the Gruber Marches. The girl had plenty of fight in her, however. She pushed. She slapped. She bit at the templar's fat, wandering fingers.

Too drunk to restrain her as intended and with festive indifference evident on his broad face, Kastner meandered through the filth and water pooling in the wheel-mulched road – the girl's wrist held in the grip of one meaty fist. She hauled at the man mountain and as he hauled back, drawing her to him, he let his pudgy palms travel across her. More slapping and scraping at the templar's face this time took him from a beer-fuelled daze to thunderous realisation. The palm of his hairy hand produced a stifled squeal from the girl and put her down in the quagmire. He blinked at her and a fat finger came up in warning but the innkeeper's daughter was already up. Filthy rainwater cascaded from her dress as she slipped and skidded away from him. Her face was fearful but her eyes full of defiance. Diederick found a squalid inspiration in the girl's determination. Pulling her drenched skirt-tails to her, she ran up the road, melting into the darkness. Kastner spat after the innkeeper's daughter, shouting something unintelligible after her. As he shrugged his disappointment and disgust away he stumbled to one side, slipping down into a wagon-cut crevasse in the road. He floundered back the other way, his boot losing purchase and putting the templar down on one knee. Furious, the knight rumbled half-heard threats to himself before slapping the pooling waters in frustration.

Diederick felt Nils standing behind him. Watching, like the page.

'Sieur Kastner is not what Sigmar intended,' Diederick said.

The squire didn't disagree, but as the beer-blind templar rose from the small lake in the road, mumbling to himself in a black mood, Nils returned to the greatsword *Terminus* and his work. Sieur Kastner listed back towards the Three Ways Inn before seeming to forget where he was going and settled on a course for the open stable door.

'Get back to work,' Nils instructed the page. Diederick nodded slowly and returned to Oberon's side.

Sieur Kastner stumbled into the stable. He tried to hold position for a moment as he glowered at Nils, furiously at work on the blade, and Diederick's back as the page selected a further shoe for the steed.

'What do you think you're looking at?' the knight slurred at them, despite the fact that no eyes had been raised in the templar's presence. Kastner fell to more grumbling, holding some kind of conversation with himself. Diederick could only make out intermittent words and phrases: 'cesspit', 'White Wolf', '...where a man of the God-King can be appreciated'.

He stomped through the straw to Oberon, who snorted his

uncertainty. When the knight was in his cups, nothing was safe from his drunken wrath. The templar wasn't above whipping the horse for some perceived fault. Snatching for the spooked animal's noble head, it became apparent that Kastner intended on mounting the horse and riding north for Middenheim.

'My lord,' Nils braved finally, amongst the commotion. 'My lord, what are you doing?' It was unwise to challenge the knight in such a state but if Kastner had ridden and fallen or if Oberon were lost, there would only be a greater price to pay the next morning. In his inebriated state, the squire could at least hope that the templar might tire easily or pass out.

'Are you telling me what to do?' Kastner growled, turning on Nils. Diederick watched the pair of them fall into a familiar routine. More slurred mumbling from the knight eventually formed the words, '...little dung-shoveller like you tell a templar of the Tail-Twinned Orb when he can ride and when he cannot...'

Nils didn't correct the knight but simply tried to convince him that the horse was without saddle, bridle and bereft of shoe.

'You want to do this?' Kastner asked with a fat snarl. His face moved between contortions of confusion and gall, falling away occasionally to the palsy of growing fatigue. Unconsciousness beckoned but the templar wouldn't let it take him. 'You want to do this, turd?'

'No, my lord,' Nils said, his voice rising with fear and his own face straining with the ordeal he knew was to come. 'Please, sir. I beg of you. My concern is but for the safety of your hallowed person. In Sigmar's name...'

Kastner's eyes closed for a moment and the fat nobleman drifted to the left. For a second it looked as if he might crash to the stable floor in a drunken malaise. His eyes shot back open suddenly at the mention of his God-King.

'You use his name to me?' the templar slurred. He advanced on the squire.

'F-f-forgive me, my lord,' Nils stammered, his eyes glassy and quivering. 'Diederick changed the shoes against my good counsel. It is he who is responsible for the unreadiness of your steed at this hour.'

Kastner turned his head towards Diederick, who stood trying to calm the snorting and disquieted Oberon. He stared at the page.

'You?' Sieur Kastner blurted.

Diederick stared back, his teenage face hard and unreadable. There was nothing of hurt and betrayal to be found there. Nils couldn't take another beating at the templar's hand. Diederick knew that. Kastner glared at him. He gave him the darkness of his eyes. As usual, the knight found it difficult to hold the boy's gaze. He always had – ever since he had reluctantly taken the young Diederick off Hieronymous Dagobert's hands. The drunken Kastner turned back to Nils.

'No, no, no,' the knight rumbled dangerously. 'The page is responsible to the squire, the squire to his lord. Punish him as you will. You are my servant. Your correction is my burden.'

With difficulty, Kastner unbuckled his belt and tossed the coils of heavy leather down on the ground before the squire. Stumbling at the stable wall, Kastner rummaged through the squire's saddlebags, hanging from a nearby stall.

'Please... sir,' Nils pleaded. The flush-faced knight found what he was looking for. He tossed a tied bundle of birching twigs and a length of knotted rope down with the thick belt. Nils almost seemed to crumble before them. Diederick watched in stony silence.

'Birch, braid or belt?' the templar put to the demolished Nils, spittle rolling down through his beard.

'No,' the squire moaned.

'What?' Kastner roared. 'I can't hear you. Birch, braid or belt. Choose your correction.' Nils just wheezed at his hulking master. 'Sigmar compels you, boy. Tell me now.'

The shoeing hammer flew across the stable, head over handle, before striking the templar in his mountainous backflesh. It thudded and fell. Kastner staggered forward, his face a mixture of pain and surprise, his brow like a growing storm. He turned slowly to look down at the hammer on the straw-strewn floor. The knight seemed to sober. He looked up at the page.

'I choose the hammer, you sack of wine,' Diederick told his master. The knight still couldn't believe what had just happened. He kicked the other implements of punishment at Nils with his boot before leaning down to pick up the hammer. He must have been seeing several because it took him several attempts to acquire it.

'So be it, you little runt,' Kastner told him, advancing with the hammer. 'I knew you were more trouble than you were worth. Since your squire has clearly failed to beat such unruliness from you, it falls to me to take charge of your re-education. You want the hammer, boy, then you shall have it.'

Nils, bawling into the straw, went to crawl away.

'Don't you move,' Kastner seethed back at him. 'You're next.'

Diederick stepped fearlessly forward, drawing the templar's eyes back to his dark-eyed defiance. 'Tell me, boy,' Kastner said, lifting the tool in readiness to strike. 'Why the hammer?'

'Because Sigmar compels me,' Diederick told the templar. Kastner grunted his drunkard's derision and went to bring the hammer down on the boy.

Oberon snorted and whinnied. The stallion suddenly reared up on its hind legs, kicking out with its front hooves. Thinking that Kastner was coming for it, the horse had gone wild. Kastner stepped back from the flash of the hooves and the steam of the destrier's breath.

'Calm, Oberon, calm,' Diederick called, reaching out for the animal, but it bucked and turned, kicking out behind it and smashing the stall bar to splinters.

'Back you blasted thing,' Kastner raged, swinging the hammer before him. As Nils scrabbled away through the straw, Diederick snatched up the stallion's halter chains from the stable wall and moved in to calm the beast before it harmed itself. Oberon's flank came around suddenly, knocking the page to one side, before the frightened horse's back hooves kicked out, striking Diederick in the head.

The page's body was knocked from his feet, smashing into the opposite stall like a child's rag doll. Everything grew dark. Oberon's hooves thundered about him and the heat of the steed's snorts washed over his face. Then, within several hoof-falls it was gone, the horse having bolted from the stable.

The lantern-light was dim. Diederick's face felt wet. There was a dull ache where his head used to be. Something bad had happened, but the page's thoughts couldn't quite make their way to what. All he knew were the beams of the stable roof above him and the tools mounted there. Two heads moved slowly into view. Everything was blurred and the light was bleeding away, but Diederick could make out Nils and Sieur Kastner looking down at him – their faces wearing the same mask of dread stupefaction. The light withered and died. It was the last thing Diederick ever saw.

Accident. Chance. Providence. Doom. These are one and the same. How many heroes have been crafted of the misfortunes that befell them? But for the roll of a die, the flip of a coin or the turn of a card they would be happy nothings to the world. All gods – those of light and of darkness – operate in the enormity of these mere moments. They are in the quiver of the string that sends the arrow wide and the glance of the sword that fails to meet its mark.

I have saved my pawn, my small piece in a larger game, from a hundred such deaths. What is life but the journey of hapless mortals through the myriad dangers of their miserable existence? It is the tedious curse of princes such as I to watch the tangled deathtraps of entwined lives form knots before me. Sometimes I cut the skein free, damning all to whom it is attached. To mortals these are the battles, massacres and disasters of the world. The labyrinthine circumstances into which the doomed have been inescapably placed. Sometimes, however, I take the time to unravel the threads of existence and free the living of their present doom. This I do when I have investment in the game. This I do for my pawn. I set him free knowing that he will similarly set me free of fate – bonds no less intricate or inescapable. And so, my pawn, I release you from a death ordinary and unknown. You are meant for greater deeds.

CHAPTER III

'But man's way
Lies through the twists and turns of forests
great and woodland dark,
Where savage and born of the earthen spite
before fancy's fearful eye,
the grotesques of the underwald come, as
they did before Sigmar.'

– Stoltz and Kramer

Near Suderberg
The Drakwald
Black Aubentag, IC 2406

Nils called but the thick darkness of the forest gave them nothing. They were alone. They were wet. Deep in the Drakwald and getting deeper. Nils held out Sieur Kastner's dress sword before him. Kastner wore the short blade when not decked in his templar's plate and required at temple or before Graf Todbringer. Nils cared little for etiquette and court protocol now. He needed to put cold steel between himself and the dank darkness through which he was advancing. Diederick – having through hard work and study, also attained the rank of squire – followed with the reins of Oberon in hand. A lantern bobbed from a saddle-mounted staff, throwing a feeble circle of light about the three of them.

It had been raining and although it had long stopped, the heavens' issue had yet to work its way down through the Drakwald's twisted canopy. The darkness was a wall of sound. A cacophony of dripping. Droplets gathering, rolling and falling from leaf to branch to muddy pools and saturated undergrowth beneath. It made for a miserable passage.

Nils called out for the templar again. The action filled both squires with dread. 'What else can we do?' Nils had put to Diederick, but the boy didn't have an answer for him. In a place so thick with trees, tangle and shadow that they might walk straight past their master and not even know it, hollering his name through the night-drenched forest was all they could do. It didn't stop the fanciful imaginations of the pair conjuring images of beastmen, fang-faced lycanthropes and the wandering dead drawn down on them by their own foolish advertisements.

'Surely the barrow can't be that much further,' Diederick said. 'We've been walking for an age.'

Nils crunched on through the sodden undergrowth.

'Perhaps it just seems that way,' the squire mused.

Sieur Kastner's drunken boasts had once again drawn them into danger. Passing through the village of Suderberg, the knight had ventured into the Crooked Boar for a stein or four of spiced brew. When he hadn't emerged, the pair of squires assumed as usual that he had forgotten about them and had taken a room at the tavern. As the next morning spent in the stables rolled into the afternoon, the boys entered the tavern to enquire as to their master's whereabouts. They found that the templar had never made it to bed and had instead entertained them with a tale told by a grieving woodsman about his children, Franz and Frieda, who had disappeared about the Six Stones Barrow. Two trappers at the tavern told the squires that the old Teutogen burial ground was due west of the village and that was the direction the knight had set off in the previous night, after stein-clashing boasts in the tap room that he would find the children or destroy the evil that had.

The squires stopped in their soggy tracks. There were sounds from beyond. Wood cracking. Branches splintering. The agony of trees with their trunks rent apart by something monstrous and unseen moving through the wet forest. Nils crouched down in the brush. Diederick did likewise, holding Oberon's head down and praying to the God-King that the dense forest smothered their lantern-light. His other hand was preoccupied with holding the sacred hammer of Sigmar, the pendant that nestled coolly against his chest. The horse snuffled and blinked its alarm. The animal smelled something, for it too fell to stillness. Listening to the departing crash of the unseen thing through the crowded forest, Nils and Diederick exchanged glances of fearful relief.

'What if we don't find him?' Diederick said as they resumed their trek through the bleak wood.

'You mean Sieur Kastner?' Nils said.

'Yes.'

'We will.'

'What if we don't?' Diederick pressed. 'This is the Drakwald. Entire companies of troops have disappeared here without a trace.'

Nils nodded. Diederick wasn't exaggerating.

'Well you for one would return to your priest and temple on the Nordland coast,' Nils said with confidence, cutting through the knotted undergrowth with the edge of Sieur Kastner's short sword.

'Father Dagobert's moved,' Diederick said. 'I mean, he was moved. The Arch Lector said he was needed in Hochland. His way temple is near Esk, at the foot of the Middle Mountains.'

'Some bad country,' Nils said. 'So I've heard.'

'What about you?'

'You don't have to worry about me,' Nils assured the squire.

'Will you return to your parents?'

'I'm an orphan,' Nils told him. 'Like you.'

Diederick stopped for a moment, bringing Oberon and the lantern to a stop. He'd never known that about Nils. The squire found that he was hacking ahead of the grim halo of light that the lantern was casting in the tight confines of the ancient forest. 'Come on,' Nils scowled, prompting Diederick to follow.

Nils's blade cut through the darkness. 'Bring the lantern up,' he instructed. As Diederick brought it forward, the squires realised that they had hit a clearing. Where there had been trees there was now a dripping, thorny tangle. Leading with Oberon's mighty hooves, the horse trampled a way through for the boys. Through the squire-drowning foliage, they found that the lantern was not needed. Mannslieb was high in the sky – although Nils and Diederick wouldn't have known it under the thick forest canopy – and blessed the clearing with its ghoulish light. The clearing was roughly circular in shape, rising in the middle and dominated by stubby stones, standing upright out of the ground in a circle. Diederick counted them. The two squires looked at one another.

'The Six Stones Barrow,' Diederick said. The trappers had been right.

Climbing up the moon-glossed hummock, the pair moved through the stones.

Nils swore.

'What?' Diederick said.

'I've got bones over here,' the squire said. 'And here. They look human.'

'Probably an animal kill,' Diederick said, upon inspection. 'See the gnawing? Besides, they look old.'

'You don't know that,' Nils told him. 'This could be like Fassberg. Or last Geheimnisnacht.'

'Dark ceremonies? Human sacrifice? Look at the moss on the stones,' Diederick assured him. 'Teutogen all right. Nothing's happened here for a long time.'

'So where is he?' Nils put to the squire.

'Wish I knew.'

Nils kicked a rock at one of the standing stones. 'Let's go.'

'We should wait,' Diederick suggested.

'Are you out of your mind?'

'We've come all the way out here,' Diederick said. 'You want to just go back?'

'He's probably returned to the Crooked Boar and is snug in a bed with a farmer's wife as we speak.'

Diederick shook his head. 'Or passed out under a tree with an empty flask.'

Sieur Kastner kept several about his massive person, for when he was out of reach of an alehouse. 'We should wait. We'll probably hear him snore or fart or something.'

Diederick smiled his reassurance. Nils's anxious mask broke and the squire joined him in the joke.

'Just look for the trees shaking...'

'Or the ground...'

'Enough to wake the dead,' Nils's chuckle died in his throat as he looked down at the bones littering the barrow. Tying Oberon to one of the stubby stones, Diederick and Nils sat down on two of the others. The cascade of droplets from the surrounding forest fell to a puddle-plopping trill. Moonlight bathed the clearing. Nils looked about him.

'Seriously,' Diederick said, attempting to take the squire's mind from the ghastly moon, the dark suggestion of the treeline and the sepulchre beneath his boots. 'You have a plan?'

'What?'

'If we couldn't find him,' Diederick clarified, 'you said not to worry about you. Where would you go?'

Nils looked uncomfortable.

'I don't want to talk about it,' the squire said. Diederick nodded. Silence dominated the stone circle. It was eerie. Sounds reached out for them from the Drakwald beyond. Every scurry, every snapped twig and flutter through the foliage drew their eye-flitting gaze. 'All right,' Nils said suddenly.

'It's fine...'

'I've waited long enough,' Nils said. 'I'm going to Altdorf. To the cathedral. To the chapterhouse. I'm going to apply to be a knight. If the Knights of the Twin-Tailed Orb will have me. If Sigmar will have me.'

Diederick mulled over what the squire had said. 'I'm sure Sigmar will accept you into the ranks as he has accepted you into his heart. That's not the problem. Squire or not, only sons of noble birth can apply to the chapterhouse.'

'It's only a matter of time,' Nils said, his thoughts wandering. 'Even if we find him, sooner or later Kastner will end up with a sword in his gullet in one of his drunken duels or a pitchfork through his heart from some farmer, whose wife or daughter he wronged. That beastman in the Schadensumpf last month almost got the better of him. Or more likely, he will just fall to a tavern floor one night and not get back up.'

'All true,' Diederick admitted. 'But that doesn't help you.'

Nils leant in conspiratorially.

'For years, Sieur Kastner has been a menace to maidens all over the province. It was going on long before I joined him. It is said that his issue routinely arrive at his estates in the Gruber Marches – sent by their commoner mothers to find their father and seek their fortune.'

'I have heard such things,' Diederick agreed.

'Have you ever met Lady Kastner?' Nils asked.

'No.'

'Neither have I,' Nils said, 'which isn't surprising considering how often Kastner returns to his estates. She keeps a townhouse in the city also. It is well known that Lady Kastner is of good heart: a giver of alms to the poor, a good mistress of the Marches and – unlike her husband – a true Sigmarite.'

'Good to hear but so what?'

'What is less known,' Nils told him, 'is that partly out of good heart and partly out of resentment for her husband's disgraceful antics, Lady Kastner sponsors his baseborns' beginnings with wealth from the estate and allows them to carry his name.'

'You would present yourself as Sieur Kastner's issue?' Diederick asked.

Nils nodded slowly, looking down at his reflection in the short sword's oiled blade. There was a self-satisfied grin on his face. 'Would you tell her of his death?'

'I would take some small proof,' Nils said, thinking on it. 'Dead or alive, Lady Kastner is mistress of the Gruber Marches. Does she not deserve to re-marry? Does she not deserve some small happiness of her own?'

Diederick never got the opportunity to answer the squire's question. 'Did you hear that?' Nils said, getting to his feet. Diederick had and even if he hadn't, Oberon's ears had pricked up. Through the curtain of dripping and nocturnal movements the forest had to offer, it sounded like a distant and angry wail: some agonising roar of fear and frustration. The two boys looked at each other, their faces pale in the moonlight. Nils took several steps towards the sound with sword in hand. Snatching up the lantern and Oberon's reins, Diederick followed.

'Come on,' Nils said grimly, cutting his way back into the blackness of the tangled forest.

As they moved through the maze of midnight trunks and snarled foliage, they heard the dreadful call again. It was Sieur Kastner. They would know it anywhere. He sounded weak. Desperate. In pain. Nils went to call out to him but Diederick's hand grabbed his shoulder. The pair stopped. Oberon snorted its anxiety. There were whisperings about them. Voices harsh and hushed, hidden in the forest night. The boys stared about in neck-craning disconcertion. Sieur Kastner called out again. This time it was more of a miserable howl of agony. Much closer. Almost an echo.

Nils pushed on through the Drakwald but once again Diederick's hand shot out for his shoulder. Nils hacked through the rampant shrubbery of the ancient forest, his blade slicing its way back through to the moon's ailing glow. His boot found nothing before it and the squire slid down a collapsed bank of shredded roots and saturated earth. Diederick's hand slipped down his shoulder and arm, the two squires grabbing for one another as they ran out of limb. Snapping his hand closed about Nils's own, Diederick was almost pulled after the squire, as the pair of them hung off the edge of a forest sinkhole. With his other hand, Diederick held onto Oberon's reins, the weight of the horse the only thing preventing the pair from plunging into the gaping hollow.

The steed, also not wishing to fall, reared – which fortunately was what the squires needed it to do. With Nils back on solid ground and Diederick regaining the use of his arm, the pair clung to the trunks of rain-drenched trees and peered into the large sinkhole. It was lined with ancient trees and foliage fortunate enough not to have fallen in. Its walls were threaded with rotten roots and jagged with stones but everything was greasy with moss and mud, as rainwater from the surrounding woodland dribbled down into the depression. Diederick went to grab the staff-lantern but discovered that he didn't need it. Mannslieb gleamed down on the Drakwald, dusting the canopy with a sickly, silver light that penetrated and illuminated the sinkhole's depths. The hollow reached into the forest's black bowels. Its bottom was uneven. A landscape of root-strangled earth, mouldering logs and depressions, deep with collected rainwater. Then they saw him.

'Heldenhammer's sweet blood,' Nils said.

It was Sieur Kastner. He was lying broken and delirious at the bottom of the sinkhole, where he had fallen the night before. The sight of people peering into the hollow drew urgent groans from the knight, who was beyond words.

'We've got to get him out,' Diederick said. Nils said nothing. He just looked down on the fallen templar. 'We've got to get him out,' Diederick repeated.

'I'm thinking,' Nils said.

'I'll climb down,' Diederick suggested.

'And how are we supposed to get the sack of wine back up here?' the squire put to him.

'The man is suffering,' Diederick told Nils.

'Perhaps he deserves to,' Nils said, looking down on his master.

'He's a servant of Sigmar.'

'Have you ever known him serve anyone but himself and his appetites?' Nils put to the squire.

'One of us could go back to Suderberg for help,' Diederick suggested, looking back into the whisper-haunted darkness of the forest.

'Alone? Through the Drakwald? In the middle of the night?' Nils said. 'You think that a good idea? Look what happened to him.'

'Exactly,' Diederick pressed. 'Look what happened to him. You can't seriously be contemplating leaving him down there.'

'What can we do?'

'Like I said,' Diederick repeated, 'I'll climb down. You drop a rope to me. I'll tie it around him and we'll use Oberon to pull him out.'

Nils seemed to consider the plan.

'The rope is back at the stable,' he said dourly.

Diederick fixed the squire in a stony stare that gleamed in the moonlight.

'Nils,' he said, 'I know what you're thinking but we're not doing this. I'm going down into that hole. You are going to rig something up here with Oberon – take apart the harness – vines, roots, anything.' Diederick handed Nils the reins. 'Yes?'

'Yes,' the squire said finally.

With that, Diederick ventured into the sinkhole. Descent wasn't a problem. Climbing down the wall of the hollow, the squire found that the earth came away in his hand in squelchy sods but that the root systems of surrounding trees gave him all the handholds he could wish for. As he climbed down, he could hear the templar's ragged breathing and his agonised moans echo about the depths. Mannslieb looked down on them from above, like a great coin in the night sky, reflecting light from its blotched, silvery surface down into the sinkhole. Nearer the bottom of the hollow, where even the roots of the ancients above failed to reach, Diederick would be forced to drop the remainder of the distance. This would make climbing out all but impossible if Nils failed to rig something for their extraction.

'How's it coming?' Diederick called up. His voice assumed an empty desperation, as though the depth of the hollow sapped all of the strength and determination from his words. There was no reply from above but Diederick could see roots twitching at the hollow edge suggesting that the squire was hacking up material for an improvised rope of some kind. Clutching the hammer about his neck and offering a small prayer to his God-King, Diederick dropped.

It felt further than it looked. Something leapt in the pit of his stomach. His boots hit the sodden ground and he slipped, falling to one side into a sunken depression of collected rainwater. Pulling his face from the water, Diederick found the stinking pool to be choked with bones. Extricating his hand from a ribcage, while staring at a skull – jawless and cracked – Diederick found himself swarmed by a plague of frogs that had made their home in the dank underpool. The disturbed colony hopped about in filthy panic, croaking their disconcertion.

Scrabbling to his feet, Diederick made his way across the pit with difficulty. The bottom was a boot-clamping mire that threatened to drag the boy down further into its foetid depths. Clambering across a log that disintegrated in his hands, liberating infestations of lice and the segmented lengths of venomous centipedes, Diederick reached the templar. Sieur Kastner looked up at his squire with unseeing eyes. The knight was feverish and out of his mind with pain. His plate was bent and buckled, while beneath there were almost certainly bones broken. He clutched the length of the greatsword *Terminus* to him like a child he feared to let go of – a lethal, mud-splattered child, whose cleaving blade and inset jewellery glinted in Mannslieb's pallid blaze.

'We're going to get you out of here,' Diederick assured his master bleakly. 'Can you move?'

When the templar didn't reply, Diederick went to inspect his legs for injury. With heart-sinking realisation, Diederick saw that Sieur Kastner's legs were no longer there. The knight moaned miserably to himself. Diederick looked about the bottom of the pit. There were wretched holes – openings – in both sides of the hollow wall. The sinkhole had collapsed into a network of excavated misery running beneath the ancient forest. Something living both beneath the Drakwald and the ruined barrows of the Empire's long-dead tribes had been liberated. Diederick stared into the darkness of the nearest opening. He strained to see what was within and was greeted by the suggestion of beady, blood-hungry eyes staring back. Diederick stumbled back through a water-logged crater, only to turn and find the tunnel entrance behind him similarly haunted. Needle-toothed monstrosities were swarming the dribbling crawlspace of the passage, eager to catch a glimpse of their next meal.

'God's wounds,' Diederick cursed. He looked back down at Sieur Kastner. Whatever infested the tunnels seemed to fear the light.

Where the knight's armoured body had fallen, in both presence of daylight filtering down through the Drakwald, and the fearful gleam of the moons during the horror of night, Sieur Kastner had remained untouched. Where his legs had lain in shadow, near the hollow's edge, things had ventured from the tight, muddy openings to feast on the knight's flesh. Opening his plate up, the monsters had begun to eat Sieur Kastner alive. Only the reach of *Terminus*, wildly swung, and the light of the sun and moons had kept the creatures at bay.

Diederick retched into the frog-writhing pool. Wiping his mouth, the squire suddenly felt something slither across his shoulder. Spinning around, the squire found a root-twined rope had fallen across him.

'Thank Sigmar,' Diederick murmured, grabbing at the improvised rope. The squire looked down at Sieur Kastner. There would be no saving him now. As his squire and a servant of the God-King, it was still Diederick's responsibility to see his master's body to a funeral pyre. He had to try. Father Dagobert would never have forgiven him otherwise.

Diederick pulled the length of entwined root. Something was wrong. Its length ran and it ran until finally the coils of its hasty construction fell down into the pit.

'Nils...' Diederick growled, his eyes drawn back up towards the forest above.

Something was happening. The squire could hear the sound of Oberon crashing about the trees. He listened to the fearful whinnying of the stallion and the thud of panicked hooves into the woodland earth.

'Nils!' Diederick called. There was something up there with them. The squire could make out the break of branch and the snapping of foliage as Oberon turned, bucked and kicked out at creatures of darkness emerging to claim him. Of Nils he heard nothing. No friendly face appeared at the sinkhole edge and no further root-twined rope dropped down to extricate him. All he could hear was the crunching of bones, the scissor-slice of needle teeth and the horrible passing of flesh down goblinoid gullets. Diederick felt a dank dread creep through him. Nils could not save him; Oberon would follow; the squire would be left in the pit with his dying master, to face a slow death by starvation or be flesh-stripped by swarms of subterranean fiends, the instant clouds covered the guardian moon.

The boy's lips tightened to a dogged snarl. He would not die here, in some arsehole of the Drakwald, as a full belly for an underclan of shadow-suckling goblinoids. This was not the death the God-King had planned for him.

Diederick turned back to Sieur Kastner. The knight still clung to *Terminus* with an almost religious fervour. Diederick looked about the grim pit for an exit. He made a decision. He needed that sword.

'My lord,' Diederick said, kneeling down in the mire beside the fallen templar. Kastner's eyes writhed about their sockets in delirium. 'Master, trust that I will see *Terminus* back to your family's lands.' The squire took hold of the great blade but Kastner would not let it go. 'Your great-grandfather, your grandfather and your father saw its honoured blade – a blade that shed blood at the side of Magnus the Pious – back to the Gruber Marches. There, Sigmar-willing, it will one day find service with one of your issue. A warrior, like yourself, pledged to the God-King's cause. Let me do this last service for you, master. Allow its example to live on. Let me see *Terminus* home.'

Diederick couldn't tell if the knight had heard him but the metal-cased digits of his gauntlets suddenly released the blade. Diederick nodded but the templar's eyes trembled shut. He fell to moaning away the last of his life – a life long with sin and regret. Despite the knight's failings, Diederick hoped he could find his way to peace.

Drawing the greatsword to him, Diederick gauged the weight. It was far too heavy for him to hurl from the pit like an anchor or grapnel. Above, a sliver of cloud was drifting before Mannslieb's full form. Diederick didn't have much time. Grabbing the rope Nils had thrown down to him, he climbed through the loop intended to haul Sieur Kastner back up the side of the hollow. The end Nils had failed to secure Diederick triple-knotted about the hilt and guard of the greatsword. Attached to *Terminus* by a line of entwined roots, Diederick held the heavy sword over his shoulder in the fashion of a pikeman or halberdier. Splashing through the bone-littered shallows, the squire launched the tip of the weapon at the sinkhole wall like a javelin. The broad blade passed into the damp earth, its weight and the keenness of its edge taking it with ease into the side of the pit.

Backing along the wall, with the horrid whispers of tunnel crawlers in his ears, Diederick prepared to save himself. He breathed in. He breathed out. With water erupting about his footfalls, the boy launched himself at the protruding hilt of the two-handed sword. Swinging about it like a tumbler or acrobat, the squire's legs came about and his boot tips reached the flat of the blade. Without waiting to lose his balance, Diederick bent his knees and pushed off from the embedded blade, leaping desperately for the wall-snaking roots of the trees. Like grapnels, his hands clawed through the strata of black soil, grasping for anything that might provide purchase. And there the squire hung, by the tips of the index and middle finger of his left hand, ensnared in a willowy root.

As the mire-smeared squire made his ascent through the under-tangle of the ancient forest, he could hear Oberon stamp and snort, whinny and haw. The steed was being attacked by the dark denizens of the below and beyond.

'I'm coming!' Diederick hollered up the sinkhole wall. He was terrified that the horse would bolt and abandon him. 'Nearly there, boy...' Diederick was exhausted, but managed to haul his mud-sleek form over the edge of the pit. There was no time to catch his breath. He could hear the steed stomping and skidding to a halt, hemmed in by the dense forest. The Drakwald darkness was sibilant with the hissing of shadow-hidden forms. Things that crawled from the earth to feast.

Diederick skidded about the edge of the pit, bathed in the silver safety of the dying moonlight. He slipped out of the roots looped about him like a harness. Upon reaching the far side of the hollow, he began to gather the rope in his arms. With the slack taken up, he hauled at the hairy roughness of the root line. His palms burned and his heels sank as he fought the sinkhole wall for possession of the embedded greatsword. Inch by inch it slipped out, until finally *Terminus* slurped free of its earthen prison, sending Diederick tumbling back into the blackness of the forest.

On his back, and with the weald about him alive with the sounds of famished evil, Diederick gathered the rope hand over hand like a sailor. Finally hauling the greatsword through the forest tangle and to him, the squire scrambled back to his feet. *Terminus* was far too heavy for the boy to wield. Grunting, Diederick laid its length across his shoulders. As he felt something come at him in the murk he used his body to lunge the blade tip at the threat, sometimes spinning on his heel to cut at his tormenters with the cleaving edge of the weapon.

The effort was back-breaking work, but through a snarl of exertion, Diederick found his way to a grim smile. He couldn't see them but he could feel the wariness of the goblinoids beyond. Even wielded in such a fashion, *Terminus* could take off a spindly limb or impale a wizened ribcage. Guided by the staff-lantern mounted on Oberon's saddle and the stallion's snorting alarm, Diederick found his way to the steed. The wildly swinging lantern had saved the animal's life under the sky-blanketing darkness of the forest canopy. Their fear no less for such artificial light than Mannslieb's gleam or the blinding fury of the sun, the night goblins had been wary of the beast. Instead of the shredded mound of horseflesh Oberon should have been, the steed had only suffered belly-bites and scratches along its muscular flanks. Allowing *Terminus* to tumble from his shoulders and stab upright in the forest soil, the mud-splattered squire held his arms up to calm the stallion.

'It's all right,' Diederick soothed. 'It's all right, boy.'

As the horse lowered its head and approached, it revealed the butchered body of Nils. The squire's ragged corpse was being dragged down a hole between the great roots of a twisted oak. The corpse twitched as the thing below attempted to wedge Nils through an opening too small to admit him.

'No!' Diederick yelled, skidding down beside the squire's corpse. As he grabbed for his body, something gave and Nils slipped suddenly below. Grabbing for his trailing hands, Diederick and the underdweller fought for the squire's body, until finally it was wrenched from the boy's grip. 'No!' Diederick roared down the hole, but something shot back out at him. A sneering mask of pallid underdweller gnarlflesh, stretched over a sordid skull and crowded with teeth like broken glass. Only its eyes sported any kind of colour – a murky crimson, like the blood its clan guzzled from the fresh corpses like piglets.

The night goblin dared not press its advantage further into the lanternlight and swiftly withdrew. Diederick kicked away from the hole and pulled *Terminus* from where it was speared in the ground. Slipping the muddy length of the templar sword down into the stallion's saddle-scabbard, the squire mounted his master's warsteed. Diederick could only imagine the hissing hordes of goblinoid hatred stalking him between the tree trunks, just out of sight. Holding the staff-lantern high, Diederick kept the monstrosities back as he guided Oberon to the sinkhole's edge.

Looking down into the hollow and with Mannslieb's waning light dying about them, Diederick found that Sieur Kastner, lying smashed and insensible on the pit bottom, was almost impossible to make out. He heard the crunching of small jaws through bone and gristle, and realised that in the twilight he was being watched. Scores of beady, red eyes peered up out of the pit at the squire. Drawn out by the dwindling glare of the moon, the night goblins had ventured out from their tunnels. They were swarming the snug shadow of the forest and were now creeping out into the open night and feasting on the Knight of the Twin-Tailed Orb. It was an ignoble end for a servant of Sigmar. Even Sieur Kastner. His body would never see the funeral pyre. His spirit would never rise to meet the God-King.

Diederick thought on the knight. His squireship was over. He thought on poor Nils and considered his daring plan. There, above the pit, Diederick came to a decision. He would not be returning to the temple. To Father Dagobert and his sermons. Diederick lifted the staff-lantern high before tossing it down into the sinkhole. The lantern smashed down on the pit bottom, splashing oil across the shallows. The flames raged, turning the pit into an inferno. Goblinoids screeched in blind agony, unable to find their way to mother-darkness. The underdwellers burned and the darkness of the surrounding forest was lit up by the blaze. The shadow creepers withdrew, spitting their simultaneous hunger and hatred of the pink flesh.

The squire felt the heat rise from the pit. With it, he hoped that Sieur Kastner's soul might reach for the skies – if only to atone to Sigmar himself for being such a despicable human being. Diederick turned the great Oberon about. He had never ridden the beast and the steed was huge. The squire gave the horse a little encouragement with his heels but Oberon didn't need it. The horse was happy to weave through the thick trunks and leave the goblin-haunted site of flame and slaughter.

Their path lay east. East of Suderberg. East of Middenland. East to the Gruber Marches –where– God-King willing – Diederick would return the sword *Terminus* to its ancestral home and lay false claim to a new one of his own.

CHAPTER IV

''pon my soul, I could a mighty tale unfold,
and upon the shoulders of our hero bestow
times of trial, transformation and woe.'

– Kaufmann, *The Saga of Faramond* (Chorus)

Flaschgang River Road
Hochland
Schlachtentide, IC 2420

It was the first warm day of the Sommerzeit and Diederick Kastner felt the sun on the metal of his plate. He rolled in the saddle to the idle rhythm of Oberon's ambling gait. The Flaschgang buzzed with darting dragonflies and gurgled its meandering journey south, on its way to join the mighty Talabec.

'And the precepts that guide us?' Kastner put to his squire.

Emil Eckhardt rode beside his master, the young squire's horse in turn trailing a third pack animal. Over the beast of burden, hands and feet bound beneath the horse's belly, was a blanket-bundled corpse.

'To strengthen,' Emil said.

'And why?'

'The servants of Sigmar must be as strong–' Emil said.

'–in both mind and body,' Kastner added.

'...as the bonds that bind them, one Imperial to another.'

'Sigmar was unifier of the warring tribes that settled these ancient lands,' Kastner said. 'He gathered their strength so that they might face trials past, and those yet to come, as one. It is our sacred duty to maintain what he created. No one man can call himself an army, a nation, a people. It was Sigmar's wish that we be part of something greater than himself. He is both a generous and modest God-King. We love him for that. Go on.'

'To honour,' Emil told his master.

'How?'

'Leading by the Heldenhammer's example,' Emil said. 'By bringing his teachings to the people through action.'

'Sigmar was no teacher,' Kastner corrected, 'no mentor in a conventional sense. There are no writings of his to study. No body of works left to follow. His instruction lay in his deeds. His ways in his character. He trusts us to keep his spirit alive in our aspiration to his example. Brave in battle and loving of his land. And the third of the precepts that guide our order?'

'To protect.'

'Go on.'

'We are the blazing omen,' Emil said with confidence, 'throwing fear into those who would bring fear to the Empire. We are the griffon's talon, tearing the heart from the darkness within our own borders. We are the hammer in Sigmar's hands, to be swung through the ages at enemies out of his reach. The innocent are our charge, the weak our burden and those who would war in the God-King's name, we call brother. Does that satisfy you, master?'

'It will serve,' Kastner said, the merest curl of pride in his otherwise grim lips.

Content that he had pleased his lord, Emil fell to self-satisfied silence.

'Tell me, squire,' Kastner said. 'Why do we drag the maggot-ridden corpse of Yulian Spartak back to Flaschfurt?'

'To burn him, master.'

'But what does that serve?'

'We burn him before the people,' Emil said, 'so that they may always remember it. So they know him as but a man and not as some dark legend of their past.'

'You can't kill a legend,' Kastner said. 'Yulian Spartak needs to be dead in the hearts of the people. Only the certainty of his end should endure on tongues and be carried far on the wings of idle gossip. They must see the monster burn, for then they will not fear him. They will not fear what he has become. They will be better prepared to stand against such evil, should they encounter it again.'

'Does such an act not carry dangers, master?' Emil asked.

'Explain yourself.'

'Are we not simply exposing the innocent to a corruption that they would rather forget or have never seen at all?'

Kastner frowned.

'Do you not understand?' Kastner said, his voice grave.

'I have doubts...' the squire admitted.

'A spider crawls across your arm,' the templar hypothesised.

'Yes?'

'You brush it away,' Kastner continued. 'Moments later, you brush your arm off again – but there was no spider there.'

'Is that not a good thing?' Emil asked.

'It is your fear returned,' Kastner told him. 'A dread that now lives on inside you, giving function and form to your nightmares. It draws you to it and makes you part of that which you abhor. In your heart you would know that there was nothing to brush away, if the spider still sat crushed in your fist. We guard the borders of Sigmar's empire. We patrol the roads and forests of his ancient land. We cannot, however, stand sentinel over the souls of each and every one of his people. Actions will speak in our absence.'

'Yes, my lord,' Emil said obediently.

'How many womenfolk wake to infant screams of horrors relived? How many sons of Flaschfurt would have set off after Yurian Spartak and his Ruinous band? How many would have wanted to but for the chill of cowardice in their bones? Victimhood eats its way through the victim, leaving a darkness that the Ruinous Powers of this world can exploit. Sigmar did not give rise to a nation of victims. The people must be allowed their peace. There is a reason we burn and bury our dead. We must be able to move on in good conscience. To live our lives without wonder of what was and what might have been.'

'Yes, master.'

Kastner was not convinced that the squire truly understood. He pulled gently on the reins, prompting Oberon to fall back. He leant across Emil's trailing packhorse and, pulling at the rope that bound the body to it, Kastner liberated the blanket-bundle. The body fell to the road with a thud and a spray of rotten mulch and maggots. The filthy blanket fell open to reveal Yulian Spartak. Spartak of the Iron River. Spartak of Chernigov. Spartak of the Horde of Change. Spartak of the Flesh Capricious. The Kislevite had taken more names than forms, which would have made him difficult to track down were it not for the series of sorcery-slaughters committed by his warband in villages and homesteads along the Drakwasser. It had begun in Flaschfurt, however, and that was where Kastner was determined it would finally end. Emil stared at the hideous champion of Chaos before instinctively looking away.

'Look at it,' Kastner instructed harshly. Emil obeyed with disgust. 'Look at this evil. Not the manflesh it has riddled its way through, but the darkness still there in its Ruinous form. Even in death it wishes to take you from your thoughts – to a place of dread and doubt, where it reigns supreme. In death it does this as it did in its disgusting half-life, putting you from your shot.'

Emil looked down at the misshapen warrior. Its crossbow bolt still sat in the hunch of one shoulder where a second horned head had grown, yearning to be flesh-separate from the first. Hideous arachnoid limbs of some fresh transformation hung uselessly from the bear furs of its armoured back, while the warrior's legs and feet were those of a terrible bird: scaly, taloned and powerful. Beyond that there was little to make out in the butchery and the rot. Kastner's sword *Terminus* had gouged, hewn and hacked pieces off the thing with cold efficiency. With its sickle-staff cleaved in two and the crowning emblem of its Ruinous patron smashed, the Knight of the Twin-Tailed Orb had spun around. His broad templar blade was like the cyclonic fleshstorm Yulion Spartak had cast through Flaschfurt, Garssen and Ahresdorf and had attempted to visit upon the Sigmarite templar. As *Terminus* had chopped through the armour and chitin of the damned warrior's back, severing the champion's spine and almost cutting the thing in half, Spartak of the Capricious Flesh had erupted in a vomit-inducing blossom of final transformations, until finally the changes slowed and grew still like solidifying wax about a candle.

'You can know your enemy,' Kastner said as the squire stared down at the ungodly corpse, 'without becoming him. That is the burden Sigmar left us to bear. It is a heavy one and it forces us to be strong for our own good. Do you understand?'

'I do,' Emil said, his eyes burning into the butchered corpse. He looked up at the knight and Kastner knew that he did.

'Shall we see this monster back to Flaschfurt?' Kastner asked.

'And watch him burn for his atrocities,' Emil said. The knight and the squire climbed down from their steeds and together bagged and replaced the miserable cadaver on the packhorse's back.

Kastner heard the scrape of sandals on the road. Meandering up the river road was Gorst. The flagellant seemed lost in his thoughts of impending doom and catastrophe to come. His head was hairless with obsession and worry – giving it the appearance of a skull – sitting inside the thick bars of an iron face-cage. His ragged robes hung off the sharp bones of his emaciated form. His lips mumbled a constant stream of madness – warnings and portents of little meaning or consequence. About his whippet-frame the flagellant had wrapped slender chains and the heavy locks that bound them to his purpose.

Kastner had found him sitting on the steps of Sigmar's mighty cathedral in Altdorf. Such doom-laden fanatics often gathered before the temple, watching for signs of some impending apocalypse or great war in the comings and goings of the God-King's priests and templars. When he left the cathedral two years before, Gorst had stood and started following the knight without explanation. The two men had never spoken of Gorst's reasons and, although seeming to understand what few instructions Kastner had given him over that time, he had never made any kind of sense in return. Kastner had come to think of the flagellant like a hound in this way. He was always following in his tracks, hanging his head for the favour of a word or scrap of food. Emil couldn't find it in his heart to take pity on the madman, taking him for at best a parasite or beggar and at worse a potential thief or slitter of throats. Kastner often joked that the squire would go before the flagellant – having given as reason the greater number of years of service.

'What was that?' Emil asked. There was a sound that if not carried on the wind, gurgled along on the lazy Flaschgang. It wasn't the rattle of Kastner's plate, nor the muffled jangle of Gorst's chains. 'Is that a child?'

Kastner bit at his bottom lip but held his tongue. Emil wandered from the packhorse to the river's edge. Kastner waited. The squire's call came. 'Master,' he said, 'it's an infant – a baby – on the water.'

Indeed, the sluggish channel carried a root-riddled sod of reeds and twigs downstream. In the nest lay a bundle of swaddling. From the swaddling came the cries of a newborn. 'My lord?'

'Go,' Kastner told him. 'If you think you need to.'

Emil trudged down the weed-strangled bank, his footfalls tearing through the foliage. Down in the water, where mud and silt attempted to claim his boots, the squire reached out for the sod and pulled it to him. The baby's cries subsided at the appearance of another face above it. With the swaddling clasped to him, Emil made the difficult ascent, careful that the infant did not fall or himself with it.

'Who could do such a thing?' Emil said as he approached his master with the rescued child. 'In Sigmar's name, have these people no shame, no decency?'

Kastner gave the squire the hardness of his eyes.

'Probably not,' he agreed. Waiting.

Emil pulled back the swaddling to inspect the child for injuries. He found none. He found something else entirely. The infant suddenly fell to the ground. The squire's arms were open. He had dropped the bundle of swaddling, the monstrous infant, the horror that the babe had been. His steps took him back towards the river. The baby screamed once more from the tall grass of the roadside. Emil looked up at Kastner and then back down at the uncovered altered form.

'You knew?'

'I suspected,' the templar said. 'It is not uncommon. The product of some deviant liaison. After carrying such a horror, a mother might not be able to bring herself to end her own issue. It is still her child, after all – despite bearing the hideous marks of dark favouring.' Emil said nothing. He just stared at the misshapen infant, screaming its misfortune to the sky. 'Perhaps she thinks her babe might find its way to someone with greater strength and stouter heart.'

Emil looked from the child to the crossbow hanging from his saddle.

'I couldn't,' the squire said.

'The servants of the Ruinous Powers will not always present themselves as Yulian Spartak, dripping with the blood of his innocent victims. You must end this thing of darkness,' the Sigmarite templar told his squire, 'as your calling dictates.'

'I can't,' Emil said miserably.

'Have you not read your Rendsberger? What would Von Bildhofen's *Daemonologie* say on the matter?'

Emil shook his head. The squire heard the sigh of *Terminus* clearing its saddle-scabbard. His head continued to shake.

'My lord, no.'

'You would defend such evil from Sigmar's steel?'

'Surely this child is not our enemy,' Emil said.

Holding the greatsword in two gauntlets, its heavy blade dangling above the screeching infant, Kastner prepared himself.

'We find our enemies on the dark path. Would you join them on it?'

'No, master.'

'Then you know what is necessary. What is needed. This thing presents with the blessings of the Ruinous Powers,' Kastner insisted grimly.

'Cannot the gods decide if it should live or die?'

'We are their instrument,' Kastner said, lifting the blade. 'It is decided.'

Emil looked away.

'I cannot watch,' the squire told him.

Kastner's gauntlets creaked about the sword's hilt. He paused.

'You have much to learn, squire,' the templar said finally, before removing his blade from above the infant's horrific form. 'Your education is my burden. I will not fail you as you fail yourself. Pick up the child.'

'My lord?' Emil said with a face contorted by mixed emotions: shame, concern and disgust. Kneeling, Emil wrapped the creature back up in its swaddling.

'Place it back on the water,' Kastner commanded. 'You will come to see the mistake in your mercy.'

Emil made his way down to the water and set the screaming child back on the sod of woven weeds before pushing it into the torpid current. By the time he returned, Kastner was in the saddle, his glare full of reproachful sadness. Knowing that he had disappointed his master, the squire remained silent.

The knight prompted Oberon on with his heels, Emil and his packhorse trailing behind with the troubled Gorst mumbling incessantly to himself in their hoof steps. Kastner kept his distance from the shrieking child, the sod carried ahead of them on the sloshing waters, bouncing along the reed banks on the opposite side of the river. The templar and his squire had little to say to one another for the next hour. Emil knew better than to disturb Sieur Kastner in such a black mood.

The infant cried. The waters lapped at the muddy banks and the horses crunched through the grit of the road. Emil watched his master who in turn was looking downstream, watching the far bank. Kastner suddenly sat up in his saddle, craning his head for a better view. Drawing Oberon to a stop, the templar slid down from the steed and led the horse to the roadside. Emil followed suit and knelt down beside his crouching master. Kastner had but one word for his squire.

'Watch.'

Peering through the long grasses lining the river road, Emil saw that the sod of reeds had become tangled in a broken branch that lay off the bank. The infant screeched – its suffering rising with the heat of the dying day. Emil watched. He waited.

The squire's heart thudded in his chest as a figure darted from the tree line and down the riverbank. Its body was covered in piebald fur and its legs were long and cloven. Looking up and down the river, the beast – with a long face and stubby horns of a nanny goat – snatched the child from the reeds and clutched it to itself. Within moments, the creature had become one with the forest again.

'The gods decided,' Kastner said. 'Just not the ones you were counting on.' Emil felt the biting reproach of his master's words. 'Now the infant is our enemy.'

'My lord...'

'Now it suckles gall from a mother born of hate,' Kastner continued, 'to take its place in a tribe of beastmen. To spread the canker of the Ruinous Powers through the ancient forests and hunt us through the darkness. To maim. To defile. To kill. To sire more of its monstrous kind for us to destroy.'

'I'm sorry, my master,' Emil told him, his eyes on the grit at his boots.

'Fortunately,' Kastner said, getting to his feet. 'Calamity is not without virtues of its own. There is a crossing not too far downstream. We shall pick up the trail at the riverbank and you will track the beast – as I have taught you – back to its foetid herd. There Sigmar's holy work will be done. Have no doubt. We shall end the beasts that walk like men, with all their foul get.'

'Yes, my lord,' Emil said. He was having difficulty finding his way to the same fervent enthusiasm for the fight ahead as his master. The feeling followed him across the Flaschgang and into the depths of the Drakwald. Light left them and the squire was forced to light a lantern. Reading tracks by lantern light was not ideal and several times the squire lost the trail, only to have the templar find a hoof print here or the broken pieces of a snapped twig there.

'Such foundlings,' Kastner told the squire, 'are considered by the beastmen to be gifts from their Dark Gods. Their ears are always open to the cries of the afflicted and abandoned.'

The tracks led the pair to the suggestion of a trail, a dark path winding its way through the broad trunks of the ancient forest. The haunting sound of creaking bark and hollowed bone-chimes hanging from the branches drifted on the dank air. Moss-ravaged stone markers started to signal the beginnings of a dark and shrouded route through the forest's ancient tangle. Once upon the winding trail, Kastner and Emil could hear the distant cries of the child. They were gaining on the beastwoman. Every step into the Drakwald depths took them into the creatures' accursed and ancient hunting grounds. Stinking water sat in leaf-choked puddles. Fungus ran rampant across dying trees while a miasma infected the very air they breathed. The stench of rot – of disease and of slow death – coated them with its rancid musk. Through it, bloated flies buzzed. Things that droned about them crawled across their skin and bit at their flesh.

At the glint of light through the blackness of the dense forest, Kastner told Emil to douse the lantern. Again the pair crouched to watch the beastwoman, foundling cradled in her filthy claws, approach some kind of concealed camp. The smothering forest broke ahead. Cankered leaves carpeted the floor – rustling with snakes, vermin and the large beetles they preyed upon – leaving the surrounding branches bare. Black birthing pools writhed with knots of foul worms. The fat trunks of dead trees seemed to thin, making way for a circle of rough menhirs and standing stones. At the centre raged a fire, threading the forest with a muggy smoke, and casting the beastwoman in silhouette.

There were others. Many others. Black outlines of muscle, hoof and horn. Some swigged blood and ale, while others roared a bestial laughter at one another. Several creatures butted thick skulls in drunken dispute as about them beasts were snarling, bleating and jostling each other in the shadows. Beyond the fire, Kastner could see a crude altar improvised atop a fallen stone, where some kind of bestial shaman was shaking a staff crowned with a star of bloodied antlers over a sacrificial offering. The creature was dressed in rags, its fur settled with moss and its flesh harvested by blooms of fungus.

A single horn curled its way out of the creature's skull. Behind the monster, the herdstone it was honouring with innocent blood ached with unnatural energies.

'Sigmar has blessed us,' Kastner hissed. Emil couldn't find it in himself to agree. 'It's a warherd. Take courage, boy. You could not kill the child – the God-King has seen fit to pave the way to enemies you can. These beasts are the very children of Chaos. We shall take their hides in Sigmar's name and bring light once more to this benighted part of his Empire.'

Carefully and quietly, Kastner drew *Terminus* from his saddle-scabbard and climbed down from Oberon. Taking his crusader shield from its saddle-mounting on the steed's flank, Kastner slid his arm through the thick leather restraints. Even in the gloom, the Imperial cross was clear on the shield's battered surface – a symbol of unity across Sigmar's lands, with the God-King bringing tribes from the north, east and west of the Empire together with the under-dwelling dwarfs under one banner. Emil climbed down also, taking his cross-bow and drawing the string back to its latch. Kastner shook his head. 'Must you? I don't mind you hunting our evening meal with that wretched thing but must it be used to slay the God-King's enemies?'

'Is this not a hunt of a kind, my lord?' Emil replied, placing a bolt in the groove. Kastner disapproved of the crossbow. It was not a knightly weapon. On the other hand, it would take little for it to slam a bolt straight through the thick plate of his armour. Or the thick hide of a beastman, for that matter. He looked back at the raucous celebration about the standing stones. The templar stared at the wizened shaman with suspicion as it conducted its primitive ritual above the butchery on the altar. Such primitives called on otherworldly powers against which a knight's armour offered as little protection as against a crossbow bolt.

'Then your first quarry can be that horned thing at the centre of the stones,' Kastner told the squire.

'You think it leads this herd?' Emil asked.

'Hopefully not for much longer,' Kastner said.

'I'll need to get closer.'

Kastner looked down at *Terminus*, the greatsword's blade shadowed by the darkness about it. 'You and me both.'

Emil thought on the deer and boar he hunted through the woods. 'Won't they smell us coming?'

Kastner nodded at the squire's packhorse. At the stinking corpse of Yurian Spartak draped over it.

'We are masked by the stench of corruption,' the templar said. He took his crusader's helm from the pommel-horn of Oberon's saddle. 'Fight well,' he said to Emil. 'Know that the God-King is with us in this desperate place. That he fights at our side in the bloodshed to come. On my signal.'

Emil nodded.

'Good luck, my lord.'

'When your sword is guided by Sigmar, good fortune is not a factor,' Kastner said. 'Remember that.' Kastner's face disappeared behind his helm. Taking slow steps through the mud and mire, leading Oberon by the reins, Kastner advanced on the warherd. As he got nearer he could see that the gors' fighting, drinking and dancing was masking their approach. With Spartak's rotten stench hiding the sweet smell of their uncorrupted flesh from the host and their warhounds, the knight and his squire made it to the outlying circle of standing stones. Roughly carved runes and daemon-honouring symbols, splashed in old blood, covered the ancient obelisks. From the leafless branches of the canopy above swung gibbet cages of petrified wood. Each contained a miserable specimen. Prisoners – men, women and children – had been gathered by bestial hunting parties to provide fresh sacrifice for their unholy gods and flesh for their grumbling bellies. The warhounds that had hunted them had been chain-staked into the ground below the prisoners. They routinely leapt and snapped at the cages, snarls and feverish drool dribbling from their jaws.

The sound of an ugly death – wet and shrill – cut through the bombast of the bestial gathering. Risking a glance about the standing stone, Kastner saw the shaman, arms outstretched, holding his staff and a gore-oozing heart in his disgusting claws. He bleated something to the stars as a disturbed cloud of flies swarmed about his filthy robes. The shaman jabbed his staff at the cages, summoning another victim to his dark altar.

Moving his helm around, Kastner peered around the other side of his stone. A hulking beastman, a wall of muscle and wiry black hair emerged from behind the swollen trunk of a diseased oak. Upon its globed, shaggy shoulders sat a squat bovine skull. The mighty horns of a bull dominated the monstrous head, while its long face bore the curse of a thing sired by daemon on livestock. Steam smoked from its nostrils as it parted the braying and bestial merry-making. Several urn-swilling beastmen failed to move swiftly enough and produced from the monster's chest a rumble of thunder. A skull-crushing fist came down on the first goatly head, sending the beastman crashing into the mud. The second was grabbed by its furry shoulders and butted into savage unconsciousness by the oxen-headed beast. It too went down to the celebratory braying and bleating of the herd. The creatures parted for the beastman, leaving only the warhounds in its way. The bull broke one of the hunting dogs across its hoof with a furious kick. The carcass flew into the air before being torn back down to the ground on its staked chain. Within moments the gnashing mongrels were flat to the forest floor, whining their submission.

Kastner watched the bull take instruction badly from its bleating shaman. Barging through the gibbet cages and setting them to creak and swing, the monster's search produced sobs and doom-laden shrieks from the prisoners within. The people were broken. They had watched as their number had dwindled, one by one succumbing to the butchery on the altar and a bone-splintering feast for the hideous herd. Only one seemed to have any fight left in her. A mere girl by the look of her. Kastner watched as her legs flailed out at the monster from the gibbet cage. The girl gagged.

'Get away from me! You stink,' the girl called. The bull reached out for her but she pulled her legs within the cage. 'Are you deaf as well as lame of brain, you abomination? Go find a spit.'

Kastner was impressed with the girl's spirit – and she was a girl, seeming no older than Emil. She was dressed in rags that might once have been robes, made from material that might once have been white. The girl had the reckless abandon and wicked tongue of youth. Her eyes were dark and defiant while her hair was boyishly short and looked as if it had been scissored about a bowl. Kastner had seen such haircuts before – on the novice-sisters and vestals of religious orders. Standing in her gibbet, she clutched a package to her stomach: a pile of tomes, bound in a pile with twine. As the beastman grasped the wooden bars of the cage, the girl kicked at it with her sandals. 'Get off, you reeking freak.'

The girl certainly didn't sound like a sister. Ire dribbled from the bull's steaming snout. Its ears rang with the bleatings of its shaman and the girl's effrontery. With an effortless flex of its muscle-bound arms and shoulders, the monster tore the cage apart, causing the novice-sister to drop into the den of dogs below. A fang-faced hound brought up its head to snap at the girl. Swinging the books around on their length of twine, the girl smacked its snout aside. A great hoof came down beside her, crunching the dog into the ground for its impudence. The girl screamed as the bull snatched her up by the legs and dragged her through the mire towards the altar. Clawing at the muddy ground, the girl discovered that she had lost her pile of books. She reached out for the length of twine but the bull's monstrous stride swiftly took her out of reach. As the beastman stomped away, the warhounds rose from their subservience and closed about the package of tomes like the gates of a snarling enclosure.

Kastner moved back around the standing stone, *Terminus* seeming to burn in his grasp. The bull laid its colossal, blood-stained hands on the girl, producing another shriek of surprise, but the monster simply grabbed her like a sack of grain and slammed her down on the altar. Lying in the butchered remains of the previous sacrifice, the novice-sister thrashed out with her feet and small fists, knocking the heads of toadstools and settled fungus from the shaman's flesh. The bull glowered at the victim, its stench overpowering and its hot breath billowing about them. The goat-headed shaman seemed amused by the girl's resistance, its yellow teeth bared and its foetid form wracked by a sickly laughter.

'I hear your shepherd calling, whey-face,' the novice said, hitting out at the ancient. She was simple and coarse of tongue but her spirit was indomitable. The shaman reached out for her with mildewed hands. 'Don't you touch me,' she said, spitting at the beast. The girl tried to get up out of the gore but the shaman's staff suddenly came down across her throat. It both held her to the altar and restricted her breathing. She clawed at it but dark energies were flowing through the monster and it was as immovable as a tree. The goatly grin was gone from the ancient's furry lips. It moved in with a claw still wet with blood. The girl tried to cover herself as its hand explored her shredded robes, pulling from them a small silver hammer on a chain. It dawned on the shaman, as it had done on Kastner, that the girl was some kind of novice or the sister of a religious order. With the last of her breath and the staff across her throat, the girl hissed: 'My... God-King... will... smite... thee...'

The shaman erupted with bleating laughter. It was infectious. The creatures of the warherd joined the celebration in savage mirth. As the concubine of an enemy god, the girl's sacrifice would bring many blessings from their dark patrons. Selecting a flint knife from the altar, its razored blade stained red by the many lives it had taken, the shaman held it above the torso of the thrashing girl. The shaman's eyes closed and its lips fell to daemon-honouring bleats and incantations.

Kastner stood, the smooth metal of his plate gliding up the moss-threaded stone. The templar was tensed. His mind and body were ready for the slaughter to come. He had been watching and waiting. Enemies had been counted. Every brute silhouette had been allowed to reveal itself, the measure of its reach and its likely intention. The knight knew by horn and frame which beasts would fight and which would scatter. He knew which creatures were far from their brute weapons and which were out of their mind on ale. He knew the things that had to die first. The ones that would test him with their gifts and savagery. The gors. The bull. The wizened shaman. He looked to Emil. The squire's crossbow was already up, resting against an opposing stone.

'Now,' Kastner told him, his helm coming down and tapping against his breastplate.

The shaman's ragged ears pricked. His eyes opened and rotated in their sockets. Interlopers. Intruders on unholy ground. Fresh sacrifices for the herdstone. His thick tongue wrapped itself around curses and ancient bewitchments.

Emil's horse reared with sudden savagery. The squire instinctively moved, sending his bolt wide. The quarrel tugged at the shaman's rags and shattered off the herdstone behind. The squire's steed was not itself. The creature was glazed of eye and flashing out with its hooves. Emil ducked and backed from out of the cover of the obelisk as his horse's shoe sparked off the stone. The packhorse was similarly affected, hawing and bucking the corpse of Yurian Spartak from its back. This had nothing to do with the dead warrior of Chaos, Kastner decided. This was the shaman asserting its control over the wild natures of its beast-kin.

Kastner watched as Oberon's eyes glazed over like a northern lake. The stallion's lips curled back from the long pegs of its teeth. The knight had to act fast. Kastner ran at the steed, his mail and plated fist bringing his crusader shield up, smashing the horse's skull aside. The animal stumbled backwards, both the sense and spell's influence knocked from it. Legs faltered and the stallion crumbled and crashed to the ground unconscious. The Sigmarite templar's gauntlet creaked about the greatsword *Terminus*. He was less sentimental about his squire's steed and packhorse, which they had recently picked up in Bergsburg. The crusader blade went up between the savage hooves of the reared steed and into its chest. Pulling the broad blade from the punctured ruin of the horse's heart, Kastner spun around. *Terminus* passed through the packhorse's throat before Emil's steed hit the ground.

'Again,' the knight bawled through his helm at the squire who was reloading his crossbow.

The fire raged. The warherd remembered themselves. Ale-jars were flung into the standing stones of the circle. Muscle-bound silhouettes came at the templar. The longhorns first. Savages already tested in battle with greenskins and ratmen. Monsters who had killed enough and had lived long enough to enjoy the appreciations of their herd. They had never met a Knight of the Twin-Tailed Orb, however. They had never met Diederick Kastner. Their beastflesh was tough and wiry, shot through with sinew and strong bone. *Terminus* cleaved through it like clotted cream. Kastner became a silhouette amongst many – the fire framing both the clean, confident movements of his training and the invention he introduced inbetween.

The beastmen, in contrast, were bludgeoners, favouring scavenged axes and stone hammers. Their weapons were rude and rusted but the strength with which they swung them was hate-fuelled and barbaric. There was no organisation or consideration of tactics, only an animal cunning and a pecking order, with monsters of greater size and length of horn engaging first. It was easy for a warrior – even a templar knight moving within the exhausting constraints of metal plate – to lose himself in battle. To become such an animal.

The lost were in the thrall of the Blood God – their rage a mindless offering. Such men were no better than the beasts Kastner was taking apart with the disciplined strokes and thrusts of his templar blade. Kastner had reasoned that the best warriors thought their way through battle. They knew where their blade would be the moment before it landed. They knew where the service of their shield would be required before the fatal landing of the axe. A man that fought by instinct alone – like even the most capable savage – could not know such things. He could not predict the lethal preferences of his enemy and he could not learn from them mid-engagement. Battle was a serious game of strategy and skill, like those played with boards and fancy pieces. Able players could rely on rehearsed moves, while simultaneously exploiting the weaknesses of opponents as they were revealed before them.

Terminus hacked limbs from muscular torsos. Shoulder-cleaving swings took heads almost from shoulders. Streams of hot beast-blood sailed about the knight as the herd's best gors carpeted the ground within the circle. Kastner's shield soaked up the frustration and desperation of axe-wielding monsters that roared at him as if it meant something. The onslaught continued as Kastner plunged his blade through the carcasses of their fellow savages. Inbetween such surgical thrusts, the templar found a moment to slam back at the creatures at his rear, smashing jaws from goat-skulls with the cross guard of his sword and kicking monstrosities back into the flames of the furious fire.

As the carnage unfolded and the warherd began to get over the drunken shock of the intrusion, the shaman slashed his flint knife through the air, motioning the hordes of lesser gors and brays on into the slaughter. As the herd's best butcherers were cleaved apart by the fearless knight, there were few beastmen that relished such a proposition. With the ale souring in their bellies and their spears and cudgels loose in their claws, they hesitated.

During a raid or the murderous slaughter of a village, the cogs of barbaric carnage were usually oiled by the blood spilled by beastlords and longhorns – the very creatures the plate-clad knight was hewing his way through. With lesser creatures and beastlings fleeing into the darkness of the forest, many of the herd's savages thought of doing the same. Several hoofsteps back, however, they were stopped in their tracks by the thunderous roar of the bull. The beast snatched a broad woodcutter's blade from a nearby creature and took its head clean off with a bellow-driven sweep. Both the sound and the violence drove the warherd on, like a storm at their backs, across the stone circle at the templar knight.

The shaman bleated its alarm at the bull, fearful of offending its gods and intent on completing the sacrifice. Spinning the axe in its colossal fist, the beast caught it and launched the weapon haft over blade at the tree supporting the gibbet cages of the prisoners. Embedding itself in the diseased trunk, the axe cut through the lines supporting them. The cages crashed to the ground amongst and on top of the herd's warhounds. Like the horses, the dogs had been driven to mindless savagery by the shaman's incantations. The prisoners shrieked their terror as their cages shattered and the diseased maws of the dogs set upon them, tearing the flesh from their bones.

The last of the beastlords was a four-horned monstrosity that Kastner thought he had put down in the first few kills. The monstrous thing, driven on by some bestial refusal to die, swung a mace made up of the embedded fangs of some sabre-toothed conquest. Twice the weapon had punctured Kastner's shield and had even plunged through his plate pauldron and into his shoulder.

As Kastner cut pieces off the beastman with his greatsword and the creature mauled him in return with its thagomizer, Emil found it difficult to take the shot. He had held the crossbow to his eye for some time. Each time he prepared to take the shot, Kastner's armoured form or the flailing body of one of his brute victims moved before the target. As Emil had moved to get a better shot, beastmen had joined the fray – some bound for the squire and intercepted by Kastner.

The shaman, eyes closed and lips mouthing ritual incantations in some dark tongue, held his flint blade over the girl's chest. The novice's bosom rose and fell rapidly in alarm, the creature's staff holding her down on the altar. She pushed up against the staff but it would not move. The mumbling ended. The knife came up. Emil's target would not wait. The squire let the bolt fly. It whistled between Diederick Kastner and the four-horned beast he was exchanging blows with, but the pair barely noticed.

The shaman did notice. The quarrel – which had flown straight and true – had found its way between the creature's unsettling eyes. It stumbled against the mighty herdstone at its back as the flint knife clattered to the altar. The macabre staff followed. Sliding back down the herdstone, the shaman was dead by the time it reached the cankered earth. The novice-sister sat upright, clutching at her throat. She was coughing, cursing and trying to get her breath.

There was snarling. There was barking. And it was getting closer. Emil turned to see that the hulking bull had stomped through the flesh-stripped prisoners and released the warhounds. The beast towered over the chain-trailing creatures, snorting its hate at the squire before thundering its way back towards the Sigmarite knight and the horde of bestial kin it had unleashed at him. Emil hooked the stirrup over his boot and feverishly reloaded the crossbow.

'My lord,' he said, the words leaving his lips like a last regret. Bringing the crossbow up, he slammed the bolt into the lead creature, pinning it to the ground. He reloaded. The pack scrambled on.

Kastner looked to the squire and then back at the four-horned beast before him which refused to die. Behind the creature was a horde of bull-spooked beastmen, charging with spears and gnarled clubs. Another hound went down. 'Master,' Emil called, hammering a third mongrel into a tree trunk.

Kastner threw *Terminus* down at the ground, the blade quivering in the soft earth, and allowed the beastman's fanged mace to bury itself in his shield. Shrugging the weapon aside and with his gauntlets free, the knight seized the creature by the horns and butted it in the snout with his crusader helm. And again. And again. With the beastman's ruined face splattered across the helm, Kastner released it, allowing the creature to fall backwards.

'Present your blade,' Kastner roared across the stone circle, retrieving his own weapon.

The pack was almost upon the squire. Emil lined up his next shot but realised the futility of the action. Allowing the crossbow to drop, he tore his short blade from his scabbard, slashing the first of the hounds to one side. Another came at him and received the same treatment. Somehow, in the unfolding havoc, Emil found his way to his training. The disciplined cuts and slashes that Kastner had taught him. Moves that suited a short blade and an inexperienced swordsman. But there were too many. Too many sets of jaws. Too many blood-crazed hounds, savaging his legs, clamping onto his arms, leaping at the squire and dragging him down. Emil became a mound of emaciated bodies, whippet tails and diseased maws, tearing his body in different directions.

Kastner saw the occasional flash of the blade and the isolated yelps of animals unfortunate enough to find themselves skewered by it. The squire was down, however, and needed help. The templar took several determined steps towards the screaming squire, but the dogs were dragging his fang-slashed body into the trees. The templar's steps became an awkward run, exhaustion and the weight of his plate dragging him down. He felt the warherd slam into his shield like a team of charging stallions at the head of a runaway coach. Kastner fell to one side, almost tripping over his own armoured boots. He almost went over, which Kastner knew would have been the end of him. Down on the ground in full plate armour, he would have been an easy sitting target for crooked spears.

Self-reproach sizzled in his chest. He could not save the squire without saving himself. He was no use to the God-King dead. Kastner dug his boots into the sloppy earth. The horde pushed. With a roar the knight heaved back.

'Sigmar,' he hissed within his crusader helm. 'My god… my king…'

Kastner heaved. He heaved again. Blows began to rain down on his armour from the flanks. He gasped as a spear slipped inbetween his plates and cut, hot and wicked, into his side. Cutting through the shaft with *Terminus,* he pushed on into the centre of the mob. Every mongrel and half-breed wanted to own his death. The yellowness of their hearts was gone. Their bare chests beating with the confidence of their number, the success of their savage blows and the knight's impending death. Diederick Kastner had no intention of meeting such an expectation.

'Sigmar, grant me the strength to cleanse this land of your foes...' the knight snarled through his efforts. He heaved at the mob before him. His teeth gritted beneath his helmet and his boots stamped footholds in the ground. He hurled himself at the shield and the shield at the warherd. '...as the light cleanses the darkness.'

One final gargantuan push had driven the monstrosities before him into the embrace of their own fire. Kastner screwed his eyes shut against the brightness that flooded his helm. He felt heat pass rapidly through the metal of his plate. In driving the throng before him, the templar had half stepped into the fire himself. The silhouettes of his enemies, thrashing at the knight with their weapons moments before, were now thrashing at themselves, bleating and screeching, as the beastmen attempted to extinguish the flames licking their way through their shaggy fur.

Kastner turned, the heat scorching its way through his plate searing the skin. With part of the horde aflame and the rest unwilling to follow them, the knight found himself alone. The hammer of blows raining down on his buckled plate had ceased. Spears failed to lance his flesh. Muscular bodies no longer clashed with his own. The beastmen huddled together. They were a wall of spear-points and the crude presenting of weaponry. Kastner had reminded them why they should fear him.

The templar's steaming plate rattled as he shook himself back to composure. He stretched his tension-knotted neck from side to side. *Terminus* ached in his gauntlet and he clashed it three times against his mangled shield.

'Come on!' the knight roared at them. 'Come on! I have the God-King's absolution in my hand. Come and get it...'

One exhausted step followed another, taking the templar into the bestial ranks. A ram-headed beast came at him with a stone hammer. It died. An antlered monstrosity tried to impale him on a pitch-forked spear. It died. A stubby-horned fiend threw itself and its serrated hatchets at him. It died. Cut. Thrust. Shield-smash. Repeat. As his plate cooled, righteous hatred for the darkbreeds burned. He would kill them all. Holding back a pair of dead-eyed goat monsters, Kastner swung *Terminus* about him, severing head after bleating head. Pushing the beastmen back he pulled the shield aside and slammed the length of the greatsword blade through the pair of carcasses. He would kill them all. The stone circle stank of death like never before. Kastner found himself striding through mounds of corpses. The beastmen stumbled through their dead. *Terminus* sang through them, its blade an instrument upon which a ballad was played. A story of drama and death. Mostly death. Even as the herd thinned and the cowardly creatures went to flee, the knight cut them down, opening their shaggy beastflesh from their broad shoulders to their buttocks. He. Would. Kill. Them. All.

But he wouldn't. The bull – a ferocious tower of bovine fury – denied him. The colossus stomped forward, shaking its mighty horns and smashing remaining beastmen aside with its huge fists. As the broken bodies of its kindred hit trees and the standing stones of the circle, the bull grabbed the herd's final gor. The goat-faced wretch bleated in terror before the bull tore it in two. With gore and intestines dribbling through its huge fingers, the monster snorted pure hate at the knight standing before him.

'Come on,' Kastner said, beckoning it on with a gesture of his shield. 'In the God-King's name, let's finish it...'

The bull stormed at him, its hooves shaking the ground like thunder. Its head came down. Its horn-points came at the templar, dark with dried blood. Kastner assumed a fighting stance. He was ready to side-step the beast and use its own momentum to take it past him. There he would deliver a strike to fell the creature – or at least slow it down. The bull was fast for something so huge and at the last moment Kastner decided that he would not be able to evade the avalanche of muscle and rage coming at him. Bracing himself behind the shield for the impact, Kastner found himself driven backwards.

Corralled between the monster's two great horns, Kastner was slammed back into the rough stone of a primitive obelisk behind. The hulking beast grabbed the standing stone with its huge hands, and trapping Kastner between the unforgiving obelisk and its thick skull proceeded to pound the knight to oblivion. Kastner felt his shield buckle and his plate crumple about him. His head bounced back and forth within his helm as the bull smashed him into the standing stone.

The assault stopped and Kastner attempted to recover his breath. The beast's huge skull moved away, once again allowing the knight to see the light of the fire, the stone circle and the shadows that lay beyond. The only other living thing within the circle was the girl, who, benefitting from the bull's distraction, had picked her way back through what was left of the hound-mauled prisoners to find her precious pile of books.

Kastner pushed himself away from the obelisk, his plate having moulded itself to the stone's imperfections. Like a prize-fighter trapped in a corner by his opponent, Kastner was pushed back. His shield battered him into the rough stone, its metal surface pounded to uselessness by the beastman's colossal fists. Suddenly the shield was gone, torn away by the bull – the creature eager to pulverise the knight's armoured form and the soft flesh that lay within. A fist came at Kastner. He ducked. Barely in time. The woolly knuckles of the beast smashed stone from the monolith. Another fist almost took the knight's head off, settling instead for shattering away a section of the obelisk.

Kastner launched himself at the colossal creature's chest. It was like the side of a building, muscles bulging like bricks – it had its own brutal architecture. Kastner slammed it again with his battered pauldron – enough to make room for *Terminus,* and the chest-opening sweep of the blade that gashed the beast from navel to nipple. The monster bellowed its pain, smacking the broad blade from the knight's exhausted grip. As the sword clanged off the standing stone and onto the wet earth, the beast back-fisted Kastner across the circle.

For moments following, the knight had little idea where he was. The brightness of the fire eclipsed all else. Its crackle was a mind-aching torment. The ground seemed to move with a sickening motion. Suddenly Kastner was up. The bull was upon him once more. It lifted the armoured templar and flung him like a sack of grain back across the circle. He hit another of the standing stones. There was a sharp pain in the back of his skull. When he opened his eyes he found that his helm had gone. He was sitting at the base of an obelisk. All he could hear was the fury spilling out of the beastman. It charged.

Kastner toppled himself to one side, his plate rattling like a wagon on a rough road. He felt himself drifting in and out of consciousness.

The brute's hoof smashed down into the base of the stone where the knight had been. Kastner crawled miserably away, plated arm over buckled arm. The creature raged above him like a storm. The knight dashed his face in the muddy pool he was crawling through, bringing him briefly back to clarity. The standing stone gave an excruciating moan as the bull tore at it, toppling it across the knight's scrabbling form. Trapping Kastner briefly, the irregularity of the obelisk and the marshiness of the ground beneath its fallen length allowed the knight to scrape his armoured legs free. Before Kastner knew it, the beast was bringing another stone down on him. The knight rolled to one side through the mud, the mire squelching in through the rents in his plate. The bull grasped a broken chunk of stone, bigger than the monster's own head, and held it above its horns. Mounting the fallen stones, the creature stood above the knight's prone form, snorting its clouded exertions into the night air. Its arms trembled. Kastner stopped crawling. He rolled back over to present himself to the bovine colossus... the squire's recovered crossbow in his muddy gauntlets. It was not a knightly weapon – but it would serve. Kastner fired.

The bolt stabbed up through the muscle of the bull's chest. The close range had buried the bolt right up to its feathered flight. The beastman snorted with sudden surprise. Its bludgeoning stone crashed to the ground, bouncing off the toppled obelisk from which it came. The bull staggered back across the slaughter of the circle. Gasping. Snorting. Moaning like a herd of frightened cattle.

Kastner pushed himself to his knees. His arms were shaking. His head felt light and the wound in his side burned with every excruciating movement. He got unsteadily to his feet, his plate rattling with exhaustion. Putting one foot in front of the other, the knight walked about the stone circle and recovered *Terminus* from where it lay, splattered with both mud and blood before the base of a rough obelisk. The sword felt heavy in his hands and the knight needed both to drag the blade across the stone circle. The bull had made it to the gore-dripping altar, bent over double, its great chest heaving with the difficulty of breathing.

With more effort than he could bear, Kastner heaved *Terminus* above his head, roaring his side-splitting agony. The greatsword crashed down on the altar surface, sending a crack through the ancient stone. The bull had pushed itself away through the slick blood on its surface and crashed down beside its shaman at the foot of the herdstone. It groaned, one hoofed slab of a leg shaking uncontrollably. It spread the fingers of one huge hand across its chest and around the bolt through its thunderous heart. Its other arm waved the Sigmarite knight away in silent pleading. With difficulty, Kastner moved around the broken altar and swayed above the bull in his own torment. The templar shook his head as clouds of the beastman's hot breath enveloped them both. The herdstone ached with the unnatural energies of its making and construction. Its wyrdstone gleamed like shadow, charged with the offering of so many souls slaughtered in the circle before it. The bull nestled its mighty horned skull against it, like an infant at its mother's bosom. Still it thought its Ruinous patrons would deliver it.

'No,' Kastner said, his lips bloodied and bruised. The beast closed eyes wet with fear and frustration. Its arm came down in monstrous acceptance. Kastner lifted *Terminus* once more and brought the blade down on the creature's thick skull with all the fury he could summon from his pain-wracked body. Blood sprayed the knight's ruined armour as he hacked down through horn and bone. The blade came down again and again, its cleaving movements becoming wilder and wilder. Although the fire in his arms succumbed to the effort, the fire in his heart did not. He. Would. Kill. Them. All.

The heavy blade went wide, missing the beastman's demolished skull and clashing through the irregularity of the herdstone. The metal of the blade rang strangely against the material and Kastner felt a sudden agony burn through his mind like the tip of a fire-stoked poker. The hurt and surprise was such that the Knight of the Twin-Tailed Orb dropped *Terminus* in the gore of his ruined foe and stumbled at the altar, his gauntlet clasped across his right eye. A groan of delicate anguish escaped his lips. Blood, hot and thick, spilled through the metal digits and down his face. He tried to see but he could not. Blinking his left eye open through the blood and the pain he found that he could not do so with the right. His heart became a whisper. He roared his fears and fell to his armoured knees. All he could see with the right was the deep darkness of the world now gone. A throbbing woe. A feverish affliction. A white-hot absence. Doom in all its pure honesty.

Snatching his gauntlet from his hand he traced the tip of a finger through the bloody socket and across the ruined eye. He felt the prick of an object within and the simultaneous agony of a pain the like of he which he had never experienced. It was like a crash of lightning through the mind, throwing everything within into the dread, darkness and disorder that followed. Kastner tried to think. To focus his way through the constant torment. *Terminus* must have struck a flinty shard from the wyrdstone and sent it like an arrow head into his eye. Clutching his other hand, the knight smashed the metal fist into the herdstone in frustration and anger. He had been stupid. Rash. Irrational. And he had paid for it. He had lost something that he couldn't possibly get back. The realisation burned him.

The templar remained before the stone for a while, kneeling in the end of his enemies. The shame of tears rolled quietly down one blood-speckled cheek. Gore steamed from the ground. The fire began to die. The raw redness of the dawn reached through the open sky.

Kastner felt something nudge his arm. It was Oberon. The stallion pushed at him gently with its nose, as though unsure whether its master was dead or alive. The knight was so still. The steed was not the only one interested. Kastner looked up. The novice-sister was kneeling before him, her bound books in her lap, her lips parted as she stared at his eye. It was a botched mess. A spider-shaped puncture wound revealing the darkness within. Blood ran like tears from its ruination. The girl tore a strip of clean material from her chemise and proceeded to wrap it about Kastner's head, covering his blind eye. She had been talking but Kastner hadn't noticed.

'So you're a knight,' the girl said.

'What?'

'You're a knight?' she repeated. Her voice was annoyingly up-beat. Sing-song and provincial. She moved the pile of books closer, as though she were protecting them. Kastner grunted. From the sound of her voice, the templar found it difficult to believe that the girl had ever looked between the covers of one. 'I've never seen a knight close up. There were some that visited the Reverend Mother, you know, with important persons and such…'

'A knight is an important person,' Kastner said. He needed something to concentrate on other than the agony in his head. The girl didn't seem to have noticed that Kastner had spoken. She rambled on.

'The one I saw up closest, well he wore the same kind of armour as you. Different symbol, though. Some kind of animal, I think. One of the girls in the scullery said it was a griffon, whatever that is…'

'You're a sister?' Kastner put to her.

'Yes, well, no – I'm a novice,' the girl admitted. 'I work in the scullery…'

'I got that,' Kastner said. The blinding agony of his eye was making him short and sarcastic. 'A Sigmarite?'

'Why, yes, sieur,' the girl said. 'The Reverend Mother said that one day I'd make a very fine Sister of the Imperial Cross.' Kastner had heard of the order. Like his own knightly order, the Sisters of the Imperial Cross answered ultimately to the Grand Theogonist in Altdorf. The order maintained priories and convents of dutiful sisters throughout the Empire and took as their symbol the Imperial cross – the same cross that adorned the pommel of *Terminus*. North, south, east and west – the Sisters of the Imperial Cross honoured Sigmar as their patron and took as their solemn duty the spiritual unity of the God-King's Empire. 'She gave me this...' the girl told him. She pulled a silver hammer from her robes from where it was hanging on a chain.

'Where's your priory, girl?' Kastner demanded, pushing himself to his feet. He wobbled and the novice went to steady him.

'The Hammerfall,' the girl told him. 'In the Middle Mountains. Going on three years now.'

Kastner turned and put his head to Oberon's.

'Good boy,' the templar told him. Then to the novice, 'Girl, get my sword and my steed.'

'I have a name, you know,' the girl scowled.

Kastner nodded to himself. The girl really wasn't bright. She clearly knew no better than to answer back to a knight. If Kastner had truly been of noble birth he might have had her answer for it. It was the same pluck he had seen in the cage, before the bull. Three years at the Hammerfall and still a novice. Little wonder, given the mouth on her. Little wonder that she had found her services indispensable in the scullery, the knight reasoned. He turned.

'What's your name, girl?'

'Giselle,' she said.

Kastner nodded slowly.

'Girl,' he said, 'get my sword and steed.'

'Don't you have...?' Giselle began.

The knight turned his head, brought up his hand and slapped it down into his gauntlet.

'All right, all right,' the girl said, heaving *Terminus* out of the gore. 'I just thought you'd have a squire for this sort of thing.'

'I do,' Kastner said, finding his footing and striding for the woods. As he passed Emil's crossbow on the ground – the unknightly weapon that had saved the knight's life – he scooped it up.

With *Terminus's* bloody blade over one shoulder, Oberon's reins in the other hand and her pile of books under an arm, Giselle followed the templar out of the stone circle. Kastner stepped over the two warhounds Emil had shot. Even in the sliver of morning sun, the tracks were easy to follow. The pads of the savage dogs were everywhere. Emil's body had been dragged through the trees. There were scraps of clothing. Blood. Even a couple of the boy's fingers. There were also bodies. The bodies of emaciated hounds that the squire had managed to gut with his short sword or skinning knife. One by one the knight stepped over the carcasses of dead dogs. There were so many that it was hard to believe any of the herd's hunting pack had been left alive. They hadn't. Kastner found the last of the beasts, its tainted jaws still wrapped around Emil's neck.

Kastner trudged down into the bloody mire about the boy's body, pulling the warhound off him. A crossbow bolt, planted there by hand, was buried in the dog's stab-thrashed belly. Emil was a mess. Kastner felt cold emotion wash through his pain-wracked chest. Giselle came up behind with Oberon. She allowed the greatsword to fall and spear the ground and looked at the templar. The girl saw the grief – the responsibility – pass across Kastner's face.

'Is he alive?' she asked. Kastner didn't answer. 'Saw a man fed to the Graf's wolves once,' the girl said absently. 'He looked much like that.'

The boy's limbs were savaged, his ragged torso was a fang-punctured mess, his handsome features all but gone. Kastner brought his ear to the squire's mauled chest. He paused. He held his own breath. Then he heard it. Faint – but there. The beating of the boy's heart. He felt it. The slight rise and fall of his ribcage. Kastner closed his eye.

'Hang on, Emil,' the knight said.

Hauling the moaning Emil out of the puddle of his own blood, Kastner laid him across Oberon's saddle.

'Get up,' Kastner told the girl. She shook her head.

'I don't ride.'

'You do today,' Kastner said. 'Give me your foot.'

'I've never ridden a horse in my life, sir. My family couldn't even afford a broken mule…'

'Girl, I need you to do this,' Kastner said. '*He* needs you to do this. There is a small temple in the foothills of the Middle Mountains, near the village of Esk.'

'A temple to Sigmar?' the girl asked, suddenly interested.

'Yes, a way temple,' the templar replied.

'I need a temple,' she said and Kastner found the girl's delicate foot in his gauntlet. He pushed her up onto the mighty Oberon. There she uncertainly took the reins with Emil laid before her. She hugged her books to her.

'There you will find a priest named Dagobert. Tell him Sieur Kastner sent you. He will recognise my steed and my squire. This is Oberon.'

'This priest,' Giselle asked, 'he is a wise man?'

'Yes,' Kastner said. 'He will know what to do.'

'I mean,' Giselle said, 'is he a learned man? My Reverend Mother bade me promise, on the blood of the Founder, that I deliver these tomes to a learned man, a priest – a true servant of Sigmar.'

'Your books be damned, girl,' Kastner said, his agonies making him sharp and impatient. 'A man's life hangs in the balance.'

'My lady was very specific,' the girl said moodily. 'A learned man, she said. A true servant of Sigmar.'

'You'll find none truer,' Kastner said irritably. He pulled Oberon to a stop. He rubbed his blood-splattered forehead with his fingers. He needed the girl more than he cared to admit to her. His trials – his agonies – were making him discourteous. 'You were taken by the beasts of the forest on your way to deliver these tomes?'

'I was.'

'The Drakwald is not to be travelled lightly,' Kastner told her. 'Take my squire to Father Dagobert. He is a good man. A learned man. He will see to your tomes and answer any questions your Reverend Mother has. But please, take my man to him first.'

'My Lady seeks no answers from the books, sir,' Giselle said. 'She said take them. Take them far from the Hammerfall. To safety.'

Kastner frowned, but he did not have time for further questions. He handed her Emil's crossbow. 'If any bar your path, you tell them you are on the temple's business and put this in their face. They will think twice, I assure you.'

Giselle took the weapon.

'How might I find this temple?'

'Oberon knows the way,' Kastner told her.

'You would entrust this man's life to a horse?'

'No, I entrust him to you,' the templar told her. 'Gorst!' Kastner called to the forest. 'Gorst, get yourself out here, you mangy beggar.'

Giselle looked about. The fingertips of red morning radiance probed the dank forest. Then she saw him, emerging like a skittish animal from behind a tree. A wretched figure. A flagellant draped in chains, his head trapped within a small cage. Giselle's lip curled with obvious disgust. 'Girl, meet Gorst. Gorst, I want you to lead Oberon to Father Dagobert. You remember the temple at Esk?'

The flagellant nodded slowly. 'Gorst, the God-King asks this of you. Do you understand? You will not fail him. You will not fail me.' The flagellant nodded. Kastner slapped Oberon's hindquarters, prompting the stallion on. As the horse reached Gorst, the flagellant broke into a run, leading it into the forest at a trot. As Emil moaned at the movement and Giselle rolled in the saddle, the novice turned back to look at Kastner.

'What are you going to do?' the girl called over her shoulder.

'The God-King's work,' Kastner told her. 'There is stone to smash and bodies to burn. I shall ensure that this dark path leads nowhere. The Empire is no place for the children of Chaos. The next warherd to pass through here will know that.'

As the Knight of the Twin-Tailed Orb became lost to her in the halo of morning sun breaking through the trees, Giselle nodded and turned back to her path. She thought on the slaughter of the stone circle. 'I think they will,' she said to herself.

CHAPTER V

'Why did chance its steps betray,
Far from friend and home –
On trails left by the hands of fate
Where only shadows roam.'

– The Brothers Ziegler

The Drakwald
Hochland
Sonstill, IC 2420

Diederick Kastner was lost.

North had not taken him north. It had taken him to another place. Somewhere the sun rarely shone – and when it did, it bled across the sky like a wound, keeping impossible consort with the moons. Diederick wandered, his mindless steps and stumbles plunging him through forest he had never known. He dragged *Terminus* behind him in one trembling, white fist. The tip of the sword's broad blade left a furrow behind the templar, cutting through the tangle of the forest earth.

Kastner's battered armour felt like a fireplace, reflecting the feverish heat of his body inwards. Droplets fell from his brow and cheeks, pitter-patting against his breastplate. He moaned his exhaustion, madness dripping from his lips like Gorst or the madmen he'd seen in hospice cages. He tried to stem its flow but even the attempt to do so became a senseless rant.

Day and night danced about him, like lovers at a fête, swinging each other around, each revolution getting faster and faster. The sensation was sickening. The land moved beneath his feet and his stomach shifted, causing the knight to heave and vomit down the trunks of trees. He tumbled. He fell, his plate clattering like a tray of tankards to a tavern floor. His sweat dropped to the black forest earth. Buds on the trees erupted and buried the knight in blossom. Leaves glowed glorious green before bronzing, withering and raining down to the ground about him. Frost crept both through the naked woodland and the templar, harbinger of snowfall which dusted everything a dirty white. Within moments it was gone, leaving puddles in its wake that were guzzled by the thirsty earth and once again the twigs and branches of the canopy were dotted with shoots of green.

Kastner crawled. He pushed himself from tree to trunk. He stabbed the toe of his boots into the dirt for purchase, like the climber of a slope or mountain. Roots slithered about his footfalls while foliage seemed to reach out for him. Insects stung, bit and ate the templar alive. Birds and bats flew at him. Forest vermin raced before his unsteady feet. All were blurred and indistinct. Afterthoughts of their own noxious existence.

A snake shot out and snapped at his foot. Kastner blundered back into a tree, disturbing an owl which flapped its great wings at him. His next footfall wasn't there and neither was the one after that. The knight tumbled. He fell for what seemed like an eternity before hitting the ground. It was a steep slope, littered with logs and boulders pushing up out of the ground. Kastner hit one before bouncing and falling against another. Some were plate-scuffing glances while others knocked him briefly from what little sense he had left. Pieces of plate were torn from his suit and the sword *Terminus* was lost to him.

A short plummet later and the templar felt his body snap straight through the rotten branches of a dead pine. While his mind struggled with the impossibility of what he was experiencing, his body cleaved straight through dry wood. His armour crumpled as he slammed stomach first into a thicker, more resilient branchlet lower down the giant. Something like a rib broke inside the knight but before he could claw himself to safety, the weight of his plate dragged him down through the living boughs and branches. They beat him and smashed him to near unconsciousness before depositing the knight in a twisted pile at the foot of its trunk, his face in the dirt.

Kastner roared like a wild animal. Fire lanced through his left thigh, cutting through the malaise of other agonies squirming through him. Something had speared down through his leg, pinning him and his plate to the forest floor. Arching his back and tearing the wound in his side, Kastner saw that the sword *Terminus* had fallen after him, the broad blade stabbing down through the knight's plate, searing through his flesh and grazing the bone. The templar smacked his head into the ground and fisted the soil with his remaining gauntlet. Bellowing once more, Kastner reached back and took the blade in hand. Hauling it upwards, the metal made an excruciating sound against the plate through which it had punctured. The pain was unbearable, but Kastner found himself willing it on – the agony cauterising its way through his dismal torments. At last the blade came free and fell heavily to one side, sticky with the templar's blood.

Dragging the greatsword like a penitent burden and limping like an animal that had ripped itself from a trap, Kastner pushed miserably on through the changing forest. Hours passed. It could have been days or weeks, for all the knight knew. His body felt as if it were aflame. The fever brought the knight's heartbeat thundering to his ears. He was everywhere, yet felt nowhere. Each twist and turn about the trees was a dark discovery. Every decision, left or right, cost the knight a little shred of his soul, yet moment by moment he felt he was becoming something more.

He was shaking. The templar willed himself to stillness but felt even his resolution tremble. The hairs on his body stood up on end with the chill of fear and excitement. In the impossible forest about him, roots snaked through the earth beneath his feet as if bifurcating networks of midnight blue threaded his pallid flesh. Like a God-King distant and lost to him, the land was Kastner and Kastner was the land. A nation of competing afflictions. A living, breathing empire to master and control.

Thunder ripped the heavens apart above the dark canopy. A storm was descending – unseen and irresistible. What feeble light from the dying sun and shine-stealing moons found its way down to the clearing floor withered to twilight. The weald became an impenetrable labyrinth of gloom and dread. Kastner drew his miserable hobble to a stop, dragging his skewered leg in line with the other. All ways looked equally foreboding. Ahead was a fat log – a toppled trunk, bulbous with growths, nests and holes. Kastner could see the glint of eyes within. The bug-riddled timber was infested with vermin and the crawling, creeping, slithering things of the world. Beyond the woodland was a chorus of sickly creaking. From within the gaping darkness of the log, Kastner heard a dreadful, booming laughter. Its jovial invitation was infectious and ripe with a doom-laden mockery.

Turning from the log, which seemingly blocked the path ahead, the knight saw to his left a colossal oak – gnarled and broad. The kind of timber from which the great cannon-carrying vessels and siege machines of the Empire were crafted. Its branches were straight like a gallows. Its bark was rough and full of furious character, giving the knots and gnarled bumps the appearance of a rising column of leering skulls that barred his path, flashed white by the lightning that opened the sky up above them. As the thunder tore the very air apart around the knight, lightning struck the branches above. With an ear-splitting crack, the bolt split the great oak in two. Flame spread rapidly through its crooks and boughs, devouring the wood with hateful abandon. Kastner drank in the power of the scene. The spectacle of wanton destruction.

The templar hobbled back from the intense heat, turning his plated back to the furious inferno. Opposite, the pathway was no more certain. Trees seemed to meld one into another, as though they were one. The bark was uniformly scarred and stripped by the wicked claws of some animal, the rents dribbling sap down the wood. The more Kastner looked at the gliding curves, the rounded beauty, the arches, the twists and bends of the trunks and branches about one another, the more he was drawn to it. It reminded him not of inanimate trees but of people, men and women, embracing one another. In the opposing flames, Kastner found his face on every one of the male figures, while the girls were every woman he had ever yearned for.

'No...' he half-gasped, and forced his gaze from the perversity. To his right he found the log – which was impossible, since that was behind him. Except it wasn't. The flaming oak now occupied that space. Kastner stared about, searching for the way he had entered the clearing, but it wasn't there. The bodies. The flames. The laughter. The flames. The laughter. The bodies. The knight was lost in every way a man could be.

Kastner roared at the spuming heavens above. He had never seen such a storm. Rolling banks of clouds swallowing one another – spreading, surging and raging with lightning of pinks and blues. His chin fell and his gaze reached the clearing floor. He found tracks – the trench the greatsword had been carving behind him cross-crossed itself many times in a pattern of madness. Lines and circles. The black earth of the clearing was churned up in the impression of a star. An eight-pointed star.

Kastner reached for the name of his God-King but found that it wasn't there. The hallowed name that had sat on his lips for decades. His patron. His god and his king. The deity to whom the templar had pledged his life and service. His name... was gone. Kastner crumbled to his armoured knees.

'My lord,' he called up into the storm. 'Why have you forsaken me!'

'You are not forsaken...'

The voice was everywhere. It was the roar of the flame. The laughter in the darkness. The doom-laden rapture. The impossible storm. Kastner turned, dragging his injured leg after him. He spun around, the forest blurring to smeared darkness. Then he saw it. For an instant. In the clearing. Right next to him. Horror incarnate, leering at mortal insignificance. Stumbling to a stop, Kastner got the impression of some hideous thing of the beyond. Fiend. Gargoyle. Daemon. Black as night, with the horns and wings of infernal favour.

'Do not see meeeee...' the being said in a voice that seemed to burst the heart.

Pain. Incredible.

Kastner clutched his head and let slip a scream of honest agony. He covered his eye, but the searing torment proceeded in the socket of the one that was no longer there. He could see lightning inside his mind. Shards of colour that defied name or description. Ghostly impressions of a world beyond that of sense and sight. He could feel with his heart. Listen with his mind. He could taste a world ripe for destruction. It was too much. It was all too much. Make it stop.

CHAPTER VI

'With a world of pleas to hark and heed,
Miracles begged and forgiveness received,
Recoveries to foster and babes to feed
How can fair Shallya offer aught but tears?'

– Fliessbach, *The Daughter of Death*

Way Temple – the Sudenpass
Hochland
Niedrigstag, IC 2420

'Get him up, get him up.'

Being the hulking fellow that he was, Dagobert's attendant, Berndt, picked Kastner's body up from the hay cart, plate and all. 'Bring him inside,' the priest said, his voice like the gravel on the road running beside the way temple. He ran stubby fingers through his greyish hair. Berndt didn't reply. The attendant was a mute.

'Also had this,' the gruff farmer said, lifting with difficulty the dead-weight of the gore-smeared *Terminus*. Dagobert ducked inside and snatched a pudgy fistful of coin from the donations box and put it in the hand of the bemused farmer who had found the Knight of the

Twin-Tailed Orb unconscious on the side of the Sudenpass. He took the greatsword *Terminus*. 'Put him in the robing room,' Dagobert instructed, 'with his squire.'

As Berndt stomped through the temple with the knight in his arms, candles guttering as he went, the clatter of Kastner's ruined plate attracted the attention of the congregation. It was mostly travellers – skinners, pedlars, merchants and the like – taking the Sudenpass from Wolfenburg to Middenheim, with a few regulars from the goat farms up in the foothills. Disturbed from their devotions, the attendees' eyes were drawn from the God-King's sculpted form to the dreadful state of the templar.

'Apologies,' Dagobert said, waddling after Berndt and the templar. 'Pray return to your thoughts, brothers and sisters.'

Moving through the way temple, Berndt pushed through the curtains of the robing room. Emil was already there – like a preserved body in an ancient tomb, the hideousness of his injuries hidden in bandages and moist salves. A portly priestess of Shallya sat beside the squire in her white robes, giving motherly instruction to Giselle who was moving back and forth with fresh dressings.

'By the Dove,' the priestess said, 'what have we here now?'

'Another servant of Sigmar, Sister Arabella,' Dagobert said. 'Deserving, I fear, of your attentions.'

'Set him down on the other bunk,' the priestess directed. Berndt obeyed. 'I am going to need assistance with his armour.' Dagobert nodded, laying *Terminus* aside and moving across to help Berndt with the smashed plate.

'His wounds are grievous,' the priestess concluded as she unwound Giselle's handiwork about the templar's eye. 'An object. It still seems to be in there,' the priestess said. 'Hand me my satchel, child.' Giselle passed the priestess her bag of instruments and potions with no little petulance. 'It's going to have to come out. It'll get infected.'

'Whatever you think is best,' Dagobert said.

'Shallya knows,' the priestess said, 'this is dangerous. He could lose more than his sight – and he has lost that already. You'll take responsibility.'

'Aye,' Dagobert said slowly. 'Aye, I will at that.'

Selecting a pair of tongs that wouldn't have been out of place on a blacksmith's rack, the priestess dipped them into the ruin of the socket and tried to grasp the shard protruding from it. As the metal of the tong scraped the stone, Kastner's hand shot up, snatching the priestess's wrist and the tongs away from his eye.

'What are you doing?' the templar snarled, his other eye writhing about its socket, his gaze roaming the room like a frightened animal.

'Diederick,' Dagobert soothed. 'Diederick, it's me. You were brought to the temple.'

As the templar lifted his head and looked about him, he fixed Arabella and Giselle in a withering stare. He let go of Arabella's wrist.

'I don't know you.'

'This is Lady Arabella, new to Shallya's shelter from Hovelhof,' Dagobert said. 'And this is Giselle, from the Hammerfall. She brought Emil to us, thank the Founder. She said you sent her.'

Kastner burned into Giselle with his gaze, making the novice-sister bridle under the intensity of his attentions.

'Yes,' he said finally. 'You were there.'

'We've been expecting you,' Dagobert said. 'It's been a few days.'

Kastner laid back down, then turned his head towards the bandage-smothered Emil.

'Will he make it?'

'Lady Arabella doesn't like his chances, out here in the provinces,' Dagobert said.

'He needs the care of the hospice in Altdorf,' the priestess said. 'As might you.'

'I'm not going to Altdorf,' Kastner told her.

'The injury to your eye requires extraction of the offending object,' Arabella told him. 'I cannot lie to you. There will be pain.'

'I have known pain.'

'A great deal of pain,' the priestess said.

'Then leave it alone.'

'It will become infected and it will kill you. You will be slain from within, good templar. Would you have that? Taken in your bed during fever and delirium. Not the end a knight of Sigmar would pray for.'

'Do what you must,' Kastner said grimly.

'Before you were insensible,' Arabella told him. 'You must be rendered so again. Father Dagobert, please bring us a bottle of your strongest spirits.'

'Well, I...'

'Come, father. The God-King praises alcohol as a gift – if enjoyed in health, peace and moderation. This purpose is medicinal, after all.'

'Save it,' Kastner spat. He looked hard at the priestess. 'Just get it out. If it's going to be as painful as you say I'll be out soon enough.'

'As you wish, my son,' Arabella said to him. 'Hold him down.'

With Berndt's great form holding the knight's broken body down and Dagobert holding his skull against the bunk, Giselle hovered over them.

'What can I do?' the girl said.

'Take these,' Lady Arabella said, thrusting a handful of clean rags at her. 'There will be blood.'

Moving in once more with the tongs, Arabella felt the knight suddenly strain against them. His body spasmed and a grim moan erupted from his pursed lips. 'Hold him,' the priestess commanded. She took the tip of the shard – which still protruded a little way out from the ruined eye – and attempted to extract it. Moans became roars and roars shrieks as the priestess used all of her strength and skill to take the stone from his skull. Dagobert held Kastner down, his face a grave mask of care and determination. Blood streamed down the side of the templar's face, where Giselle tried her best to stem the flow. Soon the gathering were covered in the knight's blood, their hands slimy with his gore.

'Hold him,' Arabella carped, her frustration getting the best of her.

'I'm trying,' Dagobert shot back. 'He's so strong. Girl, help me here,' the priest of Sigmar said to Giselle. The bunk was already awash with blood.

'Why isn't he out?' Giselle asked, the templar's screams passing straight through her. 'My brother had my father pull a rusty nail from his foot once. The pain. He went out like a candle.'

'He has a strong will,' Arabella mumbled, no less rattled by the knight's grating agonies. 'I'll give him that.'

Even with both Dagobert and the novice-sister holding his head still, the priestess could not extract the shard's infectious presence. The stone seemed wedged in the bone of the socket, as well as lancing deep into the skull. Even her bodily attempts to twist the splinter of stone free – producing from Kastner the most dismal howls she had ever heard from a patient – failed to move it.

When the knight's screams finally subsided – to the relief of everyone – the priestess thought she might be able to exert more pressure but regardless of her efforts, the stone shard was there to stay. She finally sat back, letting the tension in her shoulders go. She seemed in shock.

'You're giving up?' Dagobert asked.

'The goddess forbids harm done in her name,' Arabella said, her face almost as white as her patient's.

'You said he would get an infection if it was left in,' Dagobert protested. 'You said he would die.'

Arabella looked from Dagobert, to Giselle to Berndt.

'He's already dead,' the priestess of Shallya said, withdrawing her hand from his chest. Dagobert moved around and put his ear to Kastner's heart. There was no life to be found there. 'I have offended my mistress,' Arabella said. 'I must make amends.' She got up from the bunk. 'I'm sorry, Hieronymous – I must leave you now.'

Dagobert lifted his ear from Kastner's blood-smeared chest.

'What of Emil?' the priest said miserably, his mind elsewhere.

'I will take my ponies back to Hovelhof,' she said, 'and leave you the hospice wagon. I can do no more for him. Take the boy to the Shallya temple in Altdorf. If he survives the journey, the high priestess will care for him there.'

As Arabella left them, Dagobert turned back to Kastner's lifeless form. He leant up and kissed the knight on the forehead. Even now, in the blood-battered corpse of the warrior before him, the priest could see the boy he had raised.

'Girl,' Dagobert said, getting to his feet.

'Yes, father,' Giselle said, the tautness of teenage ill-humour and irritability gone from her face.

'Strip and bathe the body for last rites,' the priest said with difficulty, as though he were forcing every word. Giselle nodded slowly. She drew Sigmar's hammer up out of her robes on its chain – the simple token of her simple faith – and kissed the silver of its form. 'I must send word to Grand Theogonist Lutzenschlager and Grand Master Schroeder of the Knights of the Twin-Tailed Orb.' Dagobert continued. 'Berndt, you will go ahead to the temple and the chapter house with my missives. They shall learn that one of their very best, a scholar and a warrior born – a true son of Sigmar – this day is lost to us.'

There are many who would mean you harm, shadow-of-mine. Many wretched gods and their misguided servants. The weakling God-King of the Empire. Ulric of Wolves and Winter. Even the merciful maiden Shallya, who would harm as much as she heals with her potions and instruments. They will cut you with their steel. They will burn you with their faith.

You are claimed, shadow-of-mine. You were begot of havoc. Orphaned in a world you will destroy. Baptised in the susceptibilities of your enemies. You have the attention of the Dark Gods. They look down on you as I do. With dread. With hope. With possibility. You cannot deny what you are. My gift to the world. Flesh, bone and the spirit that drives it on. A living doom.

In order to realise your terrible purpose, however, you must live, my creation. Live, shadow-of-mine. The Dark Gods know you now. Show them what you can do. Give them a glimpse of the calamity to come.

CHAPTER VI

'Methinks the road to damnation cuts unfairly through lands of fair intention.'

– Frederik III (ascribed – *the Great Crusade against Araby*)

The Drakwasser Road
Middenland
Klein Frederikstag, IC 2420

Day and night. Day and night. Kastner's eyes were dry, for he could not close them. In the hours of day he endured the tedium of the world, viewed through the narrow opening between the curtains of the hospice wagon. At night he dreamt dark visions projected on the darkness beyond. He felt a living death. Every moment was so acutely experienced that it hurt to think and feel. He sensed his body healing. It was becoming stronger. More powerful. Assuming a formidability that even he, as a knight trained in the arts of death, had never enjoyed. He was becoming... something else. Something more. The flesh of his side and his leg itched as it knit itself back together. Breaks and fractures were now but dull aches and the dread fever a distant memory.

Only his eye still burned. The storm was still there, raging in the darkness of his mind. A constant torment, shredding at his nerves and his sanity. He could feel the shard of stone in his head. It was heavy and aching with wretched purpose. It was part of him now and wanted him to be part of it. The realisation of his desires and impulses might have distracted the templar from the ever-present agony that shot through his skull. A goal upon which to focus and channel the raw anguish that proceeded from the mind-splitting torture. Instead he was forced to simply lie and endure every single second of a torment without end. If a man knows his labours end as the sun goes down, then he can push on through to dusk. If a man knows his journey's destination, even though that destination might be far away, he can walk on – putting one boot ahead of the other, until finally he reaches journey's end. The agony ripping through one side of his face, his head, his mind, was a journey without destination and a day without end. At first Kastner didn't know if he could take it. Then he discovered that he didn't have a choice. He finally found that he could, but that it might have cost him his sanity.

He had awoken to horror. When he was but a small boy he would wake in the middle of the night. The temple dormitory was without windows and black with darkness. Down the corridor he could hear Dagobert snoring. It had been a reassuring noise to a boy all alone in the world. Some nights he would wake to silence, however. No sound. No light. Most dreadful of all was the feeling that there was something there in the darkness with him. Something stalking him. Watching him. He knew that to set eyes on it would be the end of him – but he had no choice because he could not move. The horror of vulnerability. It didn't matter how strong, how fast or lethal you were, if you couldn't move a muscle to defend yourself. Bumping about the cot in the back of the hospice wagon, that was what Kastner had woken to. Paralysis. Immobility. The insensitivity of the flesh.

He could not lift an arm, kick out with a leg, blink his eye or lick his lips. A fly crawling inbetween them could choke him. An insect could end him. It was the most dreadful feeling he had ever experienced. No bed wetting nightmare or courage-leeching doubt before combat could compare. He would rather feel the steel of his enemy skewer through him than live the soullessness of utter vulnerability. As he was wont to do – as it was the only thing to do – Kastner tried to reach out. He tried to sit up. He tried to move just one toe. But there was nothing. In his mind his body responded with force and enthusiasm for the task. He throbbed with possibility. The power of the things he wanted to do. The magnitude of coming accomplishment intoxicated him. His body was just waiting to catch up with such grand achievements. It was a useless study in flesh. A forgotten vessel housing a furious force. A living trap within which was buried a monster... a giant... a god.

Perhaps, when he had been able to walk, his every step had driven the shard of wyrdstone deeper into his brain. He could even have fallen and driven the sliver further into his skull. He thought on his surroundings. Perhaps some attempt to remove the object had done him more ill than good. Conversely, the thing might just have petrified its way into him and claimed him for its own. It didn't matter. What danger was he to the Empire, to others or himself lying in a cot like a cadaver? Whatever had happened, the shard had pierced into or pressed against something that had crippled him. His life as he knew it was over.

Kastner heard a moan. There was someone in the cot lining the other wall of the hospice wagon. The templar had never been able to turn his head to see who he shared the wagon with. He assumed it was Emil, his squire – although it didn't sound very much like him. Like Kastner, his injuries had warranted the long, uncomfortable journey to Altdorf, in search of healing hands at the Temple of Shallya. The boy groaned beneath his bandages and blankets – something between agony and ecstasy. Kastner hoped he was having a nice dream. The wretch would have little to look forward to upon waking.

The knight peered hard at the darkness between the doorway curtains. There used to be just darkness and light. The longer he stared at the only view he was allowed, the one constantly visited upon him, the more he came to appreciate the degrees of difference. With the rising of the sun, day was just the absence of darkness. With the setting of the sun, both the night and the knight were a canvas upon which darkness daubed its dread. Like a painter working colours on his palette, Kastner had observed darkness mixed in many shades – and found himself lost to them. They were to be his masterpiece. And he theirs.

For what seemed like forever, Kastner had watched their journey drop behind the wagon. That was how he knew for sure that they were heading for the Reikland. He had felt the winding path of the Sudenpass, the bump and crunch back up the Flaschgang Road and the rattle as they crossed the well-travelled crossways of the Old Forest. He had watched the trees change and even disappear for a spell as they trundled past the brigand-haunted Weiss Hills. Occasionally, he would spy one of the many individual homesteads and hamlets on the route. In some, peasants peered in with ghoulish curiosity. Not too close – in case the hospice wagon was carrying somebody infectious – but close enough to see the freakishness of the horrifically injured, the almost dead and the dying. Kastner watched the same disappointment cross their faces. He was the kind of freak they could not see. The kind of abomination that hid its true form and denied the morbidly inquisitive a sickening thrill.

It was with ghoulish curiosity, however, that Kastner found himself staring through the curtains as the wagon passed through the larger villages. He knew three through which they passed well: Bergendorf, Heedenhof and Gerzen-by-the-River. He knew the sounds of village life, the sing-song Hochlanden lilt and the bustle of passage on the crossroads – heavy goods moving north and south, regiments marching east-west along the Old Forest Road, both to and from Fort Schippel. The knight would not have recognised the villages through which the wagon had passed on its way south. The thoroughfares were dead but for the congress of ravens. Woodsmoke stung his nostrils and on his dry tongue he tasted the copper-tang of fresh death. He knew destruction without seeing it. Not the terror of beastmen or greenskins from the woods. Their needs were their own. Kastner sensed carnage absolute. A message in the massacre. Buildings had burned. The earth had drunk deep of innocent blood. Mutilated bodies were spread and hung as totems of annihilation. Advertisements to all who would now fear to tread where the archenemy had left its unholy works. Only the slaves to darkness worked in such ways. Ruinous doom from the north. The warriors of Chaos.

Night intruded on the hospice wagon. A kind of a moonless darkness reigned. He could hear the trees beyond, hissing in gentle movement, but he could not see them because the rear of the wagon was facing the other way. The Drakwasser sloshed and slurped not far in the distance. Kastner could hear its broadening banks and the unimpeded breeze coming off the lonely hills that the sunset positioned to the west. All of this and the smoothness of the wagon's passage through the well-worn ruts in the road told the templar that they were somewhere between Flaschfurt and Fort Denkh where the track broadened to allow camp to be made off the tree line.

The knight's hearing – growing with his other senses – drew the world beyond to him. He could hear a fire, which the low-tinged blackness outside seemed to confirm. He could hear the sizzle of a spit, and the smell of scorched meat pulled at a powerful hunger in his belly like the strings of an instrument. He was ravenous as little had passed his lips in the preceding days but liquids – water and a little broth – for fear of choking. Horses loitered somewhere nearby. Kastner could hear the soft rumble of their hearts and the gush of hot blood through their veins. They snorted and kicked gently at the earth, their tails swishing about them in agitation. Something was bothering them.

It was probably Emil. The squire's withered moans had become more insistent. Despite being unconscious, the poor boy had become increasingly aware of his agonies and the little anyone could do to alleviate them. Kastner had seen the wreckage the pack of dogs had left behind. The wagon was thick with the squire's sickly stench, which with the constant groans and lack of conversation had made Emil a poor travelling companion. At least he could move – if the rippling covers, the periods of violent shuddering and the occasional thrash of a bandage-trailing limb were anything to go by. Kastner felt for the boy and felt responsibility for him. He might have felt more if it weren't for his own dismal prospects. The warherd and whatever Ruinous abominations to which they were making sacrifices had all but finished them both. Kastner was fairly certain that they were spending their last hours together in the back of the hospice wagon.

Sounds, both within and about the wagon fell away. The knight's concentration intensified. It hurt – as if his ears were bleeding – but the tiny details beyond became his. The nibbling of mice in the grass. Grubs boring through the wood of nearby trees. The imperceptible creak of stones expanding about the fire. Like the forest-shattering felling of a mighty larch or elm, Kastner could hear the turning of the pages of a book. The desiccated leather of the tome's covers soaked up the clamminess of the hands holding them. The pages, crisp with age and rough like southern parchments, rubbed against one another with an ancient sibilance. The knight could hear the ink, hundreds of years old, still drying in the dread formations of letters on the page.

There were voices. Mind-cleaving in the volume and clarity with which they came to Kastner. Gorst mumbled booming insanities some way off, enjoying the campfire from a distance. As his face-cage and chains rattled and the flagellations quietly bled and soaked into the filthy rags at his back, the fanatic spoke of one Kastner had thought lost to him. The man who became a king. The king who became a god. Sigmar... Kastner's mind burned to hear the Heldenhammer's name but it was an old pain – remembered and welcome.

'I don't understand any of this...'

'...any of this...'

'...any of this...'

New words intruded on the scene and echoed through the cavernous emptiness of Kastner's thoughts. A girl's voice: sing-song, coarse of cant, tender with teenage years. Unbroken. Unseasoned. Untouched. The grating insolence of youth to be tamed. The knight remembered. The prisoner. The novice-sister. Giselle, the Sister of the Imperial Cross. The girl from the Hammerfall. Kastner drank in the fear and uncertainty of her words.

'I'm not so sure anyone was ever meant to...'

Kastner detected a voice from his childhood. The warm rumble of Father Dagobert. He heard the gravelly rasp of the priest's chins and the weight he carried about his belly – in turn carrying the weight of his words with authority. Despite this, the knight sensed a sweet edge of doubt to the priest's declaration. It was like the stain of harvested fruit on a knife. It was meant to be an answer. A comfort – but it was anything but.

Kastner heard the priest select another tome from a stack warming near the fire. The creak of an opening spine. The whisper of pages. The priest was consulting. Comparing. Cross-referencing. The world died away. Only the conversation mattered. The frank exchange of hushed words across the crackle of the food and fire, heard by Kastner as though he were sitting there also.

'Well I don't,' the girl said honestly. 'All this brainworking – it's not for someone like me. I work in the scullery. I'm not even a sister.'

'Tell me again,' Dagobert said. 'It's important.'

'The Reverend Mother summoned us to the Repository,' Giselle said. 'Below even the undercloisters. Deep in the mountain. My mistress told us that it was where the most dangerous tomes, papers and artefacts collected by the Sisters of the Imperial Cross were stored. Things a novice was never meant to see, I can tell you that.'

'I know of it, child,' Dagobert informed her. 'Though I have never been honoured with an invitation.'

'Well I didn't know of it,' Giselle said. 'Sister Elissa told me she thought it was a myth. I was terrified.'

'As you should be, my child,' Dagobert said. 'For the Hammerfall's vault holds centuries of recovered deviancy, the life's work of madmen and knowledge of the damned once employed – or intended as such – against the God-King's subjects. Even the Arch Lectors require the Grand Theogonist's own permission to conduct their studies there, so secure a repository for darkness it is. Only Sigmar's own cathedral in Altdorf could boast better protection for such damned things than that mountain. Pray continue.'

'My mistress was acting oddly.'

'How so?'

'Out of sorts. Like she was afeared. I'd never seen her that way,' Giselle told him. 'There was this time, Sister Elissa and I–'

'Please, my child. To the bones of the matter.'

The girl paused. A demonstration of her childish hurt.

'The Reverend Mother's patience was thin and her instruction urgent,' Giselle said. 'That's all I meant to say. She set her sisters to work destroying the artefacts and burning the tomes of the Repository. Elissa, me and the other girls from the scullery, we were scared. It felt wrong, to destroy all that the sisterhood had worked hard to protect.'

'Then?'

'She had selected a number of items that she claimed were – well, as she put it, too dark, too rich in potential or too essential to the Empire's continued existence to be put to the hammer or flame. Grand boasts, from my Reverend Mother's lips, I can tell you.'

'This scared you even more, I suspect.'

'Yes, father,' Giselle acknowledged. 'It terrifies me to know that such dark treasures exist in the world.'

'They do,' the priest assured her. 'Such tomes – studied with care and precaution – are a great boon to our crusade against the Ruinous Powers. If they were to fall into the wrong hands, however, they could spell the end of the world. I exaggerate not, child. You carried such tomes to me from the indomitable Hammerfall.'

The pair were quiet for a moment.

'"Giselle Dantziger", my Reverend Mother said, "you came into the world a rude and inconstant thing, with a mouth more at home in the gutter than the cloister",' the novice told Dagobert. '"You may have lacked the study and serenity required to achieve the rank of sister so far but the one thing you do not lack is courage, girl."'

'You were not originally intended for the sisterhood?' Dagobert said. It was not really a question.

'I call the City of the White Wolf home, sir. My father thought some time at the isolated Hammerfall would tame my wilfulness and wild ways,' Giselle said.

'Not Ulric's own wolf priests?'

'The Al-Ulric and his holy men would not have me,' Giselle said. 'The God-King took me to him and for that I am thankful.'

'You have served him well, child.'

'She gave me the collection of tomes, grimoires and papers I presented to you,' Giselle continued, 'and sent me down the mountainside with orders to deliver them to a priest – a learned man – a true servant of Sigmar. She sent some of the other novice-sisters down the mountain in other directions. All ways were treacherous. I cannot tell you the number of times I nearly lost my life on those frozen heights.'

'She sent the novices? What of the older sisters?'

'The Reverend Mother said that since they were closer in age to meeting the God-King, they deserved to face him at the Hammerfall. I still don't understand what she meant. Myself. Amalie. Karletta. Marlene. Several more of the scullery girls. Each with a bundle of books or sack of artefacts. Karletta was but four and ten. I don't know how many of them made it off the Hammerfall alive. I heard screams across the valleys, but they could have been anyone's.'

'You were brave,' Dagobert commended. 'To climb down out of the Middle Mountains would have tested the most fearless of the God-King's subjects. Your Reverend Mother sent you south?'

'South-west, sir, yes. "Don't you stop girl", she said. "Not for man nor beast, until you pass your burden on to another." Well, I would'nt've – but for the beasts that walk like men. They didn't seem interested in the tomes in my care but it was good fortune that your man came by when he did.'

'Fortune of a sort,' Dagobert conceded darkly.

'You think it was the God-King's doing?'

'Perhaps,' Dagobert said. 'My child, the letter sent with the bundle of books. Did you not read it?'

'I did not, father,' Giselle said. 'I cannot. I cannot read.'

Dagobert gave a grave chuckle.

'I think it not amusing, sir. The Reverend Mother was teaching me, but I fought her in my studies.'

'I do not laugh at you child but with the world,' the priest assured her. 'The Reverend Mother sent you with some of the most dangerous texts I have had the dubious privilege to lay eyes upon. Your ignorance protected you, child, for if you had been tempted by even the titles of some of these tomes, it would have been your end.'

'My mistress sent a letter?'

'Between the books in the bundle, bearing the wax sigil of her order,' Dagobert said. 'You would like me to read it to you?'

'If you would, sir.'

'To whom this letter finds,' Dagobert read. 'I pray to the God-King that the works with which I have burdened this poor child find their way to a keeper of the faith – a true servant of the Heldenhammer. My name is Ottoline Hentshel, Reverend Mother of the Hammerfall Priory and proud Sister of the Imperial Cross. It had been, with my sisterhood, the highest honour to stand sentry over such damned volumes as now find themselves in your possession. Two nights past, however, I was blessed with what I believe to be a vision of the God-King. He came to me. He told me that three days hence, the Hammerfall would receive a visitation from which it would not recover – from which my sisterhood would not recover. The Hammerfall, which has stood for centuries unmolested, atop the highest of peaks in the Middle Mountains, looking down on the God-King's Empire and watching over his people. If I hadn't heard it from the Heldenhammer's own lips, I would not have believed it. It has been my duty to destroy what I can of the dark hoard the Hammerfall has kept safe these generations past. There are some pieces, some texts and the dread knowledge they carry that even I am not permitted to erase from history. My sisters and I will greet our visitors in the way Sigmar intended before preparing to receive his own. Please welcome the child who carries these burdens with hospitality and care. She is a daughter of the Empire and emissary of the God-King's word. I beg you: see these dangerous works to safety, to the site of our patron's crowning – the Cathedral of Sigmar in Altdorf – where they may once more find sanctuary with the priests, scholars and holy knights of his church. The blessings of Sigmar upon you.'

Again, silence settled on the scene, with only the spitting of the fire filling the void.

'You think my mistress received the God-King?'

'I do not know,' Dagobert said. 'But the rider I stopped and had confidence with earlier today told me that Bergendorf, Gerzen and Heedenhof were not the only villages to suffer destruction. There is a storm sweeping through our lands, burning and butchering its way south with dread purpose. It has put others to the sword in our blessed ignorance. The township Esk – dear to my own heart – has similarly fallen to these fearless marauders. Perhaps Sigmar did warn your mistress. Warned her that a doom from the north was coming. A warband or host intent on destruction. Men and monsters, who move through our lands unchecked, like vengeful ghosts, who slaughter with impunity in search of god knows what. Report is, my child, that the Hammerfall too smokes like the fiery anger of the mountain and that your sisters already sleep in Sigmar's delicate care. For all we know, you might be the last of your order…'

'This cannot be,' the girl sobbed.

'And yet it is,' Dagobert said. 'It is happening. Right now. Events move swiftly about us.'

'What do these marauders want?'

'No one can tell what truly drives such mockeries of men,' Dagobert said. 'The favour of some dark god? Immortality? Daemonhood?'

'But you think not?'

'This carnage is not the random path of some northern barbarian,' Dagobert said. 'The path has purpose. I believe that this host – whoever or whatever they might be – slaughtered the Sisters of the Imperial Cross at the Hammerfall in search of one of the godforsaken works you brought to me. I think that they followed it to Esk because the tomes were taken to the way temple nearby, and that they know it travels south on this road – accounting for the butchered villages and hamlets on our route.'

'Then they are already ahead of us,' Giselle said, her words rising with panic. 'How will we reach the city with these beasts between us and safety?'

'Calm yourself, girl,' Dagobert said. 'Don't forget that Sigmar watches over us.'

'Sigmar watches over us!'

'…or that I sent Berndt on ahead with my missives to the Grand Theogonist. There are soldiers stationed at Fort Denkh. We shall appeal to the company captain for sanctuary behind his walls. It is also where I requested Lord Lutzenschlager have a contingent of his finest knights meet us to escort us back to the Altdorf.'

'How do you know that he will answer such a call?' Giselle put to the priest. 'Are you and the Grand Theogonist friends from temple?'

'Far from it, child,' Dagobert said coldly. 'But I included in my letter assertions that even the Grand Theogonist would dare not ignore.'

'Excuse me, sir. Assertions?'

Dagobert didn't answer at first, as though considering his words carefully.

'Some of the tomes you brought to me were undoubtedly dangerous and belonged in the secure vaults of the Hammerfall,' the priest said. 'But only one of the diabolic works could truly justify such a bold invasion of our lands. One worth risking so much for.'

'Which one?'

'This one, child. *The Celestine Book of Divination*,' the priest said. 'Or *The Liber Caelestior*. It was composed by a Tilean scryer or madman – depending upon whose version of history you trust – called Battista Gaspar Necrodomo. He used the stars, their relative positions and the patterns they cast across the night sky to make predictions about times that were to come to pass.'

'He knew of the future?'

'So say some,' Dagobert admitted. '*The Liber Caelestior*, however, is considered especially dangerous since it prophesises the coming of the End Times.'

'The End Times?'

'The days of doom, my child. The end of the world.'

'You have read of these End Times?' Giselle asked.

'*The Liber Caelestior* is on a list of prohibited texts that the Grand Theogonist forbids even his Sigmarite priests to read. The contents are considered too perilous to become common knowledge. As far as I know, the Grand Theogonist and his predecessors are the only ones to have read it in its entirety.'

'You *have* read this tome,' Giselle said. 'I can tell.'

Dagobert said nothing for a few moments. Then:

'Given the murderous circumstances surrounding the tome's acquisition,' Dagobert explained, 'and what presently is at stake, I thought it prudent to examine it for myself. The bundle you brought from the Hammerfall contained a primer – a text used to translate, at least in part, some of the other works. Our journey has afforded me time to translate the early sections.'

'And?'

'Though he seems to talk in dark riddles, some of what the madman says has already come to pass,' Dagobert admitted grimly.

'And what of the End Times?'

'The End Times are heralded by a coming of a warrior from the north, at the head of the greatest army in the history of man. He will be the Everchosen of the Ruinous Powers...'

'I don't know much,' Giselle said, 'but I know that does not sound good.'

'The Everchosen is a warlord bearing the favour of the Dark Gods and their blessings in equal measure. There have been few who have enjoyed such a title and unrivalled command of damnation's forces. Only a warrior worthy of the Powers' dread unity, through the completion of a series of unholy quests, can present himself to be crowned Everchosen of Chaos. Several such men have plagued the Empire and our God-King fought them even before that. As we have had our mighty champions like Magnus the Pious, so the Dark Gods have their own. To be Everchosen is to receive the gods' ultimate blessing: sole command of the legions of darkness and the honour of ushering in the End Times – the end of the world as we know it.'

'Then...' Giselle began. She seemed to be thinking. 'Who is this Lord of the End Times to be?'

'All I've learned so far is a single name,' Dagobert said. 'A name I have mercifully never heard before. The herald of the apocalypse is a man called Archaon. A southern name for a northern threat – with the Empire caught inbetween.'

'A name? Surely this Necrodomo must have said more of him than that?' Giselle argued, her tender years lending themselves to impatience. 'On account of these strange powers, and all.'

'He did,' Dagobert admitted, 'but the page bearing the burden of that secret had been torn from the tome. Perhaps someone, at some time, thought that such knowledge should be kept separate from the text. Or that it was better destroyed. Even Necrodomo himself could have removed the dangerous details of Archaon's identity upon truly considering the danger that they posed.'

'Do you think that the leader of the marauders is Archaon?' Giselle asked.

'Desiring confirmation and the secrets of his future?' the priest said. 'I think that such an idea is equally dreadful and possible, my child – and if true, makes getting this volume to Altdorf all the more necessary.'

'I can't believe this to be happening.'

'Do not fear, child,' Dagobert assured her, 'the Grand Theogonist will send his Templars for *The Liber Caelestior*, if not for us personally. Trust that they are on their way to us.'

'Did you hear that?'

Kastner's searing attentions were suddenly brought back to the hospice wagon. Beyond the incredible stench that now dominated the space, the knight could hear noises from the opposite bunk. Emil's moans had ceased. The knight could see the bottom of the squire's bunk. There were still movements beneath his bandages and blankets but they had assumed a horrid undulation, like a snake sloughing off its skin. The sounds from beneath were grisly. It was like the splinter of crackling on a roast pig and the collapse of liquefied flesh. Kastner wondered if Dagobert or the girl had checked the squire's dressings recently.

Then he heard it. Something new. In the tedium of wagon, new was usually good. The knight did not think this to be the case when he heard the slow, wet growl of what Kastner could only assume was some kind of dog. Outside, Kastner heard the horses bridle. The stink of predation was in the air.

The knight fought his body for control of his neck muscles. If he could just loll his head over to one side, he could see the thing with which he was trapped in the hospice wagon. Pleading fed the knight's frustration which in turn stoked his anger – but it was no good. He could not even form a face of fury let alone act upon it. The cot opposite creaked as the thing that was no longer Emil shifted its weight.

'I'm sure I heard something,' Kastner thought he heard Giselle say.

'It's probably that malingering oaf, Gorst,' Dagobert said, putting the girl's fears to rest. 'Here. Eat something. You will need your strength.'

Inside his head, Kastner roared his defiance. He would not die a miserable, unknown death in the back of a wagon, slowly devoured by and horribly becoming one with some Chaotic spawn of corruption. Kastner willed his body to movement. He yearned for his arms to thrash out, or his legs to kick, his head to lift from the cot or his torso to buck. His mind burned with the effort but his body betrayed him. There was no life there. Not even a promising numbness. Just a terrifying absence.

The growling grew louder. A savage announcement of territorial assertion. Except the horror cared not for forest or hills. Its claim was the templar's own precious flesh. Although he could not see it, Kastner felt the wagon lean, ever so slightly, as Emil's unmade form pushed out from the blankets in its glistening stink and moved towards Kastner – led on by a new snout and a new sense of smell.

Kastner had started to entertain his blackest fears, when suddenly something wonderful happened. Kastner passed water. He hadn't realised it at first but the templar had been soaking the blankets and the cot – urine passing down through the boards of the hospice wagon. Kastner could hear the pitter-patter of his waters beneath the wagon. He heard Giselle grunt as she realised what had happened.

'I think our patients may need us,' the knight heard Dagobert say.

'I'll go,' Giselle said. 'There are fresh blankets in the driver seat.'

Kastner felt feeling return to the tip of his little finger and the knight waggled it for all he was worth. A celebration in miniature. This led to a twitch of the shoulder and the slight drift of his head to one side. There his sore eyes beheld the thing that was now Emil. Still a festering patchwork of mauled flesh, a hairless, eyeless dog snout had pushed free of the terrible changes that had overtaken the squire's wretched form. The grotesque head snarled at the templar as it sniffed his vulnerability. Lips curled back like an opening bud and the snaggle-toothed jaw – a twisted parody of the mongrels that had infected the boy with their corruption-frothing maws – yawned open with predacious intention.

A roar built within Kastner's chest, at first a miserable rasp, building to bombast and the raw announcement that the templar wanted to live. He reached out with soul-draining effort, bringing his hand up in defence. The fresh obedience of action to thought was sweet relief. It was instinct. The spawn moved in to consume the templar's flesh. Kastner's hand came up between them but suddenly stopped. For a heart-stricken moment, the knight thought his body had once again failed him. As he heard the jangle of chains through the cot side, Kastner came to realise that this was not paralysis. It was captivity. There were manacles about his wrists and thick chains between them. As the spawn moved in to feed on him, similar restraints thunked to the wagon floor, slipping from the squire's changing form.

As threaded slime dribbled from the spawn-jaws in expectation of its first meal, Kastner tore at the chains. Passed through the cot as they were, the restraints accomplished precisely what they were designed to do. Keep the templar in place.

'God's wounds,' Kastner heard Dagobert swear. He could see the priest through the curtain opening, where Giselle stood also, the girl struggling with what she was seeing. Kastner's mouth was moving but returning from insensibility, his throat couldn't manage anything as articulate as speech. The urgency of the bellow that escaped his lungs was enough to shake the priest from the spectacle.

'The crossbow,' Dagobert rumbled. 'The crossbow.'

The spawn's own hackle-roar erupted from the nest of teeth and tongues which had once been a head. Its transformations still underway beneath the blood-soaked mound of blankets, the abomination leant in for the kill.

Kastner punched for the wagon bonnet, dragging the length of chain between his manacles up against the cot rail. Once, twice, thrice. The rail gave and clattered free – just in time for the knight to land a punch on the dog-spawn's snout. He hit it again and again with his left fist, his right forced to follow, but the ravenous monstrosity would not surrender its first conquest. Within the spawn, bones snapped and flesh rearranged itself in its aching desire to feed and make Kastner part of its metamorphosis.

Allowing it an opening, Kastner felt his own lips retract with disgust. The blind snout slipped through the opportunity the templar had allowed it, bringing its stinking maw right up to his face. A growl like buried thunder issued from the beast's transformations. Kastner bellowed back at it, coiling the length of chain between his manacles about the spawn's alteration-slick neck. Kastner heaved the beast to him, holding its horrid, squirming flesh against his own, cutting across its throat with his restraints.

'Damnable contraption,' Dagobert said, having been handed the retrieved crossbow and a bolt from Giselle, but struggling to load the weapon.

Kastner heaved. His muscles enjoyed the ecstasy of movement. He willed the corrupted spawn dead and his body answered the call. His biceps bulged and the metal of the chain cut into the thing. The thrashings of primordial panic replaced the undulations of transformation on the opposite cot. The monstrous nest of butchery that was the creature's evolving form did not like what Kastner was doing to its mongrel head. It might have been some nightmare aberration of nature but it still needed to breathe.

The spawn bucked and flailed. A foul fluid bubbled, foamed and leaked from its hissing jaws. Kastner could feel it dying in his embrace. Somewhere, in the horror of it all, the templar's arms trembled to give his squire peace. With a final roar, Kastner strangled the loathsome aberration. A crunch and wet rattle left the grotesque's throat before the beast – moments before in the flesh-euphoria of new life – convulsed its way to a messy death.

Kastner heard the crossbow relieve itself of its bolt. With the priest awkwardly behind the weapon, the quarrel cleared the creature's horrific malformation and thudded into the wooden sideboards beside it.

Kastner released the spawn's blind, skinless muzzle and allowed the fang-heavy skull to hit the wagon floor. The sweet smell of corruption lingered. Giselle turned away, the food she had just eaten returning with a retch of disgust. Dagobert allowed the crossbow to dangle at his side, the priest's face hollow and sheepish. Kastner brought up his wrists, the manacles and chains rattling together. Finally, the word came. When it did, it was cold and imperious.

'Keys…'

CHAPTER VII

'If history has taught us anything,
it's that one man fighting for his belief –
no matter how mistaken and misguided his faith,
is measured to the worth of ten faithless knights.'

– Frederik III (ascribed – *the Great Crusade against Araby*)

Fort Denkh
Middenland
Nachfrederikstag IC 2420

It was a dismal day and had started badly.

They had built a basic pyre and burned what remained of Emil Eckhardt on the mist-shrouded hills along the Drakwasser. Father Dagobert had deemed it the safest course of action, considering the extent of the boy's corruptions. The priest had reasoned that he must have been infected in some fashion from the bites he received from the beastmen's pack of hounds. He claimed that he had heard of herds hammering extra fangs into the jaws of their beasts, made from curse-carved bone and wyrdstone flints for just such a purpose.

Dagobert, Giselle and Kastner stood in attendance about the

smoking pyre, with Gorst ghosting the impromptu funeral a little way off. The fire struggled to take in the early morning drizzle and Kastner brooded in his blood-stained arming doublet and leggings, with a blanket about his shoulders. Dagobert conducted the swift service, saying some nice things about the squire and his family. When asked if he had anything to add, Kastner said nothing, limping back to the camp and wagon.

The knight spent the morning and part of the dreary afternoon the same way, sitting morosely in the saddle, guiding Oberon ahead of the wagon on the Drakwasser Road. Dagobert had tried several times to engage the templar in conversation but Kastner had been deaf to the priest's entreaties.

Erupting like a pair of fat spear-points from the forest, the towers of Fort Denkh were a welcome sight. The sight of the towers drew a smile of relief from the priest, directed at Giselle sitting beside him on the wagon.

'I will ask to speak with the company captain,' Dagobert called to Kastner, but the templar rode on in silence. The priest's syllables grew sour and accusatory. 'You can be very surly sometimes.'

Kastner drew Oberon slowly to a stop. As the wagon caught up with him, the priest did the same. The templar gave him the grim gaze of his single eye, fresh bandages tied about his head, hiding the other. Giselle had offered him the dressings from the hospice wagon supplies but the knight had taken them from her in silence and changed the dressing himself. The material masked the darkness of the ruined socket and the dull glint of the protruding shard point. What it couldn't hide was the septic star of bruising that threaded outwards from the wound, reaching through the pale flesh surrounding the injury.

'You want to do this now?' Kastner said.

'You're right I do,' Dagobert said. 'We had no choice with the chains.'

'What does a paralysed patient need with chains?'

'Lady Arabella lent us the wagon,' the priest informed him, 'for your transportation and comfort. She indicated the restraints as a precaution. We knew little of the nature of Emil's injuries, or your own – and by Sigmar we were right to do so.'

'You served me up like some kind of sacrifice.'

'I can only say sorry so many times,' the priest said. 'I did what I thought was best. These are testing times, Diederick – but know that I am truly sorry my boy, for your suffering.'

'What know *you* of my suffering?' Kastner accused.

'I know the pain of change unsought,' Dagobert said. 'I had raised you like my own. I had hoped you might want to serve with me at the temple. You wished to travel with Sieur Kastner, however – I could see that. There was a deep yearning inside you to fight for the God-King with more than words – for men's souls, but not in their hearts, from before an altar. Sigmar had other plans for you and I accepted that. Loved and encouraged you. Arranged for your squireship. Your path from there you made yourself. Think not that it did not wound – it hurt me deeper than a sword can cut or a spear can pierce.'

The templar saw the priest's eyes glisten and allowed the harshness of his own features to soften. 'I cared for you then,' Dagobert said, 'as I care for you now. Which is why I want you to let me inspect your injuries.'

'They heal,' Kastner said.

'The priestess said they could become infected,' Dagobert said. 'Your fever, your malaise. They could all be part of–'

'I am returned to health,' Kastner said. 'With the sun, Sigmar gave me back my strength and my senses. I am his again as I am yours. My infirmity, Emil's fate – these are all tests to be endured as part of the God-King's work. It is dangerous but necessary. If I heard you right in the back of this wretched wagon, you carry burdens that deserve your attention far more, father.'

'You seem at the centre of those also,' Dagobert admitted. He nodded to Giselle beside him. 'If you hadn't delivered this child and the dark treasures she carried from the forest and its dangers – paying dearly for it yourself – then we would be living the doom of the Empire. Nay, the world, if that damned volume is to be believed.'

'Our concern with these dread, otherworldly matters will soon be at an end,' Kastner told him as the towers of Fort Denkh reached into the sky above them. 'Other servants of Sigmar will carry the weight of responsibility on their shoulders. Let ancient prophecies and Ruinous lunacy be Lutzenschlager's concern. Let the people be yours and the bold advance of this invading warband mine. We shall all be the God-King's hand in this, in our different ways, according to the gifts he has given us.'

'It fills me with joy to hear you speak in such ways,' Dagobert said with a bleak smile. 'I thought I had lost you, boy.'

When Kastner didn't reply, the priest looked to him and followed the templar's glare. It was directed up at the towers and the smoke trails that wound about their rounded elevations and stained the sky.

'Crossbow,' Kastner said. Dagobert nodded, his chins wobbling with the sudden effort of passing the reins to Giselle. Stuffing the bulk of *The Liber Caelestior* and its primer, wrapped in soft cloth, into his robes, Dagobert climbed into the back of the wagon.

'What is it?' Giselle asked, but neither of the men answered the girl.

Changing places with the novice, Dagobert returned with the loaded crossbow and Emil's quiver of bolts, standing about the driver seat like a coachman with a blunderbuss.

'This cannot be,' the priest said to himself. 'This cannot be.'

Giselle heard *Terminus* clear its saddle-scabbard. Kastner held the sword upright, balancing the weight of the heavy blade. Without his plate, the templar wore only his doublet, leggings, boots and a blanket. He craned his head around and peered back at the sight of Gorst in his rags, chains and cage, tramping up the road some distance behind. The Knight of the Twin-Tailed Orb could see no one else on the road.

'Eyes open, girl,' Kastner said to Giselle at the wagon's reins, digging his heels into Oberon's side and prompting the horse ahead.

As Oberon and the hospice wagon rounded the corner approach and the fort crept out from behind the trees, the three of them saw bodies in the road. Some were merchants and farmers, cut down on the road with their packhorses and oxen where they had been waiting for admittance. The tall fort gates were open, however, with soldier sentries missing from the portly, conical-roofed half-towers of the gatehouse. Archers were also missing from the curtain wall of the fort. As they approached, Kastner cast a suspicious eye across the river but found only the fort's lonely reflection in the slow, glassy waters.

As Oberon's hooves and the wheels of the wagon hit the cobbles, the cacophony of their entrance bounced about the stone barbican and the courtyard beyond. It was eerily quiet. The buildings within the fort walls were black and burned out, trailing a breeze-blown smoke of cinders. The stables, outhouses and market exchange were gone and the gallows toppled. Only the stone of the petitioners' hall and barracks remained and the captain's quarters and company chapel still quietly smouldered. The dead carpeted the courtyard, their bodies lying broken and butchered across the blood-splattered cobbles or dumped in mounds that buzzed with feasting flies.

Crowds of crows launched themselves from the slaughter at the visitors' approach, cawing about the courtyard before settling on the fort wall.

Kastner guided Oberon through the bodies, the steed's mighty hooves stepping through travellers and traders. The horse passed over the blue and white of Middenland soldiers. State troops, garrison sentries, archers and halberdiers. All had been slaughtered where they stood. The bodies were not defiled or tainted with sorcery, and neither did they bear corruptions or display the hallmarks of butchery for butchery's sake. Despite the absence of these things, Kastner was confident that the massacre was the work of Chaotics or marauders. It wasn't something that betrayed itself to the eye or would bear explanation. The destruction had a taste to it. A murderous economy. The elegant butchery of an unsuspecting, unprepared and outclassed force, torn through by their martial superiors. Veteran dealers in death. It was a massacre – but a purposeful one, by warriors who enjoyed their work but to whom the swift and circumspect execution of their enemies was the only thing on their minds. Kastner had sensed the self-same purity of purpose as they had passed through Gerzen and Bergendorf.

'Take care, child,' Dagobert said to Giselle as the wagon bumped through the bodies, before calling across the carnage, 'Diederick?'

'It's them,' the templar confirmed. 'Expert bladework – one man, one mortal wound. No casualties. Some improvisation, with the fires. A distraction, maybe. Had to be something. The gates are open, bearing no damage of an assault. They were in without a fight.' Kastner moved Oberon around a toppled artillery piece. 'Cannon. Unfired.'

'What do we do? What do we do?' Dagobert said.

'We can't stay here,' Kastner said. 'That's for sure. You say that they're looking for that book. If they hit a provincial fort to find it, then your precious tome will only find security in the Altdorf, where the walls are thicker and their opponents more than just a borrowed weapon and a bright uniform.'

Kastner turned towards the far gate.

'Do you hear that?'

'Hear what?' Dagobert said. Giselle's confusion confirmed to the knight that he was the only one to hear the approach: the developing acuteness of his senses warning him of danger. Horses. Heavy, like his own. Plate and barding, rattling to the rhythm of a gallop. The deep breathing of both steed and rider. Eighteen. Kastner listened to the hoof falls. No. Twenty horses and riders. The knight turned to Dagobert and Giselle.

'Riders approaching,' Kastner said, turning his own steed. 'Conceal yourselves.'

Dagobert cursed, getting down from the wagon with difficulty carrying the crossbow. Giselle jumped down lightly behind him.

'Where?' the priest called, already flustered.

'Anywhere,' Kastner said, sidling Oberon up against the inside of the fort wall beside the southern gatehouse. The portcullis was open and it was through the entrance that the horses thundered in – like a battlefield charge. Kastner cast a glance across the courtyard and found that Dagobert and the girl had disappeared into the charred remains of a domed chapel.

Destriers flashed by the templar. White, wearing red barding. In the saddle, Kastner saw armoured figures in gleaming silver plate. The lead rider carried a standard advertising the host as Knights of the Fiery Heart. Templars out of Altdorf and personal guardians of the Grand Theogonist and the Cathedral of Sigmar. In their plated fists the knights carried the long hafts of silver warhammers. Their tabards bore the striking red of Imperial crosses, the arrow-points of each end terminating in the shape of a heart. The visor sights of their crowned crusader helms were cut to accommodate a similar pattern.

Despite being a vision to behold in their armour and on their magnificent steeds, the templars drew from Kastner the wrinkle of his lip. This was not a new feeling. Many of the Sigmarite Orders felt that both the Knights of the Fiery Heart and the Knights Griffon – responsible for safeguarding the God-King's temples in Altdorf and Nuln, capital city of the Empire – were glorious to behold. That they were expertly drilled and fearsome warriors. They also felt that they were far from the real work of the God-Emperor. Temples and personages needed protection but it was in the deep dark forests and provincial mountain ranges of the Empire that Sigmar's will was prosecuted – slaying greenskins, beastmen and the servants of the Dark Gods in His name. It was dirty, desperate work and the duty of orders like the Knights of the Twin-Tailed Orb, while the magnificent temples and cathedrals of the land, already situated in some of the most fortified areas of the Empire, were guarded by the Knights Griffon and the Knights of the Fiery Heart.

A preceptor riding behind the standard bearer raised the haft of his hammer, bringing the corpse-mulching entrance of the knights to a halt. As the horses slowed and stopped, the riders looked about the carnage – the smouldering of buildings and the sea of bodies. The preceptor raised his visor – a Reiklander, noble of face, black of hair and sporting the trimmed moustache and beard thought fashionable in the cities.

'Brotherhood!' the preceptor called crisply. 'Dismount.'

The templars stepped down from their steeds with hammers in hand. As Kastner motioned Oberon on in front of the open south gate, he heard Dagobert bawl from the ruined chapel.

'By Sigmar's blood, it's good to see you, sirs.'

As Dagobert and Giselle emerged – the priest resting the crossbow on a demolished wall – the preceptor ordered six of his knights forward. The templars were quite an intimidating sight, running forward in formation, glinting warhammers held in two gauntlets, their faces hidden in their crowned helms. As the Knights of the Fiery Heart surrounded them, Dagobert and Giselle slowed. Kastner felt his hand tighten about *Terminus*. Feeling the urgency of an explanation, Dagobert addressed the preceptor.

'My name is Hieronymous Dagobert of Nordland,' he said, his words fast and uncertain, 'priest of Sigmar's way temple on the Sudenpass near Esk.'

'You are the priest?' the preceptor asked.

'I am, good sir,' Dagobert replied, 'last time I checked. This is Giselle Dantziger, Sister of the Imperial Cross, late of the Hammerfall, in the Middle Mountains.' The priest looked to Giselle, not only to check that he had announced her name correctly but also to see the glow of pride on her face at hearing that she was now to be known as a Sister of the Imperial Cross. Dagobert didn't think that there would be anyone left alive at the Hammerfall to dispute the fact. Besides, the priest believed that the girl had earned it.

'Preceptor Riesenweiler of the Knights of the Fiery Heart,' the warrior told him. 'My orders come directly from the Grand Theogonist himself, Hedrich Lutzenschlager – though for the purposes of this conversation, sir, you may take them as coming from Sigmar himself.'

'Well, I don't know about tha–'

'You still have the tome?' Riesenweiler asked.

'I do, sir, by the God-King's good grace,' Dagobert said, uncomfortable being within a cordon of hammer-wielding knights. 'Though you can see from the massacre about us that you are not the only interested party.'

'I sincerely hope that you are not attempting to bargain with me you foolish old man,' Riesenweiler warned.

'No, sir,' Dagobert went on uncertainly, and with Giselle looking about them at the slowly closing templars.

'We have ridden far, at the Grand Theogonist's behest,' Riesenweiler continued. 'Be clear. Hedrich Lutzenschlager demands the whole truth of your heart, priest, and we nothing less.'

'I only meant to say that there has already been a great deal of blood spilt over these heretical works.'

'I swear, priest,' Riesenweiler spat with the impatience of nobility, 'that your man on the rack made more sense.'

'What?' Dagobert said. 'You mean Berndt? You racked him?'

'Speak up!' the knight bellowed imperiously.

'Why?'

'Because Hedrich Lutzenschlager demanded the whole truth of his heart.'

'But... he... he's a mute...'

'And yet on my master's rack, the words fell right out of him,' Riesenweiler said. 'One last time, priest. Or I shall have my man here open your skull with his hammer and search for the answers in there.'

Dagobert looked to a terrified Giselle – and then back to the preceptor with a face of stone.

'These poor fools died at the hand of marauders,' Dagobert said, nodding at the slaughter around them. 'Who, I suspect, would do as much as your master has empowered you to do – and more – to acquire the contents of the tome in our possession.'

'At last, we understand one another,' Riesenweiler said with a wolfish smile. 'The Grand Theogonist was also told that you had with you a pair of invalids. Men in need of Shallya's mercy.'

Dagobert's eyes narrowed.

'I should wonder that you did not send one of her priestesses to ease their suffering, sir,' Dagobert said, 'rather than a company of heavily armed knights. Men better equipped to inflict suffering than alleviate it.'

'I see you know us well, sir,' the preceptor said. 'Now, these men...'

'What does the Grand Theogonist want with them? Surely not to enquire as to their wellbeing?'

Riesenweiler nodded to one of the knights, who slammed the haft of his warhammer into Dagobert's ample gut, drawing a savage grunt from the priest and putting him down on his knees.

'Blackguards!' Giselle screeched at the knights.

'Do not make me ask again, you idiot provincials,' Riesenweiler said.

'The boy, Emil Eckhardt, passed,' Dagobert managed, attempting to get back his wind. 'Sieur Diederick Kastner–'

'–is right behind you.'

The courtyard echoed with the clatter of plate, as Preceptor Riesenweiler and his Knights of the Fiery Heart turned around in unison. There Kastner sat, blocking the south gate, on Oberon. He was armourless, bloodied, bandaged and holding the greatsword *Terminus* out before him. 'What would you have with him? And don't make *me* ask again, you bloody genteels.'

Something about Kastner amused the preceptor. Perhaps it was the knight's grim jest or his filthy attire, bereft of plate. It could simply have been the appalling odds. Nodding, Riesenweiler ordered his remaining templars to similarly surround Kastner and his steed. Oberon snorted and stamped as the Knights of the Fiery Heart formed a circle about him.

'Sieur Kastner – Diederick Kastner of the Gruber Marches,' Riesenweiler announced. 'By the order of the Hedrich Lutzenschlager – Grand Theogonist and Sigmar's Will in this world – you are charged with perfidy, wanton bloodshed, bringing terror to this land, the breach of your holy faith, consort with heretics and the worship of outlawed gods.

'Outrageous!' Dagobert said, getting to his feet, but the knight standing over him put him back down with another haft-slug to the gut.

'Your crimes have been weighed and measured,' Riesenweiler said, 'and your punishment devised. That punishment is death, sir. I have taken the liberty of informing your chapter master and claiming your ancestral lands.'

'Kind of you,' Kastner called, 'but you are mistaken, as the God-King is my witness.'

'And yet Sigmar stands as witness against you,' the preceptor replied, 'speaking through my master of your renouncement of his following and your service to the Ruinous Powers.'

'I don't suppose it matters that I have done none of those things.'

'You will,' Riesenweiler told him coldly. Kastner's lip curled into a snarl. It did not matter. This was no mistake. Some great betrayal had been fabricated and his life and work offered as a solution to some unknown problem. If the God-King had a failing, it was that he entrusted his Empire to sycophants and parasites that would pervert his cult for their own ends. Most who served in the ranks of his priesthood or martial orders knew this, believing that they might still do some small good in his name despite their suspicion that the leaders of his faith had lost their way. This was no mistake. The Grand Theogonist would not have sent twenty of his best templars out into the provinces with such specific accusations and orders as part of a misunderstanding. This was real and it was happening now. Kastner felt the careful life of advancement and devotion unravel about him. He had fooled himself into thinking that his next action would have great meaning and would change the direction of his life. The truth he admitted to himself was that his life had already turned a corner. There was nothing left to do but accept his fate.

'I will…'

'You will,' Riesenweiler repeated. Kastner lowered *Terminus* and pointed the tip of the broad blade at the Knight of the Fiery Heart.

'Wanton bloodshed I might grant you, preceptor,' Kastner growled.

'No,' Dagobert bawled from the ground. 'Diederick, don't. This is madness – the servants of Sigmar set against one another.'

'Diederick Kastner is no servant of Sigmar,' Riesenweiler seethed. 'Brotherhood! Do your duty.'

'No,' Dagobert roared. 'Desist in this insanity. We demand audience with the Grand Theogonist. We demand to hear this from him. We demand to hear his reasons.'

But the preceptor had done with the priest. He had heard the order from Lutzenschlager's own lips. 'The man Diederick Kastner must die…'

When Riesenweiler had proposed taking five knights, Lutzenschlager had said, 'Take twenty and see that it is done.' When Riesenweiler protested the number, the Grand Theogonist had told him, 'This man is cursed by the Dark Gods with a future of doom and damnation. A future that must be denied, for our sake as well as his own. Sigmar has granted us the opportunity to do that. He has entrusted me with this task and now I entrust you. Take twenty of your knights and end this enemy of the Empire. No life your holy weapons have taken has ever been more deserving.'

'Do your duty!' Riesenweiler commanded.

The knights moved in with their hammers, the dismal daylight reflecting off their immaculate plate. Kastner felt the pain in his eye intensify. The crackling torment felt its way through his mind like lightning searing between a thunderhead and the ground. With every snap of pain, the templar's face contorted. In the blinding after-agony of each mind-cleaving crack, he saw the bodies of brother templars cut down in the courtyard. The blood-splashed silver of their plate. Crowned helms, rolling about the cobbles with the decapitated heads of knights within. The blessed soldiers of Sigmar laid low.

'I will not be a slave to the perversity of these events any longer,' the templar told all. 'Servants of the Dark Gods or the servants of Sigmar – you all seem lost to me. I will not offer up my life in the name of such madness.'

'Diederick, no!'

But it was already done. The decision was made. With it came peace. With it came – for that moment at least – a mind free from soul-crippling pain. Oberon reared. Kastner lifted *Terminus* for a killing stroke. His first victim came in, his hammer swing drilled and predictable. Kastner would make him pay for the insult of such a routine manoeuvre. To think that Diederick Kastner could be felled by such lack of imagination. At least the forest creatures and the marauders of the north hit you with everything they had. All their skill, their passion, their blood-thirsty invention. Sigmar's knight would die for his presumption.

Suddenly there was movement.

It caught Kastner's attention, as it did his opponent – as it did his templar brothers. A nearby mound of bodies rose from the cobbles. Dead Middenlanders rained to the ground. Butchered torsos. Cleaved limbs. Spilled guts. Beneath were winged forms. Warriors in mail and plate of their own, the metal dark with age and stain. Their wings appeared to be extensions of their armour, infernal appendages of beetle-black. The warriors' helms were the colour of bronzed bone, almost seeming to be skull grown over the metal plate. They rose to their knees, their gauntlets empty, protecting themselves with the mound, shaking the blood and leakage from the surface of their wings.

'My god...' Preceptor Riesenweiler said, lifting his warhammer. He looked from Kastner to the eight marauder knights who had just revealed themselves. Oberon's hooves hit the ground once more. The templar's hammer hovered. Kastner held *Terminus* high above his head.

'The marauders!' Dagobert called out, retreating within the ruined chapel.

'Enemies of Sigmar in our midst,' Riesenweiler called to his knights. He jabbed an accusatory metal digit at Kastner. 'The forsaken reveals his dark servants. Destroy them!'

Knights of the Fiery Heart charged through the carpet of bodies at the Chaos warriors. The armoured figures walked calmly towards the templars, bringing the thumb-protrusions of their wings over their shoulders. Reaching up, the Chaos knights grabbed the protrusions with their gauntlets and withdrew from the hollow bone fingers between the wing membranes a pair of curved, bone swords. Like gnarled sabres of rachidian razors, the knights readied themselves for the charge.

It was just the kind of carnage Kastner had imagined in the courtyard. The marauder knights were cold and purposeful in their execution of their assault. While Riesenweiler's templars lifted and swung their warhammers with a confidence born of drill and prayer, the Chaos warriors were lopping, slashing and stabbing their way through their element – the blood and body parts of their victims. The Ruinous knights moved with the reactive fluidity not of one born to wear plate, like the highborn of the Empire, but of one who had become part of it. Drawing wings before them like shields, the warriors allowed silver hammers to bounce uselessly from the armoured membranes before erupting forth from behind them and scything down through gaps and between plates in the templars' silvered armour.

Kastner watched with simultaneous horror and exhilaration as the templars of Sigmar and the Ruinous knights fought for his soul. Oberon trotted about the bloodshed, with Kastner lifting *Terminus* to strike. Knights of the Fiery Heart, batted back by the wings of their silent foes, tripped through cadavers into the greatsword's reach. The rage in Kastner's belly caused *Terminus* to tremble in his grip, but he couldn't bring himself to strike Sigmar's servants down. As three silver knights smashed one of the damned warriors back through the carnage, its wings and bone blades turning the irresistible force of the warhammers aside, Kastner found himself above the knight.

Righteous fury washed through him like ice-water. The Ruinous warrior had to die. Every part of Kastner's being needed to end him. Almost every part. The wyrdstone within his skull grew warm. It was a strange sensation and the templar brought his hand up to the ruin of his punctured eye. The stone was hot to the touch. Every time Kastner brought his greatsword up, it pulsed a savage heat that he felt throughout his head. Kastner growled at himself in frustration. Within moments the Chaos warrior would turn or move out of reach. *Terminus* came up. Kastner's head came down with the searing thunder that peeled through his skull. Gritting his teeth through the agony, the templar unleashed the broad blade of his weapon. Hacking down between the warrior's wings, the sword cleaved through his neck and shoulder. Tearing *Terminus* skyward, Kastner brought the sword down through the flesh and armour fusion of the other shoulder.

Kastner didn't see the Chaos warrior crash to its armoured knees, its helm-heavy head lolling forward and falling from its gore-spuming torso. He was down on the cobbles, *Terminus* clattering to the ground beside him. Clutching his head with his hands, the templar looked up just in time to see a Knight of the Fiery Heart hammer aside the body of the winged warrior and bring his warhammer over his decorative helm. Kastner rolled across the blood-spattered courtyard, snatching for the hilt of his greatsword as he did. The warhammer came down, sparking off the cobbles. Kastner kicked back to his feet and put *Terminus* between him and the Sigmarite.

Two other knights, drawn down on the dismounted templar, charged from the right and for a moment it appeared as if Kastner would need to take the three of them. With the agony in his head subsiding, he brought his hand down and clutched his greatsword. The first of the charging knights suddenly went down, a Chaos warrior who had been matching him step for step, hacking his leg from his knee with the sweep of his heavy bone sabre. The second was knocked from his feet by a second warrior who slammed into the knight from the side. Tackling the Sigmarite to the ground in a pile of bodies, the Ruinous warrior encapsulated them both in its wings before rearing and stabbing one of its great sabres down through the knight's silver chest.

Kastner felt the God-King's wrath come down with the warhammer of the knight facing him. Holding the heavy blade of *Terminus* against the assault, the templar fought the desire to kill his opposite.

'I'm a Knight of the Twin-Tailed Orb,' Kastner roared at him. 'A templar of Sigmar. Like you.'

Kastner's protests didn't give the hammer-wielding knight a moment's pause. The weight of the weapon came down once, twice and a third time, each swing carrying more fervent force than the last.

'You are nothing like me,' the knight bellowed through his visor, his clipped and cultured voice that of a Reiklander. Kastner felt rage build within him. As the hammer's haft came down, the templar pushed it aside with his greatsword. Reaching for the knight's ornate helm with his other hand, Kastner flipped up the visor and found himself looking at a young nobleman. His couth features were screwed up with effort and righteous hatred for his enemy, the kind of righteous hatred that had once disfigured Kastner's face. Hooking his fingertips inside the crowned helm, Kastner pulled the knight violently to him. Bringing *Terminus* back with the other, he buried the cross-guard of the sword in the young knight's face. Allowing the dead Sigmarite to rattle to the courtyard cobbles, Kastner spat after him.

'You're right,' he said. 'We are nothing alike.'

He turned from the Knight of the Fiery Heart to the two marauder knights that had saved him. The templar expected vengeance. Instead he found cold acceptance. Kastner heard Riesenweiler direct his knights on with imperious disappointment, sending eager warriors his way. Kastner shook his head, raising *Terminus* before him.

'Fight me!' he bawled at the Chaos warriors. He ran at the first but it simply backed away, not even offering a bone sword or wing in defence. 'What's wrong with you? I'm your enemy.' Turning savagely at the second, Kastner brought his greatsword around with such frustration and force that it cut the Chaos knight's bone sword in two. As the marauder backed away, its skull-helm bowed in some kind of wretched deference to the templar, it reached for the gristle of a third protruding hilt and cleared a shorter bone blade from another winged finger-scabbard.

As Riesenweiler's company stormed at Kastner, the marauder knights stepped into their path, bone swords flashing in both hands – putting the holy Sigmarites from their prize. The templar felt his heart twist inside his chest. He had a cold loathing for everything in the courtyard but couldn't bring himself to butcher his damned saviours from behind with a sword in their backs. Looking about him, Kastner came to realise that the marauder knights had formed a skirmish line – a cordon of their own, facing outwards and keeping the devout Knights of the Fiery Heart from him. Sick to his soul, Kastner knew that without them he would have been bludgeoned mercilessly into the cobbles by the Grand Theogonist's armoured assassins. He knew that he wanted to live and had the marauders' intervention to thank for the possibility.

Looking beyond, Kastner saw Father Dagobert making an awkward run for the hospice wagon, his damned volume clutched to his chest. Giselle still sought the cover of the chapel ruins, while Riesenweiler put himself between the two of them. Clutching the haft of his hammer high in his hand, the preceptor rattled up behind the priest at a jog.

Grabbing Oberon's reins in his hand, Kastner mounted the horse and jabbed his heels into the animal's flanks. Urging the steed into a corpse-stomping gallop, Kastner rode for the preceptor. Pushing Dagobert against the wagon, Riesenweiler spun the priest around. *The Liber Caelestior* was buried in his chubby arms.

'Give it to me!' Riesenweiler shouted into the priest's face. As Dagobert struggled against the far stronger knight, Riesenweiler smashed the wood of the forward wagon bow to splinters with his hammer. He swung the weapon at Dagobert with murderous force. The second swing destroyed the wagon's handbrake, while the third put a hole through the sideboard. Between the weight of the weapon in one hand and the priest's struggles, the preceptor couldn't guarantee the hammer's destination. Riesenweiler roared. Dagobert roared back.

'Deviants all,' the Knight of the Fiery Heart accused the priest, the silver head of the hammer against his cheek, pinning him against the wagon. 'That tome belongs to my master now!'

With Kastner still riding through Riesenweiler's scattered company – evading the arcs of hammers and knocking the knights down with Oberon's flanks and turns – Giselle found herself grabbing at the back of the preceptor's plate.

'Leave him,' she called, but Riesenweiler shrugged her off and turned, grabbing the girl's short hair in his gauntlet. Hauling her into the wagon bed, the novice-sister hit the wood with a crack. Tearing her around, the knight found that it was the stock of the crossbow she had recovered from the derelict chapel that had made the noise rather than the girl's delicate bones. Holding it casually at her hip, Giselle pulled on the trigger. The weapon gave a buck and a sigh, sending the bolt the short distance into Riesenweiler's groin. The knight stumbled back, clutching at the mail skirt covering his lower abdomen. The chainmail had done nothing to halt the quarrel, which had slammed some depth into the preceptor's flesh.

Riesenweiler started to say something but he was distracted by the shaft of wood through his body and the blood splashing down the cuisse plates on his thighs. He went down with a cacophonous crash, looking between his gauntlet around the bolt at both Giselle and the priest.

'This is...' Riesenweiler began, 'this is not what Sigmar had planned for me.'

'Not for any of us,' Dagobert agreed, stepping forward. Black horseflesh suddenly flashed by, its passage rippling the priest's robes. Kastner rode Oberon straight through the Knight of the Fiery Heart, Riesenweiler ending up a trampled mess, some distance away – brained and broken beneath the stallion's colossal hooves.

As Kastner pulled the horse around, he discovered Father Dagobert and Giselle staring dumbfounded at him.

'Get in,' he shouted, bringing the pair back to their senses. Turning the greatsword about in his wrist, Kastner slapped the flat of the blade against Oberon's side, urging the horse on ahead of the wagon.

'On,' the priest yelled, sending ripples down the reins at the wagon horses. 'On, my beauties.'

Weaving Oberon through the silver knights, Kastner leant low and to one side, cutting down the desperate Sigmarites as he rode, creating a path for the wagon to bump across the courtyard bodies for the south gate. Turning aside warhammers and cleaving through the finest quality plate with well-aimed hacks and chops, Kastner discovered that the few knights who had made it back to their glorious white steeds had been set upon by the winged marauders.

Leaping the corpses of a Chaos warrior and the four knights whose lives it had cost to bring him down, Kastner and Oberon thundered up to the gate. Reloading the crossbow, Giselle had little skill at range, but the threat of the weapon and the glancing whoosh of crossbow bolts off stone and cobble enabled Dagobert to whip the wagon horses through the stone gateway. Slashing the ropes of the barbican winch with *Terminus*, Kastner brought his head down low and nudged Oberon swiftly through the gate with the portcullis shuddering down behind him. Hammering his horse up the road away from the decimated Fort Denkh, Kastner could hear the slaughter of the leaderless knights by the warband of winged warriors – the same warband that was massacring its way south through the Empire. As he rode past the wagon, urging Dagobert to keep up the pace, the templar couldn't help feeling that he was trying to outrun both his past and his future in leaving the Sigmarites and marauder knights behind.

'Where are we going?' the priest shouted at the passing warrior.

Kastner considered. They needed a place to rest and collect themselves. Somewhere he could think and devise a more decisive course of action. He turned to look at the red-faced Dagobert and Giselle, who was still clutching Emil's crossbow. The templar made a decision.

'Home,' Kastner told him.

CHAPTER VIII

'...on aery lips, that whisper dead men's
names
Through forests ancient and ruins new.
He, like a traveller
In cursed lands of rack and ruin, bore an
aspect
of misgiving, worn to habitude.'

– Tanhauser's *Ode to Fear*

Kastner Estates
Gruber Marches
Blutig Wellentag/Ersten Aubentag im Erntzeit, IC 2420

The trees creaked with the ropes of the innocents hanging from them. Oberon took the beech-lined path up to the mansion at a grim trot, his rider rolling in the saddle in stunned disbelief. With each crunch of gravel, it became clear that Riesenweiler and his Sigmarites had come to Fort Denkh by way of the Marches. The beautiful manor house still stood, the knights having had little time to torch it on their way to intercept Kastner and the damned tome he was escorting to safety in Altdorf.

Kastner saw Kiefer the groom, swinging in the breeze, the boy's face frozen with the horror of the moment he realised he was going to die. Old Wendal – the Lady's bailiff – had taken a monstrous beating. Even Fitchling, purser of the estate, swung for the bad fortune of attending the manor house the day of the knights' arrival. The housekeeper Frau Valda and her serving girls, all still in their aprons and strung from the branches above the Great Lawn.

Dagobert and Giselle were silent on the front of the wagon. Even Gorst, who had somehow found them again after their flight from Fort Denkh, held back his ramblings. Kastner brought Oberon along the length of the Kastner mansion, halting the steed before the large oak doors of the entrance. There was paint splashed across the worm-eaten wood, the words scrawled with passion: HERETIC. Before the accusation, Lady Kastner – Lady Angelika to those who knew her – hung like a canting scarecrow from the stone porchway. Lady Angelika, whom Kastner had come to love, not like a mother, but like a beneficent goddess or patron. Cruelly neglected by her husband, her heart was kind and her mind sharp, steering the Kastner estates through the financial ruin of her husband's foolishness and drunken abandon. Such hardships had not cooled her compassion for others, and upon arriving in the Gruber Marches with a templar's steed, an ancestral blade and a dubious story, Diederick had found not only a home but a name of his own and the opportunities that went with it. He owed Angelika Kastner his life. The life falling apart around him.

Before the templar knew it, night had fallen. His torso – healing with almost supernatural speed and determination – glistened with sweat and glinted with the reflection of stars in the dark sky above. Even his limp was fading. The shovel bit into the rich brown earth of the estate. He had been digging graves all day. His bones ached and his mind was numb. Gorst had helped him with the bodies and was now sitting behind a finely trimmed hedge, unusually quiet. As the last few shovels of earth hit the mound, Kastner patted them down. On the simple marker he had painted the name 'Trudi'. He had never known the serving girl's family name.

A lantern approached from the manor house. It was Giselle, with a stein and a jug of milk. She hung the lantern off the handle of a pick buried in the ground. It rested with Kastner's hammer swinging from its chain – the silver hammer Father Dagobert had given him before the young Diederick had left to be a knight's page. The novice poured the milk in silence and handed it to the templar. Despite all they had been through, Kastner detected fear in a face unaccustomed to such an emotion.

'What is it, girl?' Kastner demanded.

'Father Dagobert said you should keep up your strength. You're still healing,' Giselle told him. Kastner drank deep. The milk was cool from the cellars. He thrust the stein forward for more. The sister obliged him. 'My cousin Johan once–'

'Tell Dagobert that I need him,' Kastner cut her off. 'Someone should say something for these people.'

'Then why don't you?' Dagobert's voice carried through the darkness. The priest walked up behind Giselle, the heretical tome both the Knights of the Fiery Heart and the winged marauders were searching for under one arm. 'You know the words.'

'They stick in the throat,' Kastner told him grimly.

'As a servant of Sigmar, you've presided over many funerals,' Dagobert said, walking into the lantern-light.

'I knew these people...'

'All the more reason you would want to honour them.'

'You think after today, it wise to lecture me on funeral etiquette?' Kastner said, his anger rising. 'Conduct the bloody lamentations – would you, please?'

'Humour me, Diederick,' Dagobert pressed. 'Help me with first rites.'

Kastner glared at the priest. His lips parted but nothing proceeded from them. He tried again and again he failed. Kastner clenched his teeth and stabbed the shovel into the ground.

'You know the words won't come,' he said finally.

'And what of this,' Dagobert said, indicating the silver hammer he had given to the templar. The hammer he had worn around his own neck. He moved forward. Kastner flinched. Not afraid of Dagobert but himself. The priest took the lantern from the pick handle and held it up to the knight's chest. There, in the flesh, masquerading as a wound or injury, was a hammer-shaped mark. Like a burn, the silhouette was red, agitated and covered in scratches where it had irritated the templar's skin.

'You cannot speak His words, nor tolerate His sigil against your flesh,' Dagobert said.

Kastner looked down at the mark on his chest. His head rose

slowly and thoughtfully. His pain and anger was spent. He felt tired. Looking up at the priest, he stared deep into Dagobert's eyes.

'What is happening to me?' Kastner asked, his voice barely a whisper on the night air.

'You are marked,' Giselle said. 'Any fool can see that. Marked by the Dark Gods…'

'Silence, woman,' Kastner snapped. 'Don't speak such things.'

'Someone must,' Dagobert said.

'Why didn't they kill us?' Giselle asked. 'In the fort, the marauders could have killed us with all those other people. Why didn't they? The Hammerfall. The villages. The fort – but not us. Are we marked with you?'

'I'm warning you…'

'They could have taken the book from our corpses,' Dagobert said, pulling the damned tome from beneath his arm.

'I don't know,' Kastner told them, his gaze on the ground.

'I think I do,' Dagobert said. 'In the manor house, in view of what has come to pass, I thought it worth the risk to consult this Ruinous volume further. While you were out digging graves for those whose blood is on your hands…' Kastner's head came up sharply, but the harsh words the templar had for Father Dagobert died on his lips. 'I have been using the primer to translate this wretched thing. It has answers for us, Diederick, but answers you are not going to want to hear.'

'But I think that we need to hear them,' Giselle said, her arms folded before her. She looked from Kastner to the priest.

'You accuse me of being marked by Ruinous Powers,' Kastner said, kicking at the earth, 'but it is the two of you with your noses in the pages of outlawed texts.'

'We seem to be at the heart of events of some significance. The marauders. The Knights of the Fiery Heart. The Grand Theogonist of the Empire. Sigmar himself, for all we know. I have been sitting for hours, trying to conceive of why Hedrich Lutzenschlager would have ordered his knights to destroy us. You know that I have few good words to say about that man. Court politics and cult conspiracy put a toad like Lutzenschlager on the Grand Theogonist's throne, not the God-King's will. Men who opposed him were banished to the way temples of the northern coast and the wilds of Hochland. He's deluded. He's devout. His soul is a bottomless well of ambition, tapped falsely in the name of the God-King. But a murderer of convenience?'

'He's a walking corpse,' Kastner hissed through his teeth. 'That's all we need to know.'

'You're going to march into one of the most fortified cities in the land?' Dagobert challenged. 'You are already a hunted man. You mean to execute the most well-protected man in the Empire – bar the Emperor himself – in his own cathedral? I wish you a miracle in such an endeavour, my son, because you are going to need one.'

'No,' Kastner said in words of flint, 'just a blade and powerful will.'

'And a heart full of vengeance?' Dagobert said. 'Would you not know what placed such fire there?'

Kastner's expression soured, 'Pray continue.'

Dagobert held the tome up before Giselle and the templar.

'Despite its macabre appearance,' he said, 'it seems free from any kind of physical corruption. Leather cover, iron clasps, ink and vellum. If evil resides in its pages, it hides itself well. The reason, it seems, for the tome's heretical status and inclusion in the vaults of the mighty Hammerfall, is the knowledge it has faithfully carried to us through the ages. It is called *The Liber Caelestior* or *The Celestine Book of Divination*. You have helped me catalogue such books brought to us at the temple, Diederick, false prophecies that preach the God-King's absence in the world, foretellings derived from celestial congress...'

'Nonsense,' Kastner said.

'Agreed,' Dagobert said, 'the ramblings of madmen, hardly worthy of notice, hardly worthy of cataloguing and securing. These writings are nearly a thousand years old and belong to a professed Tilean seer called Battista Gaspar Necrodomo. He was an astromancer who prophesied what he called the End Times – the end of the world, my friend.'

'Doesn't mean it's not–'

'The Reman priests and inquisitors of Law and Light didn't seem to think so,' Dagobert said, 'and neither did Sigmar's devout servants. When it found its way to the Empire, it was buried in the Hammerfall.'

'Even learned men can be wrong,' Kastner assured him.

'Necrodomo tells that the End Times will be heralded by the coming of a great warrior from the north, a man who would be favoured through his deeds by all of the Ruinous Powers in unison. A man who would be their chosen – their Everchosen, as the Tilean terms it.'

'And how might one man alone bring about the end of the world?' Kastner asked darkly.

'He wouldn't,' Dagobert replied. 'Warriors flock to stand beside great men for the promise of battle, glory and victory. Harnessing their strength, Necrodomo claims he would overcome the trials set for him by the Dark Gods and earn their sponsorship. With their armies – their unified power – his advance would be irresistible. He would destroy the Empire – nay, the world. Without people to pray to them, gods like our own would be lost to history and the existence of man, with all other races, would be plunged into an eternal darkness.'

'Does this doom-monger have a name?'

'His name is Archaon.'

'Then perhaps this Archaon leads the marauders we saw yesterday,' Kastner said.

'Perhaps...'

'A dread tale indeed.'

'Not a tale, Diederick,' Dagobert said. 'Tales do not come true in the telling.' Kastner shook his head.

'It tells of truths?'

'That have already come to pass, my boy. How the tome itself came to be in our possession. The death and destruction in its wake. The doom to follow. Interpretations, true, as is the case with the translation of any ancient text. Even allowing for that, the predictions are uncanny.'

Kastner burned into Dagobert with his gaze.

'You think I am this Archaon?'

'From where I stand, it seems possible,' Dagobert said slowly.

Kastner roared, snatching up the shovel. Swinging it about him, he let the tool sail into the canopy of the surrounding trees.

'No!' Kastner bawled at the priest, as the shovel clanged its way through the branches and down into the earth below. He stabbed a finger at Dagobert. 'That cannot be so.'

'You are marked, good templar,' Giselle said.

'I should end you both for suggesting such a thing,' Kastner seethed. 'And burn that tome for the lies it tells.'

'Burning the book would not stop the prophecies coming to fruition,' Dagobert said. 'We would simply be blind to them.'

'How can you know?' Kastner said, his chest rising and falling, his face contorted and his eye filling. 'How can you know?'

'I don't,' Dagobert admitted, shamed by the pain of Kastner's reaction.

'What is your proof?'

'The north and the south meet in Archaon's blood.'

'What does that mean?' Kastner bawled.

'You were undoubtedly born here,' Dagobert said. 'You were brought to me a newborn. But look at your skin, your hair. You are a northerner from head to toe.'

'Proof of nothing...'

'Before serving the Ruinous Powers, Archaon found service in Sigmar's name.'

'So have many,' Kastner said. 'The Dark Gods delight in the corruption of virtue. Some of the God-King's boldest and best have fallen to that path.'

'Not many of his templars, I would hope, my son,' Dagobert said. 'Knights pledged in earnest to his cause. Men who were already chosen to stand as our protection against such darkness.'

'A templar?'

'The agreement of events and the people at the heart of them is compelling,' Dagobert said. 'The tome tells of this all, the unfolding tragedy of these times.'

'No,' Kastner spat. 'This is not true. You are wrong. You are deceived.'

'And sometimes we deceive ourselves,' Dagobert warned.

'I am a changed man,' Kastner admitted wretchedly. 'And events would seem to have conspired against me, certainly since this girl brought the calamitous thing into our lives. How can we know she is not a dark servant herself?'

Giselle took several steps back.

'You have already damned us all by your wretched company,' Giselle spat. 'I cannot return to the Hammerfall. This good father here will never see the inside of a temple as its priest. You wallow like a sow in its sorrow but cannot see the ruin you visit upon others.'

Giselle ran forward with her hand outstretched to slap him, but the templar's own came up, locking around her wrist. He pushed her back with a snarl, causing the novice-sister to fall across Trudi's fresh grave.

Dagobert helped her up as Kastner glowered at them both.

'My child, even if Archaon stands before us,' the priest said to Giselle, 'as far as I can glean from the early sections of the volume, the Dark Gods complot against him. He is no more to blame than the animal in the hunter's trap. He did not choose but was chosen. It is the reason I stand with him – why we should stand with him – in hope that he might be extricated from the snare he finds himself in.'

'Is there no hope?' Kastner said, crumbling slowly to his knees.

'Always, my child.'

'Should I not just select a noose from the many that hang in these trees?'

'I doubt fate would allow such an ending,' Dagobert mused.

'What does that even mean?'

'I knew a young man once,' Dagobert said. 'A man the plague had left bereft of wife and child. He tried to follow them through the noose of a rope...' Dagobert seemed to stall, the story difficult to tell. Giselle and Kastner watched the priest struggle. 'The timbers of his cottage had been as rotten as his fortune, however, and they broke under the weight of the attempt.'

'What happened to him?' Giselle asked.

'He pledged the life that had been granted him, to helping others through their difficulties, rather than sinking into his own.'

The girl nodded, still not quite understanding, and attempted a weak smile.

'I never knew that,' Kastner said, still on his knees.

'Well here's something that you should know,' Dagobert said. 'There is a page missing from *The Liber Caelestior.* An important one. Torn straight from the tome itself. The page, it seemed, was going to reveal the identity of the warrior who was to become this Archaon. Without it, we cannot be certain of anything. We need that page.'

'Where is it?' Giselle asked.

'It must reside – for safety – with the only man with authority in the land to have your matriarch grant him access to the tome in the first place.'

'The Grand Theogonist?'

'Well that is it then,' Kastner said after a pause. 'Lutzenschlager sent the knights. The page has told him who he is looking for.'

'Even learned men can be wrong,' Dagobert said, attempting a smile of his own. 'Diederick, I can continue with my translations, but you will not know any kind of peace until you know for sure. We need that page. It's time to start praying for a miracle.'

Kastner looked down at the freshly turned grave earth. He didn't think he was capable of such prayers. Not to the God-King, at any rate. The devotions would close up his throat. He pushed himself to his feet, nodding slowly in agreement. He would know what business destiny had with him. Besides, there were marvels and miracles in the world for which the God-King was not responsible. Miracles that required neither prayer nor devotions.

Picking up his arming doublet from where it lay across a hedge, disturbing Gorst from his quiet mumblings, Kastner slipped into the blood-stained garment and made his way to the manor house. The new sensitivity of his hearing – one of many changes to the way the templar was beginning to experience his doomed world – picked up the sighs of relief that fell out of Dagobert and the girl. At what should have been well out of earshot, he heard them exchange words.

'The very Cathedral of Sigmar?' Giselle said.

'The lion's den, child.'

'Will he return?'

'No,' Dagobert said. 'I seriously doubt it.'

'Then why send your friend to his death?' Giselle asked.

'I sent him because he *is* my friend,' Dagobert said. 'I hope for his sake – and our own – that he does not return. That he finds peace in the God-King's holy temple. Knight of Sigmar or not, Diederick is polluted. Dread forces twist his soul in the same way they twisted the flesh of poor Emil Eckhardt.' Dagobert's manner became grim and brooding. 'If he does indeed return, with dark answers to dark questions… well then, we shall all be doomed.'

Kastner crossed the pitch-black lawn, heading for the untruth of his ancestral home. He nodded slowly to himself, his head burning with unanswerable questions. His past was a lie. He knew that. But would his future be similarly false?

'Kastner,' Giselle called.

Her voice echoed about the empty gardens of the manor house. It was morning and even the birds seemed to be paying their respects to the dead. The air smelt of freshly turned earth. 'Sieur Kastner!' Giselle hollered across the graves.

'He's not in the house?' Father Dagobert called back. He had just completed his lamentations for the dead. With the number of bodies buried, it had taken some time.

'No, father. Last I saw him,' Giselle said, 'he was looking over the suits in the hall.'

'Sieur Kastner's ancestral suits of armour,' Dagobert said. Giselle frowned as he approached her. 'The former Sieur Kastner,' the priest clarified. 'His great-great grandfather fought alongside Magnus the Pious, you know, during the Great War against Chaos.'

'Perhaps he just left for the city early this morning,' Giselle said.

'Without talking to me first – I wouldn't have thought so.'

'Perhaps he just wanted to be alone.'

'Understandable, I suppose,' Dagobert said. 'It's not every day you discover you might be the herald of the apocalypse.'

'He'll return when he's ready, yes?'

'Yes,' Dagobert considered. If the priest was right about *The Celestine Book of Divination,* then Kastner's whole life was in there. He was going to want to come back for it. Dagobert nodded, his chins wobbling. 'The tome, yes, indeed. If we wish to know where he is, I should get back to my translations.'

'I'll make us some breakfast,' Giselle said.

'Yes, my child. You do that.'

As Giselle arrived at the well for fresh water, she discovered that the bucket had already been lowered. Heaving on the handle crank, she found that it wouldn't budge.

'The bucket is stuck,' Giselle called. While she tried her best to lever the handle round with her slight form, Dagobert walked back over to assist.

'It's probably the windlass,' the priest told her. As the pair of them heaved, the rope slowly wound its way around the spindle. 'What by gods?' Dagobert said. The weight on the rope was incredible.

'Perhaps it's caught or something.' As Giselle leant over to see the bucket rise from the darkness, leaving Dagobert on the crank, the rope almost ran. The commotion drew Gorst, who sniffed at the well like a curious hound.

'Get back on the handle, child, or all our efforts with be for naught,' the priest said, thick beads of sweat forming on his brow. 'It's caught on a root or something that's broken through the shaft wall. We're probably hauling up half a tree here.'

As the bucket rose above the stone rim of the well, Giselle and Father Dagobert could see that they were dragging no tree root. The bucket hung next to Diederick Kastner's body, the rope of which had been formed into a noose. The templar's face was a livid white – the black tracks of corruption clear to see, radiating through his flesh, away from his injured eye, like a star.

'Sigmar's blood…' Dagobert said. 'Sigmar's precious blood.'

'What does this mean?' Giselle said, her face still stricken with shock.

'It means I was wrong,' Dagobert said. 'It means that destiny cannot be compressed like a dead flower between the pages of a heavy tome. It lives. It is untamed and ever changing.' Giselle saw tears roll down the priest's rounded cheek. It was a tear of grim happiness, rather than grief. 'It means,' Dagobert said finally, 'that fate is what you make of it.'

But fate is not what you make it, shadow-of-mine. Fate is as inescapable as I choose to make it. Your fate is tied to my own and I will not let us fail. You cannot give away what isn't yours. Your soul may flee this mortal vessel at my command. When I am ready to assume the Everchosen's anointed flesh. When I am once again ready to rule a world ripe for ruin. No coward's noose will deny me my eternity.

You think it took an indomitable will to deny me? To flee your mortality and consign your flesh to corruption? No, shadow-of-mine. It takes an indomitable will to bend, nay break, the very laws of existence. It takes an indomitable will to wrestle the reins of runaway fate and yoke destiny – that tramples even gods – like a beast of my burdens. It takes an indomitable will to send you back to redress your failures and begin again. To live in ignorance and do my daemon bidding. My indomitable will.

CHAPTER VIII

'They called it the 'Miracle of Altdorf'. For years the River Reik had served as the city's latrine, with outpourings and effusions dumped straight into broad waters. It is from this time that Emperor Siegfried declared the city "The Great Reek" – the first recorded use of the term – and transferred his court to Nuln. Plagues of the Bloody Flux and Muddied Waters decimated the population. It is a little appreciated fact that the dwarf engineers tasked with constructing the Cathedral of Sigmar also established the beginnings of the first brick sewer system under the Domplatz District, on the river's southern shore.

With the diffusion of waste spread along the river's length, both the stench and the plagues abated. The network and culverts would be greatly extended during the princedom of Wilhelm III. At the time, however, the sewer system was hailed the "Miracle of Altdorf" and the dwarf engineers responsible were given freedom of the city. Many decided to stay, establishing the city's first Dwarf Quarter.'

– Emmerich Siessl, *The Great Reek*

The Sewers
The City of Altdorf
Tag von den leered Thron, IC 2420

Kastner had stowed away on a riverboat called the *Mutter's Melken* at Ahlenhof. Narrow barges were a common sight on the mighty Talabec. The waters were slow but powerful there and heavily laden with the black earth of the mountains upriver. Still, the journey was swifter than that back upstream to Talabheim, where the use of horses and well-worn towpaths were required. From what Kastner could tell from the hold in which he was hiding and overheard conversations from above, the *Mutter's Melken* was transporting grain to Marienburg, with little intention of stopping off at Altdorf. The captain was capable and the small crew busy, making it easy for the templar to maintain his concealment amongst the cargo. It also gave him time to think. To feel. To decide.

Diederick Kastner would not be a puppet of fate. He would not be hunted for being what he was not. The champions of the Dark Gods were mistaken and the God-King's servants fools. This insanity would end. Diederick Kastner would end it.

For a large part of the journey downriver, Kastner dozed amongst the grain sacks. He had left the Kastner estates before daybreak, enjoying little in the way of sleep, and took back-forest trails through the Marches to Ahlenhof. He hadn't woken Giselle or Dagobert, leaving them to enjoy the lonely luxuries of the manor house, its many rooms and soft sheets. He imagined that they would be relieved upon finding him gone. They were safer without him. Kastner was confident that the priest would know why he had left them and where he was going. On a table nearby, Kastner had seen *The Liber Caelestior* and the primer Dagobert was using to translate it. The knight had glowered at the pages with their meaningless words and symbols. The tome had been open at an early section, where, Kastner could see, a page had been torn out. He had studied the tattered edge of the vellum and the pattern of the tear, hoping to recognise it again. As he stood there, he fancied his life laid out in the macabre volume and imagined himself tearing all of the pages from its wicked spine and feeding them to the fire. His hand had hovered over the tome for a moment before he snatched his fist back.

Down in the Great Hall, Diederick had found Sieur Kastner's collection of suits. Armour belonging to the knight as a younger man. Plate worn by his father, his grandfather and his great-grandfathers. The noble family that Diederick Kastner had never had. With his own plate ruined and lost, the templar had selected a suit belonging to Sieur Kastner's great-great-grandfather. Sieur Adalbrecht Kastner – of the Gruberswald Kastners – who had fought in the Great War against Chaos beside Magnus the Pious. The irony was not lost on the knight. It wasn't an attractive suit, having suffered extensive repairs upon its return from service in Kislev. The work was of fine craftsmanship, however. It was a functional piece of mail and plate, lacking in the fashionable flourishes of the others, which were more demonstrations of status and calling. A boxy crusader helm with a protruding head-spike completed the armour, and Kastner had selected a single-handed battlehammer and round shield combination from a display in the hall that seemed to match the suit in style and brute function.

In the stables, Kastner had fed Oberon. Intending to stay off the roads and take the river downstream, the knight had decided to let Oberon sit the certain slaughter out. Patting the stallion, he had wandered to the gate where the saddle rested and unbelted the saddle-scabbard containing the greatsword *Terminus*. Belting the scabbard about his plate, Kastner settled the weapon across his back. *Terminus* had been earned at Magnus the Pious's side and complemented the style of the armour well. With that, Kastner had walked from the estates, morning breaking over the surrounding treetops.

Kastner smelled Altdorf before the calls on deck told him of the boat's approach. It was not called the Great Reek for nothing. Sieur Kastner had an untended townhouse in the Oberhausen District and Diederick had visited the capital on numerous occasions as part of his duties, the chapter house of his order and the Cathedral of Sigmar both residing in the Domplatz, south of the river. Altdorf was an abomination. A cancerous growth on the hide of the Empire. The city reached out with its slums into the Great Forest and the

Reikwald, its boundary walls routinely extended and rebuilt about the more permanent developments. Towering above the surrounding tree tops, Altdorf had the power to steal the breath – which given the stench coming off the river and rising from the narrow streets, was a welcome consequence. Its ramshackle buildings appeared like children's toys, built precariously about and on top of one another. Towers trembled and steeples leaned about constructions of finer worksmanship – the palaces, colleges and temples – with the Cathedral of Sigmar shaming them all.

It was beautiful. The exquisite brickwork. The spired towers. The glorious windows of stained-glass and lead. The colossal temple-dome marking the spot where Sigmar was crowned the first Emperor. Visits to the cathedral – on cult business or private reflection at the side altars – were the only thing about the city that had brought Kastner any pleasure. The templar suspected that his present visit would be less enjoyable. His route to the cathedral would also be very different. No clatter of horseshoes on cobble. No citizens paying subdued respects to a Sigmarite Knight of the Twin-Tailed Orb.

Kastner felt the difference as the *Mutter's Melken* crossed the confluence of the Talabec and the River Reik. The narrowboat rocked as it hadn't done before on the journey, producing angry calls from the captain and liveliness from his small crew. He could hear the bustling business of the docks nearby, with boats offloaded or loaded with cargo bound for Marienburg and the considerably slower treks upriver to Talabheim and Nuln.

Kastner pushed the fore hatch open. The boatmen were all busy with negotiating the meeting of two rivers and the arches of a towering crossing. It was called the Three Tolls Bridge – or as Kastner knew it, the Ostlander Bridge. Dank weed hung from the underside of the arch like the hulls of galleons in drydock. Skeletal smugglers sat in gibbet cages that in turn were set into the stone of the bridge exterior, waiting for their deaths while riverside ravens circled. Along the shoreline Kastner saw a muddy embankment of collapsed stone blocks, where beggars had erected a small colony of tents and shanties. He watched. He waited.

'Oi, you!' one of the crew called. The templar had been spotted. 'Stowaway, captain.'

The captain came forward as the narrow boat cut through the current and angled itself for an approach to the bridge archway nearest the southern shore.

'Bring 'im 'ere,' the captain bawled above the heavy slop of the river against the flat-bottomed hull. 'Any man that travels on my boat has to pay for his passage. You gets to save your legs. What do I gets, ay?'

As several boatmen closed in on Kastner, the templar rose from a crouch and exited the fore hatch. As the boatmen saw he was clad in mail, plate and helmet, they slowed. They knew a warrior when they saw one.

'For my passage,' Kastner called at them, 'you get to keep your lives. It's a bargain, believe me.'

Kastner saw what he was looking for. He filled his lungs with as much air as his breastplate would allow, took several heavy steps to the side of the boat and dived into the murky waters.

'Well, would you look at that,' the captain said, as Kastner's fully armoured form disappeared below the stinking surface.

The weight of the plate took Kastner down. The pressure inside his lungs built. Water gushed in through his helmet, but Kastner's eyes were already closed. You couldn't see through the waters of either the Talabec or the Reik and certainly not where they met in confluence. Using his shield as a crude paddle, Kastner pushed himself through the weight of the water, all the while the bulk of his armour dragging him to a watery grave. Suddenly his boots hit stone, angular and slimy with algae and effluence. It wasn't the river bottom. The Reik was much deeper near the harbour dock. He had sunk to the collapsed blocks of the embankment. Pushing the weight of his plate forward and clawing at the architecture of the sunken collapse with the mail on his other hand, Kastner made for the shore.

The air in his lungs burned to be free. His underwater exertions had plunged him into dizziness and disorientation. He felt his way with more than his hands now. He was developing senses he had scarcely imagined a man could possess. Despite the fact that one eye was closed and the other gone, the templar felt that he could still see. Despite the darkness of his world and the cold, wet embrace of the river water smothering him, Kastner's goal drew him like a wolf to a bleating lamb. He could hear it. He could smell it. He could feel its resistance. He could taste its possibility. He could do all of these things and none of them. They were all part of the way he was changing. It repulsed and excited him. He felt the vulnerability of its power. The promise of doom. The objective in the blinding darkness. Or perhaps he was simply addled and drowning.

Kastner's helmet spike clanged against a stone block above his head. He had found it. The overhang he was looking for. With the spent air stabbing its way out of his chest and oblivion beckoning, the templar stomped on through the depths. Beneath the overhang in the ancient collapse, Kastner found a pocket of foetid air. As the helmet broke the surface, the templar hauled it off his head and breathed deep in the funk beyond. It was disgusting. He almost wretched but there was nothing in his stomach to bring up. All he knew was that he could breathe in the darkness.

He blinked river water and filth from his eye. Kastner stared into the darkness. He had rarely been in a place so absolutely bereft of light. The forest was never this lightless. Whether it was the glint of the stars or the pervasive gloom of the clouds, there was always something to see by. Impossibly, in the blackness of the embankment hollow – where light had not ventured for possibly centuries – Kastner found he could see. Not well. Perhaps only as well as the things that crept, crawled and slithered through the feculence about him, but he could see. He was not even sure that his remaining eye was responsible for the strange sensation. It was as if Kastner himself was giving off some kind of ghostly darkness, imperceptible to others, which cast everything about him in a contrasting and ominous light.

Kastner stared about him. Every crook and irregularity of the collapsed passage that the hollow fed into caught Kastner's darkness, throwing shadows of light beyond them. It was as if this sunless and forgotten place had been dusted with the feeblest shimmer. It was fainter than faint, but it was there.

Moving his armoured form up the incline of shattered stone and sludge, he came to the thick metal bars of a subterranean entrance. Kastner put his mailed fingers about the bars. Rust came away in his hands. It was in fact an exit. Kastner had been confident in the location of the passage even if the same confidence hadn't extended to reaching it. Few people knew of its existence, since few had ever taken an interest. As a templar of Sigmar, he knew of the Grand Theogonist's security arrangements and on occasion had been part of them – even though that wasn't the primary role of the Knights of the Twin-Tailed Orb. It was more likely that Kastner's love of the Cathedral of Sigmar as a squire and young templar had brought the existence of the passage to his attention. He adored the architecture of the temple and had familiarised himself with the history of its construction as well as its cult significance. The dwarf engineers responsible for the architectural wonder had built many functional features into the cathedral as well as flourishes of spiritual grandeur. Kastner knew of the secret staircases that wound through the colossal pillars of the Great Sanctuary. He knew of the ossuary below the catacombs that connected the Sun Chapel and the chapter house of the Knights of the Fiery Heart to the cathedral. He knew of the priest passage – a hidden subterranean route constructed by the engineers as a means of escape and for the evacuation of relics, should the cathedral ever be besieged. The priest passage, connecting the cathedral to the river and providing escape by means of the miracle of the city's first functional sewer system. The sewer system in which Kastner was standing.

Slipping his battlehammer from his belt, the templar smashed at the cage door set in the bars. There was a brief and blinding spray of sparks. Kastner hit it again. This time the door fell off its rust-eaten hinges in a shower of flakes. The passage beyond was round and buckled, as though weight from above had contorted its structure and foundations. Dwarf-crafted bricks sat uneasily against one another, some protruding, some angled awkwardly and others pulverised under the pressure. As Altdorf had grown in importance and Sigmar's ruling priesthood in their overconfidence, the priest passage had been largely forgotten. But Kastner hadn't forgotten it.

Kastner's armoured form sank down into the swamp that percolated the passage. The stench was horrendous. The collective feculence of the Domplatz District, gathering, stewing and creeping slowly downhill towards the river. Each step was a putrescent struggle. Each breath was a gag-stifling ordeal.

The waste soaked through his mail and smeared his plate. With his lip set in a permanent snarl of determination, Diederick Kastner pushed on through the endless length of the tunnel.

He encountered side-passages and turn-offs, ladders, hatches, and cage-ways but he would not be put from his purpose. Kastner thought of the sweet city air, high above, through the crumbling stone and the newer Imperial sewer networks, up through the gratings and hatch-covers. Rank in its own way but like a noblewoman's perfume compared to the muck he had been breathing down in the tunnel.

Besides, Kastner had a very good reason for taking the excruciating route that he had. If the Grand Theogonist had sent twenty of his finest templars out into the provinces to destroy the man Necrodomo's words had identified as Archaon, Herald of the End Times, then Kastner could expect heightened security about the city. Kastner tried to imagine the ordeal that would be waiting for him. Altdorf's mighty gates fortified with extra sentries and soldiers. The watch doubled. Reiklanders, armed with bills and shields, swarming the Templeplatz about the prince's palace, forming with engineers and their cannons a veritable gauntlet along the Templestrasse. Templars – perhaps even of Kastner's own order – Knights of the Fiery Heart and the temple's men-at-arms, all placed on high alert and ready to respond, should a threat manifest itself. Should a champion of Chaos called Archaon and his Ruinous allies make an attempt to push into the city. It made for a vision of hopeless futility. A vision that had driven the templar to find another way into the cathedral.

In the face of any such threat, it was unthinkable to all that the Grand Theogonist was in any actual danger. That the city walls could be breached by a single man and so small a force. That the Imperial Army would not be a match for any single threat. Those people could afford to be confident. None of those people had read *The Liber Caelestior.* None but the Grand Theogonist himself, and it was no doubt on Hedrich Lutzenschlager's unquestioned orders that the city be elevated to such a state of vigilance and security.

As his every doomed step took Kastner closer to the cathedral, the waste got deeper, the rats swimming through it bigger and the corpses more frequent. Every so often, something rotting in the sludge would groan and reach out for him, prompting Kastner to smash in its skull with a merciful swing of his hammer. Just as he allowed himself to believe that his trek through the city's bowels was almost over, the knight encountered an obstacle. A colossal stone ball, as tall, broad and round as the tunnel itself. Kastner leaned against the immovable object and tried to catch his breath but he couldn't take the foul air of the sewer down far enough to make a difference without retching. The thick river of excrement was being slowly fed by a side tunnel but the ball blocked Kastner's route to the cathedral. It was one of the technological wonders the dwarfs had built into the system. Such colossal balls were employed to prevent blockages. Rolling slowly and gently downhill, they pushed the swamp before them, out into the river at different times and intervals along the shoreline – before being winched back on hook-points inset in the ball's surface. This one had been jammed in the collapsing dimensions of the tunnel.

Kastner smashed at the ball with his hammer but time had not had the same effect on the ball as on the passage. It was a solid, if slime covered, ball of solid rock. The templar might as well have been pummelling a boulder on some mountainside. Resting the battlehammer by his side, the templar tried to clear his head of the rancid stench of the sewer. The side tunnel didn't take him to where he needed to go. Climbing out of the sewers in the middle of the Templestrasse was exactly the kind of suspicious activity that would bring a company of Altdorf's finest down on him. He stared about the rancid darkness. At the ball and the irregularity of the brickwork in the surrounding wall. Kastner grunted.

Moving around the side of the ball, he smashed at the wall where the ball had become wedged. The bricks – even dwarf-crafted bricks – came apart under the hammer's insistence with a great deal more forgiveness than the ball. It was hard work, but before long the knight had decimated the side of the tunnel about the huge ball. As the impacts echoed about him, up and down the passage, it dawned on Kastner that hammering might attract unwanted attention. Holding the hammer silent he listened through the blackness and fug. Even with the weapon doing its worst and shards of brick flying, the templar's keen senses had not abandoned him. Something had shuffled up through the sludge behind him. It was broken and awkward; it groaned at the thing it sensed in the darkness but could not see.

Kastner allowed the thing to bathe in his darkness. In the rich effluvium of the sewer, the templar couldn't smell it but suspected that the shambler was dead. From what he could make out, half the thing's head was missing. He began to wonder if this was one of the bodies he had already encountered in the sewer morass. It reached out for him. Batting the cadaver back against the tunnel wall, Kastner brought up his shield and sliced its rounded edge through the rotten meat of the corpse's neck. Shearing its head off against the brick, Kastner allowed the thing to die once and for all. The body dropped and sank below the effluence.

Reinvigorated by the kill, Kastner slid his own body around the slimy circumference of the ball. With his armour plates catching on the broken brick at his back, it was difficult to edge around the object. With a final push, Kastner tore through a section of wall. The muck that had collected beyond oozed forth, dribbling around the ball and almost swamping the knight. Once again, Kastner found himself up to his neck in the mire. The Reik had been a bath of rose petals compared to the faecal deluge beyond and the templar found it difficult to keep his footing below the surface. Every slip, slide and step was a gagging agony. There simply wasn't enough air left in the tunnel-space above the slurp and fester.

Then he felt it. Where his hand expected to find the rounded wall of the tunnel, he discovered a sludge-filled alcove. Wading into it, Kastner could make out the barest impression of rungs on a rusted ladder, which his mail digits confirmed moments later. Hauling himself from the suction of the muck, Kastner climbed the short distance to a metal hatch. Feeling about its edges, he found it to be unmistakably octagonal. It was the shape of the cathedral's Great Sanctuary and the shape of the dwarf-crafted bricks used to build it. Kastner rested his crusader helm against the hatch and risked a smile. Bringing up his shield and putting his shoulder against it, the templar smashed at the metal until the long-rusted bolt locks on the other side gave way and the hatch bucked. Hooking his fingertips about the hatch, he slid its weight to one side and climbed out of the sewer.

Effluence streamed from his armour, pooling about his boots. Within the plate his doublet and leggings were soaked through. Kastner could only imagine how he appeared – covered from helm to toe in the waste of ancients, freshly crawled from the sewer like a rat or roach. The priest passage was roughly hewn and led to a dead end, with only a crack of light giving the suggestion of a false door. After the darkness of the sewer, the sliver of golden light was almost blinding. Taking several heavy steps, Kastner smashed his boot down on stone, which promptly gave with a creak and toppled. Kastner blinked his way into the next chamber, his shield held up against the harshness of the light, but found only a single stubby candle, alight but almost spent.

As his boots crossed the uneven stone floor, the templar felt suddenly weaker, as though the raw determination that had got him through the sewers had abandoned him. He stumbled to one side, reaching out for a surface, and found a skull. A human skull, amongst many. Skulls set in stone. In fact, the chamber was filled with rough stone shelves stacked high with the browning bone of skull collections and presented skeletal remains. At intervals through the chamber, full skeletons were displayed in sarcophagi – some standing upright like the one Kastner had just smashed to the ground, others on horizontal slabs. Kastner felt dizzy. It was an effort even to walk. It was as though the very stone were sapping his strength.

The templar shook his head within his helm. He was in the

ossuary – the charnel chambers below the catacombs – housing the remains of men and women who thousands of years before had pledged themselves to the cult of the God-King and the building of his holy Empire. Kastner bit at his lip. He was standing on holy ground. The stone beneath the soles of his boots – that had once filled him with such passion and devotion – now leeched his strength and plunged his heart into a deep well of dread.

He stumbled on through the ossuary, afflicted by the consecration of his surroundings. Rough steps took him up into the labyrinthine catacombs that riddled the foundations of the cathedral and the Templeplatz beyond. Here the subterranean tombs of distinguished priests, templars and even past Grand Theogonists were to be found. The catacombs marked the passing of more recent paragons and martyrs to the Sigmarite cause. Rather than be returned to a family estate to which he didn't belong, Kastner had hoped one day to earn his own place in the catacombs and be honoured as one of Sigmar's worthiest servants. Now he couldn't stand to be in the presence of such worthies. The templar slipped down to one knee at the foot of a flight of stone steps leading down into the catacombs.

The door creaked open and Kastner was forced to retreat noisily into the shadows. The door boomed shut and he heard the scuff of sandals on the steps. A priest was descending. Kastner felt his limbs tremble, as though he suffered a fever without the symptoms. Before, the Ruinous taint had fought the devotion in the templar's soul and the love, pure and true, that he held for his god and his calling. Something had prevailed, though for the life of him Kastner knew not what. Here in the catacombs, in the presence of a future not to be and surrounded on all sides by the holy ground of Sigmar's cathedral, the templar felt the corruption within him fight for its existence. Kastner clenched his mail fist. Shakes turned to quakes. Quakes to a cacophony of rattling plate.

'Is there someone there?' the priest asked with an imperious sneer. 'Present yourself. I don't have all day.'

Kastner heard the priest sniff the air. 'What is that god-awful smell? What is going on down here?' he demanded as he descended. Two steps from him, Kastner stepped out. Colour fell from the priest's harsh features. He had expected to find a novice or a sentry to be scolded, not a hammer-wielding warrior, dressed in faecal-splattered plate. Kastner fed off the fear in the priest's eyes. The shaking ceased. He brought up the hammer to strike the priest down. The hammer hovered above the terrified Sigmarite. But something in Kastner wouldn't let him do it. To murder an unarmed cleric, cowering on the cathedral steps. He turned away. 'It's you,' the priest said behind him. 'The extra men-at-arms – the templars. You're the one they're looking for.'

'And much more,' Kastner said, whipping around with his shield and dashing the priest into the stone wall of the stairwell. He bounced and fell back onto the stairs, tumbling head over shoulders down the harsh steps. Kastner looked down on his still form. He stared for what seemed like an eternity, his face a blank mask. There was blood. There was injury but the priest breathed still. 'Forgive me my sins, father,' Kastner said to the unconscious cleric, 'but I need to compound them. I'll be requiring your robes.'

CHAPTER IX

'And Friar Helstrum told of Sigmar – a
vision to behold.
Through the land his power, his virtues and
memory extolled.
Sigmar knelt amongst the divines and before
the Winter God.
A gold crown of immortality our Emperor did
don.
Sigmar comes to us timely, almighty and
reigning supreme –
This, the friar did attest, the God-King
revealed in his sleep.'

– Gottfried Hachenbacher, *the Ascended Sigmar*

The Cathedral of Sigmar
The City of Altdorf
Tag von den leered Thron, IC 2420

Kastner went down on his knees. This was a relief. He felt weak and unsteady. The knight certainly didn't want to attract any attention by falling over in his plate in the all but silent sanctuary. The floor hurt to walk upon. The stained-glass shards stung his eye. The very walls of the cathedral ached devotion. Somewhere deep inside the templar, the God-King's divinity was leeching his soul like a vampire.

His newly liberated robes barely fit about his armour but he wasn't the only visitor to the sanctuary bedecked as such. The colossal chamber – feeling ever more so below the vaulted dome above him – was playing host to a number of priests, Sigmarite sisters and templars of different orders – some also dressed in armour. Sigmar was a martial god. The wearing of armour in his place of worship did not offend him. It was a form of worship and respect. While wearing plate before the God-King was not considered disrespectful, disturbing another man's devotions was. This worked very much in Kastner's favour. Priests at prayer kept their distance from one another, spreading out about the chamber. Some favoured the side altars, others the spectacle of the magnificent stained-glass window. Some the colossus of Sigmar himself, wrought in gold and dominating the head of the chamber. Kastner suffered quietly before the mighty statue, the God-King looking down on him in silent, aureate reproach.

The priest's thick robes were doing their best to soak up the filth that covered his plate and leaked from his mail. He still reeked but there was little he could do about that and he hoped to pass for an afflicted begging Sigmar for relief. It seemed to be working. Many of those at prayer were too polite to comment on the smell or unwilling to engage such an unfortunate in conversation and simply moved away. Holding his crusader helm to his chest and pulling up his hood, the templar waited. Rather than blunder past sentries in an attempt to get in to cross to the heavily guarded Sun Chapel – the Grand Theogonist's private temple – Kastner had reckoned on waiting in the main sanctuary, confident that the Grand Theogonist would come to him. Before Kastner was the Grand Theogonist's golden, octagonal throne – the throne from the comfort of which Hedrich Lutzenschlager would enjoy morning observances.

The templar rocked slightly on his armoured knees. It was just him and the God-King, in the holiest place in all the Empire.

'You have forsaken me,' Kastner hissed to himself, his dry lips pronouncing each word slowly within the confines of the hood. The templar looked up at the statue's proud features. The statue gleamed its goldenness and from the low angle, Sigmar looked like a haughty and disdainful god. 'I have lived a devout existence. Bettered myself with study, for your good grace. Trained to my limits and served you through the sword. I have honoured you. I have loved you. I have given you everything I have. Yet you have left me lost on a path to I know not where.'

The templar was bathed in shafts of coloured light from the stained-glass window and felt his harsh whispers rise on the heat of the morning sun.

'I am no longer an instrument of your design,' Kastner said. 'A yardstick to measure the purity of others, a weapon for you to wield in punishment and a shield to protect your Empire from foes near and far. I am changing. I am changed. I know it. Circumstance has turned me from my purpose, in service of others unknown. Like the warped arrow, I fly untrue, yet hit the mark. I will not be a nothing in your eyes. A dog to be put down in the street. I am not an error. An aberration. I am not history to be re-written. I am not a mistake to be corrected. Speak to me, my lord. My Emperor-of-all. My God-King. Show my heart the way. Lead me back to your light and love. I did all in service of you. Like the arrow shaft, I can be softened and straightened. Like the imperfect blade, I can be re-forged. I beg of you, my lord. Find use for me again.'

About Kastner, priests had started to gather for the morning observance. They stood in clusters, the daily business of cult politics dominating the conversation. The templar even heard several speak of the Grand Theogonist's mysterious orders and the extra security around the cathedral. Clusters became crowds as the numbers grew and the domed sanctuary filled with clerics standing before the colossal figure of their god. Still they gave the stinking templar a wide berth. Kastner rose to his feet. He felt sick to his stomach. His knees felt weak.

'Don't leave me,' Kastner pleaded with his lord, 'the plaything of fate. Show me a sign – in this place of all places. Anything, curse you.' But nothing came. Kastner's lifetime of devotion and service was rewarded with the kind of monumental silence only a towering statue could deliver. As the priestly gathering hushed and parted, Hedrich Lutzenschlager entered the Great Sanctuary. In robes of glorious white and golden thread, which trailed behind the Grand Theogonist for half the hall, the High Sigmarite made his way towards the throne. Lutzenschlager was known as an ardent but cold servant of the God-King. A puritanical and inflexible executor of his faith, his displeasure was easily earned. He wasn't a physically imposing man. He didn't need to be. The six Knights of the Fiery Heart escorting him in were imposing enough, in the gilding of their gold and silver plate, carrying the lengths of hammer-crowning pole-axes in their glorious gauntlets. Lutzenschlager's short steps took him with business-like speed through the masses. With him hurried a small group of attendants, bearing the Grand Theogonist's own ceremonial hammer, staff-sceptre and rolled readings. Lutzenschlager's head was shaved short, leaving a black shadow that almost gave the appearance of a skullcap, while his feathered brow framed hard eyes and a beaked nose.

As the Grand Theogonist made his long approach, Kastner glowered back up at the impassive mask of the golden god. Pulling back his hood, he slipped his crusader helm back over a snarl that threatened to split his face.

'You speak not,' Kastner mouthed within the darkness of his helmet, 'but I hear everything. Silence will be met with silence, God-King. Nothing so singularly personifies the prayer unanswered as a god powerless to save his people. So be it. You will watch your worshippers suffer and die – as I drag down your Empire into the embers of Armageddon. You will hear me then, God-King. You will hear me in the pleading prayers of your people, held under my blade. You will hear me in the ravenous fires that will eat all you have lived to build. You will hear me in the deafening silence of the End Times, where I will leave your petty Empire no world left to conquer. Though half blind, I see you for the fraud you have always been. The appealing ramblings of a mad friar. I renounce your false majesty – and will forge a path of my own making. I will champion my undoing and accept allegiance of those that already answer the hatred in my heart. I do this out of hatred for you, my lord. Out of hatred for all the fickle Powers of this world, who play at destiny with men's souls. With darkness lies a new beginning, as with me lies the end of man and all godkind.'

'Yessssss,' something dark and deep within him said. With the word, Kastner felt his heart suddenly thud within his chest. Like the unfastening of a lock, the heavy chains and shackles of his infirmity fell away. A dread potential had bloomed within the knight, at once allowing him to access all he once had been and the fearful doom he would one day become. Kastner savoured the troubled birth of darkness within his soul. The feeling was new. It was exciting. And yet it had always been there, its mouldering seed forever planted in his heart. He knew nothing of birth. It was lost to the darkness of ignorance. He had been begotten by darkness and to darkness he would return. Kastner allowed the cold rage to build within him, honing it like a blade on the eve of battle. It was time.

As Hedrich Lutzenschlager passed Kastner, he heard furious mutterings from within Kastner's helm. He turned to one of his escorting knights before ascending the steps leading to the statue of Sigmar, to take his place on the throne. The Knight of the Fiery Heart came to a stop beside Kastner and laid a gleaming gauntlet on his pauldron.

'Silence, brother,' the knight warned from within his own ornate helmet.

Kastner's mail fist came up behind his helmet and reached down the back of his hood. As the knight turned to retake his place in the Grand Theogonist's honour guard, *Terminus* cleared the scabbard at Kastner's back. The blade sang overhead, before Kastner brought its cleaving edge down through the knight's own armoured shoulder. With the force of the storm stirring within Kastner behind it, the greatsword cut through the ceremonial plate like ripe cheese. Blood fountained from the stump as the arm clattered to the ground, the knight falling swiftly after it. Like the sigh of a stirring volcano, shock passed through the congregation. But Kastner had barely begun.

While Reikland reinforcements milled on the Templeplatz and horses dragged cannons across the Three Tolls Bridge, a gauntlet of knights in full plate sat tall in saddles. Sentries and men-at-arms stood in double their number at the cathedral's archways and entrances. All waited without the great cathedral walls and doors for a threat that would never come.

Kastner had already announced his arrival within in blood. He called to his enemies with the death of their own. The world flooded him with its new sensations. He could hear the echo of confusion in Sigmarite hearts. He could taste the questions on their lips and drank in deep the fear filling their bellies. The rear three knights attempted the clatter of an urgent turn. Kastner wished them dead. And it was so.

The gold and silver of the knights' ceremonial plate did not look as impressive with Kastner's blade exploding from the chest plate or leaving the crimson of slashed throats cascading down its polished surface. There was running. And shouting. And screaming. The Great Sanctuary was emptying of Sigmar's false prophets. They shrieked with unmanly abandon, tearing at each other's vestments to get through the chamber doors and arches.

As his attendants fled with the only weapons the Grand Theogonist had – and called for the cathedral's men-at-arms – Hedrich Lutzenschlager fell back into his throne. He wore the shock of a man watching an accident unfold but feeling powerless to stop it. His face was a paralysed mask of horrified acceptance. Two Knights of the Fiery Heart crossed their pole-axes before the throne to prevent Kastner getting through, while the remaining warrior came for him with the kind of confidence and fervour Kastner himself had once reserved for the enemies of Sigmar. He swung the pole-axe with the full length of its haft, expertly guiding the weight of the hammer at its far end towards Kastner with irresistible force who brought up his shield and leaned into the impact. As it smashed into the shield surface, Kastner was sent skidding to the side. As tiles came up before the sliding side of his boot, Kastner threw himself straight back at the knight. Circling in a graceful arc, the pole-axe came at Kastner again – from the other side. Again the hammer fell like a thunderbolt at him and again he got his shield before it. Crunching up through the shattered tiles and sliding *Terminus* between his arm and the shield, Kastner slipped the toe of his boot beneath the haft of a pole-axe lying across the body of one of his victims. Scooping the weapon up with his foot, he caught it in his mail fist before launching it at the knight. The armoured warrior caught the haft-spike of the axehead in his chestplate, the point rupturing the knight's heart.

'Your god has abandoned you, sieurs,' Kastner told the two remaining honour guardsmen. 'As he has done me.'

The knights were not interested in exchanging conversation with heretics and as the first grabbed his master below the arm and manhandled him from the throne, the second came forward to keep Kastner occupied.

'One at a time,' Kastner questioned. 'Really?'

The Sigmarite held his pole-axe in two gauntlets, jabbing and thrusting at Kastner with well-practiced lunges. Kastner didn't even move to take *Terminus* from where the weapon was resting behind the handles of his shield. He watched the spear-point on the head of the weapon come for him and merely leaned back out of the weapon's path. To one side. Then the other. Having pushed the stunned Grand Theogonist in the direction of his escape, the second knight rattled up behind to aid his compatriot.

Kastner slapped the haft of the first knight's weapon aside with his shield before running straight at him. There was a clatter as the plate of the two knights clashed. Kastner had knocked the warrior back at the throne with his shield before turning to meet the oncoming head of the other knight's pole-axe. The Grand Theogonist, meanwhile, was backing rapidly towards the hordes of exiting priests, unable to take his eyes from the blood being spilled in Sigmar's Great Sanctuary.

Kastner allowed the head of the pole-axe to glance from the rounded surface of the shield, turning with the force of the weapon and moving out to one side. His hand slapped down at his side to remove the battlehammer from his belt. The Grand Theogonist had not heeded the calls and entreaties of his priests to follow them, but upon spying Kastner move in on him with the hammer, Lutzenschlager turned and ran. Three more steps took Kastner to the trailing tails of Lutzenschlager's extravagant robes. Stamping down on the material, Kastner stopped the Grand Theogonist in his tracks. As Lutzenschlager turned, gathering the robes in his hands to heave for his freedom, Kastner tossed his battlehammer with murderous force. Passing head over haft, the hammer struck Lutzenschlager in the chest, knocking him from his feet and turning him into a lifeless mound of robe and limbs.

The first mistake that Kastner's opponent made was turning his helm to check on his master. The second was turning back. Pulling *Terminus* from where it nestled behind his shield, Kastner cleaved through the knight's helmet. Dropping his pole-axe, the Knight of the Fiery Heart crashed onto his backside, struggling to push the rent visor up from his ruined face. Kastner could hear the footsteps of the knight behind him and didn't even turn to meet his attacker. The steps were not even, like those of a knight making a charge. They sounded irregular, like the kind you might make to throw a ball or the weight of a pole-axe around on the length of its haft. Kastner waited. He allowed the knight to line up his target. Kastner took a step closer to the knight on the floor, fighting to pull the mess of his face from the mess of his helmet. Then Kastner suddenly lowered his head and swooped to one side. The crowning hammer of the pole-axe came straight down on the head of the sitting knight, smashing what was left of his skull to mulch. The knight couldn't believe what he had just done to his knightly comrade and his body remained frozen in stunned realisation. The Knight of the Fiery Heart had little time to contemplate the harrowing accident, as *Terminus* came down like the blade of an executioner's axe and took off his stricken head and helm.

Tearing the priest's robes from his muck-smeared plate, Kastner slipped his greatsword back in its scabbard on his back. Walking with a brisk clatter, he stood over the Grand Theogonist. Lutzenschlager – his former spiritual master. He picked up his battlehammer in one hand and the leg of the robed Grand Theogonist in the other. A novice priest stood apart from the fleeing crowd of Sigmarite priests. He looked at Kastner in stunned amazement, his eyes needlepoints of searing naivety and accusation.

'Come on,' another novice begged, pulling the boy but he resisted.

'That's it, boy,' Kastner mocked. 'Run along.'

He dragged Lutzenschlager back through the gore on the floor and towards his throne.

'For Sigmar's sake,' the novice priest's friend pleaded once more. 'Let's go. The Knights of the Fiery Heart will handle this.'

'They will try,' Kastner said to himself, as the novice was pulled away.

'Wherever you go,' the boy shouted, his voice tender with his years, 'wherever you run, wherever you hide, the God-King will find you.'

'He will not,' Kastner barked back, his words echoing about the Great Sanctuary. 'For I am already lost to him.'

'He will punish you,' the novice's voice faded as he was pulled back through the fearful confusion of priests exiting the chamber. 'For the desecration of his temple and the dark path your soul has taken.'

'A path my craven god put me on,' Kastner roared.

'You are deceived…'

'About a great many things,' Kastner said, turning and looking up at Sigmar's golden face. With the words dying on his lips, he set about tying the Grand Theogonist's wrists and ankles to arms and legs of his throne with belts from his ample robes.

Kastner sensed them coming. He heard the rhythmic clack of plate: Reiksguard, Sigmarite knights and templars summoned and running across the Templeplatz. The flutter of confusion and fear to be found in the chests of common soldiery – fighting men forming a perimeter with their halberds and spears. The patience of cannons, loaded, primed and dragged into position across the cobbles. There was shouting and the clearing of swords from scabbards as armoured figures strode into the cathedral and began issuing orders. As the last of the priests fled the Great Sanctuary, a river of plate cut through their numbers. Knights of the Fiery Heart, full of imperious dread to learn that their defences had been breached, accompanied by Sigmarite warriors of other orders, at liberty in the Domplatz to aid their knightly brothers and highlight further their failure. Knights Griffon. The Hammers. The Knights of Sigmar's Blood. Even a few of his own order: the Knights of the Twin-Tailed Orb. Grand Master Schroeder was present but at the head of the deluge of devout fury was Grand Master Boschkowitz of the Fiery Heart. Helmless, immaculate in silver and temple gold and with his huge warhammer already in his hands, Boschkowitz's great beard trembled with anger at the sight of the Grand Theogonist's honour guard cut down before Sigmar.

Using the head of his battlehammer, Kastner lifted Lutzenschlager's chin and held the unconscious Grand Theogonist's head against the back of the throne. The gesture slowed Boschkowitz and the advance of the knights.

'You'll be Diederick Kastner,' Boschkowitz bawled across the chamber, 'out of the Gruber Marches. Late of the shadow of the Middle Mountains. The deep shadow.'

Kastner said nothing to confirm or deny the Grand Master's accusation. He was not there to oblige Etzel Boschkowitz.

'If you take another step further,' Kastner assured the Grand Master, 'he dies.'

The serpentine certainty of Kastner's words halted the furious Boschkowitz, causing the knights to clash into one another. 'You storm the sanctuary – he dies. If you still grace my sight at the end of ten seconds – he dies.'

'You can't expect us to leave the Grand Theogonist,' Schroeder said, his eyes full of loathing for his own knight.

'One.'

'Would you?'

'Two... Three...'

'Out!' Grand Master Boschkowitz commanded.

'Four...'

'We can rush him,' Schroeder said.

'Out, I say,' Boschkowitz bawled, backing his knights out of the chamber and holding his warhammer out in front of the Master of the Twin-Tailed Orb. 'Care for the Grand Theogonist's person still falls to me and my knights. I have the Arch Lector's confidence and you will do as you're commanded.'

'Six... Seven...'

As the knights withdrew, Boschkowitz gestured to Kastner with his warhammer.

'I'll kill you, Kastner,' the Grand Master told him. 'In Sigmar's name, your life is mine.'

'Hedrich Lutzenschlager is Sigmar's representative in this world, Master Boschkowitz,' Kastner said. 'Concern yourself with his life, for it is only your cooperation and my forbearance that keeps him breathing. Now get out of my sight, blind pawn of a false god.'

Etzel Boschkowitz bit back a righteous retort and stepped back out of the Great Sanctuary, closing the archway doors with a boom. When Kastner turned his dark attentions back on Lutzenschlager, he found the Grand Theogonist's eyes open and staring at him up the haft of the battlehammer.

'What do you want?' Lutzenschlager said. His words spoke of cold indifference but the beads of sweat forming at his temples said otherwise. Kastner removed the hammer, allowing the Grand Theogonist to support his own head. He slipped his head out of his crusader helm and placed it on the floor before the throne. He looked down on the Grand Theogonist.

'What all men want,' Kastner told him. 'Answers.'

'The God-King has nothing for you,' Lutzenschlager said. 'You have spilt blood, the blood of his servants, in his great temple. Sigmar only has vengeance in his mighty heart for you.'

'I'm not asking Sigmar,' Kastner said. 'I'm asking you.'

'I have nothing for you either,' Lutzenschlager said, 'but the assurance that it does not matter whether I live or die and the promise that you will fail. Every true son of Sigmar will stand against you. You will be a thing hunted. Your life will not be worth living. End yourself, dark pilgrim, here in this place – before the god you once loved, and receive his forgiveness.'

'I'm not going to kill you, Lutzenschlager,' Kastner told him, the words of comfort cold on his lips like a nonchalant threat. 'You are weak. A weak man. A weak leader of the Sigmarite church. I like you just where you are. On the throne – divisive, inept, a slave to vanity. The God-King deserves you. As for killing myself, I already feel I've died a thousand times over. No more. No more. Death is easy. Death is quick. Only through the suffering and affliction that is a life long-lived can we expect to learn all of the answers to all of the questions that plague us. I'll start with yours.'

Kastner brought the battlehammer down hard on the arm of the throne. The domed roof of the Great Sanctuary rang with the shrieking anguish that ripped its way out of Hedrich Lutzenschlager.

'The heretic text I was escorting from the Hammerfall, back to the safety of these hallowed halls,' Kastner said, his patience wearing away with every moment. '*The Liber Caelestior*. It had a page missing. A page torn from the tome, bearing the identity of a man who would be end to the world. You have this page? From your visits to the Hammerfall.'

'You think... I would aid,' Lutzenschlager half-sobbed through his agony, '...a chosen of the Dark Powers?' An irrational guffaw burst forth from the man.

'I think you might save yourself further suffering,' Kastner said, 'knowing before your weakling god and in your coward's heart that you had no choice. Because you do not.'

'I will never...'

The battlehammer came down again. Hard. Blood sprayed Kastner's plate. The scream was longer this time. It tailed off into a livid moan that haunted the chamber with its miserable insistence before dying further to a dread whimper. Lutzenschlager began to fade.

'Wake up!' Kastner roared, slapping the Grand Theogonist about his pale and stricken face. 'The page...' Kastner said, kneeling slowly before the throne. Lutzenschlager looked at him through pain-clouded eyes. 'It contained details of this man – this chosen – this Archaon.'

When the Grand Theogonist didn't respond, Kastner raised the battlehammer again. 'Don't make me destroy what's left of you,' he told him. Kastner tapped the hammer against the gilding of the seat, making Lutzenschlager jump at each impact. The Grand Theogonist let out a wretched moan before nodding his pain and conflict-contorted face.

'Names?'

Lutzenschlager shook his head.

'Places?'

'No,' Lutzenschlager answered, miserably.

'A description,' Kastner demanded, pointing to his face. 'Some defining scar or mark of birth?'

'Sigmar forgive me,' the Grand Theogonist blubbered. 'No...'

'What then!' Kastner snapped. 'There have been others – knights, templars, good men of Sigmar who have fallen to the Ruinous

Powers. How can you know that I am this Archaon? Without such details, how can you be so certain that you would have me, one of the most loyal and devoted of Sigmar's servants, hunted down by his brother templars and killed on sight?'

Kastner smashed the battlehammer back and forth between the sides of the throne, drawing wails of terror from the Grand Theogonist.

'Tell me! Tell me now – while some semblance of humanity yet remains within me.'

Lutzenschlager's strangled howls found their way to the words Kastner demanded but did not expect.

'He is the only one...'

'The only one?'

'The only one prophesised to come in search of his name,' Lutzenschlager wheezed.

Kastner dropped the battlehammer down before the throne and rose slowly to his feet. He turned away, his mind wrestling with what he had just heard. 'The page predicted its own accidental tearing from the tome.'

'What?' Kastner said, half listening, half thinking, half feeling. 'It what?'

'The page contained a prediction of its own removal,' Lutzenschlager said, his words punctuated by sobs of torment. 'Discovered only after its first translation. *The Liber Caelestior* told of the living end – a man called Archaon who would kill the world. He was a man both of the Empire and not of it. And yes, one of the Sigmar's most loyal and devoted servants. A knight of the God-King's realm.'

'You suspected I was this Archaon...'

'Your priest sent word that you were coming to the cathedral with *The Celestine Book of Divination*,' Lutzenschlager said, his voice struggling under the weight of the words. 'The tome, the attack on the Hammerfall and the villages on your route – the fact that you were, even Master Schroeder admits you were, one of the finest knights of his order.'

'But when I arrived, you knew.'

'Only Archaon himself is to come searching for confirmation of his true self – so the page claimed.'

Kastner stood in silence. He could hear the crowds outside on the Templeplatz. The orders being barked. The perimeter being established.

'Why not destroy both the page and the damned book?' Kastner asked. 'Why didn't you just wipe it from the face of the world?'

'You know better than anyone what we do,' Lutzenschlager croaked his suffering. 'Such texts have to be studied, despite their dangers. It was felt long ago, by one of my predecessors, that the knowledge in the tome itself could be used to combat the evil knowledge therein. That the best chance to destroy this harbinger of doom was to allow him to come. Grand Master Boschkowitz was uncomfortable with the risk and sent his men to intercept you – but I assume they failed, as they were destined to do.'

Kastner looked up at the golden face of Sigmar and then down at Lutzenschlager's demolished form, bound to the throne.

'And the Grand Master is unlikely to fail twice,' Kastner said, looking about the sanctuary. 'If you knew this was going to happen, what were your orders?'

'It doesn't matter.'

'It matters to me,' Kastner growled.

'Right at this moment,' the Grand Theogonist said, the ghost of a wicked smile crossing his pain-strained face, 'every fighting man in the city is being summoned to the Domplatz. Reinforcements have been called from Carroburg, Castle Reikguard and the surrounding weald. Any man of Sigmar has been promised eternity at the God-King's side for your death. On top of that, the palace great cannons and batteries have been turned on the cathedral. My orders are to level Sigmar's holy temple rather than allow one of his greatest foes to escape. I don't care if they have to fish both of our bodies out of the rubble. You will not leave this place.'

Kastner wandered about the chamber, his gaze drifting from the incense burners to the tapestries to the side altars to the Great Sanctuary doors. An army waited for him outside the cathedral. Sigmarites, drunk on their staunch devotions, baying for a heretic's blood. Would Kastner be cut down? Would he be burned on the Templeplatz for all to see or hung, drawn and quartered in the palace courtyard before the crowds? Would he be imprisoned, living out the last of his miserable days in some dank cell below a distant castle, buried in unbreakable chains with only daily tortures to look forward to? There was no end to the miseries the Empire could visit upon him. There was nothing left.

The priests and templar knights he had served now wanted him dead. The nobility, whose duchies, baronies and marches he had purged of evil, would come to regard *him* as evil, the very same. Worst of all, the people – who had enjoyed the protection of his knightly deeds – would forget the name Diederick Kastner and revel in his downfall. His execution would be a form of entertainment to the blood-thirsty crowds and his story would become a wretched ballad, the cautionary tale of a monster and virtue fallen from grace.

Kastner felt their future loathing and he hated them for it. He despised their double-dealing god and his Empire that sheltered them from the true darkness of the world. With the toe of his boot he pushed the stand of an incense burner forward, allowing the trailing material of a Sigmarite tapestry to dangle in the embers and catch light. The flame – simple flame – had Kastner entranced. The flame became a flicker and the flicker a dance. Soon fire was raging up the ancient cloth, devouring the material, the ink and the history it depicted in image and the language of the long dead Unberogens. Sigmar's comet-commemorating birth and his glorious deeds – the uniting of the tribes of men; his battle with Morkar, the first Everchosen of the Chaos gods; the Battle of Black Fire Pass and undeath from the south. Kastner watched the fires spread. Sigmar's trek towards the Worlds Edge with its dark peaks and crowning sunset finally fell to the flame. It was the last Diederick Kastner saw of the God-King. Sigmar was facing adventures new in unknown lands and had his back to the Empire he had built. His back turned to Kastner. Within moments, the scene was lost, raining to the floor as soot – for even the God-King couldn't outrun the ravenous fires of destruction, hungry for history and intent on turning all to ash and darkness.

As the fires crackled up the tapestries and scorched stone sanctuary walls, feasting on the beams and staining the great domed ceiling with soot, Kastner felt a rage build within him. The injustice of it turned his blood to ice. His heart froze and shattered within his chest. He had come so far on the God-King's path and yet had reached no destination. He had survived obscurity, sacrificed all in the God-King's devoted name, worked his whole life in study and training and taken the fight to Sigmar's enemies, defeating them with a scholar's mind and a warrior's nerve. All for naught.

His hard work, his accomplishments, his pain and his sacrifice had brought him to betrayal. Of Sigmar and his servants. The promise of Kastner's treachery, as written in the stars. The bottomless doom Archaon intended to fulfil. Archaon would avenge him. Archaon would bring the Empire, nay the world, to its knees and punish the gods that plagued it for their falsehood. The lesser races of the world – like maggots infesting the lands in their ignorance and indifference – would be alleviated of the burden of their meaningless lives. Their existence would find new expression in servitude or an end to all suffering in death. He would drown the sun and smash the moons. He would tear down the sky and turn the world inside out – a world of darkness and flame, worthy only of the blackest souls and the evil that they may commit upon one other. A doom perpetual. The End Times would be his for the earning.

Kastner turned towards the golden statue of his accursed god.

'This I pledge,' Kastner spat. 'I renounce your worship and the doubt ensconced in my heart. I curse you in word and deed, my craven-king. Your servants will be mine to slaughter. Your lands mine to burn. My body and soul I give to the darkness. This is my oath. Here – in this place – on the very spot where your Empire began, I pronounce myself as its living end…'

Kastner felt the warmth of Sigmar's hammer on its chain about his neck. A gift from Father Dagobert. The hammer began to melt, scarring the flesh beneath his plate and dribbling molten metal down his chest.

Taking several armoured steps towards the statue, Kastner tossed his battlehammer with all his terrible might. The hammer cut through the smoke gathering in the chamber, head over haft, until it smashed into Sigmar's aureate face. The soft gold of the sculpture crumpled about the heavy hammer-head, turning one half of the God-King's impassive face to unsightly ruin, leaving the haft of the weapon protruding from Sigmar's right eye.

'The Darkness is not without a sense of humour,' Kastner said, satisfied. 'Unlike you.'

Suddenly the flames about the chamber roared and jumped domeward, as though extra fuel had been poured upon them from above. Kastner drew *Terminus* from the scabbard at his back, at first suspecting that the forces outside had grown desperate enough to employ battle wizards from the colleges. Kastner felt a warmth pass through his body. The metal of his plate and the rings of his mail were growing hot to the touch. The knight felt his hair singe and his skin roast where it was in contact with the crusader armour. Before the Grand Theogonist's throne, Kastner watched his helm smoulder. Like his armour, its surface charred. Unlike Kastner, now pledged to the Ruinous Powers of the world and enjoying their protection, such instruments in service of darkness were scalded by their presence on the cathedral's holy ground. Kastner's helm and plate were scorched to a burnished black. Even the greatsword *Terminus* – which had done so much in Sigmar's service – suddenly erupted in strange flame, its blade a nexus of twisting and turning tongues, the colours of all damnation.

'This won't save your pig-priest,' Kastner said, marching up the steps towards Hedrich Lutzenschlager, still tied to his throne. Shouldering his shield on its straps, Kastner scooped up the hot metal of his helm and slammed it down on his head in defiance, the scorched smell stinging his nostrils. He lifted the burning *Terminus* above his head. The Grand Theogonist's eyes, weak and barely open suddenly came to fear-stung life. He tore at his bindings, his brave words to Kastner fleeing from his craven heart. 'You want to be a martyr, Lutzenschlager?' Kastner put to the Grand Theogonist. 'Let's go together – you to your doomed gods and me to mine...'

Thunder. Everywhere. An ear-splitting flash. A dazzling boom. The sanctuary dome rang like a bell. A great force passed furiously through the chamber. The smoke cleared. And Kastner with it.

Kastner was no longer on the steps. He was back on the sanctuary floor, bathed in grit and surrounded by chunks of crafted stone – some of which had struck his shielded shoulder and armoured body. This wasn't battle wizards or the wrath of a vengeful deity. This was *Big Bathilda*. The greatest of the palace great cannons, crafted at the Imperial Gunnery School in Nuln. It was famous more for the circumstances surrounding its crafting than the power of its broad barrel and gaping muzzle. It had been intended as a gift from the Emperor Dieter to his cousin Prince Wilhelm but had been insensitively named after the city prince's mother, Lady Bathilda. As a consequence, it had never been fired. Until now.

Kastner blinked brick-dust from his eye. It was everywhere. On the floor. In his helmet. Swirling about the chamber like a thick mist. Disorientated, and with *Big Bathilda*'s boom still between his ears, Kastner squinted about him. The blast – if not the cannonball – had blown him across the slippery stone floor of the chamber. He could make out the infernal blush of flames about him and the glow of daylight, presumably streaming in through a *Bathilda*-blasted hole in the cathedral wall. The glow flickered and it took Kastner a few moments to find his way back to his thoughts and the danger he was in. The flicker was the single-file entrance of knights and soldiers through the freshly created entrance.

Kastner slapped his gauntlet about the floor for his *Terminus*. Fortunately, the blade was still aflame with the purity of the place and Kastner found it just in time. Murky silhouettes closed in on him as he pushed himself to his feet. He could hear Lutzenschlager screeching for help and Kastner assumed that the Grand Theogonist was still bound to the throne where he had left him. He could also hear Grand Master Boschkowitz's Reikwald drawl through the dust, giving orders to his Knights of the Fiery Heart. There were shapes and shadows everywhere. The knights were cautious. In the chalky gloom, and in the heart of their sacred temple, they didn't want to injure or kill one of their own. Kastner didn't have to worry about that.

Rising into a swing, Kastner took down an armoured unfortunate with his blade. The warrior's death cry drew knights down on Kastner, as well as barking orders from Boschkowitz. *Terminus* clashed with a warhammer, lopping its ugly head from its haft before doing the same to its wielder. Another hammer glanced off Kastner's pauldron as he worked his way around. With knights coming down on him faster and in building numbers, he couldn't afford drawn-out textbook engagements. He didn't need to fight these men. There were no accolades to win for technique or tournamentship. The Dark Gods only demanded deaths: so that's what Kastner gave them.

He buried his blade through a breastplate. Withdrew it. Turned a broadsword aside, one hand on his hilt, while grabbing a hammer haft to stop it coming down on him. Kastner smashed Boschkowitz's man back with the cross-guard of *Terminus*, before dropping to his knees and sweeping the blade straight through the legs of the other knight. As he went down, Kastner saw that he was one of his own order. The warhammer was back. He turned it away with a swipe of his sword, allowing the swung weight of the weapon to take it off target. The silhouettes spliced. They doubled and took form. Soon there were knights all about him, all hungry for victory in the presence of their God-King. Kastner made them pay for their overconfidence. Regardless of the teeth-clenching effort behind their visors, the knights still fought in the way they had been trained. Their movements were restricted and measured for economy, trust being placed firmly in their plate's ability to resist the impact of enemy weapons. Kastner knew their manoeuvres. Their combinations of attack and defence. He was an expert in such pedestrian combat. He knew the weak spots of their plate, for so long he had been forced to guard them for his own survival.

With each death – with each limb-lopping, head-cleaving, heart-stabbing death – Kastner felt the favour of darkness flow through him. Plate clattered about him, forming a mound of metal bodies that Kastner ascended. The dust thinned. He could see the knights flooding into the chamber: the Reiksguard, the Knights of Sigmar's Blood, the Knights Griffon and the God-King's champions – the Knights of the Fiery Heart. Amongst their number were a selection from other orders, including Kastner's own, as well as temple men-at-arms and city state troops – though no common soldier would come between an honour-bound knight and his quarry. Like a sea of polished plate, catching the tinted sunlight of a stained-glass window, the knights were like waves crashing up against the shore of their demolished dead.

Like the captain of a ship reading the weather, Kastner guided the stroke of his sword through the parting plate and spuming surf of his enemies' end. The island of the fallen at the centre of the sanctuary became his to defend and step by step, death by death, he reclaimed lost territory from the silver seas. *Terminus* trailed unnatural flame like a banner, flapping from the blade. It cleaved lesser blades in half, struck the ponderous heads from warhammers and sliced shields in two. The broad blade clutched in his gauntlets was everywhere it needed to be. Turning aside the practiced clash of knightly sweeps and the thrusted points of halberds and tapering blades. Cleaving through helms. Smashing down through armoured torsos. Opening up silver bellies and trailing the guts that spilled from his brother templars.

An otherworldly exaltation had Kastner's heart in its grip. Something hidden in the shearing of armour, the crunch of bones and ugly parting of flesh was pleased. He could almost see its horrific form in the spectacular spraying of blood from lopped limbs and severed heads. He could smell its ambitions for him on the copper-tinged air. He could hear its encouragement ring in the ghastly peel of screams echoing about the helmets of his victims. He felt the presence of darkness in this death he dealt.

Like two farmer's sons fighting for the reins of a cart on its way to market, Kastner felt a fight within him for the murderous path and the plunge of the crusader blade. At moments, the vengeful thrust of the weapon's broad tip into a crunching helm or the unyielding, stone cold parry of a halberd blade that should have hewn him apart were his own. He was a knight. A templar. A battle-tempered warrior at the peak of his training and physical fitness. He still was, of a different following. At other moments, lives were taken before he had conceived of their ending. Feats of incredible strength or unknowable skill were performed by his hand. His body raged in fires of exhaustion and the weight of the greatsword was an agony in his arms but this didn't stop Kastner smashing knight after Sigmarite knight into the sanctuary floor, punching visors and jaws from his mailed fist and cutting clean through Gotz Schroeder – the Master of his own order – *Terminus* finding a path through every chink, hinge and weakness in the knight's finely crafted plate.

As the horror followed the blade everywhere it went and the torso and legs of Grand Master Schroeder fell to one side, Kastner suddenly realised that his eye was firmly shut. He was a raging bonfire, blinding in the darkness he threw across the stinging purity of the temple sanctuary. Blotted out by the brightness of the cathedral walls and the holy ground upon which they charged, the knights of Sigmar caught the full glare of Kastner's burgeoning malevolence and cast shadows of light – some blazing with the pious nobility of their hearts, some long and sallow with the doubt and dark secrets they hid deep within themselves. Kastner saw through their plate and the armour of their souls. He read them like heretical texts: their hopes, their needs, their flaws and their fears. He knew what they were going to do to him before they did and he killed them for it.

Kastner's darkness was only eclipsed by the deep inscrutability falling from the great, round stained-glass window in the cathedral wall. A great black sun, it looked down on him like a lens and Kastner felt the dread ancients of existence take turns to peer down on his miserable mortality in simultaneous celebration and judgement. As he hacked and skewered the God-King's warriors on *Terminus's* blazing length, Kastner both grew and withered under their infernal gaze. Stronger. Faster. More adamant and savage in mind and form. Hope shrivelled and crumbled within him like leaves during the Great Fall. His love of life, the architecture of his beliefs and the nobility of a man never to be, all turned to dust within him. It rained like loss through his soul, leaving a terrible emptiness for the darkness to fill. Perhaps it was this last moment of doubt – this scintilla of shattered honour – that allowed Etzel Boschkowitz through.

Kastner felt the Grand Master's warhammer smash into his back, pulverising his shield and the pauldron beneath it. Kastner was spun off balance by the weapon's brute force and was tossed off his mound of bodies and into a forest of halberd spikes and blades. Caught off-guard, the weapons clattered against his armour rather than through it, but as Kastner became swamped by knights eager for the kill, he rediscovered the hot sensation of steel passing through his plate and flesh. Pushing himself back and forth in the metallic throng, with knights finding it difficult to bring their weapons to bear on an enemy so close, Kastner gave back to his brothers. Messily grabbing knights from behind their helms, Kastner plunged the searing blade of *Terminus* blindly at guts, groins and thighs, feeling his enemies go down before him.

Suddenly the sound of clashing metal subsided and the knights pulled back. Kastner attempted a tight turn in his armour. It was difficult. *Terminus* was employed in swiping away the thrustings of spear-points and angled blades and he was off balance. He turned to see Boschkowitz before him, his beard shaking with righteous rage. He felt a mind-splitting smash as the Grand Master battered his helm aside with a swing of his hammer. The world suddenly spun. It felt as though the Grand Master had taken his head clean off. He hadn't. He had just sent Kastner tumbling back into the wall of knights and blades. Steel squealed once again through his armour. Pain lanced through his back and thigh.

Shaking sense back into his concussed skull, Kastner turned *Terminus* about and thrust the anguished blade straight into the knight behind. He pulled it out and forced it back into the armoured warrior unfortunate enough to take his place. Once again, the disorderly throng withdrew. Like Sigmar's fist, Boschkowitz's warhammer came down on Kastner. He went down on one knee to receive the God-King's blessing before bringing the flaming *Terminus* up, his gauntlet on both the hilt and blade like a staff to intercept the incredible force of the weapon. The warhammer's haft hit the blade, Kastner holding his sword above his head and keeping the weapon from smashing him into the flagstones of the sanctuary. A combination of the Grand Master's own strength and the cleaving edge of Kastner's crusader blade took the head of the hammer from it haft. Kastner stood to press his advantage but Boschkowitz kicked him straight in the breastplate, knocking him back into his knights.

'Hold him,' the Grand Master roared like a lion through his beard. 'Hold the Ruinous slave.'

A Knight Griffon took Kastner about the throat with his arm, while a gauntlet grabbed out for his plate, holding him fast. He felt his helmet crumple as Boschkowitz slammed into his helm with his great mail fists. One-two. One-two.

'Kill him!' Kastner heard the Grand Theogonist screech. 'Kill him now, Boschkowitz!'

Grand Master Boschkowitz held his mighty fists out to receive a pair of warhammers, tossed to him by Knights of the Fiery Heart on either side of the parting. He clenched his teeth and smashed the pair of hammers at each other, causing them to spark.

'Now you die,' Boschkowitz spat, bringing one of the warhammers up to strike Kastner's battered helm from his armoured shoulders. Kastner had no doubt that this time the Grand Master would send his head flying across the Great Sanctuary. Pulling on every ounce of strength he had left, Kastner dived. Lowering his head like a bull, he lurched forward, dragging the knights holding him from behind with him. As Grand Master Boschkowitz's warhammer pulverised its way through skull after knightly skull – several belonging to knights of his own order – the gauntlets released their grip on Kastner who surged on, his battered helm lowered and its head-spike aimed at the exposed chest of the Grand Master. As his helm hammered into Boschkowitz's chestplate, the knight gave a grunt. The spike had slammed straight into his heart. Drawing on the strength of the God-King himself, still the knight fought on, holding Kastner to him and smashing down on his back with his other hammer.

Kastner pulled his head from his helm, leaving the head-spike buried in the Grand Master's chest, and stumbled into a fighting stance. Boschkowitz stared down at the spike and then back at Kastner, bringing both warhammers at him with as much force as the knight could muster. This time Kastner was ready for him, turning aside one warhammer, then the other, before sweeping *Terminus* back across the Grand Master's throat. All fell silent for a moment in the Great Sanctuary. Boschkowitz started to say something, but his final words were lost in the awful sound his neck made as his head lolled backwards to hang down between his shoulders. The chamber echoed with the clatter of his knees on the flagstones and the crash of his armoured body to the ground.

Silence reigned for a few moments more as the ring of the Grand Master's metal plate endured. It was broken by the imperious shrieks of Grand Theogonist Lutzenschlager as he was removed to safety from the chamber, throne and all.

'The cannon,' he called in a panic driven by the fact that only he of all Sigmar's servants in the sanctuary knew the extreme importance of Kastner's death. 'Fire the cannon. Destroy the interloper. Somebody end this now!'

As Lutzenschlager was removed through the brick-ragged hole in the cathedral wall, Kastner saw the monstrous muzzle of *Big Bathilda* wheeled awkwardly up to the opening. It didn't matter; the response from the knights was instantaneous. At the Grand Theogonist's order they fell on Kastner. *Terminus* smacked away the first hammers and halberds, but Kastner was soon clamped between the armoured bodies of knights. Some were driven by simple glory. Others by the grief of fallen brothers. Others still by the blessings of their God-King. Within seconds it became a plate-pulverising crush, with those most ardent in their attempts to end Kastner pushed against him by knights further away, eager to play their part in the downfall of a dangerous foe.

Kastner tore his body this way and that, attempting to create some room about him – at least enough to bring *Terminus* up from where it was trapped between the vice-like bodies of two Sigmarite knights. It was no use. There were too many knights, with a never-ending stream of armoured warriors filing into the Great Sanctuary from the blasted opening and the main doors. Beyond that, *Big Bathilda* was being loaded and primed. Kastner had no doubt that the Grand Theogonist would order the great cannon fired as soon as possible and wouldn't let a consideration like the lives of his knights get in the way of such a decision. Not to kill a man who would become the Everchosen of Chaos and the Lord of the End Times.

Kastner felt the axe blade of a halberd bite into him. The wicked point of a spear slid into his shoulder, cutting its hot way through meat and bone. Sword tips waggled their way between joints and split chainmail rings to knife at his flesh. These hot agonies and more, Kastner felt through his trapped form. He heaved. He pushed. He tried to extract the broad blade of *Terminus* where it sat extinguished between the backs of two equally immobile knights, but the greatsword would not budge. The tip of a crusader sword stabbed wildly at his face, opening up gashes across Kastner's forehead and cheek, but he couldn't even crane his neck out of the way. It suddenly became difficult to breathe as the spear-tip of a halberd that had been burrowing into his torso breached his plate and sank into his side.

Kastner reached up at the multi-coloured light coming in through the stained glass. His fingertips scraped at dust-defined beams. In his last moments, even a monster like Kastner could appreciate its beauty. He watched as he waited. Waited for the killing strike through the clash of bodies. Waited for the thunder of the great cannon turned on the mad throng of knights. Waited for a death well-earned.

It was raining. Inside the temple. Glass fell across the bloody scene, glinting as it caught sunlight that had blasted its way into the cathedral. The stained-glass window was no more. Dark shapes, like fallen angels, rocketed down towards the mob of Sigmarites. They landed in a circle about Kastner, crushing surrounding knights into the floor of the Great Sanctuary beneath their boots, producing fountains of gore that rained about them. The figures rose. Their dark armour was unmistakable. Their skull-helms of bronzed bone. Their armoured wings, now extended about them like the lengths of shields. They drew their bone swords from the finger-sheathes of the wings, one in each hand. The marauders. The Ruinous Warriors. The Swords of Chaos that Kastner had left behind at Fort Denkh to finish Riesenweiler's knights. It seemed that they had not left him.

The slaughter began almost immediately. The razored rachidian edge of the warriors' bone swords cut a bloody swathe through the confusion of plate. They stabbed. They sliced. They cleaved. The air was thick with a bloody haze and the death that accompanied it. Like a closing star, the Swords of Chaos moved in on Kastner. The throng loosened in the knights' panicked attempt to turn their weapons outward to defend against the new threat. The winged marauders were like an elemental force. Overwhelming. Unstoppable.

As the bodies parted, Kastner fell to his knees. His armour was slick with gore and he was kneeling in a pool of blood – much of it his own. He swung *Terminus* wildly at passing knights, hamstringing several with the remaining strength he had left. Mostly he just drove knights into the armour-opening slashes of bone swords as the Chaos warriors closed in. They were suddenly about him. One winged marauder either side of Kastner. They were cold and deathly to the touch and promptly re-sheathed their weapons in their leathery wings. The other marauders had turned, forming a ring of bone swords about Kastner as the dark warriors supported him. Knights of the Fiery Heart stared in disbelief at the slaughter of fellow Sigmarites. Butchery in the temple of the God-King. There would be bellows of righteous revenge and a renewed call to charge the hated foe, but the knights were weary and their numbers decimated. Even knights and men-at-arms fresh to the death and destruction were given reason to pause.

The knights of Sigmar stared at their enemy, swaying in their armour and exhaustion. The winged marauders stared back before sheathing their bone swords, bending their knees and surging for the domed ceiling of the Great Sanctuary. Still clutching *Terminus* loosely in one hand, Kastner was held between two of them, who dragged him horribly up into the heavens. With powerful beats of their wings the warriors were soon high off the holy ground. There was a colossal crash. *Big Bathilda* had once again visited her fury on the scene of slaughter, the fat cannonball blasting through the bodies – both dead and dying – and out through the other wall. Knights still on their feet were knocked to the ground and slid through the gore of their brothers while a cloud of brick-dust erupted from the far wall, obscuring the horror below.

Kastner fell in and out of consciousness. The blood loss had made him faint. He felt pity for the birds and the bats. Flight was not a pleasant sensation.

He was high above the Cathedral of Sigmar. It was a sight not even the dwarf engineers had enjoyed during its construction. The wretched city of Altdorf fell away, its reek and rooftops melting into the tangled woodland of the Reikwald and the Great Forest. Roads cut sharply through the canopy while rivers snaked their lazy meandering way into the distance. His tense limbs slackened and his head slumped. As consciousness left him and obscurity crept in from the edges of his sight like the ash of a ravaged wasteland claiming everything he could see, Kastner saw his homeland and Sigmar's Empire darken.

It was a vision he promised himself he would realise... upon his doomed return.

VOLUME TWO

THE CHANGER OF WAYS

'Doom hath drowned more men than the sea.'

– Ignatz van Offen, *Offered Truths*

'So the doom of man travelled north –
north through forests and shadows cold,
Through lands of iron, spice and ice –
through man-eating ogres and trolls.

'Bitter like winter's bite he was,
with the God-King's lands at his back.
His darkened heart beat to vengeance,
echoing with questions unasked.

'A new path lay before the knight,
a way of blood and butchery:
On which no sacred life was spared
and his dark patrons were appeased.

'Northern Wastes and warrior met,
where men's forlorn hopes go to die.
Accepting he was damned and lost,
to his gods he made sacrifice.

'Warrior of the Empire dead,
subject of the God-King deceived.
Great warlord of the Shadowlands,
of Ruinous treasures received.'

– Necrodomo the Insane,
The Liber Caelestior (The Celestine Book of Divination)

CHAPTER X

'There are many ways north, for the path is well-trodden,
There are none from the south, for the route is forgotten.'

– Ungol proverb

The Worlds Edge Mountains
The Northlands
Poslekogot/Month of the After-Claw (Gospodarin Calendar)

Hieronymous Dagobert had found the bloodied and broken knight in the stable, saddling Oberon. He looked like suffering itself. The priest had tensed as he discovered that they were not alone. The armoured marauders, the winged knights that had slaughtered the soldiers and templars at Fort Denkh, were leading some of Lady Kastner's finest horses from stalls deeper within. Dagobert looked to the templar, to the Ruinous knights and then back to his friend.

'So it has come to pass,' Dagobert said gravely.

The templar grunted. He sounded different, Dagobert decided.

'I'm in no mood for riddles, old man.'

It was still his voice, but there was something… more. Potent. Powerful. A slight echo, like that created when speaking in some great hall or chamber. A dark authority, even at a grunt or a whisper.

'You are Archaon.'

'I am… Archaon.'

'To be the Everchosen of the Dark Gods and Herald of the End Times.'

'In the flesh.'

The Chaos knights, deathly things with their dark armour, skull-helms and wings, led their steeds outside leaving the two men alone.

'Well, you will always be Diederick Kastner to me,' Dagobert said.

The knight tightened Oberon's harness and took *Terminus* from where it hung off the stalls on its cross-guard. The blade sizzled to afflicted flame at the templar's touch, a ghostly torment seething about the weapon's honourable history and service to the God-King. The knight slammed the greatsword down in the scabbard attached to Oberon's saddle.

'One of those names I stole,' the templar said. 'The other was given to me as an act of pitiable charity. You'll forgive me if I choose not to hear either of them ever again.'

'You expect me to call you… by that name?'

'It is the only one that is truly mine,' Archaon told him. 'Where's Gorst?'

'I think you frightened him off.'

'And the girl?'

'In the hall, with the crossbow,' Dagobert said.

'Whereas you opted for one of Sieur Kastner's duelling pistols from the mounting on the hall wall,' Archaon said. He could hear the weapon rattling in the priest's nervous grip. The warrior turned. 'Have you ever fired one of those things before?'

Dagobert shook his head and looked down. As he did he felt the razor tip of a bone sword dimple his double-chin. One of the Chaos knights was beside him, arm and weapon outstretched.

'The weapon of a coward,' Archaon said, 'in the hands of a man who is anything but. Do not fear me, father.'

'Fear you?'

'I mean you no harm,' Archaon told him. 'You. Gorst. The girl. This horse. You're the only kindly souls I know in the entire world.'

'I don't fear you,' Dagobert said. 'I fear what you will become.'

'What I have already become,' Archaon said. 'Destiny has made its play. Fate has chosen a side. Now it's my turn. The gods of light and darkness have created this doom between them. Well, they will get more than they bargained for with my miserable soul. If I am to be end to all then all will end. Man and god will fear me for the annihilation I will bring. The rise and fall of the sun, the ever-lengthening horizon – wretched covenants with deathless damnation. Nothing will stop me. Do you hear?'

'I'm trying to save you, child,' Dagobert said desperately.

'And I you, father,' Archaon said. 'Lutzenschlager and his Sigmarites are out in force. They will scour their miserable Empire for me and any associated with me. They will capture you. They will torture you. They will kill you. I would save you from that. For the kindnesses you have done me, priest.'

'You would have me come with you?' Dagobert said incredulously. 'Betray my god? An entire lifetime's worth of prayer and devotion?'

'Your god is a liar,' Archaon hissed. 'A trader in souls who would betray those most in love with him. Those who, for him, have fought the hardest.'

'I cannot follow you into damnation.'

'Then come to save my soul, Dagobert,' Archaon said, lightening a little. 'I don't care for your reason. I care that you are by my side. With me or not, I would have the counsel of a man of the world – a wise man – in these tumultuous times.'

'So that we may all become the playthings of Dark Powers?'

'Dagobert,' Archaon said. 'We have a book of tomorrows and the means to translate and interpret its riddles. I mean not to be the pawn of the infernal powers any more than your pig of a God-King. Help me forge my own path – and save your life into the bargain.'

The tip of the bone sword tapped the priest on the chin. 'You'll have to excuse them,' Archaon said. 'They seem tediously intent on my continued existence.'

After a moment's reflection, the priest dropped the pistol to the stable floor with a thud. Archaon nodded. The tip of the bone sword drifted from the priest's chins.

'Just as well,' Archaon said. 'Wouldn't want you to hurt yourself. Balls, barrels, black powder. I don't trust them. The thing is just as likely to blow up in your hand as put its shot through me.'

But Dagobert couldn't find it in himself to derive any humour from the situation. He turned and the winged Chaos knight stood to one side. As he walked away, the lines of his face cutting deep with the gravest concern, Archaon stopped him at the stable door.

'Father.'

Dagobert looked down to one side at the straw on the floor in grim acknowledgement. 'Pack up the wagon with the tools and provisions for a considerable journey,' Archaon said. 'If you please. Have the girl and Gorst, if you can find him, assist you. Take anything from the manor house for your comfort. The rest will be put to the flame. Do you understand?'

Hieronymous Dagobert did understand. He understood that he was damning himself to Ruinous confederacy. He understood that he was doing it for the love he still bore both the man and the boy he had known.

'I understand,' the priest said, and left the stable.

And so Archaon went north. North through the dark woods of Hochland. Across the Middle Mountains, where the Hammerfall still smoked among the peaks, and through the wilds of Ostland and the Forest of Shadows. Riding at the head of the wagon, the white bonnet of which soon became a blood-splattered brown, Archaon watched the world of men unfold before him. His good eye took it all in. The life of the place was intoxicating. He had never really appreciated it before. The trees. The buzzing insects. The birds calling through the canopy. The people, everywhere, a plague on the land – living out their selfish existence in ignorance and obedience to lesser gods. Archaon had never appreciated the complex vitality of the world until he had wanted to destroy it. Though his ruined socket was covered by a leather eye-patch, the dark templar could still see. He saw ash. He saw smoke. He saw bodies burning beneath benighted skies. He saw the doom of the north clawing its way south and he the herald of its annihilation.

Behind him the wagon was flanked by four of his winged warriors on horseback. Archaon's Swords, as he came to call them, were five in number. There was little to tell the silent warriors apart and they were not much interested in conversation, so it was difficult for Archaon to set them apart in terms of character: they didn't seem to have any. Archaon let his imagination fill in the details, assuming that at some time, perhaps long before they were lost to Chaos, they had been men with hopes, dreams and fears, like everyone else. In the end, the dark templar simply took *Terminus* and cut numerals into the black of their pauldrons, naming the warrior who seemed to shadow him most closely 'Eins'. The other Swords became 'Zwei' and 'Drei' – who seemed to Archaon closer than the others, and Archaon fancied them brothers in a former existence. 'Vier' and 'Fünf' appeared to hold each other at a distance and the templar imagined that perhaps they harboured some secret dislike for one another, in the days before their dreadful damnation.

Archaon had two Swords travel on either side of the wagon at an ambling gait, while Eins drifted at the rear to ensure no one was following them. Gorst was always following them, but Archaon had informed the Swords that the flagellant wasn't a threat, and on occasion even had his uses.

Father Dagobert, sullen and silent since leaving the inferno of the Kastner estates, thought of the Swords as a prisoner escort. He couldn't so much as pass water in the trees without one of their number loitering nearby. There was little need for such precautions. He had decided to stay with Archaon and as the warrior had put it, attempt to 'save his soul'.

The girl Giselle had been another case entirely. The sister had no relationship with Archaon. She had not known him... before. She owed him her life, and that was about it. Being not especially bright, for Giselle the choice was simple. Travel with Archaon and Dagobert north into the terrifying unknown and damnation, or remain in the Empire. With the simple honesty of a girl innocent in the ways of the world, she had confessed to Dagobert that she intended to quietly leave the party and present herself to a temple or convent. It was not Archaon or his Swords that prevented the sister from leaving. Echoing Archaon's own words, Father Dagobert found himself warning her to stay. He told her that she would be turned over to the Grand Theogonist's men by any of Sigmar's servants. That she would be tortured for what she knew, imprisoned and executed as a heretic. He told her that he was protecting her – as Archaon had done Dagobert.

In reality, she became Dagobert's prisoner, the priest watching her as the Swords watched him. In truth, Dagobert saw his salvation in her. The girl was so stubborn and her simple faith so enduring that Dagobert found the fight in her something of an inspiration. In the insanity of such dark times, he found her to be a compass to guide him back to the light. He could trust in her unbreakable will. In order to save Archaon's soul, he needed to preserve his own: which meant he needed Sister Dantziger. This meant that on several occasions he was forced to betray her confidences. Sometimes the girl would just slip away. On other occasions, she simply ran for her life, appealing to those they encountered on the dismal roads of the Empire for assistance. Dagobert brought her back. Sometimes forcefully. When she slipped into the hamlet of Smallhof, begging the villagers to be hidden, the priest had been forced to tell Archaon, for their own safety, as well as the girl's. Archaon set his Swords on the hamlet, with instructions to find her. The search soon descended into a bloodbath, with Archaon and Dagobert looking on, as the Swords tore the village apart searching for the girl. They slaughtered all who would hide her, all who would inform on them and send word to the soldiers, templars and witch hunters on their tail. After Smallhof, Archaon had Father Dagobert chain one of the sister's wrists to the driver seat of the wagon. It was better than breaking her leg, which had been Archaon's other suggestion.

As time went on, the forests of the Empire gave way to the grim cold of Kislev. The sun was lower in the sickly sky, its light struggling to reach through the northern haze. The dreadful days and nightmares inbetween seemed to stretch into weeks uncounted and months that were marked by whether and how hard the snows came. The companies of soldiers and lone Sigmarite knights that had hunted them through the Imperial provinces were a mercifully rare experience in the lands of the Gospodar. Step by step, the warband's progress became less of an escape and more of a dark pilgrimage. They were no longer hunted, it seemed – bar the occasional and wretched attempt of lone witch hunters to bring them to Sigmar's justice. The dawn, feeble as it was, began to promise more to the warband than just an opportunity to put more distance between them and their persecutors.

The Kislevites themselves were as welcoming as their ice-threaded hovels. They were a backward and superstitious people, bleak and hard as iron. Unlike villagers in the Empire, they didn't run for their homes or send for their lord or baron at the sight of Archaon and his warband. They did nothing but work their farmsteads and watch with ghoulish, hollow expressions as another madman rode north to his destiny. Their only luxury seemed to be in the greasy extravagance of their facial hair and the impregnation of their womenfolk, who went about their backbreaking chores with swollen bellies and small armies of bedraggled urchins. Some said it was the cold that drove Kislevite men to their beds, since they were not known to be especially accomplished lovers. Some said that they spent much of their time this way with their wives out of necessity. It was part of their culture. To be ready – for the next incursion, the next invasion, the next war against Chaos. As Archaon rode along frost-shattered roads and through the smoky homesteads of the northern division he understood that the wastrels clinging to their mothers' dirty skirts were simply the hardened savages and horsemen he would have to fight on his way back through Kislev on his return to the Empire. The idea amused Archaon and on one occasion he even drank to Kislevite courage, toasting the northerners with their own potato swill, in an all but empty watering hole.

The crows gave way to vultures, the spice on the air to the cold, copper tang of old blood. The warband started to lose the little light they had across the Troll Country. There were no friendly faces to be found there. Even Ungol nomads and archers on horseback, despatched by the Tsarina to cull the beasts of the borderlands, were open in their hostility. On the frost-bitten plains and amongst the howling hills, Archaon encountered all manner of winter savagery. Prides of white sabretusks that slashed the wagon bonnet and leapt at Archaon in the saddle. Hordes of gnoblar cannibals, driven insensible with hunger and feasting on each other as well as themselves. Herds of northern rhinox and great mammoths, stampeding across the icy plain: hormone-fuelled and aggressive, charging anything in sight. Savage tribes of albino orcs, mounted on blind boars of war, observing the warband's passing from a distance. A pack of direwolves, struck down by some monstrous and unnatural mange, howling their torment through the blackened stakes of a dead forest. All manner of blood-crazed creatures, eking out an existence on the shadowy frontier of the Chaos realm. Monsters that would have long died out, were it not for the game trails leading north out of the Tsarina's lands, carrying lone maniacs and defectors. Men of death and destiny.

The savage lands tested Archaon and his Swords, more than their escape from the Empire or the harsh indifference of the Gospodars. Beyond the torchings of the God-King's way temples en route and the bloodshed necessary to secure passage, the warband had tasted little of the murder required to honour new and Dark Gods. Crossing the borderlands, Archaon had traded a magnificent bear skin for the life of the Ungol chieftain that wore it. With the cloak, Archaon received the blessing of the Ursun, father of the Bears and patron god of Kislev, from the nomad chief. It could have been custom, fearful courtesy or even an insult. Archaon didn't know. He did know that blessings from any power other than the dark, primordial entities he now served scorched his soul and within moments the Chaos warrior had reneged upon his deal and ended the chieftain as an offering to the Star of Universal Ruin. With the shaggy hide about his shoulders, keeping the worst of the chill from his bones, Archaon wiped the innocent blood of the Ungol from the searing blade of *Terminus* and bade his Swords slaughter the Ursun-worshipping nomads for the same purpose.

In the Troll Country the warband made scabbards of the low beasts – things of horn and fang, some that walked on four legs and some that walked on two. Though the monstrosities had all the advantage of number and brute nature, they had only been lightly bathed in the darkness of the north. Though hard won, the warband's victories were ones of survival against packs and predators, and as such, were squalid offerings to the dread pantheon. Oddly for a place with such a name, the warband never encountered such a thing as a troll.

All through their journey, with the ancient forests of the Empire behind them and the cruel Kislevite winter a recent memory, Dagobert continued his translations. Having the miserable Giselle take the wagon's reins and with the wind and the beast-things howling through the tears in the bonnet, Dagobert tried to unlock the secrets of their destination and destiny. Like everything *The Liber Caelestior* had delivered, all but the most significant of details were vague and open to interpretation. Deliberately so, the priest thought. Necrodomo the Insane had a dark gift, but he was no less a charlatan than other prophets of his ilk. Sometimes, Necrodomo hedged his bets. For such a prognosticator the unfolding moments in an hour, a day, a year or a lifetime were like drops of water in a river, flowing by. Sometimes the waters were crystal clear. At other times, the waters were white with the violent churning of their passage or murky with the silty burden of past meanderings.

Archaon would routinely interrogate the priest as to the tome and its secrets. Whereas before, Dagobert's interest ran to Archaon's salvation and opportunities the volume might provide. Now, reading Necrodomo's revelations had become a duty. As the warband's steeds climbed and the wagon struggled through the heavy snow of Black Blood Pass, Dagobert read of the northmen's ambush. The avalanche of ice and rock that tumbled down before the warband, blocking its path and the riders that rode up behind them. The greasy marauders of Edric Ulfensbane seated on their shaggy mounts, cutting silhouettes of horn, fur and axe into the blinding glare of the Worlds Edge Mountains. The northman was known as Red Edric in the Jottenheim and it was said that he and his Norscans charged a heavy toll for those travelling the pass. One traveller – one life. The horsemeat of accompanying steeds was considered an added bonus for a job well done, and Red Edric's men had grown fat on a diet of horsemeat and death.

Archaon and his Swords were outnumbered four to one by the marauders, but it made little difference. Ulfensbane's murderers were no match for the dark templar and his knights of Chaos. Archaon decorated the snow with their lopped limbs and livid gushings. With their winter steeds slain and axe-brothers butchered, the last of the northmen abandoned their leader to the Chaos warriors, choosing to leap from the crag upon which Archaon had cornered them. Taking their chances with gravity, rather than the certainty of a horrible and immediate death at Archaon's hand, the northmen might have made the terrible drop if the snows below had been deep enough. They weren't, and the marauders became bloody smears on the rock and ice of the slope below. Edric Ulfensbane wouldn't take such a cowardly course and presented his icicle-encrusted axes to Archaon. Sliding the steaming blade of *Terminus* in the drift, the Chaos warrior crunched along the crag towards him. Reading the northman like a hunter might the tracks of a wild animal, Archaon reared back and to the side, out of reach of Red Edric's wild and murderous swings.

'Drown me in snow, would you, northman?' Archaon seethed, before ducking beneath the arc of the Norscan's weapons and grabbing him by his furs. Throwing him down into the drift, Archaon proceeded to bury the man alive, drowning him as he might in a stream or river. Red Edric's arms and legs flailed as he choked on the snow, held there in Archaon's feverish grip. Leaving the northman's body to freeze, Archaon recovered *Terminus* and trudged past Dagobert and Giselle, who had watched from the wagon.

'That wretched book earned the trouble of its keeping today,' Archaon told him, pointing his crusader blade back up at the pass blocked with a small sea of settling snow. Dagobert nodded, shivering to think what it might have been like for them buried in the avalanche. 'Keep reading,' Archaon said. 'I wish to know more of the misfortunes that are to befall us... before they actually do, of course.'

'It doesn't work like that,' Dagobert said, a little harshly. Archaon turned on the priest. Dagobert's frost-rosy cheeks paled, while Giselle – chained to the wagon – wouldn't even look at the Chaos warrior. 'I mean, my lord,' Dagobert said, 'that much of the translation is educated guesswork and interpretation.'

'Then guess well, priest,' Archaon told him, walking on through the snow, 'lest we all die for the sake of secrets already in our possession.' Calling through the crystal cold air, Archaon ordered Zwei and Drei to find them an alternative route through the pass. On the way back down the mountainside, the warband and wagon encountered a frost-bitten Gorst, the flagellant, weighed down with his chains, only just having caught up to them.

Hieronymous Dagobert did as he was bade by his master. As the warband passed over the very spine of the world, the damned tome told Dagobert of death from the skies in the form of a flock of harpies, nesting in the north-eastern slopes, and the manflesh they intended to regurgitate for their screeching, cliff-bound young. It did not tell of the Skewered Skull hobgoblin clan that bounded out of the foothills of the Dark Lands at them on long-legged war mongrels. The foothills formed part of their slave grounds. Attempting to catch and imprison Archaon was more foolish than trying to kill him, however, as the hobgoblin half-khan and his clan discovered too late. The warband decimated the clan to the very last rider and gangling, lupine steed, wiping the Skewered Skull clan and its ruling khanate from the face of the Dark Lands forever.

Leaving the slave grounds for some other foetid breed of greenskin to assume, Dagobert steered Archaon from the different types of doom to be found at the fortress of Uzkulak with Hashut, Father of Darkness, and the contested dwarf stronghold of Karak Dum. *The Liber Caelestior* also suggested that the infamous Road of Skulls held nothing but foes unworthy of Archaon's blade and led out onto the Eastern Steppes, where men went mad for want of landmarks on the endless expanse of the horizon. So at Dagobert's word the warband braved the treacheries of the Shattered Shore, where land and ice were indistinguishable and the world looked as though it had been smashed by the fist of an angry god.

It was here, in the howling desolation of a desert of ice that Archaon began to truly feel as though he were drawing nearer to his goal. Here on the edge of doom, where the gloomy heavens were like no other and where the seas sat frozen and unnatural, he found a kind of peace. He discovered that the buzz of insanity on the air soothed the ever-present pain in his ruined eye. That the petty concerns of the Empire and its bordering nations were long behind him and that the world was opening up before him. The scale of the place was heart-stopping. On one side, a range of frost-shattered peaks reached into the heavens as though they owned them, with the cragginess of splintered obsidian. On the other, searing depths plummeted below a covering of broken bergs in a darkness that threatened to swallow the world. Between them, Archaon had only a sky in mourning and the ice-riven shore. He could feel the black heart of the lands beating beneath his boots, calling him on with every distant quake. Despite standing in a land barren and lifeless, the Chaos warrior had never felt such life. Such will. Such possibility. It lifted the darkness of his spirit and put him in a murder-happy mood.

'Tell me again, priest,' Archaon called through the freeze. The air almost shattered about his words. Dagobert was seated up front in the wagon, buried in a nest of thick, lice-infested furs. Giselle drove the wagon. She would rather have spat on Archaon or Dagobert than accept a kindness from either of them, but with the air around able to freeze the blood in her veins, the Sister of the Imperial Cross had no option but to take the offer of furs for her own trembling body. 'Tell me how I might achieve an end to eternity,' Archaon said with a laugh that echoed about the face-scalding wasteland of white. 'How might a mortal man end a world?'

Dagobert cleared his throat. Calling through the frost-threaded air was an effort.

'With a nature indomitable,' the priest said, 'like the land, at one with its savage calling. With a heart's desire deeper than the ocean depths. With steel, cold and true, my lord.' With every passing day, Hieronymous Dagobert read more of Necrodomo the Insane's twisted prophecies and with every day the priest sounded more like him. 'To earn the honour of ender of worlds, Lord Archaon, you must offer yourself as a weapon to be wielded by the very powers that would test you. You must become the Everchosen of the great gods of darkness. You must become an acolyte of the Waste's insanities, a disciple of the Ruinous Star like there has never been and doom to all who cross your path.'

Archaon thought on the warriors he was to meet. The warbands who had made the trek north like his own. The madmen who deceived themselves into the belief that they were worthy of ancient evil and its infernal sponsorship. The Chaos warrior smiled to himself. It almost cracked his frozen face. He felt a kind of savage pity for such victims of fate. Their journeys, their trials, their lives had all been in vain, for they were yet to meet their end. Their end had a name – and it was Archaon.

'They will join me or die,' Archaon spat, his words misting on the razored air. 'Tell me more, priest. For I long to hear of my saga again.'

'Words,' Dagobert said. 'Just words. Any fool can tell a story.'

'Then there is no better choice for my own,' Archaon replied harshly, 'than you.'

'Words are nothing without action,' Dagobert said. 'Words are but fantasy to the reality of the blade plunged through the heart or passed across the throat. You will have to kill more men alone than entire armies leave behind them on the battlefield, than the lives taken by sea and storm and the victims claimed by pox and plague. And that, just to get the attention of the dread pantheon.'

'I have their attention already,' the dark templar proclaimed. 'I am Archaon. Past and future ring with my name. I have been selected by fate and will soon be Everchosen of the Ruinous Powers. They want sacrifices. They shall have them. I'm no blood-blind barbarian. This is no madness or malaise. I'm no pawn to be played and I enjoy not what I do. Men will die because they have to. Because they stand between me and my destiny. These monstrous powers shall have the souls they demand…' The wind rose to howl about the warband and the wagon, dusting them with ice. 'Yes, you hear me you calamitous monsters. I will be your weapon – but no more than the sword or spear issued to the soldier of state in prosecution of his duties. I am no more your instrument in the great unknown workings of the world than you are mine. You desire the doom of men, which with your assistance, I can deliver. The gods need a champion no less than the champion needs their blessing. I will be the Everchosen of Chaos not because I beg for it. I will not utter a word in entreaty – I will be chosen as the champion of the Ruinous Star, bearing the favour of all darkness, because darkness will not have a choice in my choosing. Only I will succeed where others have failed. Only I will bring an end to all and plunge the world of men into a futureless abyss.'

'Master, please,' Dagobert pleaded, as a screeching ice storm whipped up about them. 'You offend your patrons. The entities of the Wastes.'

'Soil your robes alone, priest,' Archaon said. 'Your fear proceeds from a cowardly soul – as it does in all men. Well, I am more than man. I am mine enemy's failure incarnate. I am the morrow. I am the world's end to come. Hear me, Dark Gods: warn your warriors, your doomed champions, corpses-in-waiting. You tell them Archaon is coming and the inevitability of their death is coming with me.'

The ice storm died. Crystals rained slowly to the shore as Dagobert peered fearfully up into the heavens. Beyond the storm-stored miasma of white, the warband could hear the grumble of thunder, distant and fading.

'Dagobert,' Archaon called. 'What must I do beyond the ease of killing, to get the attention of these daemon deities? These dogs of damnation.' Again, Dagobert peered through the ice-blind for some thunderbolt of displeasure or daemonic punishment.

'Speak, curse it!' Archaon roared in jubilant fury. 'I would know what that monstrous tome has to say.'

'The translations are difficult, master,' Dagobert told him. 'Some sections require primers, references and keystone texts we don't have.'

'Then we shall find them,' Archaon said.

'Even the sections we can translate are vague and open to interpretation.'

'Then interpret…'

'The Everchosen of Chaos will be known by the six treasures of dread antiquity he carries,' the priest called. 'Six trials to be passed – six gifts of the Ruinous gods, my lord, to be earned and recovered from the Wastes and the servants of darkness.'

'They shall be mine,' Archaon said.

'They are spread to the perversity of the northern winds, my lord,' Dagobert said as Giselle crunched the wagon along the ice of the shore. 'Hidden. Lost. Claimed by others.'

'Others that aspire to be Everchosen?'

'Others who believe they are,' the priest said.

'Such pretenders would have my pity,' Archaon said, 'that they come so far for failure. Instead they shall get my blade, through their deluded skulls.'

'These treasures, lord, are separated by great distance and watched over by guardians of the gods – powerful and unknown.'

'Then what do we know?'

'Two must be earned and two must be stolen,' Dagobert told him. 'One must be found…'

'And the other?'

'Will find you.'

Archaon laughed, hard and harsh.

'The Ruinous Powers wish to play. We shall indulge them, for now. Where does this perverse game of the gods begin?' the dark templar demanded.

'As yet I have discovered the location of only one of the treasures, master,' Dagobert said.

'What is this gift of Chaos?' Archaon asked.

'I know not,' Dagobert said, 'but whatever dark thing it is, it resides in the Altar of Ultimate Darkness.'

Archaon nodded. 'Where does fate take us?'

'To the New World, my lord,' the priest told him. 'The land of murder. Where the Witch King rules in the name of gods with bloody hands.'

'You speak of one of the elder races,' Archaon said. The dark templar had had occasion to kill a number of the secretive forest folk in the Laurelorn – wood elves, as frightened villagers would call them. He had never seen their cousins from across the sea but knew, as many did, of the aid they had offered Magnus the Pious during the Great War against Chaos. Of those who lived further still across the icy oceans, Archaon had heard little. He certainly had not enjoyed an encounter with a member of their weakling race.

'I do, my lord,' Dagobert said.

'Speak on.'

'I know little more than you, my lord. Rumour and dread legend from across the seas.'

'Speak on, priest,' Archaon commanded.

'An outcast species, master,' Dagobert told him, reaching for details from the heretical texts it had been his duty to keep from the world. 'Turned from the light and long separated from their kin – ousted after civil war.'

'Turned from the light,' Archaon echoed, 'to darkness. Do these *dark elves* worship our gods?'

'They do not, master. They venerate the deathless embodiment of murder itself.'

'A race of assassins, perhaps,' Archaon acknowledged, 'but one blessed with losing wars and fleeing from them.'

'From what I have read they are not to be underestimated, lord,' Dagobert warned. 'Their kind infests the New World. They have held their kingdom of Naggaroth safe from the clutches of Chaos for thousands of years. Their watchtowers line the border where the Wastes meet the lands of murder. They benefit from the God of Murder's blessing and sorcerous servants, who will know of our approach before we make it.'

The icy haze about Archaon cleared, revealing once more the black and white immensity of the landscape about them. They were still on the Shattered Shore, with great bergs of ice creaking against one another in the frozen sea to the west and the colossal range of midnight mountains to the east. Archaon knew that there was no east and west where he was heading. No maps or guides that could show the way. Only the whim of the Wastes and the will of his Ruinous patrons.

'It seems we shall need an army,' Archaon announced. 'Fortunately for us, our gods have seen fit to furnish us with one – for it has long been in the ramblings of heretics and madmen that the greatest concentration of fighting men in the world can be found in the dread lands that are our path. We shall cross the Wastes. We shall kill the weak, conquer the strong and build an army of our own from the very best our enemies have to offer. Our banner shall bear the Ruinous Star of Chaos in all its glory. We shall best, commandeer and welcome warriors of all Dark Gods and creeds beneath the folds of its foetid fabric. It will be an army without equal. The Wastes will never know its like again, unless the gods of Chaos themselves decree so. I shall lead this army into the land of murder, where these ancient watchtowers will fall. The secrets of this Altar of Ultimate Darkness shall be mine and my host shall be sacrificed to the Ruinous Powers in its taking. This I pledge to my daemon gods – as always – with the blackness of my lost soul.'

CHAPTER XI

'It is known by many different names. The Wastes. The northlands. The Top of the World. The Realm of Chaos. The last madman I met simply called it Inevitability. I like that. Anyway. It is known by many different names. The Wastes. The northlands. The Top of the World. The Realm of Chaos. The last madman I met simply called it Inevitability. I like that. Anyway. It is known by many names...'

– Lanfranc the Unchanging (the wall of his cell, in an unnamed prison of his own making)

Inevitability
The Northern Wastes
Date unknown

The Wastes were nothing like Archaon expected – and the Chaos warrior had few expectations – but it was everything that he had desired. To Dagobert and Giselle – miserable in their different ways – the months and possibly years were passed in the gale-battered confines of the wagon, trying not to die of the cold, contaminated food or from some misshapen maniac coming out of the storm with an axe. Archaon's Swords were as stoic and uncommunicative as ever. For them, already very much part of the havoc of the north, they had simply come home. Unlike his winged warriors who were indifferent to the forlorn horror of the landscape or the woebegone priest and sister, who regarded their surroundings with dread, Archaon experienced the Wastes in all of their unseen glory. Where the warband saw the simple darkness of the skies, Archaon could stare back defiantly with a darkness of his own. His ruined eye and the shard of wyrdstone that still lay trapped within its socket was no longer a loss or disability. He saw with it what others could, in a way that others could not. He saw the winds of Chaos, impossible to detect on the rawness of the face or goosebumps of the skin, streaming about them in indescribable colour and shadow. He saw the way it had dusted and stained the pole-facing surfaces of hillsides, mountains and valleys. The way that it howled in silence through the sparse structures of the Wastes and damned souls that wandered its wilderness. The way its essence collected in the hearts of the daemons that stalked them unseen by all else in the shadows.

As they rode north, the temperature dropped. Mere existence became a numb ache. Madmen and mongrel beasts fell to their knees before Archaon and the wagon, pledging their souls to his service in exchange for a scrap of food from their stores or a moment by their fire. At first, the Chaos champion tolerated such squabbling vermin. They were a distraction from the cold. Only the strongest survived the Wastes and the miserable wretches Archaon met on his way north were untested. Their tongues knew not trust and their savage instinct for survival led them to butcher each other in their sleep and feast on the remains. They were not worthy of Archaon and so he ended them.

Even to the eye untrained in evil, the Wastes were a time and place at war with itself. A land of mournful madness. The bizarre weather; the sunless, starless skies; the rise and drop in temperature; the strange behaviour of water; the land itself – the rock, the earth and ice, almost a living thing, alien and aggressive. Features of apparent claw and tooth, landscapes of suggestive undulation and meagre thorn forests of twisted trunk and withered branch. Unforgiving ranges of mountains, freshly erupted from the ground. Volcanic peaks that glowered in the distance. Quakes and flash floods. Waterfalls that were anything but. Rivers that flowed uphill and backwards. Lakes and inland seas that just seemed to bleed up from the depths of the earth. Polar deserts of frosted grit and glacial wastes. The only things to eat slithered and crawled, while strange lights danced and poisonous gases brumed like glowing streams through the terrain. Storms were common. Wind. Rain. Sleet. Hail. Snow. Dust storms. Ice storms. Storms of energies strange and unnatural. The heavens would churn. The Dark Gods would grumble their nerve-shredding thunder and lightning would crash across the land, of every colour and intensity.

All these things Archaon took in his stride. The one quality of the Wastes that even the Chaos warrior found difficult to manage was the way in which time and distance seemed to have no meaning. With light of different oppressive hues finding its desperate way down through the tumultuous heavens, it was almost impossible to tell what time of day it was. On the occasions that the clouds did clear, the sky above was black and empty – like the dead, glassy inside of a shark's eye. The warband could ride for days and get nowhere. At other times, they were barely out of sight of their last camp before entering a landscape new and markedly different from the one they had just left.

Archaon turned to what he had brought to the Wastes, rather than the insanity he found there, for some kind of measurement. It would be easy to lose himself in a labyrinth of distractions. In the absence of sun, map or fixed mark on the ever-changing horizon, he needed a way to judge his progress. Something more than guesswork or the timeless ramblings of *The Liber Caelestior*. To know how far he had come and judge how far he might have to go. The answers to these questions were invariably 'too far' and 'as far as is needed', but it helped to have a system. Something concrete and not at the whim of change.

Ultimately he had to use Giselle and Dagobert as some kind of marker. Archaon could not trust the enhancements of his own form. As a dark templar of the Chaos Powers, his impossible existence leeching from their potency, he was faster, stronger and more resilient in body, mind and soul than he had ever been as a knight of the weakling God-King. Regardless of where the sun had gone to die in the sky, a day's worth of travel exhausted the pair. They were hungry. They were thirsty. They were tired. It was in these physical necessities that Archaon put his faith. Still, time was difficult to trust in the Wastes.

As Oberon's hooves kicked up the ice and dust and the rickety wagon meandered its way north, Archaon passed the false-witnessing hours in brooding silence. When he wasn't lost in some dark thought, some deep fury at his fate or a scorching recrimination of the soul, then he was killing the miserable wretches that crossed their path. Beastmen. Lunatics. Half-starved warriors looking for answers at the top of the world. They found their answers in the reflection of Archaon's blade, moments before its cleaving edge passed through their unworthy bodies. Occasional wretches would impress Archaon with their pluck – usually their insistence on not dying immediately – or the usefulness of their servitude. They fell into line behind the wagon, trudging after Archaon like the wounded soldiers of some massacre or battlefield defeat, following in the footsteps of an indefatigable general who would not let them die.

They were watched by Archaon's warrior-henchmen. His Swords of Chaos. They rode silently in their blank bone helms. Occasionally stretching their wings, they rolled uneasily in the saddle, flanking both Archaon and the wandering mongrels he chose to add to the number of their growing warband. Ever mindful of their master. Ever watchful of the traitorous dogs that fell into line behind the warrior of Chaos. Marauders, beastmen and armoured warriors, eager to share in the spoils of Archaon's growing celebrity, like a pack of scavengers on the murderous scent of a lone predator, stripping the butchered remains left in its wake for scraps.

Casting his gaze behind, at the tainted path taking him north into destiny, Archaon found the others he had enslaved on the road to damnation. The Swords and the rag-tag cavalcade of recruited savagery that were already very much part of the damnation about them. Gorst, always a stumbling silhouette in the dust, dragging his chains and back-lashed carcass after Archaon as he had done after the distant memory that was Diederick Kastner. Giselle, who just stared back at Archaon from the wagon. Her face wore the weariness of horror and disgust. At first such horror had been laced with pity at what Archaon had become. She, better than most, knew that the darkness of the templar's future had not been of his choosing. Such sentiment was soon lost in the hatred of the hostage, but even that had faded. Gone was the childish futility of a foul mouth and violent outbursts. She was as unbreakable as she had ever been. Her strength lay now in the tautness of her lips, the censure of her eyes and the burning silence that met any words Archaon had for her. When Archaon looked to the girl, he found only fear and abhorrence. He was a thing to her now. A force of unnatural nature that could be denied no more than the howling wind or raging sea.

When not punishing himself or other warriors of the Wastes, Archaon would demand of Father Dagobert answers to dangerous questions.

'For years we were the caretakers of damned tomes and the tales of men who searched for evil of their own making. Did you ever think that it would be like this?'

Dagobert sent ripples of encouragement through the reins, prompting the beasts whose burden it was to drag the wagon on through the bleakness of the Shadowlands. The priest was still the kind-hearted scholar that Archaon had known and loved. Such a heart and the affection the priest bore for the boy who had been Little Diederick, the man who had been Sieur Kastner the Sigmarite Knight, now weighed him down like a millstone. Dagobert had decided to follow the boy that had been his charge and the man who had been his friend into damnation's embrace. Perhaps he could have saved him once. With every step that took them north, such a hope became a fading possibility. A good intention that had become a bitter hope – that had become a lunatic's fantasy. He answered his master's questions as best he could, calling upon a lifetime's study of combated darkness and the recorded untruths of Ruination.

'I suspect,' Dagobert said, 'that it's an intense, personal and inconstant state. As a punishment might match the crime for which it was devised. Reading of such things, by so many in so many different kinds of spiritual torment, I imagine that we share common miseries as we share common joys. The searing reality of any one man's damnation seems specific to him, my master. You and I are both here as far as the chill in my bones and our words clouding on the air can tell me, but we live very different definitions of dread and darkness.'

Archaon nodded in the saddle. For years he had hunted men whose desire it had been to find this bleak and unforgiving place. Others who had returned from it, their souls and desires twisted by the horror of what they had found in both the Wastes and within themselves as they traversed such lands of torment and blood.

Ruins dotted the landscape, mostly the smashed and burned out remnants of fortifications, built from the dark stone of the region.

Towers. Keeps. Forts. Bastions. Even the isolated derelicts of half-built castles and buried citadels. The only other buildings the warband happened upon were the tents of hastily abandoned camps and rough temples honouring one dire god or another. The structures also appeared not to obey the passage of time. Despite their state of ruination, the stone of some seemed freshly carved, while the walls of others were weathered and cracked, infested with stunted mosses, lichens and withered roots.

Beyond that, there were the bodies. The dead and the dying. Corpses. Everywhere. The Wastes were a warzone. Some of the unfortunate warriors and champions had clearly died in battle. The butchered torsos. The headless. The limbless. The unrecognisable. The ground soaked with blood and decorated with trailing gut. Others had been the victims of ritual sacrifice, impaled on stakes, cut to pieces or burned as part of daemon-appeasing ceremonies. Like the derelict structures, the cadavers appeared to defy the days, months and years. Some were waxy and cold to the touch, slow to rot in the climate, while others became infested with fat maggots and spoiled to puddle and bone within days, for little obvious reason. The strangest sensation for Archaon was accidentally happening upon the same smouldering ruin days later, only to find the bodies carpeting the grit and ice to be in a better state than when he had initially left them. Bodies he may have put on the ground himself. Freshly butchered corpses, rather than the clouds of flies, stripped skulls and mounds of spoilage the dark templar had left days before.

Archaon never truly got used to the perversities of the Wastes. The strangeness of the land and the weather. Its unpredictable effects on things both living and dead. The Chaos warrior understood that this was very much the point of the Wastes' existence – if the land had such a thing as a point. Its very nature resisted definition and defied expectation. Its inhabitants could be anywhere, at any time. They could be alive. They could be dead. The Wastes could be a promised land – a paradise – or it could be some kind of eternal punishment. It was everything and it was nothing. To Archaon it was a means to an end. The dark templar's intentions extended beyond its borders – he ruled his ambitions, they did not rule him. He brought death to his enemies but was not there to feed his blood lust. His black heart sought satisfaction from the goal upon which it was set, but he didn't lose himself to indulgence – a prisoner in gratification's loose embrace. Neither did he become lost in the infectious malaise of the place. He would not forget himself and remain. He was there with purpose. His movement was ever forward. Even if the path he was on led to nowhere.

'And what of the gods of Ruination that call the top of the world their home, trading in dark deeds and the souls of lost men? I have fought their servants for what already seems like a lifetime. I have stood sentry over those they would claim with their myriad and wicked ways. I have frustrated their desires with word, deed and blade. Though they curse me with gifts unasked for and invite me to their realm with prophecies and deceit, I hate them with all my heart. As I hate the God-King and the feeble powers of this broken and decrepit world. I hate them, yet I feel that I know them not. How can a man hate nothingness?'

'The Ruinous Powers are all things to all men,' Dagobert said cryptically, drawing upon his careful studies of dark arts and the pledges men have made – their very souls for desires they thought denied to them. 'This land is not their home. They are the land and the land is an expression of them. They dwell in the dark corners of men's hearts. A place warm and ripe for corruption. They prey on the fickleness of fancy and the inescapability of need. We hide behind the stone walls of temples and the false hope of daily rituals, half-remembered history and symbols that jangle about our necks, but the truth is that we are defenceless against their predations.'

Men were feeble things, Archaon knew. Mostly spoiling meat and the selfish desires that drove inconsequential existence. It took nothing to twist the hearts of such beings. Desires of the flesh. The blood of one's enemy. The promise of alleviated suffering. The granting of paltry ambitions. It cost nothing for the dark powers of the world to build temples in the blackest reaches of such hearts. Nothing for such beings to draw the twilight from men's souls. Like the leech within, they infected their host with a little of their own filth, to keep the darkness flowing. Most men harboured such a covenant, many unknown to themselves, masked by ignorance and denial. For few could tolerate the knowledge that they are truly evil without the comfort of a path or purpose. For those men, the path always led north. Through the Wastes and the Shadowlands. To the insanity beyond. To darkness, pure and true.

Like the lodestone, the desires of those who would kill in the name of ancient evil took them to the top of the world. Archaon was set on a course not of murderous malice or self-glorification. He travelled not for unknown pleasures or the alleviation of torments past. He was at the top of the world simply because the route to Armaggedon led through the Ruinous Wastes. If that was where he would find the means to end a world, then so be it. Nothing could quell his appetite for annihilation. Oblivion beckoned.

And so, the Chaos Wastes. There mindless marauders, who had ravaged, robbed and butchered their way north, gathered. They knew not why. The road to damnation was a lonely one and perhaps, Archaon considered, it gave the doomed comfort. To know that there were those who shared their madness. In truth, they were there to fight the foes of their dread patrons, each other and themselves – since there was only so much pain and bloodshed a single man, even a man devoted to Chaos, could achieve. Marauders found each other on the path and gathered about the suggestions of greatness in their ranks. Warbands formed. Warbands joined together to create hordes and hosts about emerging warriors and sorcerers, whose worthiness was tested before the growing number of the damned.

Like hungry wolves they fought each other for the wretched right to lead others of their ill-breed. Some became dark beacons in the cold havoc of the north, attracting hordes of their battle-kin to their banner, bringing the souls of hundreds under the yoke of their dark celebrity. Such men might even earn the loyalty of beastmen and greenskins or the fallen of the elder races. Such dark light in the world might then snare the service of monsters and daemons. From such a melting pot of savagery, the champions of Chaos are crafted. Some received the kind of infernal gifts and sponsorship required to exalt them to infamy. Dark heroes to those in their service. They became names known by others, known by the names of other great warriors whose heads they had claimed and followers they had taken for their own. Some became Chaos lords and generals, commanding armies that would threaten to conquer the very Wastes themselves. Such was the dark path to damnation and greatness. The path that the man who had never been Diederick Kastner found himself upon. The path of the Ruinous Powers.

'What are these gods of havoc and darkness?' Archaon had put to Father Dagobert. 'What do they want with me?'

'There are as many creatures of dread haunting the Wastes and the corruption of men's souls as there are evil desires in the world, master,' the priest had told him. 'Of the Ruinous pantheon, most find themselves afflicted by the dark will of four. Four ancient misfortunes of existence. Like the four walls of a prison cell, holding the conflicting hopes and fears in men's hearts hostage. He who would war with all else – the spiller of blood, the flame that heats the ire in men's souls, causing it to bubble over into the world.'

'I have felt this torment...'

'As all men have,' Dagobert said, 'since the first fist or the first stone was lifted in violence.'

'Go on, priest.'

'He whose dark desires are the very nature of desire itself,' Dagobert said. 'He who lusts. He who thirsts. He who both tempts and is temptation.'

'You said there were four,' Archaon pushed.

'He who is the end of all,' the priest continued. 'The constancy of suffering and desperation – whose sign is seen the world over in the diseased and the gasping hopes of the dying.'

'And?'

'He who is the very storm of change,' Dagobert said. 'The volatility and vitality of a world ever in motion. The embodiment of men's appetite for... more.'

Archaon nodded.

'I have known all of these afflictions,' the dark templar said.

'And they have known you, my lord,' Dagobert told him. 'As they know all men.'

'How can one man serve such opposites?' Archaon asked, the desires as described to him seeming at odds with one another. 'How can a man be both desire and death that would end it? Constancy yet the drive of change.'

Dagobert considered. He thought back to fearful texts read by candle-light in the temple vaults and long forgotten.

'He must not be the pots that keep the paint separate,' Dagobert said. 'He must be the ever-darkening canvas, burdened with colour upon colour until he becomes a shade of ruin pleasing to all the Chaos Powers to look upon.'

Once again Archaon nodded, for once again the priest's words had cut through the confusion that burned in his mind. Digging his heels into Oberon's flanks, the Chaos warrior urged the steed onwards.

The daemon-haunted north was ever calling. There damnation exerted its great influence and the gifts of Ruination were showered on the fearless, the accepting and the doomed. The endless darkness of the unstable region about the pole was more dream than reality. It was where gateways to unearthly realms stood tall and the raw promise of Chaos bubbled up through the appearance of reality. It was where lie became truth, a never-beginning eternity where men could lose and find themselves a thousand times over. Where fantasy and nightmare bred realities anew and mortals could stand like mirrors in the soul-shattering presence of gods. It was not Archaon's destination, however. He was no pilgrim of darkness. He was not there to prostrate himself at the feet of his daemon overlords. He had not travelled across continents to jostle and squeal like a piglet before the bounty of a sow's belly, begging for blessings, with a bottomless appetite for attention and favour. That was a path to greatness unworthy of one who might call himself the Everchosen of Chaos. A calling beneath the Lord of the End Times. Archaon would not seek damnation. It would find him. He would not curry favour with his infernal patrons. They would come to him when the time was right. When he was needed. When he had earned their power.

Instead, Archaon went west. In reality, there was no such thing in the Wastes. There was only the instinct of west. A direction that most of the time was signified by a general trend in the warband's wanderings. Without open sky or elevation to believe in, there were only two seeming constants in the Wastes – and even they, on occasion, were playful in their perversity. Archaon trusted that, if he kept the berg-shattered coast on his left and the daemon darkness of the pole on his right, his progress should generally be west. Taking care that their exploration of the Wastes had not taken them too far into the twilight insanity of the polar interior, Archaon routinely meandered away from its agonising attraction and every few weeks would reach the frozen, storm-battered shore, before turning inland once more. In the gloomy hinterlands between, the ring of shadow that encompassed the continent's dark heart, Archaon used the winds of Chaos to guide his path.

Thus, the saga of Archaon – warrior of Chaos and champion of the Dark Gods – began. He was no northern marauder or tribal chieftain, leading his brothers in the perpetual darkness of murderous territoriality. He was no blood-baptised champion, looking for the way to become lost. He was no fool sorcerer, searching for secrets, only to become one. He was Archaon. He would achieve the horror of the entire world. He was a living legend. Great things were his to achieve – and to achieve them he would need great men.

The first of these great men, Archaon slayed. They were new arrivals, like the dark templar himself. Untried and untested, leading small bands that were equally so. Men of the Empire, haughty Bretons, grim Ungols and Gospodars, even the occasional southerner. Some bore Ruinous favour for the terrible evil already wrought in their homelands: claws, spines, venomous fangs, horns or some other type of deformative horror – acid-dribbling maws, an overpowering stench or scaly, armoured skin. A hundred different aberrations of the mind or body, received as blessings for terrors rendered. Their conception of their pantheon or patron powers was simple and savage. They had carved symbols into their faces and flesh, indulged affliction, wrath, vice or dread powers they did not understand. They honoured their gods with insanity and the weakness of wild abandon. They did not know what they had become or the part they had to play in the circus of delirium and death that was the Wastes. They thought of themselves as victors when in actual fact they were victims. Of folly. Of fate. Of Archaon's irresistible path. Souls caught in the slipstream of the dark templar's supremacy.

So many died. Some even of note. Fastred the Bold, veteran of the Field of Green; Baba Kosch, witch of the Grovod Wood; Herrick von Raukov, the sickly seventh son of Ostland; the Knight of Brass, who Archaon had always assumed was just the subject of ballads and tales; Hjalmar Deathstrider, the famed axe man of Vidarheim and some hulking, corpulent thing calling itself the Gutwrencher, which had dragged itself north from the Mountains of Mourn. Few had been worthy of Archaon's blade, despite their infamy. Even fewer were chosen to join his warband's number.

As Archaon worked his bloody way west, he cut a swathe through the tribal lands of the dark continent. Northerners who truly called the Wastes their home and whose clans and castes observed the will of their gods with breeding, bleeding their last and the vile existence inbetween. They knew nothing of the fine lands of the south but the unworthies that travelled from there in pilgrimage and spilt their sweet civilised blood in tribal territory. What the marauding nomads, savage hordes and horsemen called existence was life in its lowliest form. The choice between starving and eating your enemy. Between the solitude of victimhood or the brotherhood of darkness in your heart. Between being butchered as a weakling or fighting strong. Between living a life of murderous survival or not living at all. The tribes had no true lands to call their own. The Wastes were ever changing, ever moving beneath their feet and the hooves of their hardy steeds. There was only the way of their wanderings and wars on the move. Tribes would routinely clash over the ugly Shadowlands, daubing the clan symbols of their kind in blood on smouldering ruins, erecting totems to their favoured gods and leaving skinned victims on stakes as a warning to others. Sometimes hours later, two different hosts would gut and bludgeon each other to extinction for the same miserable valley, derelict temple or storm-racked plain. The insanity was unending but such existence bred harsh peoples, worthy of the dark lands about them.

Archaon came to know them across the blade, with their ragged corpses under his boot. The Norse: fur-clad raiders of hairy brawn, they were pale of flesh but dark of soul, dragging the dragon-prows of their clinker longships up the frozen shore to unleash the fury of their number on the Southern Wastes. The Hung: squat orientals born in the saddle, as swift and savage as the spear thrown and the shattered-glass winds at their backs. The Kurgan: swarthy-skinned warriors of the Eastern Steppes, most at home under the shadow of Chaos. Indomitable. Innumerable. A melting pot of competing cruelty, the tribe had the greatest presence amongst the armies of the Ruinous Powers and produced some of their hardiest heroes and enduring leaders.

Archaon fought his way through them all. The Kurgan Kul, the sons and grandsons of Asavar the Everchosen. Archaon taunted them with the failure of their Father in Darkness, savagely cutting them down in favour of his own worthy claim to the title. The Dolgans, whose gypsy queen used her sorceries to curse her tribe's enemies with foul fortune and the misstep of luck. Any who fought the Dolgans had to battle with the terrain and weather against them, as well as the witch's inbred army of lover-marauders roaring for their blood. Archaon did not require luck to win his battles. For the dark templar, belief, skill and cold steel won the day, and he broke the Dolgans like a spine across his own indomitable will.

The Hastlings and the Tahmaks, who Archaon and his Swords met as they battled each other at the leaning citadel of Karda Fell. The Hastlings, with their flowing raven hair and beards almost forming manes about the savagery of their dark faces, and the Tahmaks who armoured themselves with the inset bone and skulls of their fallen enemies, had both spawned mighty warrior chieftains – Drach-Mal the Black and Radzseekl of the Burning Plain. After Archaon had killed enough of their tribesmen and the Fell was flooded with blood, the dark templar fought them together, forcing the warring pair to join forces against him. Both died badly and it fell to Drach-Mal's brothers and Radzseekl of the Burning Plain to hastily agree a slash-palmed truce and pull their tribesmen out from under Archaon's gore-splashed sword while there were still warriors to withdraw.

The Gharhars of the Upper Shroudlands received Archaon with submission and reverence at first. Having lost their warlord to a flesh-melding pestilence that had claimed a full quarter of the tribe, however, the skin-sloughers resorted to treachery, attempting to sacrifice Archaon as a daemon offering to reverse the Gharhars' fortunes. Many Shroudlanders died for their underestimation of the knight and his Swords of Chaos. The far Kurganites, known as the Dark Arghols, conversely were openly hostile from the outset. The Arghol women fought alongside their men in battle, all famine-thin, body-painted and criss-crossed in strips of cured flesh-leather. They seemed not to notice the scalding cold of the climate or the losses Archaon and his knights inflicted on their tribe. Again and again they attacked the warband. They attacked at that nest of debauchery, the Maidenhead, on the killing fields of the Red Decimation and during a blizzard of ash and ice that reached inside the vast ruins of Caer Targul. On one occasion warrior women, she-devils of the Dark Arghol, attempted to drag a screaming Giselle off into the gloom and would have done so if it weren't for the chain connecting her to the wagon.

While the degenerate Kurgans plagued the Shadowlands through which Archaon's warband fought, the dark templar sought worthiness both poleward and out on the continent's blasted shore. Horn-helmed Vargs from the Kraken Coast, in the Norscan north, had been yoked under the brutal leadership of King Ingvar the Ravager. The Ravager's marauder fleet rode the berg-storms of the shattered coast, burning and slaughtering their way inland like a river of lava. After halting Ingvar's invasions the Ravager King personally led an incursion north into the Ruinous gloom with the oath-answering Baldrgrim of the Bloody Beard and the Norse dwarfs of the Hel Peaks. Ingvar had but one intention – to end the mysterious Chaos warrior known as Archaon. Ingvar and his marauder army found the dark templar and his Swords of Chaos between the unscalable heights of the Vagassa Pass. There Archaon and his Chaos knights held them with sword, shield and armoured wing, butchering the bearded Norscans, their dwarf allies and their battleaxe-wielding king, in mounds of their fallen.

The Graelings tribe, meanwhile, saw fit to unleash the Werekin of Fjirgard upon Archaon's warband. For weeks the lycanthropes dogged their progress, tracking the rank scent of Gorst as the flagellant followed the dark templar and his warband this way and that across the insanity of the Shadowlands.

In the stunted pines of a withering wood, the Werekin of Fjirgard came for them through the mist, their howls echoing ominously about the contorted landscape beyond. Archaon and his Swords fought their combined savagery amongst the wasted trees. They would have dined on priestflesh, however, if it hadn't been for Dagobert prising the rusty chain of a spiked flail from the skeletal hand of a long-dead warrior of Chaos and beating back the pack of shapeshifters – very much as he had done to their wolf-kin above Archaon's infant form years before.

Further into the frozen continent's interior, Archaon's warband found the misshapen Tong – easterners with hunched backs, sharp teeth and a talent for the dark arts. Their warlocks were all whiskers and squinting hatred, withstanding the deep cold of the Wastes with the warmth of their mammoth-hair coats, their charmed fires and hulking Kurgan slaves, unfortunates snatched from the lands of the Tokmar and Yusak and worked to death. When Archaon had sliced and stabbed through enough of their slave-stock, the warlocks came at the warband with enchanted incendiaries, urns that unleashed firestorms of green flame. As Archaon butchered Yusak bodyguards, whose bodies had been warped and mutilated enough by their Tong slave masters, working his way to the warlocks, the templar was surprised to find larger urns raining from the sky.

With the frosted wilderness and the obscene shapes of standing stones erupting with unnatural infernos, Archaon realised that he had been led into a trap. The warlocks thrashed in the green flame, apparently having been sacrificed by their own witchbreed brethren. With little choice, Archaon crunched through the ice and grit at a run. His Swords were pinned down and at any moment the wagon – with Giselle and Father Dagobert within it – could turn into a fiery, green wreck. His heavy footsteps took him through the sky-striving blossoms of green fire, as the larger urns dropped and hit the ground. As he saw the lobbed urns fall before him, the templar was forced to skid and scramble in the opposite direction to evade a fiery death. Charging through the dying blaze of a short fallen urn, Archaon arrived before a pair of ramshackle mangonels, manned and manoeuvred by Tokmar slaves. Tong warlocks were overseeing the trajectory and loading of the weapon from a rhinox-hauled cart of prepared urns, protecting the fur tents of an encampment beyond. Archaon made short work of the brutalised mangonel crews and their vicious warlock overseers, thundering on through the cold and into the camp. Slashing his way through the hide shelters, the dark templar conducted the massacre alone, hacking his way through the privacy of each tent in turn and slaying without ceremony the wicked old men, their hags and chained slaves within.

Upon returning to his own warband, drenched in the blood of the easterners, Archaon found that one of the Tong's projectile urns had indeed come close to destroying the wagon, torching the horse that dragged it instead. Ordering Vier and Fünf to retrieve the two-headed rhinox from the cart of urns and yoke it to the wagon, Archaon moved around to find Hieronymous Dagobert clutching *The Celestine Book of Divination* to his chest, ready to save the tome from the fires.

Meanwhile, Giselle hid stoic and silent in the wagon itself, giving Archaon the enmity of her eyes, knowing that if the enchanted fireball had hit the wagon there would have been no escape for her. Archaon thought on the Kurgan slaves that had attacked him in the encampment and the way he had found them chain-staked to the tent floor. Bringing up *Terminus*, the blade of the Sigmarite weapon still aflame with ghostly torment, the dark templar chopped down through the freezing chain, freeing the girl. The Sister of the Imperial Cross was shocked – as was Dagobert – but both said nothing.

That night Archaon had expected the girl Giselle to leave, but in reality, there was nowhere she could go. She was hundreds, possibly thousands of miles away from the nearest civilised land, where the sweet flesh of a Sister of the Imperial Cross would not be cooked and cannibalised as an offering to a dark god. Even if she could make it out of the Wastes alive – which was unthinkable – where could she go? Naggaroth? Norsca? The Troll Country? The Darklands? How would she navigate? How could she even get there? The perversity of the situation started to amuse the Chaos warrior as he scoured the Tong encampment with Zwei and Drei for useful supplies. Even without her chains, the sister was still a prisoner and it was with some dark satisfaction that he saw her still sitting at the reins of the wagon upon his return.

As Archaon rode on, leading the Swords and the wagon up the

snaking valley, he began to think on the reasons he had brought the girl with them. The Swords were soulless, expert and unquestioning warriors – a valuable luxury in the Wastes. Father Dagobert – although priest of the God-King no more and almost feverish in the madness that was his devotion to *The Liber Caelestior* and his translations of its futures – was eminently useful. Like mighty Oberon and the stalwart blade *Terminus*, he was the only part of Archaon's past that the Chaos warrior was willing to keep around. Such reminders helped keep the dark templar in the present rather than becoming a slave to the Wastes' myriad distractions, like losing himself in wrath, obsession, temptation or hopelessness. Giselle Dantziger was something else. She was not really part of his past and although he searched for a reason to include her in his future he could not find one. As he rolled in the saddle, with ungainly scavengers screeching and flapping overhead, it started to bother the Chaos warrior.

At first, Archaon thought it was some dark manifestation of his new existence. The sadistic streak that was working its way through his very being. As a devout Sister of the Imperial Cross, who unlike the rest of the warband, had not lost her faith in the face of the Wastes' insanity, he considered that he might enjoy her suffering. Something pure and resilient burned inside her no less than the Sigmarite blade *Terminus* did in the dark templar's hands. Perhaps, Archaon considered, it was not a sadistic streak but a masochism that had wormed its way into his soul. It physically hurt to be near the sister. Her simple faith, the light she kept alive for the God-King within her, was like an inferno for the Chaos warrior. A soul-roasting agony to endure. Yet endure it he had. He had kept her alive. Despite her obvious hatred for everything he had become, Archaon had retained her as an unlikely member of the warband.

The dark templar's thoughts took refuge in the idea that his actions might have a more straightforward explanation. The effect she had on him was the same effect she had on every other wretched thing of the Wastes. Like *Terminus*, the girl was a useful weapon against the evil of the world – the evil that even as a warrior of the Ruinous Powers, Archaon spent much of his time battling. Then he thought that it might be lust, pure and simple. Archaon had never thought of the girl as particularly attractive. Now that her hair had grown out of the harsh style required by the temple, however, it framed a comely face, like that of a farmer's wife or innkeeper's daughter. The kind of young women Sieur Kastner had spent a lifetime visiting unintentional heirs upon. Plain. Pretty even, when not screwed up in perpetual disgust and detestation.

Such thoughts were not without peril for the Chaos warrior. They bordered dangerously close to mercy, a notion that ordinarily would have prompted the dark templar to turn Oberon around and execute the girl in the wilderness. A man like Archaon – a living embodiment of the end of the world – could afford no such sentimentality. He could spare lives because it served his needs or even for perversity's sake but not simply because his heart told him to. As a Sigmarite templar Archaon had long understood that good and evil were not absolutes. A man's actions in service to the devotion of his cause – whatever that might be – determined the degree to which he could be called good or bad, virtuous or evil, devout or corrupt. He had known thoroughly despicable men who claimed to be ardent Sigmarites. He had also known the fallen find their way to damnation through the virtues of their faith. Archaon knew that himself, only too well. He knew also that there was a small part of him, a scintilla of light in the darkness of his soul, which still yearned to end every evil thing in the world – including himself. A sliver of regret, like the beaten child that runs away from home but still wishes to return and feel the embrace of the parent that beat him.

Archaon knew this truth about himself. He knew that it was the lost love he had for his God-King that poisoned him as much as the shard of wyrdstone embedded in his skull, leaking its corruption into his mind. Rather than return home to the arms of a loving parent, Archaon wanted to burn down the house. The God-King and his servants would pay for his neglect and abuses. The tiny glimmer of stale hope that afflicted Archaon scared him. It scared him that it might be the reason he was keeping Giselle Dantziger alive. She represented a way back from the darkness. Escape from the shadow. Though it was a spiritual agony to be in her presence, perhaps she was keeping some part of Diederick Kastner alive.

Such dread concerns accompanied Archaon and his warband west. West through miserable moorlands and out into open country. A mountain-framed tundra that was home to the horse tribes of the mighty Mung. The Mung were known among the Wastes to possess the finest steeds of any tribe on account of the way their witch-doctors unlocked the simple animal souls of their horses to devils and evil spirits. The eyes of Mung mounts burned with the spectral fury of beasts possessed. They could run faster and for longer than any equivalent mount in the Wastes and with herds of the black beasts, the Mung's territories were wide and ever expanding. Unbeknownst to Archaon at the time, his warband had ridden into the territory of a brutal chieftain calling himself the Hu-Mung-us, a chariot-riding giant of a marauder, nearly twice as tall as his stunted Mung tribesman. Considering Archaon and his warband to be mercenaries brought in by the centigor herd of a nearby territory, which had defiled Mung steeds and fathered filth filthy offspring upon them, the Hu-Mung-us sent his fastest spirit-steeds and horseback-mounted archers to run them off. He sent them in their hundreds.

Caught out in the open, Archaon and the warband were at the mercy of the colossal war party. Mung horsemen swept down on them like a flock of birds, wheeling and swerving, attempting to cut them down with their wyrdstone edged blades. The rhinox-hauled wagon was never going to outrun the Mung horses and Archaon feared that Oberon and the steeds of the Swords would fare little better against the marauders' possessed mounts. With the tundra swarming with the Mung, Archaon ordered his warband to head for the mountains where speed counted for less and they could thin the horsemen's numbers. The escape turned into a running battle, however, with the Mung war party moving almost as one, slicing through Archaon's band at blazing speed before routinely withdrawing and turning the sky black with launched arrows. Shooting in unison from the saddle, the Mung appeared to be expert archers as well as riders and it became apparent to Archaon that they might all be skewered alive on the wyrdstone flint-tips of the arrows.

Pushing Oberon to his flesh-steaming limits and with his Swords riding alongside, their wings outstretched like shields to the sky, the warband just got out of range of the tundra-stabbing shafts. The Chaos warrior turned to find that the wagon had fared less well. The material of the bonnet had been punctured to ribbons. Dagobert and Giselle were hiding between the wheels, the wagon bed soaking up the swarm of arrows like a wooden target. The two-headed rhinox had gone down beneath the barrage, appearing more like some kind of giant porcupine with so many shafts buried in its shaggy flesh. The creature was not dead, however. It was too stupid and its hide too thick to succumb. At the site of each arrow-inflicted injury, the beast suffered the horror of a rapid transformation. It swiftly became a moaning mound of hairy mutation, spawning new appendages, tentacles and growths. With these new gifts it dragged its spiny form across the tundra towards the wagon and the pair taking refuge beneath it.

Archaon turned Oberon about and started to ride for the wagon.

'Target the horses,' the dark templar ordered, as the Swords followed on their own steeds. The Mung swept in again, like a shoal of fish darting in and out of its prey. Instead of turning aside their flint-edged blades of corruption, Archaon swung *Terminus* about him, turning the flaming blade in his wrist and cleaving down either side of him as the swarm of marauder steeds passed by either side. The horses were bedevilled and fast but they were also light and lacking in armour. The plain became a cacophony of equine shrieks as Archaon cut through legs, opened up throats and chopped entire heads from oncoming beasts. With the Swords of Chaos following suit with their own bone blades, the warband cut a bloody, screeching path through the stampede. Encouraged by the progress Archaon was making against their enemies, a herd of centigor rode down out of the mountains, spearing the unsaddled Mung with the long shafts of their wicked weapons.

With arrows shot awkwardly from the confusion on the ground glancing and splintering off his plate, Archaon leaned from one side of Oberon to the other, cleaving through the Mung mounts until finally he heard the sound of a chariot, rattling at tundra-tearing speed towards him, blades whooshing through the air as they spun with the turn of the wheel. The Hu-Mung-us drove on a pair of demented steeds, with archers either side of him, bows at the ready. Archaon roared Oberon into a charge. The Hu-Mung-us whipped at his horses with spiked reins and Archaon and the Mung chieftain blazed across the bloody field towards one another.

Holding *Terminus* out in front of him, Archaon angled the blade to turn aside the arrows flying from the chariot. With the blades swishing either side of it there was no way the Chaos warrior was going to get near enough to take the chieftain's head off his shoulders. Hauling at the reins, Archaon brought Oberon to a sudden stop, using the momentum to slip down out of the saddle and onto the frozen earth. The field was littered with the bodies of horses. Slapping Oberon away, Archaon advanced on foot as the Mung chieftain's chariot thundered down on him. The Hu-Mung-us clenched his teeth in rage as he drove the horses hauling the vehicle, who frothed at the mouth, directly at Archaon. Sliding down onto his side in the frozen mud, the dark templar slipped between the ferocious horses as their hooves pounded the earth either side of him. As Archaon heard the swooshing scythe pass, he struck out with his own blade, cleaving through the right wheel, smashing one side of it to pieces. Clambering awkwardly to his feet, Archaon watched as the broken wheel stabbed into the hard ground, anchoring one side of the chariot to the earth. The vehicle bucked and was thrown suddenly in confusion, the horses knocked senseless by the sudden stop and the archers thrown forward onto their hindquarters. Only the Hu-Mung-us seemed to have held himself in place, although the towering marauder was bleeding from a gash on his head.

'Come on!' Archaon bellowed, running at a slight crouch towards the ruined chariot, *Terminus* held out to one side in both of the Chaos warrior's gauntlets. The huge chieftain slid a colossal scimitar, serrated with wyrdstone flints, from the vehicle before abandoning it and moving to meet the dark templar. Archaon readied himself for the impact of the giant's mighty blows and the satisfaction of his crusader blade punching through the marauder's body. It was a satisfaction that never came, however. A centigor bounded up behind the Hu-Mung-us and launched its spear, slamming it straight into the Mung chieftain's back, straight down between the shoulder blades. The Hu-Mung-us took two more unsteady steps before letting his scimitar fall from his grasp and crash down onto his knees.

'No!' Archaon roared, denied of his victory. The centigor heard his furious challenge and a savage smile formed on its bestial face. Moments later it was gone. Along with the hybrid's head, which had been sliced clean off its muscular torso by a bone sword wielded by Eins who had ridden up behind it to defend his master. As the blood steamed off the tundra and both horse tribe and beasts scattered, Archaon had to content himself with the howls of the dying and the unearthly shrieks of the rhinox spawn, put out of its misery by two more of the knight's Swords.

When Archaon wasn't slaying the subjects of the Ruinous Powers, he was actively attempting to recruit them. As Dagobert translated more of *The Liber Caelestior* and unlocked the secrets of Archaon's further damnation, it became obvious that an excursion into the chill lands of Naggaroth to access the so-called Altar of Ultimate Darkness would be impossible without a full incursion from the Wastes as a distraction.

'The Witch King's mother is a sorceress of great power,' Dagobert told his master.

'The Witch King's mother?'

'Yes, my lord,' Dagobert said. 'The head of a coven of sorcerous hags. They will see us coming, master. They will know our dark intent.'

'Then we shall hide it within an even darker intent,' Archaon had told the priest. 'We shall invade the kingdom of Naggaroth from the north at the head of an immense army.'

'Where shall we find such a force, my lord?' Dagobert said. 'Warriors worthy of your leadership.'

'Finding men willing to die for greatness is not the problem,' Archaon told him. 'Certainly not here in the Wastes, where nearly every marauder, warrior and fiend is determined to bring glory to his daemon patron in blood. Finding men to lead such slaves to darkness in my name... much more difficult.'

And it was.

On his journey north, Archaon had met men like him. The damned. The doomed. Men who thought themselves bound for legend. Men who thought they could catch the fleeting eye of an uncaring god. The dark templar had travelled their path; he had fought and he had killed such men. He became to such accursed hopefuls as much a part of the Wastes as the perversity of the land and the howling ruination that swept across it. He became the test the aspirant flotsam and jetsam that washed up along insanity's coast had to pass. The yardstick of worthiness. A touchstone of warrior skill, dogged ingenuity and will irrepressible. A question of faith. The longer he spent in the Wastes, the more of a test Archaon became. As he travelled and slaughtered his way poleward, the knight found warriors more worthy of his blade and the time spent slaying them. These were men who had been to the darkness and back. Who had fought their way to the heart of it and returned. They had survived. They had survived others like themselves. This was a credit to them and Archaon began to think that they could be a credit to him also.

Those unfortunate souls that had returned from the lands of midnight delirium in the continent core were different. They were changed. Like Archaon, their bodies and minds had acclimatised to the abnormality and lethality of their environment. The mind-bending rulelessness of the place, its stomach-churning grotesquery, the constant demands of defence and slaughter. In the Wastes, you were only safe if you were dead, and there was no guarantee even of that. Those that had returned from the Gatelands at the centre of the Wastes and had not completely lost their minds were physically altered. They were not just stronger in mind, will and body, not just faster in thought and reflex, like Archaon had become. The world had confused them with something else. Their skin was no longer their own. They were gifted with extra limbs, some of use and some anatomical studies in uselessness. They returned unmade, malformed and inconstant of flesh. Their minds also seemed similarly fragmented. Their sanity had been smashed by what they had seen and even been subjected to. They had picked up the shattered pieces and reassembled them as best they could. They had not just returned themselves. They had returned at the head of sometimes hundreds of others, attracted to their possibility like a dwarf to a vein of gold. Archaon would use these champions of the Chaos gods. They would be the battering ram he would use to smash his way into the realm of Naggaroth.

Archaon's Swords of Chaos were a beginning – but only that. The winged warriors had proved themselves over and again. They were his personal bodyguard, however – their bone swords and shielding wings were always where he needed them to be. Their first concern always seemed to be Archaon's person. They were not an army. They were the honour guard of a dark hero. An armed escort into eternity.

Despite their silent obedience and life-saving interventions, Archaon was still wary of his knights of Chaos. He found himself studying their fighting style, in case one day they turned assassin and he was forced to fight them himself. He still didn't know where they had come from or how they knew where to find him. They said nothing of their origins, although the wings on their armoured backs and the weapons of bone drawn from their own bodies testified to time spent in the Wastes and the damned interior of the dark continent. They said absolutely nothing. Nothing about their lives before their fall to Chaos. Nothing about their time in the Wastes. Nothing about who had sent them or their reasons for seeking out the dark templar as their master. In turn, *The Liber Caelestior* had little to say about them, apart from the fact that they were Archaon's constant companions. His Swords. His Swords of Chaos. Only the markings of their plate said anything about their past. The eight points of the Ruinous Star suggested that they honoured all gods of Chaos with equal reverence and disdain. Glyphs and designs woven into the black of their armour and even the bone of their skull-helms told of their subservience to former warrior overlords and daemon masters:

Hordrak the Prodigal, Khardunn the Gloried, Engra Deathsword.

Archaon needed more than guardians and henchmen. It was time for him to do more than wage war. He had to become a warlord. Not just a warrior, but a general. He needed to show the gods that he could harness their dogs of differing allegiance and sworn enmity to one sled. The one that would carry Archaon to a greatness impossible to ignore. For that he needed loyal lieutenants, whose talents, warbands, tribes and hosts would combine to create the army of lost souls Archaon would need.

Some – despite their warped minds and bodily blessings – were deemed undeserving of such honour. Haarlax Shrike, despite his death-dealing prowess, would not leave the tower of skulls he was constructing to honour his Blood God to join Archaon's band. He had to die with his followers and his tower had to fall. Lord Mortriss and his Knights of Ruin had been wandering the Wastes so long in the service of Nurgle that they literally fell apart – rusted plate and bone – at the swing of Archaon's sword and the smash of his shield. The spindly sorcerer Zartas Uthezarn had impressed Archaon with his mastery of pink and blue flame that poured from horrific holes in his palms. Only days after Archaon recruited the Changer's servant to his cause, the sorcerer had been showered with infernal gifts and degenerated into a sickly spawn. Archaon might still have found use for the malformed horror but for the fact that Uthezarn, on some level truly knowing what he had become, set himself alight in a purple blaze.

There were others who travelled as part of Archaon's growing warband but did not prove to be up to the task. Slaug of the Twin-Axes went mad in the Shimmering Hills. One day his drool turned to froth and the Khornate warrior cut through Wernher Ichelheimer, Gismund the Mad, Durgrim Trollcleaver and his Longshanks before Archaon and his Swords could put him down. Archaon lost Nikitia Vang and her warriors of the Annointed to the decimation that was Ogvaldr the Aesling and his fiend-tempered sword *Snaga*. The dark templar lost his Bronze Company to the last man in his attempt to bring Ogvaldr to battle again in the great depression known as the *Odea-Ossis* or 'Arena of Bones'. By the time he met the Aeslinger's warband again it was a shadow of its former self. Many of his best had been immortalised in stone with a single glance of the cockatrice that haunted the Inconsolable Mountain. With some regret, Archaon ended Ogvaldr the Aesling on the Arga Floe and with even more watched the daemon blade *Snaga* lost to a bottomless crevasse in the ice. Archaon executed much of the dross that surrendered to him from the Ogvaldr's warband but took the scampering plague that was the giant rat-thing Stenomys. Even the monster proved more trouble than it was worth, the infestations making their home in its fur afflicting Archaon's Kvellig cult warriors. The hairless tribesmen and their shamans suffered a pox that turned them into a herd of shambling corpses that couldn't be shepherded and ultimately ended up walking into the Wastes in all directions.

The witch Grastlana le Faux had her uses. In unleashing her dark illusions to make Archaon's warband appear larger than it was at the time, she assisted the Chaos warrior in dissuading some of the Wastes' larger monstrosities from attacking them. Her spectral additions had also impressed the disdainful Prince Aleghast and his warrior-entourage enough to join the warband rather than fight Archaon for the blood-right to cross the Burning Bridge – the only crossing for hundreds of miles across the glowing channel of molten rock known as the River Sunder. Aleghast proved incapable of taking orders, and not long after Archaon allowed the prince and his entourage to be eaten by the Ravening – a nomadic band of barbaric Kurgans that worshipped, as an incarnation of Khorne, a huge ogre in Archaon's ranks called the Great Spleen. Grastlana le Faux herself had to be ended after Archaon discovered that she had been assuming the illusion of his form and issuing orders to his men that furthered the witch's own Tzeentchian undertakings.

The last of Archaon's failures to recruit able warriors to his growing host was Bhorgl the Obscene. Bhorgl – like his Prince of Pleasure worshipping warherd – was a beastman. He was a bald, fleshy thing of shaved fur, muscle, piercings, tattoos and looted jewellery. He came to Archaon willingly, professing with his thick goat's tongue that Slaanesh admired the beacon of pride and self-adulation that was the Chaos warrior Archaon. Archaon didn't believe the beast's praise and didn't like him either but had to admit that the extra muscle would be useful. Bhorgl proved popular in the warband. His brute warriors brought with them the secret of brewing fungus ale from the black mushrooms to be found about ruined buildings. A number of his warriors were also crude musicians, with their suggestive horn arrangements and rough voices. Their songs were coarse and invariably about relations with livestock.

While away with his Swords, reconnoitring a distant temple to some renegade god of the Chaos pantheon, an unnatural storm swept in that seemed to turn the world about, losing the dark templar and his warriors in the maelstrom. Archaon was unconcerned. He had left the warband with Iskavar Gan. Iskavar was a pale and capable Kurgan warrior, whose warband had been slain by Archaon's own. The Kurgan's spear arm had been something to behold, several of Archaon's warriors ending up with javelins through them from impossible distances away. Always dressed in the filth of furs and the spikes of his black armour and shield, the Kurgan had accepted a place at Archaon's side as a lieutenant. He was easy to like and used to show off his aim by launching javelins into the sky and spearing vultures as they circled. In the spirit of the evening, with the fire roaring, vermin crackling on the spit and drink being passed around, Iskavar Gan took of the potent ale.

As the storm intensified and the warband huddled about the fire, Bhorgl's musicians played. Meanwhile, their muscle-bound beastlord and two of his Slaaneshi gors found their way through the material of the wagon bonnet and inside, looking for what treasures of the Wastes and supplies Archaon secreted there. To his pleasure, Bhorgl the Obscene found Sister Giselle trying to sleep. His hoof falls on the wooden floor of the wagon had disturbed her. In truth, like everyone else in the Wastes, the girl barely slept at all and when she did it was with one eye open. Hieronymous Dagobert had been sheltering in the wagon also, studying *The Liber Caelestior* in the meagre light of a candle. Bhorgl the Obscene wasn't interested in ancient tomes. The beastman couldn't read anything beyond the fear in his victims' faces. Licking his thin lips with his thick tongue, Bhorgl instructed his gors to restrain the pair.

'What do you think you are doing?' the priest demanded, the gor manhandling him around. 'Gan!' Dagobert roared. 'Gan!' But Iskavar Gan wasn't coming. Any members of the wider warband that might have cared that an atrocity was about to take place in the wagon – and there were few – had their ears occupied with the roar of the fire, the storm and the cacophony of bestial pipehorns. Iskavar Gan, a canvas water satchel of ale lying empty beside him, was unconscious, like a wrestler out for the count.

Dagobert blustered his anger at the intrusion and hollow threats, while Giselle fought, her screams punctuated with vulgar insults. Bhorgl let slip a wet chuckle. There was the sudden glint of a thin, curved blade amongst the thrashing covers. Giselle always kept a surgical shiv – long stolen from the hospice wagon's depleted supplies – beneath her pillow. The girl hit out, passing the blade across the gor's pink throat. It split open like a ripe fruit. Giselle kicked the beast from the bunk. Clutching its gushing neck, it fell back out of the wagon. Giselle scrambled back against the wagon sideboards.

'Are we having fun yet?' the Sister of the Imperial Cross asked with a snarl, holding the razor-sharp shiv blade out before her. Bhorgl drew a bulbous billy club from his studded belt. It was the beast lord's weapon of choice for subduing his victims or rendering them unconscious.

'I've changed my mind,' Bhorgl told her. 'I won't touch your flesh.'

'You'd better believe it, milksop,' Giselle taunted, waving the scalpel.

'Your flesh shall touch the inside of my gullet as it goes down my throat,' Bhorgl promised. 'You'll still be alive, of course. Raw flesh tastes better off the bone. Warm and with screams.'

An armoured shape stepped up through the bonnet canvas behind Bhorgl the Obscene.

'I'll ask the Great Spleen and his Ravening horde,' Archaon said, snatching the billy club out of the Slaangor's fist and knocking him to the ground senseless with a single smash to the beastlord's horny skull. A bone sword slipped effortlessly through the wagon material and round in an arc, stopping just before the hairless throat of the gor pinning Father Dagobert to the bunk. The beastman glared its salacious hatred of Archaon. Eins came up behind his master. They were both frosted with the ash and ice of the tumultuous storm. 'Get their beast-compatriots. Take these reprobates out to whatever cave the Great Spleen has crawled into and feed them to Khorne's chosen. He'll like that.'

Archaon had the monster sleep away from their camp. The ogre was too dangerous to keep nearby. He might wake like a furious bear from hibernation and kill them all. His pilgrim-barbarians – the Kurgan degenerates that worshipped the Spleen as some representative of their god – slept like dogs nearby. Like the Great Spleen, it paid to keep the cannibals' bellies full.

As the Swords dragged the Slaangor away, it licked at Archaon with its fat tongue.

'Timely,' Father Dagobert said.

'We have you to thank for that,' Archaon told him. 'We were lost in the storm.'

'And?'

'You scream louder than she does, old man,' Archaon said. The priest raised his eyebrows and shrugged. When Archaon looked at Giselle, she still had the curved shiv pointed at them. Her eyes glistened with confusion and loathing. Eins moved in to take it from her. 'Leave it,' Archaon commanded. 'She's not a prisoner.'

'We're all prisoners in this place,' Giselle said.

It shocked Archaon. He hadn't heard her speak to him in a long time – and only then in hisses of hatred. Beneath the rags of her old order and the grime on her skin and in her tangled hair, she had grown up. Her voice had lost the annoying insistence of youth and ignorance. She was older and wiser. Her dread existence in the dark corners of the world had gifted her that at least. He found himself transfixed. She hurt to look upon. She had, impossibly, retained some essence of simple purity in the Wastes. Hiding in the wagon. Hiding beneath the blankets of her bunk. Exposing herself only to Dagobert's obsessions and growing insanity. It was an impressive achievement. She was something to be admired. Or destroyed. When she spoke again, the words, uttered with a savage belief, cut through him. 'A prison without walls. Serving a sentence without end. Shackled to your doom.'

'Leave...' Archaon said. His voice was but a whisper.

'I leave, I die,' Giselle said. 'Here, in the shadow of your great darkness – a warning to the terrible things of this place – my light at least shines on.'

'Your light...'

'My burning hatred for you, *my lord*,' Giselle said through clenched teeth. 'And I would not have it extinguished for all the world, you abomination. If here, in this enforced exile, this prison, this cell of shadow about you – if here is the only place I can abhor you then here I will be. Sigmar hears all prayers, even in this cursed place.'

Archaon nodded slowly. The God-King's name, said with such bitter reverence, stung his soul.

'But he does not answer them,' the Chaos warrior told her. Slipping the wavy blade of a kris dagger he had taken from the butchered body of a Khazag horse-chieftain from its sheath of petrified wood, Archaon tossed the blade onto Giselle's bunk. 'You need to defend yourself,' Archaon said. 'I can see that. I keep company with the damned and I won't always be there to protect you from them. Put your faith not in prayers to weakling gods. Put it – as I do – in cold steel. Put it in a will of the same, and have the courage to put the blade where it is most needed.' Archaon looked about the miserable interior of the wagon. 'Get some sleep.' With that the dark templar left.

But Giselle Dantziger couldn't sleep. She felt like she never slept. From the secluded cloisters of the Hammerfall, her life had now become a living nightmare. A nightmare from which she wanted to wake up. She saw *The Liber Caelestior* in Father Dagobert's sleeping embrace. She wondered if the tome held the secrets of what she planned to do next. Such a notion took her out onto the freezing grit. The chill wind felt its way through her tattered robes like the hands of death. Above the sky was dark and heavy, although it was impossible to tell if it were truly night or not. Archaon's men were sleeping around the flames of the dying fire. Grunting through their own bad dreams. Snoring. Farting. She found one that was not. Iskavar Gan's hand reached out for her filthy skirt-tails. The Kurgan had been skewered into the ground on his own willowy javelins. Demotion, to be sure. Punishment for his lack of leadership, in the face of Bhorgl's little insurrection. Death with the coming dawn. Archaon liked the warrior, but as his lieutenant Iskavar Gan had failed him and an example had had to be made.

'Forgive...' the Chaos warrior said as the Sister of the Imperial Cross pulled her skirts from his bloody fingers.

Giselle tip-toed through the limbs of sleeping warriors and tribesmen, the cold and horror of the gloom beyond the fire's light requiring her to stay close. Who knew what daemon things lurked in the shadows beyond the fire, waiting to rend flesh and swallow souls. Beyond she could hear the Great Spleen, as the warband often did, disturbed from its hulking slumber by such a twilight fiend. She could imagine the bald, fat-bellied ogre snatching the devil from the shadows and smashing it with the Blood God's own wrath into the rocky landscape thereabouts – for the Great Spleen did not deign to use weapons beyond the huge hands that its god had gifted it with. The cannibal barbarians of the Ravening would eat well tonight, with both beastmen and daemonflesh in the offering.

Beyond the fire, Giselle found the mammoth-skin tent the Swords regularly had the warband's lesser servants erect for their master. Oberon stood nearby, nibbling at stunted black lichen and grasses that were trying to force their way up through the frozen soil. The stallion's flesh was matted with scars and fresh wounds. It should have died long ago but some infernal force kept it alive, serving its master. Archaon regularly had Dagobert stitch the horse's flesh, as he had the priest do with his own. Dagobert was a fumble-fingered seamstress but the ragged repairs were enough to close both the steed and its master up and allow their bodies to unnaturally heal.

At the entrance, the heavy hide of the malformed mammoth keeping the worst of the wind and cold out, the sister found Eins. The winged knight of Chaos stood impassive in its armour and skull helmet. It had its arms folded and regarded her with the silent menace of a vampire. Its bone swords were sheathed and its wings creaked as it spread them – blocking the girl's passage. The girl and the killer regarded one another.

'You are here for your master's protection,' Giselle told him. 'And you think he needs protecting from me?' The scorn of the girl's forced laughter had little effect on the Chaos knight. 'I think he might consider it an insult to suggest that the chosen of the Ruinous Powers would need such protection.' Giselle put up her hair, winding it into a messy bun, to demonstrate her true intentions to the deathly henchman. She steeled herself and reached out to touch the thing's black wing. Her intention was to move it aside, but Eins slowly retracted it from her reach, unwilling to let the Sister of the Imperial Cross scald it with her unpolluted touch. With that, Giselle pushed her way inside.

It was warm. There was a small fire, providing both heat and low light. Archaon's armour decorated a rack made from the skeletal frame of a withered and twisted shrub. His shield and the crusader sword *Terminus* sat there also, the Sigmarite blade shimmering in its afflicted agony. Spectral flame no longer danced across its comet-carved surface as it did when the dark templar held the weapon in his God-King hating hands. Archaon was wrapped in a mound of furs by the fire. Giselle approached. She felt not quite in charge of her own movements. She knelt. She drew the Khazag kris from its petrified scabbard and held it over the mound. The blade glimmered in the light from the fire, trembling in the girl's grip. The sister held her breath. Time and again she tried to force it down. Again and again the serpentine blade stopped at dimpling the furs. She exhaled with the effort and slammed the knife down beside the sleeping Chaos warrior.

'What am I doing?' Giselle hissed to herself. 'What am I becoming? Blessed Sigmar forgive. I don't know what is happening to me.'

Leaving the blade warming by the fire, she pulled the layers of furs aside to join Archaon beneath them. She found only more furs.

'Have you come to return that to me?'

Archaon's voice was everywhere. Giselle turned. She squinted. He was kneeling in the shadows of the tent, beyond the fire, where Giselle's eyes struggled to acquire him. 'Perhaps to slide it into my heart?'

Giselle turned, fearful. Her fingers slid down the furs and back towards the kris. Archaon reared to his full height in the murk of the tent. He was all doom-laden melancholy and physical prowess. He wore only his eye-patch. The dark templar's flesh was both ugly and impressive. Horrific bruising. Patchworks of old scars. Fresh wounds – some stitched, some cauterised, some yet to be dressed. A black web of corruption reaching out from his ruined eye in the eight-pointed star of his Dark Gods, running beneath the flesh of his face like some savage's tattoo. 'Why are you here, girl?' Archaon asked. 'To kiss me, or kill me?'

Giselle's anger and disgust returned to her in a cold rush. Archaon was so ghoulishly confident. Like everything else, she hated him for it.

'I've come to save you,' the Sister of the Imperial Cross said.

'I thought that was Father Dagobert's hope.'

'It is a shared honour, my lord.'

'My lord?' Archaon marvelled. 'Not Ruinous dog? Son of the Dark Gods? Scum of all the world?'

'Can a man not be more than one thing at once, master?' Giselle said.

The knight allowed himself a cruel chuckle.

'Pray what have you come to save me from?'

'Why yourself, of course,' the girl told him. 'And the world from the plague that is both of you.'

Archaon smiled. 'Go ahead, girl… Save me.'

The taunt was too much for the sister. The Khazag knife was in her hand. She pushed herself up at him, the slight weight of her malnourished body behind the tip of the blade. Archaon was predictably fast. Killers of all breeds of darkness tried to destroy him every day. His reflexes came from some unearthly place and the strength in his hands and arms was like cold iron. He brought around his hand and snatched the girl's wrist from between them. The blazing manoeuvre was shocking enough but Giselle let out a half-scream as Archaon came at her. He followed with some kind of combat roll, a choreographed tumble that took him over her and then she over him, the kris held between them. Giselle ended up in the furs, Archaon on top of her, both her wrist and the knife pinned above her head.

'Save me!' Archaon roared. The rawness of the command echoed about Giselle's heart. It was daring, barbed and bombastic in delivery – but behind the volume was a desperation. A pleading behind the words. An inviting vulnerability in the trailing last syllable. She felt Archaon's grip tighten about her wrist. Giselle got her fingers to the messy bun she had tied in her hair outside the tent. There she had secreted the surgical shiv she had used to slice the beastmen open. Within moments it was out and clutched in her white-knuckled fist.

She stabbed at Archaon's snarling face. The razor tip of the blade shot for the knight's good eye. For that second, the darkness of Archaon's eye became her world. The play of pupil and the beautiful colours about it, tinged to an unnatural hue. She saw the momentary surprise – the fear even. Then a terrifying acceptance. He said nothing. The searing intensity of his gaze did all the talking. He invited her into the darkness. The shiv lurched forward. Giselle Dantziger would change the world in the God-King's name. She would slay the chosen of the Dark Gods. And he would let her.

But she faltered. The strength died in her arms. Like a fire doused, the struggle left her. With his hand about her wrist, the dark templar slowly moved the blade aside and pinned her to the furs. He burned into her with his gaze. The fight suddenly returned but she was only half there. She spat at the Chaos warrior and bit at his face like some wild animal. He kissed her back. The bloodshed of the Wastes, the laughter of the Dark Gods and the appetite for apocalypse were washed away. The immaculate fire that burned on his lips and in his chest could not be ignored. Archaon's heart felt as if it were broiling in his own blood. It thumped against the inside of his ribcage, slowing. Slowing. Searing to a stop.

He pulled his lips from Giselle's. The dark templar's face was strained with a panic he had not known for a long time. A bugle horn that drowned out his racing thoughts and sounded the end of Archaon. The blood settled in his veins. His lips stung. His heart felt fit to burst.

Giselle squealed as Archaon's fists squeezed about her wrists, threatening to pulverise the bones in each. The kris knife and shiv tumbled from her grip and fell down the side of the furs. Archaon released her, grabbing at her ragged robes and tearing them. There, around her neck, Archaon found it. On a tarnished chain, he found Sigmar's hammer. It was only half there, the silver bearing the harsh marks of a file – probably taken, like the surgical shank, from the hospice wagon's supplies. In the light and with the girl already covered in the grime of the Wastes, Archaon hadn't noticed. He stared down at her in disbelief. She had smeared the sacred silver on her lips. The sister just looked back through him, watching the warrior of Chaos die. There were no taunting words to be had. No death-bed threats. No recriminations. A silence racked Archaon's body.

The dark templar's face contorted about a snarl. He would not be purified. He would not be burned in the fires of his God-King foe. He would not allow the world to go on without him. He was the end of existence, not the other way around.

Giselle watched the agonising battle rage on in the knight. To be. To not be. The dark templar's forehead glistened with cold sweat. The muscles in his face were taut to the point where the sister thought they might break it. He suddenly thrust his left shoulder at her, as though popping back in a dislocated arm. They both heard it. The distant thunder of Archaon's heart – willed back to beating. It thumped rhythmically and insistently between them.

A chill terror crept through Giselle. She had tried to kill Archaon – chosen of the Chaos gods – and failed. She had tried to save him but instead had damned herself. She could not quite imagine what horrors awaited her. She lay there then, in the furs, expecting vengeance to come... but it did not. Archaon faltered. The presence of the God-King within him had weakened the Chaos warrior. He lowered himself slowly and lay his head against her chest. The pair lay there for a long time, the fire crackling beside them and the winds of the Wastes battering the heavy hide of the tent. Archaon held her. To the sister's surprise, she held him back. She felt his breathing slow. Archaon was asleep. As she drifted into oblivion herself – for the first time in a long time – Giselle Dantziger's thoughts were not on murder. She dreamed not of death, but of life. Of hope in the darkness. Of a fool's paradise in the hearts of doomed men. A place where the dying fire of noble gods might be stoked once again.

CHAPTER XII

'Khaela Mensha Khaine, for hate's sake, hear our petition – as blood answers the throat slit. Keep the hearts of the druchii cold and bitter, wherein the murderous will of our survivor-civilisation be preserved for all eternity. Bring death, just and swift, to the weak. Daub the revenger's blade with the blood of enemies old. Watch over the inconstant north. Grant the wild men and their wilderness your darkness. Let blade and bolt bring sacrifice to your altar. Bless the druchii, ever your acolytes and assassins, with murder in your name and victories as certain as spite.'

– Hellebron, the Hag Queen of Har Ganeth,
The Pact of the Pitiless

Eisarnagga Glacier
The Watchlands of Naggaroth
The Soul Harvest – First Blood (Druchii Remembrance)

The will of the Dark Gods took Archaon west. It did not matter that west was the direction the dark templar had chosen for himself – he was the chosen of the Ruinous Gods in all but name and a regular doom would not do for him. While other warriors and chieftains stumbled onwards into their doom, the incomprehension and darkness of the continent interior waiting for them, Archaon was reserved a greater fate. He would not be showered with gifts that ushered others through greatness and on into spawndom because he asked for none. He would not be a simple pleasure. A mind lost. A bloody fate. A soul to be played with. He would not be a pawn moving through a perpetual war or a player in a never-ending round of gladiatorial games. Not even for the gods' entertainment. Archaon's will burned bright in the maelstrom and like a gratification denied or a tasty morsel on the plate left for last, his journey would be savoured.

By the time he passed over the Anvil of the Gods, where dark heroes were forged and the mountainous ridges of Damnation's Teeth and the Arkhang Peaks fought for supremacy of the skies, Archaon commanded a considerable force. With a mighty army made up of champions of the Chaos gods, glory-hungry warriors, amalgamated warbands and tribesmen of the infernal north, Archaon crossed the impossibilities of the Abyssal Plain. He tested the mettle of his men at the great gathering known only as the *Wars of Omission* – fought between and within the colossal black walls of star-shaped ziggurats that pervaded the land and towered over the blood-soaked earth of the Wastes. His host was nearly burned alive in the deep freeze of the Kankgari Basin before facing the Golden Horde of the savage Chi-An, the Serpent Cults of the Tu-Kara and the fleshless warlords of the marauder Yin.

All Archaon did was give battle to the lesser existences of the world – either as general or blade to bloodied blade – or sleep. He gave his everything to fighting his way across the warping landscape of the Wastes. When you knew not where you were, when you knew not the time of day – let alone the week, month or year – progress was everything. Archaon fought on. The madness of the Shadowlands was his mentor, and the murderous intentions of his myriad enemies his teachers. He learned much of combat and of death. As the knight of a weakling god, decked in protective plate, he was an expert with broadsword and shield, on horseback or face to face-plate. In the Wastes he had come to understand the limitations of such strength, such technique and practice. He learned more than he could have imagined in the Wastes – because he had to. He had learned to be deadly with bow and crossbow, and a confident thrower of javelin and spear. He made it his goal to become proficient with every exotic weapon used in failed attempts to end him and acquired the speed and agility necessary to evade attacks rather than trust their failure to his plate and shield. *Terminus* was his constant and tortured companion, but Archaon learned new ways to wield the weapon, unthinkable techniques and handling learned from the barbarian Kurgan, the warrior Hung and damned companions of the elder races.

Archaon even learned how to kill and defend himself without weapons – with the hand and mind, learning both eastern secrets of empty-handed death and manipulation of the strange energies of the Wastes about him in the form of basic wards and protections. He learned how to slay with effortless proficiency, not just the vulgarities of decapitation, the removal of limbs or the stabbing butchery he had acquired in the knightly orders. He came to know the precise vulnerabilities of man, his bestial aberration, the warriors of other races, the monster and the daemon.

When exhaustion or injury finally sent him to his bed his sleep was fitful and feverish. His flesh would roast or it would cool to ice. He would sometimes be out for days or on other occasions wake with a terrified roar, disturbing Giselle as she nestled next to him or others from their own nightmares about the camp. It was not unusual. In the Wastes – so close to the infernal darkness of the world – all dreamt of the dread things trying to find their way into their consciousness and feast on their souls.

For Archaon the nightmare was even more intense and had become increasingly so as they worked their way west. It wasn't a dream or some fanciful notion of vulnerability. It wasn't the work of a sorcerer or infernal servant of the Chaos Powers. It wasn't even the darkness that he had always carried, bubbling below the surface of his understanding. It wasn't subtle. It wasn't the exploratory thoughts of a dark intelligence. It was powerful. Overwhelming. It was something else. Something predatory was stalking his soul. Something unimaginably ancient. A thing of bottomless evil. Dead of colossal heart. Thunderous in the world-trembling rumble of an infernal throat. A thing of savage nature, at war with itself. Churning with change, yet always the same. Both sensing and insensible. Its presence seemed to press up against his own. Horribly, Archaon found himself within the monstrosity's consciousness as much as it had crashed through his own. It was always the same. He was trapped in something dangerous and alien. A womb-like darkness, like an abyss. The infernal fog that made him gag. The sensation of inhabiting a mind savage and primordial, warped to bestial distraction. The hiss of lethal things unseen, hunting him like murderous thoughts through the darkness. Sometimes they would find him and Archaon would roar himself conscious. At other times they would stalk him for days, through a clammy feverishness from which the Chaos warrior could not wake. The horrors of the Wastes, of malformed men, of monsters and daemons held little dread for Archaon compared with the thing waiting for him behind the patch and closing lid of his eyes.

Archaon woke. He breathed in sharply. He blinked the darkness from his eyes. The thud of a monstrous heartbeat faded to nothing and the rasp and rattle of his dark prison bled away. He was cool and clammy, despite the warmth of the fire in the tent. Dogs were barking.

'You were dreaming,' Giselle said. The girl was sitting at a makeshift table beyond the fire, wrapped in a fur. As usual, she couldn't look at him. The Sister of the Imperial Cross wore a mask of disgust and self-reproach. 'Making strange noises.'

'How long was I asleep?' Archaon asked.

'About a day,' Giselle said. 'Who can say out here?'

Archaon felt his neck. It was wet. There was blood from a tiny nick across his throat. He stood and walked about the fire.

'You tried again,' Archaon said. Giselle still had her kris in her hand. She was picking a symbol into the rough wood of the table. A twin-tailed comet. The comet heralding Sigmar's birth. Archaon bridled. The engraving sent a ghastly shiver through him.

'Tried,' the Sister of the Imperial Cross said. 'Failed.'

He reached for Giselle's chin, moving it up with his finger. She looked at him for a moment and then away. Lust – love even – drained from her face. Archaon was the doom of the entire world. His gaze seared with dark destinies to come. He would raze ancient lands. His hands would drip with the blood of entire races. He would drive gods to extinction. He was entrancing… and abhorrent. Giselle couldn't look at him. Archaon pushed her chin up. What remained of her hammer of Sigmar dangled about her neck. Archaon found himself forming a snarl at the sacred object. Above the chain, however – just like those across his own throat – the Chaos warrior found the nicks and slices of a blade danced lightly across the flesh.

'You tried again,' Archaon said, almost to himself. It was a little routine the pair had grown accustomed to. Now and then the girl would try to end the man whose fate it was to end everything else. Predictably, she failed and failure drove her to consider taking her own life. The fire and obstinacy of her youth had not quite abandoned her, however, and at the last moment – the moment before the kris did its worst – Giselle found the crestfallen strength to draw the blade from where it had sliced at her soft skin. Archaon knelt before her.

'Your God-King does this to you,' the dark templar said. 'You feel the hopelessness of his failure. Abandon him as he has abandoned you.'

'And pray to your dread gods?' Giselle said, glassy-eyed.

'No,' Archaon said. 'For I have none. Let the powers of darkness favour me if they will. Let them lend me their strength and draw strength from my victories, if that is their want. You will not see me kneel to them even as I kneel before you now. All gods are fickle. Don't trust in them. I don't. Believe as much as you need to or not at all. Ultimately, the only thing you can really believe in is yourself.'

'You serve the Chaos gods…'

'They serve themselves,' Archaon said. 'As do I. This world is not fit for man or god. The Empire and nations of old, the exotic lands beyond and even here – the cruel Wastes. All will fall and all will burn for me. I will be the Lord of the End Times. The harbinger of doom for all – man and god – for in a world of the slain, with no men, no savages, no ancients of the elder races to pray to them and erect their temples, what will become of these gods, their heroes and their daemons?'

Archaon saw Giselle nod, even if it was just a little. Archaon stood, grabbing the furs about the girl and drawing her to him. They kissed. It was gentle. Tender even. Then he pushed her, spinning her naked form out of the furs and back onto the bed. The playful movement drew from Giselle a laugh. It was stifled and forlorn but it was the first time he had heard honest joy from the girl's lips. In a world of vile threats, screams and thunder, it was pleasing to the ear. For a moment the pair of them could have been young lovers, a servant girl and a farm hand kissing in a barn or a woodcutter and his wife, enjoying a simple life of contentment. As Archaon gathered the furs about him, Giselle's laughter died and her smile faded. They were not young lovers or enjoyers of a simple life. They were the unimaginable horror such people feared. They were the end to such life. They were death to warmth, affection and love – the very things other people lived for.

Giselle's blood ran cold. Her heart felt like stone. She started to say something to Archaon, but the dark templar was gone.

Outside, it was brighter than usual. Archaon's army had been making their way south for weeks and the Chaos warrior had started to feel the intensity of the continent's dark interior ebb away. It took a moment for Archaon's eyes to adjust to the dazzle off the ice. The army was camped out on the Eisarnagga Glacier – an ice floe meandering out of the twisted landscape of the Wastes, reaching down into the northernmost watchlands of Naggaroth. Here the druchii – or dark elves, as those who lived through the misfortune of meeting their kind had described them – defended their malicious lands with a continent-spanning line of sky-piercing watchtowers. A day did not pass without a madman, warband or marauder tribe testing the unbreakable resolve of the elves. The druchii lived for murder, however. They were organised, fortified and unimpressed by the horrors that came out of the north. Not even the most determined of Chaos incursions – with the mountains of iron and spite awash with Ruinous degenerates – had succeeded in any lasting invasion of the Land of Chill. The curdled spirit of the dark elves and their twisted witch-masters would not allow it.

Fortunately for Archaon, he did not need to conquer Naggaroth – at least not yet, nor with the army under his present command. The dark elves' time would come. With half the world aflame and with Archaon commanding the legions of evil, the druchii lands would fall as all were destined to do. But not today. Today an excursion into their frosted realm was required rather than an incursion to conquer it.

Archaon's tents – shelters of shaggy mammoth tusk and hide – were mobile and set on a wooden platform. The platform sat on a set of carved wooden blades, like a sled or sleigh that cut through the ice and was dragged by a team of black woolly rhinox. The tents incorporated a number of chambers, including the general's own quarters, those belonging to Giselle and Father Dagobert respectively, a tusk-arched stable for Archaon's steed Oberon and a tabernacle for the gathering of his warlords. The tabernacle also included a small shrine to the Ruinous Star, though the dark templar didn't care for it, preferring to appease the daemon deities of the Wastes only when he had to and through the spilling of enemy blood.

The dogs were barking. Nearby Escoffier was feeding his hounds. The mad Bretonnian had a sack full of bones, the carcass of some beast he had murdered in the night. Escoffier kept the swarming pack of warhounds ravenous on purpose. He had no idea when Archaon would call on him and his emaciated monsters. He kept them ever hungry. Ever ready to tear Archaon's enemies – and sometimes his wayward allies – apart, at the warlord's command. Buried in a shaggy mound of flea-infested dog skins, which kept the cold from the Bretonnian's own bones, Escoffier moved through the pack. The skinny beasts were all claw, drawn lips and dribbling jaws and the packmaster had to beat them back with the bones with which he was feeding them. The dogs were noisy but Archaon had instructed Escoffier to stake them out close to his tent. More than once the hackle and snap of the voracious hounds had warned the Chaos warlord of uninvited visitors approaching the tent.

Archaon already had protection, however. Turning he saw Zwei and Drei, perched up amongst the tusk-tips of the shaggy hide tents like a pair of black raptors, stretching their wings and keeping watch over their master while he had slept. Fitch, a hunchbacked thing, spindled of limb, served both as skinner for the rhinox-train and ostler for beasts of burden, including Oberon. Having just milked the shaggy beast-cows and returning with a bucket of suspect-smelling produce, Fitch splashed the liquid into a wooden cup for Archaon.

'Master,' Fitch said, his eyes averted and head low. He extended his long arm and offered the cup to the Chaos warrior. Archaon took the drink, allowing Fitch to withdraw from his presence and go about his business with the wretched, whip-mauled animals. Archaon went to drink the milk but his nose told him that there was something wrong with it and he tossed it out onto the ice and slush. His army was camped about the shelter. As a pair of warriors in fur and spike walked by, they noticed their warlord standing at the bone rail that ran around the tabernacle platform.

They lowered their horned helms before walking on. This was more out of animal subservience than military etiquette. Archaon was a warlord of the north, a leader amongst leaders, a general of a sizeable Chaos host. He did not waste his time with drills or formalised expectations. His army was not a state troop of the Empire or even a free company of irregular militia. They were savages, maniacs and madmen. The vast majority of them amounted to little more than rabid dogs. You did not harness such strength with uniforms and codes of conduct. You put them on chains and released them when you needed to. Since chains themselves were impractical, warbands and tribesmen were kept in line by their own chosen and chieftains, some of whom Archaon controlled by adopting them as his lieutenants. Others served the Chaos warrior purely out of fearful respect. They were drawn to his singularity of purpose and the ruthlessness with which he prosecuted his will. He claimed to be the chosen of the Dark Gods and acted like it. The damned were lost and always looking for powerful forces to guide and orient themselves to in the insanity of the Wastes – and Archaon was indeed a powerful force. He had confidence and direction and these were all lesser men who needed to make the leap of faith necessary to join Archaon in his doomed quest.

There were, of course, some of Archaon's warriors that actually did require chains. The dark templar could see the Great Spleen like a small mountain of flesh, out on the floe, a little way distant of the camp. The gore-drenched ogre was a chosen of Khorne, an almost unstoppable bloody avalanche of bone-breaking destruction. He was staked out on four colossal chains that he barely noticed on account of the crushed flowers that were rubbed into the links and which acted as a soporific. Archaon's army had fallen foul of the strange flowers in an otherwise bleak, bone-filled basin that nearly claimed them. Many of Archaon's men had settled to sleep there amongst the skeletons of other unfortunates who had never woken. Before they had stumbled out of the depression, Archaon had ordered some of the flowers gathered, which then had been rubbed on the Great Spleen's restraints, in an effort to keep the frenzied brute from smashing through the camp. As it slept on the ice, the barbarous marauders known as the Ravening that followed in its huge footsteps and honoured the Great Spleen as a manifestation of the Blood God, conducted some primitive cannibal ceremony before the statuesque corpulence of the thing.

Corsair-Captain Vayne also favoured chains. Archaon had been searching for a champion from the south, a warrior that knew Naggaroth and could advise him on the enemy he would face. Vayne – as Archaon knew him – was a druchii slaver. A reaver, who while transporting a mysterious cargo for Morathi the Hag Queen across the Sea of Chaos, had lost both his floating fortress the *Citadel of Spite* and the cargo to an unnatural tempest. Washed up on the icy shore of the Wastes and guided by his witch lover Sularii, Vayne had taken the remainder of his corsair crew inland. His lover's visions of the mighty *Citadel of Spite* beached in the Shadowlands prompted Vayne to gather a small army of slaves. The Chaos god Slaanesh was merely toying with the sorceress, however, and the corsairs' wandering led them into the Prince of Pleasure's embrace.

Polluted, bereft of vessel, having lost the Hag Queen's mysterious prize and unable to return to their homelands, the druchii lovers had wandered the Wastes for the better part of two hundred years before Archaon found them and put the corsair-captain's Slaaneshi slave army and knowledge of Naggaroth to good use. Archaon could see Vayne's reaver-officers in their scale cloaks, walking up and down the lines of their slaves – desperate wretches, caught in the Wastes and shackled to the corsairs' colossal chain gang army. The Slaaneshi slaves were surprisingly little trouble under the expert thraldom of the druchii. What little food was allowed them was drugged to keep the dire creatures in a perverse state of shared delirium. With their irons loose and scavenged weapons handed out moments before battle, the slaves had little choice but to maintain formation and fight for their lives against the enemies of the corsair-captain and his witch lover.

Archaon's compact with the druchii pair was simple. Once the dark templar had done with the gathered depravity that made up his army, he had promised them as prisoners to Vayne and Sularii. Archaon didn't tell them that he expected the challenges with which he would present his host to fully decimate their number. The agreement was rendered further pointless by the fact that those necessary losses might very well include the dark elves themselves. Still, it was easier for both Vayne and Archaon to agree to such arrangement rather than have the inconvenience of killing one another in advance – and following the death of Iskavar Gan and the doomed attempts to replace him with Balduin the Blooded, the Chevalier Malraux, Xandressa Headtaker and Tangrul-Targ as the army's second-in-command, Vayne had made a capable and entertaining subordinate.

Archaon could not see Vayne and the sorceress Sularii amongst the druchii number. The dark templar finally spotted the dangerous pair approaching his tent, accompanied by an animated Father Dagobert, who was fingering through the pages of *The Liber Caelestior*. The three of them were matched in number by the Chaos knight Eins and his accompanying pair of winged Swords. Like a delegation they were making their way through the Tusker herd of the beastlord Gorghas Hornsqualor. Muscular and shaggy, Hornsqualor's beastmen were covered with fur of dour white, almost matching the ice of the glacier about them. Like the beastlord, the beastmen had each been blessed with a single horn, similar to a narwhal, making the herd appear grizzled, rearing unicorns.

From the slavers and beasts, Archaon's army spread out across the ice, enjoying the meagre comfort of small fires and the less-oppressive heavens. The largest contingent to have joined Archaon's army of Chaos was the celestial Hundun. Under their eastern warlord, Fengshen Ku, the Hundun marauder clan belonged to the Dreaded Wo tribe and were made up of mounted members of the respected sword clans and their retainers that formed hordes of pike-wielding supporters. With their black, lacquered armour, pairs of curved long swords and iron masks – forged in expressions of horror and dismay – Fengshen Ku and the sword clan of the Dreaded Wo were a dark and determined force. Archaon had been told by Vayne that the Hundun very much resembled the celestial warriors of the Dragon Kingdom, manning the empire-spanning wall of the Great Bastian, which kept the marauders of Chaos at bay.

Both Fengshen Ku and Gorghas Hornsqualor – in the latter's own primitive way – honoured the Chaos Powers equally, as Archaon professed to do. The army was infested with lone aspirants and Chaos warriors, claiming various infernal patrons and eager to prove themselves in the army of a Chaos general like Archaon. The daemonsmith Zorn and the dawi-zharr, called 'the Mechanicals', paid homage to their bull-headed Father in Darkness and the infernal entities by possessing the hellcannons *Tauriax* and *Wrath of Hashut*. The daemon Shzmodeous, who most of the time took the form of a living darkness, revered only itself. Beyond the Great Spleen, whose followers in the barbarian Ravening thought him the living embodiment of the Blood God and Dravik Vayne, who was firmly in the barbed clutches of the Prince of Pleasure, there were two others who had brought the worshippers of individual Ruinous Powers in any number under Archaon's leadership, in their own individual and disturbing ways.

The dark templar had found Mother Fecundus in the thawing mires of Al-Quagoon. The witch had given herself body and soul to the Plague Lord – or as she called her patron, Father Nurgle. Mother Fecundus was carried by her followers on a palanquin. She could not walk. She was too massive – a bloated breeder of men. Her palanquin was more of a birthing throne than a litter and from it her obscene, malformed body dropped large, writhing pupae. Mother Fecundus's army was made up of warriors birthed in this way, for like an insect queen, she only mothered males – a plague upon the world. Emerging from their disgusting cocoons, the fully-grown warriors had already received the blessings of their father in the form of chitinous plates that grew out of their bodies like armour. Many came forth too twisted for use but the vast majority of Mother Fecundus's plague of men took their place amongst the ranks of their dour brothers. Old souls taken by Father Nurgle and placed in rank new bodies.

No less disgusting were the Brothers Spasskov. Vladimir and Vladislav Spasskov had been aspiring ice mages in the court of Kattarin the Bloody. Eager to impress their Tsarina, the competitive desire of one brother to outdo the other took them further and further north, where the temperatures plummeted and the winds of Chaos that fuelled their enchantments were most powerful. Their rivalry took them into the Wastes, where finally the two brothers fought a terrible battle of hail and storm, cutting each other to shreds in a shard storm of ice. Attracted by the terrible war of enchantments, the Changer of Ways had the bloody blizzard reform and freeze. With a change in the weather, the patron-pleasing sculpture thawed and melted, to reveal that Tzeentch had cursed the rivals with a single body. The dark god had given Vladimir and Vladislav a leg each and both of their spell-casting arms, but their torsos and skulls had been fused back to back, to form a fraternal fusion of flesh, with twice the skill and power of a single sorcerer. This did not prevent the brothers trying to outcompete each other, using their powers, amongst other things, to craft the bodies of their enemies into god-pleasing spawn of ever-increasing horror and invention. Their macabre army of victims were called the Fleshstorm, an ever-changing scourge of spawn that could divide or join together like a single monstrosity.

Archaon cast his gaze across his Ruinous army of Chaos. They were battle-hardened by the butchery of the Wastes. They were harnessed in a single purpose and fearful of Archaon's wrath. They were assured that the dark templar was indeed chosen of the gods, needing to believe that their own path to immortality lay in his shadow. They were ready to be unleashed on the Land of Chill – as Archaon was ready, damnation-blessed by a bloody passage through the Wastes and the deaths of all foes that had put themselves between him and his objective. He had achieved the impossible in earning favour from the capricious Powers of the accursed north. It was time to demand their joint sponsorship. To yoke the dark pantheon to the unstoppable wagon train that was his destiny. Only the Everchosen of Chaos was granted the right to lead the infernal armies in their collective daemon glory across the burning surface of the world. Archaon had pledged on the blood in his veins and his empty soul that the title would be his. It was time to honour his gods in the passing of their perverse trials and tests. To collect the great treasures and artefacts of power that had marked his predecessors as Chaos-favoured of all. His search for such hidden treasures had driven Archaon, by force of will alone, to gather an army of the depraved and despoiling and mount an invasion of dread Naggaroth and the druchii lands of conquest.

'My lord,' Dagobert began, as the approaching group crunched up through the ice. 'I have great news. The Swords have located the resting place of the Altar of Ultimate Darkness. It was exactly where *The Liber Caelestior* said it would be.'

'And this surprised you, priest?' Archaon said with withering impatience. Dagobert was long used to such treatment from his Chaos overlord.

'It resides in a great war shrine to the south,' Dagobert said. 'A dark citadel of black stone, towers tall and twisted architecture.'

'I will see the doom of our destination for myself,' the dark templar said, stepping down from the shelter and barefoot onto the ice. Pulling the furs of an all-encompassing cloak of shaggy mammoth hide about him, Archaon set off through the encampment. As he passed between the miserable fires his marauders, Chaos warriors and champions were warming themselves before, the considerable length of the furs trailed through the snow behind him. Many servants of evil rose in respect. Other warriors bowed. Some hammered fists into the Ruinous Star to be found in the madness of their tattoos, scarring or the inscriptions on their armour. Even the lowliest beastmen, slave or spawn acknowledged their general. The man in whose soul-crushing fist their fate resided. They snatched at the furs winding their way through the camp at his back and kissed them, they lowered their heads in primitive deference or simply withdrew before his glower like the beaten dogs they ultimately were.

'Master,' Dagobert continued behind him, 'the Dark Gods have truly favoured this venture.'

'Again,' Archaon growled, 'this surprises you?'

'This citadel is a blessing for both yourself and Corsair-Captain Vayne,' Dagobert informed him. Archaon slowed suspiciously. He turned to find Dravik Vayne smiling behind him. As usual the druchii was intoxicated on his favoured blood-mixed wine, some infusion, or a depraved and recent union. The sorceress Sularii was working her magic on him as Vayne and Archaon beheld one another, her tongue and a stream of indecent enchantments in his pointed ear.

'Service to the Dark Gods and their chosen should be blessing enough for the captain,' Archaon said dangerously. Dravik Vayne was easy to like. He was an incredibly useful lieutenant, the dark templar had to admit, and with his slick wit, intelligence and the convivial abandon of his leadership, always managed to keep the myriad factions of Archaon's army as one in the warlord's absence. He couldn't trust the druchii as far as he could spit, however.

'Why, Archaon,' Vayne slurred away blithely, 'whatever do you mean?' Sularii laughed at her lover's joke. Archaon gave his own savage smile. A warning before he turned and marched on through the encampment and across the open ice.

'Priest, an explanation – before I gut and bone this cur like a fish and feed him to his own slaves.'

'The citadel, my lord...'

'It's the *Citadel of Spite*,' Dravik Vayne interrupted. Archaon frowned.

'Your vessel?' the dark templar asked.

'The same,' Vayne insisted. 'The Prince of Excess has had his fill and has seen fit to return my *Spite* to me. Archaon, you must help me get it back.'

Archaon ignored the druchii and stomped on through the ice. The sorcerous twins, the Brothers Spasskov, were standing on the precipice of the ice. Each Tzeentchian brother held an identical staff of warped crystal, one tinged blue, the other pink. Beneath their feet, and under their elemental control, the Eisarnagga Glacier was growing. A moving wall of ice, it cracked, reached and froze its way south out of the

Wastes. It shattered forests and pulverised rock beneath its accelerated and irresistible advance down through the dark valleys and evergreen expanse of Naggaroth. Using the sorcerer's ice magic had meant that Archaon's army had only needed to camp on the ice floe and allow a frozen tendril of the glacier to take them into enemy territory.

Archaon said nothing to the Chaos sorcerer. Both brothers had their eyes closed in concentration. Vayne shrugged Sularii off, allowing the sorceress to playfully hang her arms around the Brothers Spasskov with a mock pout instead. Vayne pointed the long nail of a slender finger. Some way distant, above the pinetops, between the crooked mountain peaks and through the winding valleys, Archaon could see a collection of jagged towers, lithe and leaning.

'There,' Vayne said. 'The *Spite*. My *Citadel of Spite*. I'd know those mast towers anywhere.'

'All right,' Archaon said. 'It's the *Spite*. What in the eight points is it doing here?'

'It was lost in a storm,' Vayne told him. 'Vast and unnatural, coming out of the north and across the Sea of Chaos. A storm that took my vessel.'

'And deposited it… here?'

The corsair-captain gave a pained smile. 'Come now, Archaon. The Chaos Powers are not without a sense of humour. You should know that better than anyone. Their nature is the very definition of irony.'

'While you wandered the timeless Wastes, looking for your floating fortress,' Archaon said, 'the Dark Gods had placed it here. In your ancestral homelands. In Naggaroth, where you were returning with your slaves and cargo.'

Vayne nodded. 'So it seems.'

'These beings we serve,' Archaon said, 'are truly twisted in their treatment of their subjects.'

'To Mathlann my course belonged, to Atharti my heart and to Khaine my soul,' Vayne admitted, taking a dusky bottle offered to him by Sularii and drinking deep. 'The Prince of Pleasure did not enjoy me until after I lost the *Spite*. Slaanesh saw me and like some trinket or bauble for sale, decided I must be his.'

'We may take more from them yet,' Archaon said, thinking of the End Times to come and the unforeseen consequences for all of the soul-trading gods of the world.

'What we should do is take the *Citadel of Spite* back,' Dravik Vayne said. 'Archaon, you must help me.'

'*Must* is not a word used to the chosen of the Ruinous Powers,' Archaon warned the dark elf.

'It is because you are the chosen, my lord,' Vayne said, such pleading an ill fit for his thin lips, 'that this is possible. Think, Archaon, my ship – but your flagship. Think what a glorious command she would make, bringing the wrath of the Dark Gods to the wine-dark seas. You have an army, chosen one – why not a floating fortress from which to plan and launch your reign of terror?'

Archaon considered. It was an appealing prospect but all too often the champions of Chaos lost their way to true greatness on side paths of distracting endeavours, calling to them like sirens on the breeze.

'You may lust for such glories, sybarite,' Archaon told him, 'but I live only for the treasure contained within your abominate vessel and the glory it may bring my cause. What was the nature of the cargo you were transporting for your Hag Queen?' Archaon looked from Vayne to his sorceress. The corsair-captain nodded.

'An archaeological find from the Wastes,' Sularii said. 'Recovered stone and architecture. A temple of some kind with a centrepiece.'

'A temple?' Archaon questioned her. She nodded.

'An altar?' Again the dark elf sorceress nodded.

'The gods are to be praised and cursed in equal measure. So it truly is here,' the dark templar said to himself.

'This is magnificent news, my lord,' Dagobert said. 'But I'm afraid that the Ruinous Powers have seen fit to set other obstacles before us for their entertainment.'

'Speak, priest.'

'The Swords report an engagement before the citadel of which you talk. A druchii warhost...'

'Likely the garrison of a local dreadlord or sorceress securing the polluted place,' Vayne offered.

'Or the Hag Queen's own spears, having claimed it for herself,' Sularii said.

'Some resistance was to be expected,'

'The Swords claim the druchii warhost to number in the thousands, lord,' Dagobert interjected. Archaon looked to Vayne, who shrugged.

'Either the Hag really wants your Ruinous treasure,' the dark elf said, 'or she wants to prevent others from claiming it.' Archaon's withering gaze didn't change. 'Really wants.' Vayne added with a smile. 'Plus, we have no idea how long it's been here. Time flows unnaturally in the Wastes.'

'That's not all, my lord,' Dagobert said. 'And you're not going to like it.'

'I already don't like what I'm hearing.'

'The Swords have sighted another force,' the priest said, 'coming out of the north-east. A force that currently lays siege to the druchii, the *Spite* war shrine and its contents.'

'Not…'

'Servants of the Gorequeen, my lord – and her monstrous consort, the Blood God himself.'

'Gorath…'

'And his Bloodsworn, master,' Dagobert said. A snarl crept across Archaon's face.

'Curse the gods for their childish games,' the dark templar said, 'their confluences and coincidences.'

Even Dravik Vayne didn't offer some blithe joke or doom-laden encouragement. The druchii out in force was understandable, expected even. Dark elves would have been assigned to cordon off and isolate the tainted fortress. Shields and spears in even greater number would have been sent from watchtowers to the east, west and those residing in the country. The Hag Queen's witch covens would certainly have seen the coming of Gorath's incursion into the Lands of Chill. Gorath the Ravager. Gorath the Decimate. Gorath the Slayer-Son of Valkia, daemon princess of Khorne. Gorath of the Skull Mountain. A knight like Archaon, of some foreign land and forgotten god. His star would have burned bright on the horizon. A warrior of Khorne without equal. A killer of legendary prowess in the Wastes. A lord of cold fury.

'His head shall be yours,' Vayne pledged solemnly.

'Or ours his,' Dagobert replied. 'More skulls for his mountain.'

The priest and the Champion of the Prince of Pleasure began to argue but Archaon silenced them with a hand. Dagobert was right. Archaon had faced Gorath and his army of Bloodsworn knights several times in the Shadowlands. The knight was an imposing sight in the red of his bronze, baroque armour. Not that Archaon would have known it was the Ravager. His knights were all armed and armoured the same. In their murderous wake, the Bloodsworn attracted all manner of gore-praising deviancy. Berserker Norscans. Shadowland savages. Bestial dog soldiers and their flesh-rending hounds. Daemon slayers. Each time the dark templar's warband had met the Bloodsworn in battle, Archaon's warriors had been forced to withdraw, savaged and broken by the Ravager and the implacable advance of his knights. Some claimed that they were not men at all, but things of infernal construction. That they were built of daemon-brass in the Blood God's forge. An army of clockwork knights – bronze warriors of cog and steam. Impassive. Unstoppable. Unbreakable. They would fight all day and all night in Gorath's name, as Gorath did in turn for his Blood God.

Archaon was silent for a moment. There had been others. Other champions of Chaos. Other chosen. Morbius the Unliving at the head of a thousand corpse-warriors that Nurgle had blessed with a diseased kind of life. Goldemar the Great. Theoderic Rageblade. The Newfangled. Kudren Drax, warlord of the north. Chosen of the gods. Favoured of the Ruinous Star. Those who would be Everchosen of Chaos. All had fallen before Archaon's blade. Gorath was different. Archaon was a legendary warrior. A strategist. A leader of dark and depraved men. He was admired by the dread pantheon for his ingenuity, his singularity of purpose and his many gifts. Gorath had but one gift. The ending of life. He was the blood-blessed chosen of Khorne. Archaon had barely escaped with his life and the remnants of a warband the last time they met. And the time before that. If their clashes had taught Archaon anything, it was that of all the dread warriors of the Wastes, it was the Gorequeen's champion that would probably end up standing over his corpse.

'I can't beat him... can I?' Archaon said. Vayne and Dagobert left the question hanging in the chill air. No one would dare tell Archaon what he could and could not do. Neither did the pair rush to foolish affirmations of a doomed battle with the Bloodsworn. Archaon hadn't been the only one to barely escape with his life. 'Dagobert?'

'My lord,' the priest said. 'The Ravager is of the Gorequeen's daemon blood. Khorne's chosen in these mighty affairs. Gorath and his Bloodsworn are here in the Land of Chill for one reason. They have been guided here by destiny – or some ill force – as we have. He means to claim the terrible treasure contained within the Altar of Ultimate Darkness. He means to usurp your fate, master. He means to become the Everchosen of the Chaos Powers.'

Sularii moved round behind Archaon and draped herself across his muscular shoulders. She nibbled at his ear and allowed her thin fingers to drift down across his chest.

'Archaon is the greatest champion the Wastes have ever produced,' the sorceress said playfully. 'That Gorath could kill us all in his sleep doesn't change that fact. If the Blood God's followers were truly unbeatable then the lands would already be theirs. Killing is undeniably Gorath's strength but that doesn't mean that he is without weaknesses. We have to find them and exploit them. What say you, my lord?'

Archaon looked out across the peaks and the twisted treetops to the crooked towers of the black citadel, Vayne's *Spite*. He thought of the death waiting for them in the valleys below. The armies of the Hag Queen securing their prize. The Gorequeen-favoured Gorath and his mechanical slayers. The horrors and trials of darkness waiting for him in the citadel itself. He thought on his own small army. His rising star about to be extinguished in an ocean of blood. That would not happen. He wouldn't allow it.

Sularii's hand dipped down through the furs, trailing down the scars on Archaon's chest. He grabbed the slender hand in his crushing grip and removed it from his flesh. He heard Sularii moan slightly. Archaon looked at the Slaaneshi's sorcerous hand. He stared down at the glacier ice that burned beneath his bare feet. And it came to him. A chuckle built deep within him, finding expression in a mirth that seemed to ill fit the certain death they were facing.

'My lord?' Dagobert asked. Vayne allowed himself a smirk of contagious madness. The Brothers Spasskov continued their mumbling incantations. The Swords – as usual – said nothing. Archaon shrugged Sularii from his shoulders and turned, marching back up through the ice and towards the camp.

'Ready our forces,' Archaon said. 'Get the army off the glacier and into the mountains. We shall attack both the druchii and the Bloodsworn from the forests on the higher ground.'

As the warlord walked away, Vayne looked to Dagobert.

'The Hag Queen's warriors will mount a determined defence,' the dark elf said. 'The Bloodsworn won't stop until they have their mountain of skulls. I hope he has more of a plan than attack from the high ground.'

Dagobert looked thoughtfully after his master.

'You cannot command the legions through bloodlust alone,' the priest said. 'That is why Gorath the Ravager will never become the Everchosen of Chaos. Such a title belongs to a man who is a living contradiction of both the strengths and weaknesses of the Ruinous Powers. Our master is such a man. Trust in that, druchii savage. You shall have your dread vessel and Archaon shall have his prize.'

'How can you know?' Dravik Vayne said. 'What does your tome say, priest?'

Dagobert hugged *The Celestine Book of Divination* to his belly. Dravik could see the insanity in the priest's eyes.

'It says that sometimes you just have to have faith.' With that, Hieronymous Dagobert turned in the slush and followed his master.

CHAPTER XIII

'All praise to the screaming darkness of the world
Receive these untimely ends as dread offering
May their blood-glory bring you calamitous concord
May their screams carry your names into forever
May their spirits lend you terrible strength
Bestow on this reaper of souls your dark blessings
Let him bear the Mark that burns eternal
And in him see the Ruinous wonder of the world'.

– Inscription, 'Ara Ultimesh Noxa'
(The Altar of Ultimate Darkness)

The Iron Mountains
The Watchlands of Naggaroth
The Soul Harvest – First Blood (Druchii Remembrance)

The battle was difficult to watch. Bringing his army down through the rust-tinged peaks of the Iron Mountains and the dark forests of twisted fir and pine, Archaon had his men observe the slaughter from the highlands. Over the jagged treetops, Archaon and his horsemen, his marauders, his monsters and slaves to darkness, waited in silence. Their warlord was in the saddle and silent. His Swords, his chieftains and champions remained the same, drawing from the army a dark calmness. Among their ranks there was dread, there was envy, there was mindless need. Archaon and his army watched as blood was spilt and man, elf and infernal machine died.

The druchii were savage warriors indeed. They were ice and they were fire. Their ranks were cold, determined and disciplined in the execution of their duties, while murderous glee danced across their faces as they licked their thin lips in the delicious taking of life. Stunted watchtowers – nowhere near the size of the skygrazers on the northern borders – had been constructed about the tainted citadel. They bore bulbous keeps in their tower-tops that glowed with a ghastly light like spectral lighthouses. The elegant parapets swarmed with rotations of druchii crossbows and bristled with bolt throwers that peeped over the jagged crenellations. Between the tower perimeters, formations of dark elves held their ground with beautiful choreography, locking their longshields for the enemy's impact before sliding their serrated spears over the top and into the opposing lines. Up to their boots in northern savages and berserker blood, the Hag Queen's murderers clearly took pleasure in their work but never did they lose themselves in the bloody moment, break formation or push on into the valley to build on their success. When their dreadlords called them back to their lines, the dark elves retreated, the plates of their slender armour rattling rhythmically with their return.

Archaon watched as black clouds of bolts drifted across the battlefield, cutting through Gorath's red-skinned beasts and dog soldiers. Small groups of swordsmen ran through the carnage with the grace of acrobats, finishing tribesmen and Khornate marauders with economical butchery. They then withdrew before the streaking death of tower-shot spears and the dark energies unleashed by the druchii witches. The flanks of the Ravager's army were savaged by dark elf riders, slashing through tribal horsemen with their serrated blades. Their cold-blooded, scaly steeds bounded up the lines on powerful legs, their tails stiff like rudders, guiding their fore-talons and jaws through the delicious horseflesh of the Khornate cavalry.

All the while the *Citadel of Spite* towered above the battlefield like a bad dream. Beyond the citadel towers of black stone and metal from which Dravik Vayne's corsair colours still flew like shredded rags, willowy mast-towers bore yards and furled black, leathery sails in great lateen configurations. Like much of druchii architectural deviancy, the fortress was both imposing and elegant – a midnight study in svelte stone fortification, storm-harnessing sailcraft and the macabre. Its stern was a mighty portcullis, while its prow was the tapering black skull of some twisted, abyssal behemoth. Like a talon, the *Spite*'s cluster of towers seemed to reach out of a cragged berg of obsidian that was buried in the valley floor like a keel or colossal flint spear-tip. The rock was dangling with dead weed and riddled with caves, hollows and grottos.

The druchii were defending well. The dark garrison was drilled to perfection and their safeguarding of the Ruinous citadel, warped and tainted by its time spent in the stormy Wastes and on the Chaos seas, looked likely to hold. It seemed likely the *Spite* would remain in the Hag Queen's possession. As well as the willowy field pieces mounted on the sentry towers, the druchii had positioned deadly bolt throwers in the treelines. Gorath's approach had been direct, bold and merciless – as befitting a champion of the Blood God. His forces had ripped up the valley like an elemental force and had crashed straight into the dark elf defences. The druchii had positioned bolt throwers in the evergreen woodland growing out of the steep valley sides, and they were slamming spears into the marauder host's withering flanks. Archaon couldn't see them but druchii scouts were also amongst the trees, giving the thrower crews cover and cutting down axemen, enraged beasts and both Bloodsworn riders and their gore-splattered mounts as they attempted to rush the ballistas.

Leading his horde from the west, down the valley side and through the bleak woodland, Archaon knew that he too would have to face the same druchii defences. He had little desire to aid Gorath's assault but it would take nothing for the bolt throwers to turn back into the forest and skewer Archaon's men. Similarly, the dark elf scouts would cut his advancing forces to shreds with repeaters fired from their hiding places. This, Archaon could not allow. Signalling Escoffier, the mad Bretonnian, Archaon ordered his warhounds released. The mangy pack of whippets tore away from their chains, their skeletal frames and hunger carrying their throat-tearing maws through the forest at a scrabbling weave. Archaon waited. The warlord listened. Then he heard it. The shrill screams of elves being savaged and torn on the treeline below. He heard the carnage of the bolt throwers slow as their crews fought off the mindless beasts. For the druchii scouts there would be no hiding from the blood-hungry hounds. They would be torn from their crooks and hollows and ripped apart by the frenzied pack.

Fengshen Ku trotted forward on his steed. Archaon nodded to the marauder lord. Digging his leather boots into the horse's sides, the Hundun warlord led his mounted sword clansmen down the valleyside after the hounds. Retainers and pikemen of the Dreaded Wo followed on foot. It was the easterner's honour to finish what the hounds had begun. The throats of surviving druchii scouts and ballista crews were destined for the marauders' curved blades.

Undoubtedly the relief offered to the Bloodsworn's western flank would provide them with an advantage. Gorath wouldn't need it. Archaon had seen the Ravager at work before. He had suffered it before. Gorath the Ravager was a merciless servant of the Blood God. He thought little of the souls he sacrificed in the name of achieving his deity's dark will. Blood-blessed beastmen, Shadowland savages and Norscan berserkers were nothing to him. He granted them the mindless end they deserved. They slaughtered and were slaughtered in Khorne's booming name. Their skulls joined those of their victims on Gorath's growing mountain.

The dark elves enjoyed the distraction of marauder incursions. They broke up the weeks and months of miserable guard duty in the wintry watchlands. They had not, however, faced a champion of Chaos like Gorath the Ravager. A warlord of hate, who saw all – his enemies, his own warriors and the innocents often caught inbetween – as sacks of flesh to be butchered and blood to be spilled. He allowed the druchii their overconfidence. He sacrificed his front lines of barbarians and gors to their storms of bolt and spear, the serrated steel of their swordsmen and the cool discipline of their ranks.

Archaon watched and his warhost watched. The hope. The belief. Victory, certain in druchii minds and the sibilant orders of their captains and dreadlords. Then it came. The unleashing of Gorath's brazen Bloodsworn. His baroque army of clockwork knights, some on armoured clockwork steeds, punching up through their own ranks and advancing through the bloody haze with the unbreakable certitude of infernal machines. Hidden in their number was the Ravager himself, no less infernal in his slaughterous rampage. All died before his blood-hungry blade: beastmen, berserkers, reptilian monsters, dark warriors of the elder race. Horned daemons – red like the depths of that which had spawned them – moved through stomping ranks of knights like howling slipstreams of gore, leaving the drizzle of death in their wake. Archaon watched the tide turn. He watched the Khorne-worshipping warriors of doom sacrifice their own ranks in open celebration of the slaughter to come. Then, the thunder. The Ravager's irresistible advance. The unfolding storm of the Bloodsworn smashed their way through the blizzards of bolts and shield walls that so far had held the illusion of being unbreakable. With a stomach-turning realisation, the druchii began to die in horrible number.

Archaon could imagine his own army decimated before the unstoppable onslaught of the Ravager's ranks. All that he had fought for. All that he had created. Gone in mere moments of mindless rage. The glory of the Ruinous Star, followers of disparate gods fighting under one banner, one warlord, one cause, unified in the even greater glory of a single apocalyptic goal: all sacrificed to appease alone the Blood God's wrath. He could not allow such waste. The Dark Gods stood for more than just momentary spectacle – the soul-shattering scream or the fountain of blood. Their very best champions – their chosen – their Everchosen should be more than just slayers, regardless of their infamy and considerable skill. Such warriors and chieftains had their uses but they were both solution and problem. The wide world would not be conquered by such goremongers. The legions of darkness would be led by a man of darkness, not of blood. A warlord who saw victory through the twilight of black skies, devoid of hope and sun – through the gloom of the End Times to come, not a rage-red haze of blood.

'Will you be leading the attack, master?' Dravik Vayne put to Archaon.

'I will,' the Chaos warlord told his Slaaneshi lieutenant.

'Would you like my forces to secure the *Citadel*?' Vayne volunteered, eager to be both on board his vessel-fortress and out from under Gorath the Ravager's blade. Archaon allowed himself a smile.

'You will sound the retreat,' Archaon told him.

'My lord?'

'Have your forces hold position in the trees, above the snowline,' the dark templar said.

'Hold, sir?' Vayne asked, confused.

'I will take the horde down after the Hundun,' Archaon told him. 'I'll punch through the Ravager's flank with the witch's maggot-men and Hornsqualor's beastmen.' Archaon nodded to himself. He would need the staying power of the Plague Lord's afflicted and the gors to carry him through the Blood God's marauder madmen and on to the Ravager himself.

'My lord, you will need–'

'–you to do as you are ordered, druchii-swine,' Archaon barked back at him. 'Remain here and sound the retreat, Corsair-Captain Vayne.'

For a moment, words failed the slaver. He had never known Archaon to order a retreat – and certainly not before a battle had begun. 'Do you hear me, corsair-captain? Hold position here... I shall bring your floating fortress to you.'

Archaon dug his heels into Oberon's black, scaly flanks. The stallion moved on down the incline and through the snow-dusted forest.

'Now, my lord?' Dagobert said, the fat priest buried in the folds of robes and shaggy furs.

'Now...' Archaon said, his voice cutting through the thin mountain air. Dagobert signalled to a Hundun archer the priest had requested of Fengshen Ku from the ranks of the Dreaded Wo. The celestial dipped his signal arrow in pitch and had another marauder set it aflame. Aiming up high through the treeline, north, in the direction of the Eisarnagga Glacier and the Wastes, the Hundun archer pulled back on his ivory bow as far as the taut weapon would allow before releasing the flaming arrow into the Naggaroth sky.

As Archaon rolled in the saddle, Oberon stomping and skidding his way down through the woodland scree and snow, he could hear the sound of battle beyond. Druchii screeching their last. The whoosh of spears and bolts through the air. The rattle of armour and the march of Bloodsworn knights. The hack and slash of decapitation. The steam of hot blood on the glass-cut breeze.

Turning the stallion to one side, Archaon rode out onto the bare mountainside, where the pines were thin and roots could not cling. Though high above them, Archaon had broken the cover of the forest and was now in full view of bolt thrower crews on the dark elf tower keeps and the clash of druchii and Chaos warriors on the valley floor. About him his Swords of Chaos rode. The maggot-warriors of Mother Fecundus stormed down the slope in their thick, chitinous armour. Shaggy beastmen crushed grit beneath their hooves as they raged their way down towards the Ravager's forces. With his horde roaring down the mountainside after him and Fengshen Ku's sword clansmen standing aside amid the slaughter of druchii scouts, Archaon rode out across the blood-soaked dirt of the valley floor.

Within moments the cool air and the serenity of Oberon at full gallop was gone. It was like hitting a wall. Archaon didn't have to worry about spears and arrows from Gorath's horde. It was not the Khornate champion's style. His Bloodsworn lived for the judder of their blades through enemy torsos and the spray of hot gore across their furs and armour. As Oberon smashed through beasts and marauders, horribly trampling unfortunates under hoof, Archaon swung *Terminus* about him. The Blood God's rabid servants came at him. Cleaving through helm, horn and bone, Archaon hacked his way in through the ranks. Norscans. Khorngors. Skull-draped savages. All died as the Chaos warrior cut a path into the side of the Ravager's horde, his own marauders following in his bloody path. If Archaon was the spear-tip of the assault – deadly and irresistible – his Swords were the wedge that opened the foe-host's side like a grievous wound. Hacking and slashing from the saddle with their bone swords, the winged warriors followed Archaon into the chaos and confusion of the battle, leading Archaon's marauders into the bloody fight.

Archaon had only just got used to the brighter skies of the southern lands. When they disappeared, the warlord looked up into the sky to find a haze of repeater bolts blotting out the heavens.

'Shields!' Archaon roared back at his horde. Bringing his own body shield up and holding it to the sky, the Chaos warrior covered himself and his steed as best he could. The willowy shafts of crossbow bolts rained down on the valley. The druchii were hiding behind the distance created by their cowardly weapons. As the shield drummed with the pitter-patter of slender bolts, Archaon growled. About him the Swords of Chaos took cover behind the open expanse of their gargoylesque wings. Maggot-men hid behind their chitinous shields, while Hornsqualor's warriors did their best to weather the slaughter. Fengshen Ku's clansmen shielded themselves with the bodies of their enemies while Escoffier's warhounds were pinned to the valley floor like crucified mongrels.

The Ravager's horde was cut to ribbons but it didn't seem to bother the maniacs. Bloodshot of eye and foaming at the mouth, Gorath's marauders seemed not to care about the bone-grazing bolts embedded in their flesh. They fought on in their excruciating pain, intent on butchering their way to the craven druchii that had fired upon them. Oberon half-whinnied, half-growled as bolts found their way from the sky, past Archaon's shield and into the steed's flesh. As the shower of death died away, Archaon urged the beast on into the murderous fray.

Archaon stabbed and slashed down through Gorath's slayers with his templar blade. He caved in skulls with its gore-stained pommel. He punched berserkers away with its cross-guard. A northman's spear found its way under his pauldron and into the white-hotness of his skewered flesh. A warrior's axe cut at his side, exploiting the damage created in the wake of a previous injury and hacking at his scarred flesh. His shield was an arm-numbing nexus of furious blows. Every blood-thirsty lunatic in the Ravager's army wanted his steel through the Chaos warrior and it was only Archaon's desperate bladework and the positioning of his shield between him and such furious intent that kept both the dark templar and his steed alive in the sea of murder. If the Khornate horde's attentions had not been split between his attacking force and the wall of locked druchii shields barring their path to victory, Archaon was in such a position that he would have gone down under the deluge of wrath that perpetually threatened to crash over him.

The air was thick with the haze of blood. Archaon was there. In the chaos, in the havoc. Amongst the pushing and pulling. The crimson flash of blades. The hot agony of injuries sustained. The glory of inelegant violence visited upon others. There were shouts. Challenges. Screaming. There was death everywhere. The sky darkened to a doom-laden red. Black lightning stained the sky. Moments seemed to grind to a halt.

The horned head of the red-skinned beastman Archaon was about to end suddenly exploded. Skull fragments and what passed for the mindless brute's brain were spread across Archaon's breastplate. As the creature's muscle-bound body dropped, the brazen flash of an axe betrayed another warrior of Chaos. One of Gorath's Bloodsworn. One of the Ravager's infernal contraptions. The thing moved with clockwork assuredness, its plate barely containing the daemon-force that drove the mechanical nightmare. Its steed was the thick-set parody of a horse. A brimstone-snorting beast of cog, mail and clinkered plate.

Archaon should have been impressed. He wasn't. He had faced the Ravager's clockwork knights before. Flinging his battered shield around, Archaon smashed the knight's head from its shoulders in a shower of metal intricacies and ichor. The blood-cursed thing that possessed the suit of armour howled from its confinement with a forge-spitting fury. The knights were there, about him. They had hacked through their own to get to the Chaos warrior. Their steam-snorting steeds were suddenly everywhere, as were their axes. Archaon's Swords rode at the knights, smashing them aside with their own midnight steeds, engaging the warriors and preventing them from burying their master in blades.

Gorath the Ravager had decided that his prize could wait, however. He would honour both his Blood God and his Gorequeen with the death of a warrior equal. Smacking aside the rage of the knights' colossal axes, Archaon stabbed his greatsword straight through the breastplate of one – only to find that no heart resided behind it – and rent open the back of another as it passed on its daemon-fuelled mount.

Gorath the Ravager was ready for him. Smashing aside two more of his daemon knights, the champion of Khorne rode forth. Archaon knew this was his foe. Decked in gore-bathed brass and mounted on an infernal metal steed, Gorath was all but indistinguishable from his Bloodsworn knights. His armour did not glow with the same daemon radiance, however. His suit was more than just a prison for some daemon machine. Beneath his breastplate hammered something far more dangerous than cog or piston. Beneath it beat the heart of a thrice-cursed warrior. A man who had pledged his soul to the Lord of All Hate. A man who had promised his god a world drowning in blood. Like Archaon he was committed to a singular doom. His axeblades had never known defeat. His name threatened to burn itself into eternity.

Archaon got his shield between the first of the weapons and an axe-cleaved torso – but only just. The force took him from the saddle and into the bloody mire below. As Gorath turned his infernal steed, he ran down on Archaon again, smashing the shield and Archaon with it back into the ground. The Chaos warrior was barely back on his feet when he found the steed standing over him, the fury of its hooves smashing at the shield. Archaon backed from the onslaught, only to find that Gorath was no longer in the saddle. The Bloodsworn's serrated axes opened Archaon up, both his plate and the flesh beneath ragged with gouges and gashes. The dark templar's shield and greatsword rang with the pneumatic impact of the blows as they rained down one after another on the warrior of Chaos.

For a moment, Archaon came to believe the Blood God's champion unconquerable. Every time he rallied, every time he pushed back the rhythmic storm of axeblows and managed to plunge the tip of his blade into the monstrous warrior, he found little to suggest a man. Something that could be killed. Stabbing blows to the thigh, to the shoulder and Gorath's back only revealed the arcane working of infernal machinery. The Gorequeen's chosen did not slow. Did not stumble. Did not stop. It was all Archaon could do to withdraw *Terminus* from the screeching metal embrace of the damaged bronze to smash aside the Ravager's furious whirlwind of axeblows. Archaon's world became the seconds he snatched from death as the Khornate champion pushed him to his limits. Axe. Axe. Axe. Axe. Axe. Occasionally the Ravager would butt him with his extravagant helm or bury the chisel-tip of an armoured boot into Archaon's stomach. Mostly Archaon was just a moment's doom away from being hacked apart by the Ravager's relentless axes. Their barbed edges ripped through his plate where they managed to make contact, while the flat of the blade bludgeoned Archaon from side to side, sending the Chaos warrior tumbling into brawny marauders and druchii shields, necessitating swift kills before he was forced to face the flashing storm of the Ravager's blades once more.

As Archaon fell through the druchii shield wall again, he turned – battle-drunk – and took the head from a dark elf warrior. As he did, the bloody glower of the sky blinked darkness. Archaon readied himself for the Ravager's axes but suddenly they weren't there. Archaon looked to the Khornate champion to find that he too had noticed the brief darkness and was staring up into the sky. Concerned at the progress the combined marauder hosts were making through their bolt throwers, their hail of repeater bolts and ranks of spearmen, the druchii had despatched one of their great beasts to destroy them.

The drake was a youngling. Broad of wing but slender of black body. A reptilian nightmare, it was a thing of sinuous, serpentine beauty. Seated on its midnight shoulders, between its beating black wings sat a druchii sorceress. Guiding the young beast left and right with her thighs, the dragon witch screeched her intention to own the field of battle. Her skin was the white of ice, while behind her an impossible length of sable hair twisted and turned with the drake's sky-slithering manoeuvres.

Gorath the Ravager roared at both the battered Archaon and the dragon witch. The champion's voice seemed to proceed from deep within his infernal armour. It was the sound of roaring forge-fires and contorted steel. He would take them both for the glory of his Blood God.

As the sorceress directed her beast down at him, the drake spewed forth a stream of corrosive gas that turned a column of his Bloodsworn marauders to molten flesh and steaming bones. As both Gorath and Archaon had to roll away from one another and out of the drake's stream of corrosive horror, the dragon witch hauled the beast skyward and turned it around for another pass. Holding her willowy black staff high, the witch visited upon the battlefield a howling gale of phantom blades that cut those enveloped in its swirling course to strips of flesh. Again and again Archaon and the Ravager managed to evade the sorcerous storm, with their warriors dying about them. With every pass, the Blood God's champion roared his challenge to the witch but the only way the screeching druchii hag would oblige him was by bathing him in the blood of his mulched marauders.

With the valley floor a red mire about him, swallowing armour and bone that steamed as it sank, Archaon felt a quake beneath his slipping boots. A rumble that proceeded from the very ground itself. The herald of a doom he had arranged for all of them. It was time.

Looking up he saw Dravik Vayne on the valley side. Horns were being sounded. Several of his Swords looked up from the butchery they were committing in his name. They seemed loath to leave the field of battle as he had ordered.

'Go!' he roared. 'Get the host to high ground.'

With hesitation the winged warriors rode for the western slope, waving Archaon's army on with their bone blades. The marauder host were retreating back to the treeline at the corsair-captain's insistence, leaving their warlord alone amongst the enemy. There wasn't much time. Cleaving a nearby druchii warrior in two, Archaon watched the dragon witch bring her midnight drake down low across the carnage. Gorath was waiting for her, directing her on with his axes. Archaon had to act now. It had to be now. Slipping his gore-smeared blade into his back-scabbard and shouldering his mauled shield, the Chaos warrior ran at the Ravager. Stamping through sizzling bones and with pools of blood erupting about his footfalls, Archaon came at his enemy, his hands empty of weapons.

Looking from the foul drake as it swooped down on them to Archaon's madness, Gorath's mindless certainty abandoned him for a moment. Turning, the Ravager went to hack the defenceless Archaon in two but the dark templar dropped into a roll at the last moment. He rose as the champion's axe passed overhead, sinking his armoured digits into the baroque armour's busy design. Hauling the Ravager to him, Archaon threw Gorath's armoured form over his own and rolled the two of them through the slaughter-swamp. With Archaon sinking into the gore and Gorath the Ravager held on top of him, the Chaos warrior waited. The drake was coming straight at the pair. The dragon witch held her staff high and unleashed her bladestorm. The razor-gale sliced up the mire about them and tore up through the Ravager's back. Gorath roared with infernal insistence and hauled himself away from Archaon but the dark templar held his foe to him, using the brazen-armoured warrior as a shield against the dragon witch's stream of phantom blades. Archaon felt the druchii magic tear through Gorath. Through his ornate plate. Through his brass workings and the workings of his infernal enhancements. Then finally through what remained of the Ravager's hate-blessed flesh. As the remains of the Blood God's champion were torn from his grip by the bladestorm, Archaon felt the drake pass overhead.

Archaon lay there for a moment. Drenched in blood. His soul fired by murderous desire. He felt the Blood God's favour in his heart. His own blood boiled within his veins. The moment was mindlessly intoxicating.

'Get up…' Archaon told himself. Scrabbling out of the gore, the warrior of Chaos watched the dragon witch take her monster up into the sky. Staring about the havoc of the battlefield, Archaon found himself surrounded by the carnage of the decimated Bloodsworn. In the face of his own host's retreat back up the valley side, rallying druchii forces were rushing down on him with their slender spears and jagged blades. With the bolts of repeaters plucking at the marshy slaughter, Archaon ran for Oberon. The stallion was rearing and kicking out with its hooves at a pair of dark elf spearmen. Archaon came up behind and twisted one of the druchii's head from its shoulders. The second he grabbed from the back, drawing the spearman's own weapon across his face. Hauling the shaft of the spear towards him, Archaon felt the warrior's jaw break before he worked the weapon most of the way through his shearing skull. Tossing the body of the druchii aside, Archaon mounted Oberon and rode for the eastern slope of the valley. Like the west, through which Archaon had brought his host, it was sparsely wooded. Bolt throwers blasted spears down at him and scouts fired their repeaters from their hiding places. Weaving through the fired spears and with Oberon soaking up a number of wicked-tip bolts in his stallion-flesh, Archaon rode into the trees. He didn't wait to engage the ballista crews he passed, or scouts appearing from behind the rusty-brown trunks of evergreen giants with slender swords. Archaon knew what was coming. Knew what he had unleashed on the valley. He knew he had to get as far up the valley side as possible.

Behind him he heard the battlefield slaughter die away. Dreadlords would have ordered their weapons turned on the fleeing champion. Riders and their reptilian mounts would have clawed their way up the incline to engage him and Gorath's daemons would have hunted him through the trees. None of these things happened. Chaotic and druchii alike were transfixed by a spectacle so horrifying that they had even stopped slaying one another.

The tendrils of mountain mist feeling their way through the trees fled like scared spirits. A serpentine hiss descended upon the valley and the pines shook with a sudden gust of icy wind. Archaon's hair whipped about him. Everything felt cold. Then the valley echoed with the cataclysmic boom of the terrible things about to happen.

The freezing water crashed around the valley's meandering course, spuming and foaming up the slopes and mountainsides that guided its scalding wrath. It shattered the lower reaches of the highland forest, rending fir and splintering pine, leaving naught but smashed stumps as the waters cascaded back down into the raging advance of the thunderous flood. The deluge tore up the black soil of the valley floor and carried with it the collected debris of its destructive path and mighty bergs of ice.

Archaon patted his steed. The show was about to begin. An offering to the dark pantheon. Ruin. Havoc. Fear. Death. A gift worthy of a true champion of Chaos. Catastrophe. He was no butcher. No expert in the bloody arts like Gorath. He was a living expression of the apocalypse to come. He was Archaon. Herald of the End Times. He rode fate like a ship slicing through the waves. He would not be driven from his course. He would not sacrifice his destiny for blood, not for pleasures unimaginable or limitless power. He would not exchange it for immortality. It was his name that would echo through the ages, until there was no one left to hear it, to utter it, to fear it. Archaon looked down into the valley at his sacrifice. He saw the ice-waters smash into the Bloodsworn's rearguard. Furious bodies went everywhere. Backs were broken and brains bludgeoned from warrior skulls by huge chunks of ice. Weapons glinted uselessly in the coursing depths. The raging flood was an enemy even the chosen of Khorne could not fight. Archaon watched. Enjoyed. Like toy soldiers his enemies had their legs washed out from under them. They rose on the seething froth before disappearing into frozen waters. Their rag doll bodies were mangled in the tumbling logs, rocks and debris rolling across the valley floor and became part of the elemental force that smashed into their compatriots.

'Run, you bladeslaves,' Archaon said, his words hot on the breeze. 'Run.'

The Chaos warriors could not outrun their doom, however. Beastmen hammered into the ranks of Shadowland barbarians. Berserkers cannoned through Gorath's clockwork knights. Even the unearthly band of bloodletting daemons and mounted Bloodsworn riding at full speed couldn't evade the wrath of the valley-swallowing flood. A smile split the frozen mask that was Archaon's face as the Bloodsworn host – the infamous butcherers of Gorath the Ravager, the Rage-blessed of Khorne – were snatched, mechanical steeds and all, by the rising waters and dragged into the glacial maelstrom.

Archaon did not fool himself into thinking that the wall of furious water would be enough to kill all of the Blood God's champions. Gorath might be gone but the infernal Bloodsworn knights and the slayer daemons that haunted his warhost might stand a chance of surviving the watery doom. Being tossed about in the thrashing currents, buried in an ice-stabbing havoc of water, berg and black earth, might have given Gorath pause for thought. He might come to understand that there were others who coveted the treasures of Chaos. Others who might be Everchosen of the Dark Gods. Archaon's army was small but tempered in the relentless battle of the Wastes. They were not the Bloodsworn, however, and a champion – even a champion of such Ruinous patrons – needed to think of victories beyond the blade.

When Archaon had thought of his army at Gorath's boots, chunks of hacked flesh and puddles of gore, it was more than he could bear. It wasn't sentiment. It wasn't ownership. It wasn't pride. Every useless death represented a backward step on his dark path. He would sacrifice them all in a heartbeat if it advanced his interests – taking the world but one moment closer to Armageddon. The very blackness of his soul yearned for the doom of all the world. He was the instrument of the Dark Gods. Their key to dark and shackled futures. Hang mercy, loyalty and rank presumption. His appetite for the end was the irresistible force that kept him moving forwards. Fatewards. Determined to see the destruction of all. Blade, flame, flood or famine. Archaon didn't care – as long as there were fewer souls to plague the world than there had been moments before.

That had been the reason Archaon had instructed a retreat and saved his army from death. A swift and bloody death at the hands of Gorath the Ravager and his Bloodsworn. It had been the reason he'd had the Hundun archer signal the Brothers Spasskov. It had been the reason he had left orders with the Tzeentchian sorcerer to halt the creaking advance of the Eisarnagga Glacier and unleash the howling energies of change on the colossal ice floe. Like an unbroken stallion, free of chain and halter, the glacier had charged away. A seething wasteland of ice had crumbled to a thick, berg-clashing slush that in turn had given way to the scalding torrent that had swamped, flooded and crashed its inescapable way south through the gorges and valleys of the Iron Mountains.

Within several heart-stopping seconds, the tsunami of ice and dark water had smashed through both Gorath's army of hate and the druchii formations that were standing their ground against him. Thrashing dark elves and Bloodsworn warriors were carried away by the thunderous current. The Hag Queen's minion-soldiers at first thought to make for their stubby garrison towers but it swiftly became apparent that the fortifications – including the thorny crown of their keeps – were going to be under water. Some desperate druchii even contemplated climbing the tainted berg of dread rock upon which the *Citadel of Spite* sat. They were not given the chance to seal their doom in such a fashion, however, as the crashing meltwaters of the Eisarnagga snatched them from their purchase.

Archaon nodded. That was better. The battlefield was much transformed. It was no longer a field, for a start. It was a rising, coursing body of black water as wide as the wooded mountains either side would permit. Even above the waters sloshing and creeping up the mountainside, Archaon could feel the freeze coming off the crystal cold river of ice. Amongst the tessellation of smashed bergs and slush, Archaon watched druchii and Chaos marauders drowning. They were dragged to the depths by their armour. They were smashed senseless into ice, rock and each other. They swam past one another – oblivious now to the threat each other presented. Archaon had poured cold water on both the dark elves' murderous glee and the fiery rage that burned within the warrior-acolytes of the Blood God. Archaon allowed the water to do its worst. Druchii and marauder began to grasp for one another, pulling each other down below the surface of the black water. It wasn't murder or battle – it was survival. Too far from anything that might be described as a shore, those dark elves and Chaos warriors not bouncing along the valley bottom or smashed by the tumbling logs and debris were claimed by the cold.

Archaon slowed Oberon. The steed's flesh was steaming with the exertion of galloping up the mountainside. As the berg-crashing waters slushed rapidly up the slope, Archaon urged the horse on a little further at a slow trot, the Chaos warrior enjoying the carnage he had caused on the field of battle. He did not hear the druchii run up behind him. The silent assassin had trailed through the trees, up the mountainside, moments ahead of the rising waters. Archaon turned to find the athletic dark elf already behind him. He drew *Terminus* but by the time he had the druchii had cast his cloak aside and revealed the twisted blades of two longknives in his gloved hands. Leaping up onto Oberon's rump, the assassin was sitting behind the dark templar as he drove the knives down through Archaon's armour. With the twisted blades skewered down through his flesh, Archaon roared his pain and anger. Both *Terminus* and his shield fell from his grasp. With the assassin turning the cruel blades inside him, Archaon too was tumbled from the saddle.

Getting to his feet, Archaon could still feel the assassin on his back. Working his blades deeper into him. The druchii had no intention of letting go until the Chaos warrior had been well and truly skewered. Stumbling at a tree, Archaon ran at the trunk. Turning and smashing the assassin between him and the unforgiving wood, the dark templar bellowed his pain. He felt something crunch in the druchii, however, and the assassin allowed a gasp of his own agony to escape his slight frame. Again and again Archaon smashed the assassin into the ice-threaded bark until finally he felt the murderous dark elf slacken his hold. Reaching back, Archaon grasped for the assassin's wrist and wrenched it around in his gauntlet's grip. Bones splintered in the wrist. Turning the assassin's broken arm around he forced the druchii from his back and slammed him back against the tree. The assassin hissed his pain and intention to kill the Chaos warrior. Holding him against the tree by his throat, Archaon reached for one of the knives in his back. It was excruciating to withdraw the twisted blade. Once he had done so, he stabbed the longknife straight through the chest of its owner. The druchii gasped as the blade twisted straight through him and pinned him to the trunk. Extricating the second, Archaon stared into the assassin's eyes as he used it to cut the druchii's heart out and held the still-beating organ before him. Both warrior and assassin shared a moment of horrific understanding before the dark elf's head fell forward. Stumbling away from the dead assassin, Archaon roared as he held the heart up to the sky and crushed it in his fist. As gore dribbled from his fingers, black lightning split the heavens.

When he turned to find Oberon he found that the horse was still and stricken with fear. Hovering above the tree tops was the midnight drake and the druchii witch. She had destroyed Gorath the Ravager. Now she would kill Archaon. The dark templar looked back down the slope to where he had dropped *Terminus* and his shield.

Archaon looked from his bloody fist back up to the heavens, where the clouds had been rent asunder. From the swirling maelstrom above dropped a fireball that left a blood-murky trail of smoke. The witch lifted her staff. The drake's slender maw opened wide. Archaon instinctively lifted his arms in front of his face. Instead of corrosive breath or a bladestorm of dark magic, the fiery heat of daemon hate washed over him. The fireball struck the dragon and its rider, slamming them into the mountainside with explosive fury. An inferno roared about witch and her monster. Peering through the gaps between the digits of his gauntlet, Archaon watched as some furious infernal entity fought through the flames. A daemon princess, of a terrible martial beauty, had descended. In crimson armour forged in Khorne's own hate and bearing two great horns from her head, Archaon recognised the horrific creature as Valkia the Bloody – the Gorequeen sponsor of Gorath's atrocities. The daemon had descended in celebration of the slaughter wrought in the valley below and in honour of her champion's blood. Swinging a monstrous spear about her armoured form, she took the dragon witch's head off, allowing the shock of its pale face and its lustrous length of hair to bounce down the wooded slope past Archaon.

As the Gorequeen batted the drake's jaws aside with a daemonshield bearing the teeth of its own horrific maw, Archaon took Oberon's reins. Skidding down the slope, Archaon recovered *Terminus* and his shield. He left the doomed drake to the Gorequeen's wrath, knowing that the daemon princess would need no assistance in despatching even such a beast. Shouldering the shield and sliding his greatsword into its scabbard, Archaon mounted his steed. As he rode back down towards the rising shoreline, he cast a glance back at Khorne's dread consort. It was agony with the knife wounds in his shoulders but worth it to watch the monstrous daemon slice through the drake's throat and bury her spear in the beast. Watching her, Archaon wondered if he too might one day earn the infernal patronage of a daemon sponsor. Some dark thing from the beyond to further his interests in the apocalyptic times to come. Riding for the waters, Archaon found himself snarling. Unlike Gorath the Ravager, he did not need such Ruinous favour. He would fulfil his destiny and become the Everchosen of Chaos with or without the help of the gods and their wretched servants.

Still Archaon urged Oberon on. He did not want to be around when the Gorequeen looked for other challenges with which to slake her bottomless thirst for blood and battle.

As Archaon reached the rising fury of the frozen waters, he smiled to himself. The Ruinous Powers had never known a victory so devastating and complete. The dark templar promised them many more. At the water's edge Archaon found several Bloodsworn knights clawing their way out of the coursing glacial flood. They were bereft of their smashed, mechanical mounts. Their joints of infernal workings were frozen and riven with ice. The appearance of their Gorequeen on the field of battle had driven them on but there they stood, like statues, waiting for an end. Archaon granted their wish. Splashing down into the freezing shallows, he drew *Terminus* and cleaved helmets from Chaotic constructs. A rusty ichor that passed for blood dribbled down their breastplates and into the water, staining the shore brown.

Archaon slapped his stallion's scaly flanks with the flat of his smouldering sword, urging the beast on into the frozen waters. Clamping the saddle between his armoured thighs and taking the reins harshly with one gauntlet he swung *Terminus* about him with the other. Guiding the horse, who was now swimming through the black meltwater with his big, broad hooves, Archaon went with the current. As he headed for the rocky foundations of the *Citadel of Spite* – the Chaos war shrine now baptised in the rising waters that battered their way through the valley – the Chaos warrior slapped the water with scything sweeps of his blade. Each cut and thrust put flailing marauders and drowning druchii out of their ice-rimed misery.

Archaon dug his heels into Oberon, forcing the steed to swim for their lives towards the horrific outline of the *Spite*. The dark templar could feel the horse struggling with the temperature. Archaon's plate also had frosted and burned with cold through his leggings, numbing his limbs. Death kept them both busy. Screeching elves and current-fighting northmen swirled past them – an invitation to Archaon's smoking blade. He hacked the slender appendages from freezing dark elves and through the Norscan plaits and wild facial hair of hoar-frosted skulls. A biped reptilian steed, which had long thrown its druchii rider into the chaos of the crashing spume, suddenly reared out of the white waters churning along the *Spite*'s glistening bedrock. It snapped at Oberon, eager that Archaon and his steed not supplant the beast's precarious claw-tip purchase on the *Citadel*'s rocky hull. Oberon reared – whinnying his surprise and dipping Archaon waist-deep into the freeze. The dark templar smashed the reptile's jaws aside with the pommel of his greatsword but the thing's jaws snapped again with almost elastic insistence. Oberon instinctively leant away, nearly toppling Archaon into the rising waters that were racing away down the valley. Throwing himself back at the beast, Archaon sliced the reptile's scabby throat clean open. Working its jaw in gushing disbelief, the reptile scraped free of its purchase and was dragged down the valley by the coursing waters.

Sheathing *Terminus*, Archaon slapped the reins either side at Oberon's thick neck, urging the stallion on up the same outcrop of rock to which the reptilian beast had been clinging. The dark templar needed to get them both out of the water. Skidding and sliding up the wet rock, the steed managed to mount the outcrop and Archaon urged them into the dry hollow into which the rock shelf led. Climbing down, Archaon turned back and watched the glacial waters climb up the slopes of the valley side, swirling up through the pines and firs, bouncing mangled clusters of corpses along the forested shore. Looking up, Archaon could see the dark stone of the *Spite*'s walls and the towers grasping for the sky beyond. Had the Chaos warrior not spent what seemed like an immeasurable eternity in the impossibility of the Wastes, the vessel might seem strange. A citadel that floated on a bedrock-berg of cavern-riddled stone. A floating fortress that harnessed the wind in its colossal, tower-spanning sails and drifted across the oceans, guided by dark magics. Vayne had been right. The *Spite* would make him a mighty flagship. First he must make the corrupted shrine to Chaos his own. He must discover her secrets and claim the treasures she had held onto for so long. Treasures denied even to the inquisitive Hag Queen of Naggaroth.

Leading Oberon into the hollow, Archaon found his progress blocked by the rusty bars of a portcullis. Vayne had warned him about this. He had told the Chaos warrior that the dark elves enslaved all manner of deep-ocean beasts in the system of caves running through the fortress bedrock. Exterior gates allowed water in but imprisoned the creatures until they were unleashed on the druchii's enemies on the high seas. Archaon knew that all manner of aquatic horror lay between him and his prize. Horrors that were all the more so for being exposed to the corruptibility of the Wastes. Stepping down from his steed, the dark templar took *Terminus* in hand and advanced on the portcullis. The darkness beyond was thick and stank of the deep. There was no way to open the gate from the hollow. All the gates were controlled by capstans in the floating fortress. Resting his back against the bars, Archaon took one in each hand and heaved skyward. After an extended grunt of exertion, the dark templar forced the portcullis back up into rocky ceiling.

There was a hiss. Something beyond was stirring. Archaon turned to find it slithering down the tunnel towards him. The thing was horrible to behold. A colossal black eel, with huge glazed eyes and an extendible jaw of curved glass fangs, each the length of *Terminus*. Despite its large disc-like eyes, the creature snapped blindly at the portcullis that Archaon had raised a handspan from the floor. Its fangs clashed against the rusty metal as the famished monster battered its head against the gate in a frenzy. Archaon watched the horrid thing for a moment, feeling the simplicity of its dark purpose. He stepped forward to let it sense the satisfaction of the meal he would make. The beast went wild, smashing its head bloody against the portcullis. Archaon leaned back and then thrust *Terminus* forward. The blade passed through the bars and straight into the rubbery flesh of the sea monster's head. He held it there, the metal of the crusader sword sat in the thing's brain as death throes rippled repulsively down its length. When he withdrew the weapon, the monster fell still.

Forcing the portcullis up through its rusty workings, Archaon advanced up the creature's slimy length, leading Oberon into the darkness. The knight wouldn't ordinarily bring his horse into such a confined space, but with the waters rising up the bedrock of the *Citadel of Spite* and threatening to flood its labyrinth of caves and tunnels, Archaon had little choice but to allow the steed freedom to follow him.

As the daylight diminished behind him, Archaon's eyesight adjusted to his surroundings. It was a primordial blackness. The darkness of the deep. The druchii had imprisoned beasts of the ocean abyss. Then the warping powers of Chaos had crept in through the rock and shadow to re-craft the creatures into new horrors. Archaon could imagine few places more damning and desperate. Somewhere in this dread place he was to find the first treasures of his Ruinous masters. The Chaos warrior cursed them for their twisted games.

Desiccated weed hung from the rocky ceiling and the broad passage opened into a cavern. Archaon found himself smiling in the darkness. He could imagine how such a labyrinth might eat away at the nerve of those attempting to penetrate the depths of the lightless place. Even a lantern or torch would provide little illumination in such an environment. The rock was black. It soaked up the light, leaving nothing for the eye. At best a light source would simply show a foolhardy wanderer in the tunnels where next to place his boot. Tunnels would only be obvious to a traveller already within their craggy confines, while vast caverns and cave systems might pass totally unnoticed in the blanket of gloom.

That most natural of fears – the dread of that which you could not see – had little effect on Archaon. Like the monstrous beasts haunting the inky blackness, the Chaos warrior was part of that dread. Unlike many of his brothers of the damned, fighting their way through the insanity of the north, Archaon did not need to trust in light alone. He had been blessed with other ways of seeing. His soul was a blazing inferno of dark intent that cast all about him in the dreadlight of stinging shadow. Archaon's time in the northern murk of the Wastes had only enhanced his talent further. This place – that would rob the worthy of their senses and feel its way into their chest with the chill talon of fear – was nothing to the Chaos warrior. He crunched through the twisting tunnels of the caves, across vaulted caverns and through the foetid shallows of groundwater lakes. Monsters waited for him there. Ravenous. Feasting upon one another in the absence of their ocean feeding grounds until only the most deadly of creatures remained.

Taking *Terminus* – which struggled to summon even an anguished glow in a place of such degenerate evil – and the shield upon which he carried the Ruinous Star of his calling, Archaon slapped Oberon on the hindquarters with the flat of his blade. The horse whinnied and clopped off into the darkness. The steed did not need much persuading to leave the warlord. Its skittish sense told it what Archaon already knew. That starved beasts from throughout the subterranean realm had been drawn down on him, led to their doom by his fresh stench. Archaon made it easy for them. Clashing *Terminus* against his shield, he roared his dares into the darkness. Then he saw them. Crawling. Slithering. Skittering their way towards him. Monstrosities of the deep of every shape and size. The only similarity they shared was the growl of their bellies.

'Come on, you wretched things,' Archaon hissed through the gloom. 'Hungry? Come get some.'

The killing began. Chitinous nightmares migrated across the cavern roofs, withdrawing into their shells before dropping like cannonballs against the Chaos warrior's upheld shield. Twitching shrimp swarms clicked about him in the darkness, trying to get through his armour and burrow into his flesh. Giant, malformed crustaceans erupted from tight grottos – all spine and pincer – aiming to cut the dark templar in two. Lakes disappeared to reveal tentacular behemoths that glissaded across the cavern floor on their own slime, coming at the knight with glutinous feelers and blasting him with jets of stinking water streaming from blowholes in their octopod flesh. Coiled serpents launched at him, their trapjaw maws a pit of teeth framed with leathery frills that opened as they struck. Beasts that seemed all gulping mouth and stomach attempted to swallow him whole. Things that draped feathery tendrils about him from above burned both armour and flesh. Scaly monsters with shovel-shaped heads and clamping jaws that attempted to drag the Chaos warrior into their cave lairs.

Suddenly Archaon heard the shriek of his horse through the darkness. Taking the heads from humanoid things with snapping jaws and shells, Archaon scrambled across the slippery rock. Clipping tentacles and grasping appendages reaching from crevasses and grottos as he passed, Archaon slammed *Terminus* through the slimy skulls of serpents that slithered into his path. He saw the ghostly outline of his steed pinned to the cavern floor by some crustacean horror. The crab-beast was an armoured monstrosity of shell, chitinous legs and webbing between for the unholy creature's propulsion through the water. A nest of pearlescent eyes danced about on thick stalks while the beast went to work with the crushing pincers of its four muscular claws. Oberon shrieked its animal horror. The crab-beast had the horse clamped between the rocky floor and the bottom of its clickety body. The thing opened its chunk-claw above the terrified horse.

'No!' Archaon bawled, his announcement echoing about the caves.

Batting away one opportunistic claw with *Terminus,* Archaon ran at the beast, chopping the top half of a second pincer away with a savage flash of the broad blade. The thing reared horribly, allowing Oberon a hoof-scrabbling moment of hope, but the horse was still firmly held against the ground by the crab's shifting weight. A thick claw, as big as the Chaos warrior himself, swept in from behind, snatching his armoured form up in its crushing embrace. Archaon felt his plate buckle and mail split under the cleaving pressure. It was a second crab-beast, bigger than the first and intent on stealing the colossal crustacean's prize. Turning *Terminus* about in his gauntlets, Archaon smashed the blade down through the chitinous crux of the claw in which he was clamped. Twisting the blade through the meat and sinew of the claw's inner workings, the dark templar felt the beast release him. Dropping between the creatures, Archaon found his shrieking steed beside him. It was straining its neck to be free and Archaon laid a gauntlet on the horse's nose before turning his attentions back to the monstrosities battling pincer and claw above them.

Plunging his crusader blade into the second creature's exposed belly, Archaon sawed through the softer shell, opening the creature up from below. It was slow to react but when the beast realised that half of its innards were trailing across the craggy floor, it withdrew behind its snapping claws. As the tips of crushing pincers glanced off the dark templar's sword, Archaon worked his way within the beast's feverish grasp. With a sweep of the blade Archaon took the monster's eyes from their twitchy stalks, blinding the thing. *Terminus* crashed down through the chitin, breaching the shell. Another cleaving swing over the Chaos warrior's head broke through the thing's armour and mulched what passed for its primitive brain. Taking a moment to catch his breath, Archaon dragged the tip of his messy blade along the rocky floor of the cave. Oberon had stopped shrieking. The horse was dead. Its thick, muscular neck was now just a bloody stump. The stallion's magnificent head lay a little distance away. The crab-beast had sheared through its neck with one chunk-claw and discarded the animal's head.

Archaon felt the searing heat of fury run through his veins like lava. He charged the monster who had already started picking flesh from the carcass. Smashing two claws aside with his great sword he chopped an insistent third from an armoured appendage. Leaping up off the stallion's body and from one of the monstrosity's scuttling legs, Archaon heaved down on *Terminus*, his gauntlets hanging from the crossbars and his weight driving the broad blade down through the crab-beast's shell like a spear. The blade slid straight through the creature and Archaon hung there for a moment as the clicking stopped and the creature's limbs dropped and fell still.

Tearing *Terminus* from the butchered crustacean, Archaon settled down on one armoured knee beside the dead steed. His steed. Oberon had been there through it all. His training as a knight. His life as a templar. He had followed the Chaos warrior north to his doom and had survived the insanity of the Wastes. He laid a gauntlet on the horse's scarred flesh. Archaon felt a strange warmth wash through his chest. It was an alien sensation, feeling like some kind of illness or infirmity. A remembered weakness. He had killed so much and cared so little for so long that he had forgotten his affection for the stallion. It was hard to believe that the pair of them would never ride again.

Archaon moved his hand across the beast's still warm hide and through part of its midnight mane.

'Thanks for always being there,' Archaon managed. He looked up. He sensed hunger in the darkness. Creatures were closing in. They smelled carrion. Hot blood, freshly spilled and horseflesh. They would pay for their curiosity. The dark templar pushed himself to his feet. Oberon was dead but he was still alive. The killing had to continue.

Archaon cut, hacked, stabbed, sliced and smashed his way through the relentless onslaught of nightmares. Dripping with ichor and crunching through shattered shell and bone, Archaon fought them. He saw them slither and crawl at him, thinking he was blind to their advance, that he was easy prey. The emaciated creatures of the deep paid for their cruel instincts. Archaon cast their ugliness in the darklight of his being. He turned with speed and bloody assurance, cleaving claws, tentacles and wicked appendages from beasts who in turn were defenceless without them. The dark templar buried *Terminus* in the grim, fishy flesh of the sea monstrosities about him, opening the beasts up and filling the dank air with the foul odour of the depths. Soon Archaon was taking the fight to the beasts, slaying the warped, the scaly and the spined as they fed on the banquet of dead monstrosities about the Chaos warrior. Ravenous creatures feasting on each other's foetid flesh, allowing Archaon to move through them, indiscriminately ending beasts lost in their own gluttony.

Standing in the thick murk, his chestplate rising and falling with the efforts of dealing death, Archaon stopped. Salty gore dripped from his plate and chunks of gloopy flesh dribbled from *Terminus*. The shallows gathered about him as freezing glacial waters climbed the bedrock foundations of the floating fortress and flooded the cave systems that riddled its buoyant architecture. With the slaughter sinking into the freezing waters, the monstrosities retreated. Their element called to them – as did freedom – and they could smell the scent of easier prey flailing and bleeding in the waters outside the caverns. Washing the ichor from his armour and shield, Archaon sheathed and shouldered his weaponry and started to climb. He was certain his prize lay in the dark citadel above. Every crag, handhold and cutting purchase took him closer to it.

The agonising ascent took him up the rocky sides of midnight chambers, through the abandoned grottos of fled monsters and up an abyssal dropshaft that weaved its crooked way through other cave systems and the inky vastness of open caverns. The climb was murderous. The rock was like obsidian. All edges were sharp and surfaces greasy. The drops were dizzying – even in darkness – and the Chaos warrior had to risk heavy leaps of faith across razor-sharp chasms he could barely see.

As his body burned with the unending exertion of the climb, Archaon's hands felt the crumbling architecture of crafted stone. It was ancient and came apart in his fingers. It lacked the twisted angularity of the cave rock below and before long the dark templar found himself in the pulverised foundations of the druchii citadel. Staring about the lightless environs and heaving himself onto a precarious ledge, Archaon found he was in a dungeon, out of which the bottom had fallen. The stones about the dungeon walls – the ones the knight was perched exhausted upon – were the only ones to remain. Something attracted Archaon's attention immediately. A door of black metal set in the opposite wall. It wasn't the mouldering metal of the ancient door or the shattered stone about it that held the Chaos warrior's gaze. Between the dungeon door and the floor, Archaon could see a darklight that was not his own. A powerful evil lay in the passageways and chambers beyond. One so potent and pervasive that its darkness reflected off the walls and about the corners of the labyrinth in which it sat like the light and heat of a blinding inferno.

Standing and edging carefully around the loose flagstones about the edge of the chamber, Archaon found himself before the entrance. He could feel the dark radiance through the metal of the door, even though the metal of the door itself was cool. Levelling his armoured shoulder against the ancient metal, Archaon heaved at the door. He would not be denied. Not this close to his prize. Not this close to the Altar of Ultimate Darkness. With some surprise, the dark templar went straight through the door. The dungeon door did not open. Its locks were firmer in their resolve than the door's constitution and the black metal disintegrated about the warrior.

Shrugging off the splintered shards of withered metal, Archaon brought up his gauntlet to shield his eyes. Even in a corridor of simple, black stone – like many that made up the dungeon vaults of the *Citadel of Spite* – Archaon found the brilliance of the darkness blinding. The walls were saturated with the sheer malevolence of the treasure the labyrinth contained. Its darklight shone off the floor, the stone and the walls. It burned to stare upon. He closed his eye but it made no difference. There was no blinding glare to block with a squinting lid. The socket of his other eye, covered in its black leather patch and within his helmet, could not be closed to such wonder. It saw the darkness of all the world. A truth that could not be seen to be believed. The shard of stone within his skull bled its warping potential throughout the Chaos warrior's mind. A growl erupted from the dark templar's chest. Something savage and animalistic. Like food, drink, physical gratification or to breathe, Archaon needed the evil beyond. It sang to him, blazing into his being with its scarring potency. He hungered for it. He lusted for it. He began to realise that he would simply die without it.

Blinded though he was, Archaon sensed movement in the oblivion. He grunted the barbaric acknowledgement of an enemy. Many enemies. The labyrinth was swarming with the hunchbacked, the flesh-smeared, the shambling, the fang-faced and formed that were impaled on their own bones. Here were the druchii. The slaves. The unfortunates taken with the *Spite* by the unnatural storm. The miserable army of wretches that Dravik Vayne had left behind. The soul-ravaged remnants of dark elf corsairs and the *Citadel*'s legion of slaves. They only knew allegiance to the altar now. The Altar of Ultimate Darkness that Vayne had recovered and transported across the ocean for his power-hungry Hag Queen. Its corrupting influence had spread throughout the dungeon decks, the caverns below and the crew towers above. It had drawn them all to it. It had made mindless acolytes of them, twisting their minds beyond depravity and into the unknowing savagery of oblivion. Naked in their barbarity, their skin bleached to transparency by the darkness, they knew only that an interloper had entered the labyrinth. That the interloper was a threat to their mind-scalding shrine. That the interloper had to be torn apart. Groaning where mouths would still allow, the troglodytes lurched and shambled into one another, choking the passageways with their malformed number.

Not unlike the army of unfortunates swarming about him, Archaon grunted with brute intention. He needed to kill. They needed to die. It was agony to hold the simple sense it made in his head. Archaon drew *Terminus*. Any remaining essence of the God-King's intentions for the blade were gone. It had been forever polluted. Like Archaon, it was being re-forged in the fiery darklight. Like a furnace, the labyrinthine sanctum that housed the Altar of Ultimate Darkness – blazing with the abyssal radiance of immaculate evil – was remaking them both. The crusader blade burned no longer with the torment of its godly service. The sword was swathed in a bloody flame. It seethed in silence. It gave itself, its cleaving edge, the profanity of its pommel and the upturned smile of its cross-guard over to the darkness it had once fought. The blade had turned. Archaon smiled with his weapon. It spread to the insanity of a death-drunk grin.

The troglodytes chattered with their needle teeth. They drooled in the darkness. Bones broke as withered, claw-like limbs were brought to readiness. Archaon ran at them, his steps shattering the black stone beneath his boots. His roar sent great cracks and splits through the sanctum walls. He slammed into the freakish horde with his shield. No one troglodyte was his equal. Their twisted frames were lank and light. The passage was wall to wall with groaning bodies and the first few ranks of wretches were just smashed into oblivion by the sheer force. Skeletons shattered. Heads and malformed organs burst like ripe fruit. Archaon pushed at the mess. The floor became slick with blood and the dark templar skidded. There were simply too many troglodytes. Their obscene carcasses were crammed into the corridor and flesh and bone would give no more. Like a wave of misshapen flesh they rolled up behind the Chaos warrior. Within moments they were everywhere. Clawing, tearing finger-talons. Biting needle-jaws. Bludgeoning limbs that ended in bone growths. Emaciated arms and legs that stamped and strangled with a madman's strength. They were before him. They were behind him. Those Archaon put on the floor still ripped at his legs, eager to find flesh through the plate and mail. Others hooked their way up his back and tore at his face and helm. The dark templar became lost in the blinding evil, adrift in a sea of corrupted flesh.

He punched his blade through the horrid creatures and smashed them into the walls and floor with the unrelenting force of his shield. He smashed through skulls with the pommel of the greatsword and butted druchii malforms into a brain-splattered mess with his helmet. The dark templar pushed on through the labyrinth, feeling his way not only through the carnage but along the walls. Every junction was an agony. A wrong turn would mean minutes more of meaningless slaughter. The knight's darksight didn't abandon him, though. Although it was soul-razing to look upon, Archaon forced himself to stare into the blinding glare of doom reflected off the walls. Where the mind-scalding radiance was brightest, Archaon made his bloody path.

The sea of bodies kept rolling in like a tide. Archaon was unyielding but step by step, death by merciless death, the gibbering droves wore him down. The thrust of his arm wouldn't falter. His legs would stomp on through the meat at his feet. He would never surrender to the horde – even in their combined strength, tearing at him like a single creature of innumerable arms, claws and jaws. The troglodytes tore at the dark templar, their sharp nails like hooks in his armour and flesh. They wrenched pieces of plate from his body. They ripped his mail to shreds. The padding of his doublet became rags in their clutching, filthy claws. Archaon's shield – bearing the Ruinous Star of the Chaos pantheon united – was torn from his arm and *Terminus* was taken from his blood-slick grip by the unrelenting throng.

This did not stop the Chaos warrior. Fumble-fighting his way through the darkness, he was shrine-blind. He was without weapons, without armour, naked as a newborn and sliced to ribbons. But Archaon fought on. Dripping with blood – his own and everyone else's – he used his fists, his feet, his knees, his elbows and his head to beat the monstrosities about him to death. He wrestled the troglodytes for their lives, breaking necks and spines, tearing withered limbs from their sockets and wrenching deformed skulls from torsos. He screamed his sacrifice to the sanctum ceiling and punched through ribcages to rip feeble hearts from malformed chests. He didn't know where he was. Darkness had become his world and the blinding darklight of the altar was everywhere. Bodies carpeted the floor beneath his bare feet. The walls and surrounding architecture were wet with blood. Archaon became an infernal instrument of decimation. Some of the creatures he just broke to hear the chorus of their suffering. Others he killed quickly. Mindlessly. A number he played with, allowing them hope before cruelly finishing them. He savoured the rest, enjoying their victimhood and the last gasps of their worthless lives. His guiding star – his star of Ruination – was always the end of all. His limbs felt like lead. His mind was overcome with his dark purpose. His heart thundered beneath the sliced flesh of his chest.

Suddenly there were no more. There was nothing left to kill. It was a shock. Archaon grabbed out at the darkness – to make sure that there was nothing left hiding or cowering in the shadows. Archaon stumbled through the butchered bodies and fell against a stone column. The column was slick with spilled blood. On it Archaon's bruised fingertips traced a symbol carved into the stone. He stared at the column as hard as he could but blinded by the absolute blackness in which he sat and the darklight all about him he could make out nothing. All he had was what he could feel. The bloody steam rising from his aching body. The air thick with the stench of fresh death. The stone beneath his gore-stained fingers. He knew the symbol instantly. It had been worn with dark pride by those he had fought and killed in the Wastes and those that had joined him in the killing.

He stumbled across from the column and fell, almost braining himself on another. It bore the horror of another symbol. Another expression of another dark god, commanding followers in the Wastes and beyond. Archaon crawled through the bodies, eager to confirm the terrible picture he held in his mind. He found more columns and more symbols. Four larger pillars, each bearing the dread symbols of the gods of Chaos. The four Ruinous Powers of Chaos. The four horrific forces in the world to which the lost and damned pledged their souls – each holding the others in delicate balance. The obelisks formed the four points of a star, the four tips of a cross, the four corners of a square. Between each one Archaon found other columns, further out from the original four, which bore a multitude of other symbols – some the dark templar recognised and some he did not. Renegade entities, daemon princes of Chaos, Dark Gods masquerading as the barbarian deities of other races. Archaon had found it. One of the dark treasures of Chaos. The Altar of Ultimate Darkness. Holding one of the obelisks in his filthy hands, Archaon lowered his head in exhaustion and subservience. The darkness denied him the horror and beauty of the shrine. The Altar of Ultimate Darkness was not meant to be seen. It was meant to be experienced. It was a means by which a mortal might achieve communion with the gods. Its medium was darkness. And blood. About him Archaon heard the ooze and thick drip of blood from the bodies he had butchered. He had reconsecrated the dark altar without even realising it.

Archaon got unsteadily to his feet. He glowered into the blackness. He saw only darkness. He heard only blood. He waited but nothing happened. His glower dropped to a smile of madness that swiftly became a snarl.

'This unholy quest is complete,' Archaon announced to oblivion. 'Now give me what you owe me, you abominable wretches…'

Archaon was suddenly struck from all sides by powerful bolts of dark energy that seared from the tips of the columns. The experience was beyond pain. Beyond feeling. Archaon roared and thrust his fists at the ceiling. The energies crackled across his flesh, burning the hair from his head and his body. The darkness sizzled over his skin, cauterising gashes and open wounds. The bolts of energy lanced through his mind and met in the dark templar. He felt the shard of wyrdstone rattle horribly in his skull. He felt his scalp burn where the energies seared into him, creating an eight-point crown of pain and black-scarring around his hairless head. Archaon felt the presence of darkness within him. His soul howled at the centre of damnation's storm, being torn this way and that, but never straying from the serenity within the swirling havoc of dark voices, dreams and feelings that enveloped his being. He felt the darkness change him, as the height of the sun in the sky transformed the day into dusk and the dead of night into the dawn.

Then as quickly as it had begun, the magnificent ordeal was over. Archaon was on his knees surrounded by corpses. His flesh was the bronze of dried blood. His body ached with the agony of battle. He trembled with power and potential undreamt of. The gods of Chaos were with him. They had blessed the venture that was his life of death. They had scarred their union into him: eight black, ever-smouldering marks, charred around his head like a Ruinous crown.

Archaon pushed himself up and stumbled through the bodies. He fell from the Altar of Ultimate Darkness and clawed his way through the carnage to the wall. With his back to the overpowering evil of the blinding darklight of the shrine, he walked away with all the strength he could muster. He walked through the ruined sanctums, through the labyrinthine slave pits and the citadel underbarbicans. He felt his way along sharp passageways and through chambers of black stone. He met no opposition. He had killed all who had haunted the *Citadel of Spite*'s corrupted architecture.

Grasping the slender bars of a warped and wicked portcullis, Archaon flung it up into the stone of the gate it barred. He strode through the archway, feeling the bite of the cold night air on his naked flesh. At first the gloom coming off the surrounding mountains and the searing stars in the open sky dazzled him. As his eye adjusted from the absolute darkness of the floating fortress's inner sanctums to the twilight outside, he wandered across the stone deck. Towers reared above him, colossal and crooked, challenging the mountain peaks for supremacy. Beyond, Archaon could hear the slosh of water and the clash of ice. Beneath the soles of his feet he could feel the gentle sway of the floating fortress – ever so slightly. As the glacier had melted and rampaged through the valleys, building in strength and volume, the *Spite* had started to rise on its freezing waters. Between the natural buoyancy of the cavern-riddled foundations of the floating fortress and the dark magics re-awoken by its baptism in the calamitous body of water forming about it, the jagged keel-ridge of the floating fortress had almost cleared the valley floor.

Reaching the black stone battlements of the *Citadel*, Archaon looked down at the glossy, berg-choked waters that crashed along the druchii vessel. He then looked up the mountain slopes. The valley floor was gone. As were the bodies of the Hag Queen's druchii army and Gorath's Bloodsworn marauders. They had long been washed through the mountains and out towards the nearby western coast of Naggaroth. In the valley's place was the broad, flowing course of a meltwater river. It was black with depth and white with shattered ice. On the mountainside nearby, the forest was ablaze. Archaon could see his army camped out on the water's edge, above the snowline. Dravik Vayne had ordered the great pines and firs of the mountainside cut for huge bonfires. Even from the towering deck of the *Spite*, Archaon could see that victory over the druchii and the Bloodsworn had resulted in a celebratory mood. There was drinking, eating and the enjoyment of the fires. There was a union among Archaon's army of the apocalypse that the dark templar had never known.

He stood and watched for a minute before spotting Vayne, his sorceress and his corsairs down by the new shoreline. By the raging meltwater, Sularii and the Brothers Spasskov inspected the Tzeentchian's sorcerous handiwork. Further along the shore, Archaon could see a line of armoured figures, kneeling and frozen in the snow. The battered remnants of Gorath the Ravager's Bloodsworn knights – infernal warrior contraptions that had sunk in the glacial waters and slowly marched their way to shore to find their leader dead and their allegiance transferred. Archaon could see that Vayne was taking no chances with the clockwork knights and had them under his Slaaneshi guard. The corsair-captain himself paced the snowy shore, not taking his eyes off his beloved *Spite*. When he finally saw his warlord and master standing at the battlements and looking down upon the encampment, the dark elf's laughter echoed up and down the mountainsides. He clapped his hands in grinning approval before picking up Sularii and savagely kissing the sorceress.

'I told you he would do it,' Dravik Vayne laughed. He called up at Archaon. 'Permission to come aboard!'

As Vayne's carrying jubilation drew the eyes of the celebrating army to the *Spite*'s towering battlements, as marauders, beastmen and Chaos warriors saw their general's blood-drenched form, horns were sounded, swords and shields were clashed and a roar of supremacy rose to meet him.

'Permission granted,' the Chaos warlord told them.

CHAPTER XIV

'Always know that you know nothing...'
'The Way of the Kyu-Shinobi is the way of death unseen, proceeding from every darkness and shadow...'
'Even monkeys sometimes fall from the trees...'
'The arts of death did not fail you – know that it was not the art that failed – it was you...'
'Victory is ever in your grasp – even if you fail to achieve it...'

– Dark Empress Shotoko of the Invisible Army,
from *The Nine Disciplines of the Kyu-Shinobi*
(Trans: *The Bloody Pool of Myriad Rivers Merging*)

The Saturnine Sea
The Great Eastern Ocean
Vermintide

And so Archaon headed out across the expanse known as the Great Eastern Ocean. It rivalled the Wastes or the Steppes beyond the

Worlds Edge Mountains for its mind-breaking endlessness. Dark, choppy seas gave way to glassy waters. Land was a rare treat.

The *Spite* kept no log. No records of where the floating fortress and its growing corsair flotilla had been or where it was going. The weather changed so regularly that there was little point in following its fickle nature in ink. The floating fortress crashed through intruding ice, struggled through furious squalls and cut across the crystal calm of sun-scorched seas. With the ocean so vast and open and the heavens so changeable, it became difficult to keep track of time. The sun did rise and set but the days ran into one another like paint on canvas.

Like Father Dagobert with his torturous translations of *The Liber Caelestior*, the floating fortress and its flotilla of captured vessels pushed on into the unknown. Brooding in his throne, atop the *Spite*'s tallest tower, scope in hand, Archaon would have the priest read the insanity to him. It didn't make much sense to the Chaos warrior. Dagobert – the portly priest wrapped up in his moth-eaten furs – was never without the damned tome. His wild, grey hair draped both his fat face and the book over which he was perpetually hunched, creating a private booth for his distractions. The mind-twisting translations had driven him to madness and back, at some times convincing the priest that he knew everything and at other times that he knew nothing. When Archaon's anger got the better of him – threatening to pitch both the tome that toyed with his existence and the priest translating it over the tower battlements – it took Giselle's entreaties and distractions to calm him. In less dangerous moods, Dagobert tried to placate the dark templar with analogies and comparisons. He told Archaon *The Celestine Book of Divination* was very much like the telescope through which he scanned oceans and his future the horizon. He insisted that the same spot in the distance might appear very different from different approaches or through the perversities of changing light and weather. This did not please the Chaos warlord any more.

Archaon's destiny ate away at him. He had achieved the first treasure of the Chaos gods and had been blessed with their Mark. As the years passed and he made the ocean his own, Archaon noticed the changes such a blessing had brought him. Like an animal, his senses had grown keen. He smelled the fear in those about him. His teeth had grown sharp and his tongue tasted his impending victories on the air. He could hear the blood gush through his enemies' veins.

Staring hard enough, he could see through the very flesh of his opponents. He could see the horror of their innards and the exposed vulnerabilities their weakling bodies presented. He could see the cracks of former breakages in bone, the positions of organs hiding within cages of rib, hearts that beat like entrancing targets. His own muscle and sinew was taut – like a spring-loaded trap – making his attacks savage, blistering in speed and frenzied in execution.

Within, Archaon was like cold stone. His own doubts and fears were afterthoughts. Every action had the full commitment of body, mind and soul. Every stab and sweep of his sword was blessed with boldness. He believed he had overcome every failing, every challenge, every enemy and like wings that belief took him far. Between his blade and their secret doubts, his enemies undid themselves before him. Archaon would entertain no fantasies of death, no delusions of grand failure. He walked, thought and killed with the assurance of a god, though unlike many of his calling, he had no aspirations to be one. Such figments of fancy were a weakness – and Archaon believed he had none.

Other changes were more physically obvious. Networks of blue veins appeared through his pallid flesh, forming insane patterns across the surface of his body. Showing Dagobert, the priest did not seem to know the dialect but the Brothers Spasskov recognised it instantly, telling Archaon that he was bleeding the incantations of ancient magical wards through his skin like a tattoo that covered his body. The warlord was suspicious but the sorcerers told him that it was a blessing from the gods – the veins and letters forming an enchantment, like a suit of ringmail beneath the surface of his skin.

When Archaon had his sword, shield and crusader armour recovered by Vayne's corsairs from the caves below the *Citadel*, they were all a mess. His battered shield was covered in sucker marks from a great squid beast he had fought and the greatsword *Terminus* was stained with gore. His plate was scratched and his chainmail in shreds. Upon reassembling the mess, he discovered that the suit of armour had an infestation. A cloud of tiny black flies – so tiny, they were all but impossible to make out individually. All attempts to rid the rank plate of the infestation failed. When still, the flies settled and accumulated on the armour, making Archaon one with the darkness in poor light. When the Chaos warrior moved, the disturbed flies formed a haze drifting about him like a miasma or black mist. In combat Archaon found that the mist distracted his enemies and masked some of his movements and evasions. Over time, the dark templar's intentions to rid himself of the infestation faded, adapting his ducks and weaves to the mist's movements.

Such gifts and adaptations made Archaon only hunger more for the treasures and blessings of Chaos. He was the chosen of the Dark Gods but not the Everchosen. Not general of the daemonic legions, not herald of the End Times and the coming apocalypse. Unlike the Altar of Ultimate Darkness that the *Citadel of Spite* carried within its depths, Father Dagobert's heretical volume said little about the location of his next treasure. All the priest could tell him from the twisted translations was that it was an ancient relic of infernal significance. The priest gleaned that the artefact was to be found in a tomb, in an undiscovered land, somewhere in the Great Eastern Ocean. It had been the torment of such details that had driven Archaon to adopt the life of a buccaneer. For years he had had warriors and captains chasing every clue and scrap of information regarding the treasure's nature, location and existence. Many failed to return, while others returned to the *Spite* with little more than their lives. In some of the warlord's most desperate moments he deprived them even of those, but most he simply sent off again in pursuit of some new intelligence or possibility.

Archaon had sent his marauders to their deaths in the jungles of Pahaulaxa, to the south sea islands of cannibal giants, the Hinterlands of Khuresh and the Witch seas of Naggaroth. His warbands plundered lost cities, put entire islands and their primitive civilisations to the flame and fought savage southerners of similar ilk and madness from the bottom of the world. Those that did return carried with them innumerable tales of lost treasures, cursed artefacts and lands of the lost. There was little to narrow Archaon's miserable search. Poring over maps recovered with enemy ships, ancient scraps, charts and improvised scribblings, Archaon discovered nothing that would tell him of the treasure's location. The Chaos warrior thought he might go mad.

For a year or two, insanity did indeed prevail and the ocean ran red with the blood the warlord spilled in mortification. Every sign of civilisation sighted through the warlord's scope was destroyed. Coastlines were ravaged. Forests were torched. Ancient city-ports were turned to sunken rubble. Lone vessels, convoys and fleets were attacked on sight. Crews were butchered and ships blasted from the waves. Archaon's armada left thousands of bone-littered wrecks in its wandering wake. Portly merchantmen and greatships from the west; slavers, pirates, raiders and marauders; flotillas of oriental and druchii designation.

Archaon became the terror of the Eastern Ocean. The Dragon Emperor despatched fleets of mighty war junks to destroy Archaon's armada after Heyang was sacked and burned. The druchii corsair kings of the Broken Lands called him the Red Death. The Hobgobbla Khan slavehulks avoided the Chaos armada like a plague, while the actual plaguefleet of Papa Feste failed to bring the guns of his bloated galleons on Archaon on several occasions. Both the maritime empires of the Man-Chu marauders and the Nipponese pirates of the Kironshima Wan swore blood oaths on Archaon's end. The cannibal civilisations of volcanic island chains in their skull-adorned catamarans and outriggers prayed to their fire gods for aid against Archaon's dread fleet while the lizard men of Hexoatl and the Emerald Empire sacrificed each other to Tzunki and their Old Ones to rid them of the raiding warlord.

Dravik Vayne and the armada's Chaos lieutenants knew they had lost their master to madness the day he left aboard a flotilla of recently recruited junk-raiders with their defecting Man-Chu crews for company. The *Spite* had sighted a clanfleet bearing the markings of the Eshin. Vayne had told Archaon it was a trap and that the skaven assassins of the Ind and the Lords of Decay had long plotted his downfall. This did not sway the mindless warrior, who sailed straight into the brown, stinking filth that was the Saturnine Sea and the fleet of fat, filthy dhows waiting there. The verminships were armed with cannons that projected unnatural flame that set many of Archaon's black junk-raiders ablaze. The dhows were also swarming with skaven decked in the black headdress and rag robes of warrior-assassins. Bare-pawed and armed with an assortment of curved sabres, cleaver falchions and kris-blades – each glazed with all manner of exotic poisons – the creatures were nimble and trained in the low arts of death. The clanships vomited forth skaven in such number – swimming, swinging and leaping from their fat vessels – that Archaon's flotilla of marauder junk-raiders was swiftly swamped with Eshin vermin.

Vayne knew better than to disobey his master's orders but when the flotilla didn't return, the corsair-captain set a course for the brown miasma that was the Saturnine Sea on the horizon. The effluent waters bobbed with the corpses of Man-Chu raiders and ratmen alike, many bearing the trademark butchery of the warlord, both enemy and ally. Vayne considered it unlikely that despite being new additions to the armada, the piratical raiders of the Man-Chu would turn on Archaon. Vayne had every flaming wreck and piece of wreckage searched. They found him in the belly of a verminship. The vessel was listing badly and still aflame. Within they discovered their lord amongst a tangled nest of dead assassins. The ratmen had been broken, smashed and gutted. Some of their death-smeared weapons had found their mark, however. Archaon had been cut and stabbed by the assassins but had fought his way to bloody victory. Vayne found him still smashing what remained of a skaven's skull into the hull of the verminship with groaning insistence – the victim of some murderous delirium.

'Secure the ship,' Vayne told Archaon's Swords as the grim sentinels stood over their crazed master. When Eins and Zwei didn't move, Vayne pushed, 'The master will want the wonder of the ratmen's cannons at his command. This hulk is going down. Have the vessel jury-rigged for return to the *Spite*'s drydocks in accordance with your overlord's wishes as well as his wellbeing.'

Taking a moment to demonstrate their displeasure, the silent Swords left the site of degenerate massacre and attended to the skaven ship. The sorceress Sularii watched them go, flanked by a pair of Vayne's druchii corsairs. As the winged warriors left, excitement cut through the mask of dour concern that sat on her sharp features.

'Are we going to do it?' the sorceress asked.

Vayne allowed himself a wolfish smile.

'There'll never be a better time,' the dark elf captain told her, stepping daintily through the carnage, limbs and dismembered bodies. He turned to the corsairs. 'Go. Watch the Swords. Ensure they are distracted with the doom of this vessel.'

The druchii nodded. The corsairs nodded and left to attend to their duties of subversion and sabotage. Archaon moaned as what remained of the skaven's skull disintegrated in his hands. He looked up at Vayne and his sorceress with an unseeing eye. He wasn't blood-drunk. This was no blessing or affliction of the Blood God. Quite the opposite. He was lost in a storm of sensual savagery. A storm of the corsair-captain's arrangement. The experience was more than a gift from the lieutenant and his Prince of Pleasure. It was a dreamy distraction. The air was muggy with death and the passion that had brought about such endings.

Vayne soaked up his master's ecstatic sufferings. He knelt down behind the warlord, laying his slender hands on the Chaos warrior's shoulders. He leant in to Archaon's ear. The chosen of Chaos seemed not to know he was there. His neck spasmed and his head twitched in some private heaven of his murderous making. Vayne kissed the brawn of Archaon's blood-speckled neck and nibbled at his master's ear.

'I wish I could be in there with you,' he hissed lasciviously. Turning his head, for a moment, it seemed that the warlord had understood him.

'Dravik...' Sularii warned, coming up behind the corsair-captain and needling the druchii's shoulders with her own dagger-sharp nails. The realisation that Archaon might not be as lost in his never-ending moment of bliss as first thought sent a thrill of horror through the dark elves. The Chaos warrior could snatch for his heretical blade – buried in the muscle-bound body of some rat monster half-breed – and end them for their treacheries. 'Dravik...' Sularii groaned, sensing the imminence of her end. Even the prospect of her death excited the dark elf sorceress. Archaon seemed to be fighting the deviancies he was experiencing. A snarl wrinkled its way through his lip. The warlord had been locked in the sensual sanctum of his own mind and Dravik Vayne had thrown away the key. Taking his face in the digits of his willowy fingers, the druchii leant in and kissed the chosen of darkness, the chosen of the Ruinous Powers and now the sole chosen of Slaanesh.

'Dravik...' Sularii moaned once more. The sorceress ached for her captain. It was his genius that had led them to this. To the darkness below the *Citadel* and a shrine of Chaos unseen. Blind to both the dangers of treason and the blood-drenched altar before which he kneeled, Dravik Vayne – champion-subject of Slaanesh – had run his fingers over the symbols and sigils crafted into the erotic suggestion of the shrine's stone. The Prince of Pleasure had promised him such raptures. Such satisfactions. Such sorrows. Gone were notions of fearful allegiance. The Ruinous Powers unified in one goal and behind one champion. The god-serpent that had him in the snaking, crushing coils of euphoria had whispered secrets to the dark elf's soul. That Archaon the Chosen was a false prophet of darkness. That Slaanesh did not share glory. Slaanesh the Selfish. Slaanesh the Craving. That the Hag Queen of all Naggaroth was but the Prince of Pleasure's concubine. That she would be Dravik Vayne's also and see him to the Witch King's throne.

'Dravik...'

The serpent promised him such wondrous things. Arousing within him appetites unknown. The depths of bottomless greed. Lust for absolute power. The serpent wounded him with taunts and accusations. It laughed through the echo of his excuses and passed water on his pride. The Prince of Chaos told him that above this Altar of Ultimate Darkness lay a vessel that was his to command alone and an army that awaited enslavement. Above lay a legend to be claimed, that Archaon's great accomplishments could become his own. That in a death claimed, the Chaos warlord and his infamy would become Vayne's own. Dravik Vayne – corsair, captain and champion of Slaanesh. Slayer of slayers. Averter of the World's End. The times would not be Archaon's to end – for without the endless pleasures of the world and time to enjoy them, there would be no need for a prince to champion them.

'Dravik...'

The bright rising star that was Archaon's soul would belong to Slaanesh. He would not be fought or brought to battle. Such delusions were suicide. Rather than face the certain slaughter of Archaon's sword, Vayne had used the blade against him. The corsair-captain had his sorceress – who was not without skill in outlandish potions and poisons – concoct an intoxicant of power and potency.

Without wanting to risk discovery in the poisoning of his overlord's meat or wine, or the swift death that would come of spilling even a single drop of his master's unholy blood with bane-smeared needle-knife or stiletto blade, Vayne decided on *Terminus* as the mode of deathly transmission. At opportunity and in secret, Vayne massaged the metal of the weapon with Sularii's intoxicant. A poison of the soul, it moved quickly through the blood. With every foe that fell beneath the blade, the intoxicant spread, entering the unfortunate victim on the sword and infecting their blood with an unthinking ecstasy. Each soul in such taking became the Prince of Pleasure's own. As Archaon finished his infected foes with skill and economic butchery, he breathed the blood of the fallen that hung on the air like a red mist in the warlord's murderous wake. Speck by speck, droplet by airborne droplet, Vayne found a way through the Chaos warrior's considerable defences without even having to lift a blade of his own. Day by day and death by death, Archaon fell into the Prince of Pleasure's embrace. He became a degenerate. A wanton savage. Moaning the incomprehension of what was happening to him. Insensible to everything but the murderlust of his flesh's own fire, Archaon fell from the certitude of his apocalyptic path and into an exultant bliss.

Dravik Vayne had been an adoring follower of both Khaine and the Prince of Chaos. He was a lover rather than a fighter. He was not some bludgeoning champion of the Blood God or the Ruinous Star, mindlessly swinging his weapon like a woodcutter at the trunks of trees in a forest without end. His talents lay in the glories of murder. In the taking of a life before his foes knew that it had even been lost to them. So it was with his master Archaon.

'Dravik…'

And it was done. The corsair's wicked dagger had passed through Archaon's throat as though it were rancid butter. Blood gushed between them, splashing Vayne's neck and scale armour with the heat of his master's blood. The druchii pulled his lips from those of the warlord. The snarl was gone. Archaon didn't grab for the grievous wound or rise and stumble for help. He sat there in the gore of others, in gore of his own pooling about him. Allowing. Accepting. Enjoying. He grinned like a lust-drunk idiot. The Prince of Pleasure's glorious torments waited for him beyond a necessary death. Archaon willed it on. Waiting. Wanting. As Archaon died before them, Vayne and the sorceress became lost in their own pleasures. The Chaos warrior was barely aware of the pair as they rolled through the blood and carnage about him. He was lost in death-raptures of his own. The end was coming.

Perhaps I chose unwisely? There is time. There is time, before the end. To start again. To twist the destinies of men unborn and create calamities of my own making. Perhaps the failure is in my blood, forever to repeat itself. Ambition that is blind unto itself. Treachery. Murder. The service of the Ruinous Powers accomplished through the service of the self? The dark nectar of the gods. But in whose service is my pawn? My gods? My daemon need? Doom, plain and simple it seems. His own. And the doom of all else. What kind of corruption is this? What kind of perversity? Nothing I slipped into the ripe fruit of his soul. No blessing he was given by my abyssal overlords. Not my patrons. Not my princely foes. It is a kind of mortal madness. What kind of man lives not for the gifts of greed – for power, for supremacy and eternity? What kind of man exists only to end all other forms of existence? Cannot a man's future be corralled? Must it buck the saddle, the chains and halters of fate? This soul must be tamed. But not by me. As we all come to learn, the best lessons are those taught to us by our enemies.

CHAPTER XIV

'To be the hammer or the anvil. Destiny affords only these choices.'

– Khureshi proverb

The Hellespont
The Great Eastern Ocean
The Festival of Ghosts – Year of the Jackal

'You're awake.'

Archaon was. It was a statement, but in the accent sounded like a question. Through the haze of a befuddled mind, the Chaos warrior thought it sounded like a celestial or easterner. Archaon began to fade. A slap across the face brought him back to consciousness. He grabbed at the wrist to which the hand belonged and found it to be spindly and ancient, but possessing great strength for such a withered limb. He tore the wrist back from the Chaos warrior's grasp. 'You have slept enough,' the ancient told him.

Rubbing the crusty confusion from his eye, all Archaon could see was a ghoulish blue light. It faded. Then there was movement. Bodies. Rippling skin. Writhing bodies. Archaon kicked back across the rocky floor and found that but for his eye-patch, he too was naked. His mind raced to catch up. He didn't know where he was or what was happening. Then, in the eerie blue light that illuminated the cave, he recognised the horrific mass. It was the Fleshstorm – the spawn that fought for the Brothers Spasskov, and by extension himself, when their disgusting talents were needed. Unfortunates of the Great Lord of Change, the Fleshstorm was a single morphing entity, made up of thousands of assimilated bodies. Bone creaked, snapped and fused into monstrous frames while the naked flesh of the spawn writhed and stretched, seamlessly melting into one another. Arms reached out for him, while faces pushed through the horror in silent screams. Some individual spawn managed to break free and slowly, painfully tried to crawl away. They were all mangled limb and insanity, however, and rarely got far before the Fleshstorm reclaimed and reabsorbed them.

Archaon's palms were suddenly wet. He had backed through something warm and slick on the cave floor. He turned and found his face splattered with the same disgusting residue. Archaon had been a slayer of men long enough to know the temperature and copper-tang of blood. Tearing flaps of dribbling flesh from his face and back, Archaon flung them back at the mound of flesh and innards he had backed through. In the blue light the pool of blood and butchery appeared purple and seemed to be dripping from the rocky ceiling above the mound. It appeared as though someone had exploded or been turned inside out.

'What in the Netherhell do you think you're doing?' the cracked, ancient voice complained. 'So surprised to see these monstrosities that fight in your name? Eh? These things of darkness you gather about you?'

Archaon grunted. He was not used to seeing their insides on display. He felt the bile rise up the back of his throat. The voice was intensely annoying – like a distant scream that would not end or a mosquito buzzing continuously beside the ear.

'Who are you?' Archaon demanded to know. 'Where are we? How did I get down here?'

'Questions,' the voice bounced about the cave. 'So many questions, Archaon – chosen of the Infernals, the Daemon-Emperors of the north, the greater darkness beyond the Great Bastion. Perhaps they gave their blessing too easily? Eh? Perhaps you were judged worthy before your time?'

'Show yourself!' Archaon roared, smearing blood from his eyes. He squinted into the intensity of the blue light. It seemed to be moving about the rocky chamber with an ungainly motion. Archaon walked straight into the blinding blueness and found the wizened silhouette of a hunchbacked old man. He grabbed the ancient by the neck, despite the intensity of the blue light emanating from his forehead. Lifting the man from his feet, one of which Archaon found to be scaly and clawed like the talon of a bird, he throttled the ancient, shaking him back and forth. The old man shrieked like a strangled hawk as his body bounced about like a bag of bones.

'Who are you?' Archaon demanded.

Suddenly the blinding blue light was gone, glowing and growing in another part of the cave. In his murderous grip Archaon held a thing of knotted bone, flesh stretched to transparency and multiple limbs like some kind of human spider. Of the ancient there was no sign. Archaon cursed. The ancient was some kind of sorcerer or magician. Tossing the useless spawn back into the mountain of morphing bodies, Archaon ran at the blue light. It was emanating from the wasted ancient, who was getting to his feet with difficulty after assuming the form of some misshapen thing that was crawling away from the Fleshstorm.

The multiple limbed horror shrivelled to the wizened torso and willowy arms and legs of the ancient. It was as though he had morphed into the unfortunate thing and assumed its flesh for his own form. He squawked in terror as Archaon kicked at him. Taking a second head clean off the spawn, the Chaos warrior snatched up a small boulder of black stone from the cave floor and heaved it above his head. The transformation now complete, Archaon beheld a shrivelled old man, squinting at him in fear from the floor. Like Archaon he was naked but for a brilliant blue jewel – an oval sapphire – that was embedded in the flesh of his forehead. Like a third eye, the jewel was shot through with a sliver of darkness at the heart of its blinding brilliance that made it appear like the eye of some great reptile or dragon. The sliver widened and the ghoulish glow from the gem dimmed while the ancient's wasted limbs waved out in front of him in panic. The old man was stuck – unable to roll away because of his hunched back.

'Who are you?' Archaon bellowed, the bludgeoning rock towering dangerously over the frail form of the old man. Disorientated and agitated like some tormented beast, Archaon was in no mood for games. He wanted answers or people would die.

'All right, all right, all right,' the ancient bleated. What was left of his long, grey hair and the lustrous strands of his moustache plastered his age-mottled skull. 'Help me.'

Archaon tossed the rock aside and took the old man by one gnarled and bony hand. The ancient dusted himself off, untangling his wrinkled head from his hair.

'Your name,' Archaon demanded.

'That is no way to treat your saviour,' the ancient told him, prompting Archaon to bring up his hand to strike the old man. 'All right, all right, all right.' The ancient bent down with difficulty to pick up a bone – a femur – from the floor. He scooped up some scraps of shredded clothing. Filthy rags littered the cave where the Fleshstorm had assimilated fresh unfortunates fed to it by the Brothers Spasskov. As he pulled the shredded Man-Chu robes over his mountainous hunch and his sharp bones, the femur grew in his hand to the length of a warped staff. Without effort, the blue sapphire simply popped from the ancient's forehead, without leaving a cavity or as much as a dimple in his flesh. Catching the glorious gem, he slotted the eye-gem into the crowning joint-crook of the bone. Archaon found the new dullness of its glow entrancing. The potent energy the jewel seemed to give off made him lightheaded.

'You are Sheerian…' Archaon said.

'I am Khezula Sheerian,' the ancient repeated.

Except he wasn't repeating anything. Archaon had the information moments before the sorcerer uttered it in his outlandish accent. The old man emphasised every syllable.

'Sheeriang,' Archaon said, but the ancient shook his head with swift anger and annoyance.

'I am Khezula Sheerian…' the sorcerer said. 'Not *Sheeriang,* you simpleton with your sharp teeth and bullock's tongue.'

'You are a daemon sorcerer…'

'I am daemon sorcerer of the Great Changer of Ways.'

The ancient's ugly squint proved even ghastlier with his attempt at a smile. 'Do not mind the Eye,' he said, shaking the glorious blue jewel in the head of the staff. 'It sometimes has that effect on the weak of mind. Like the spyglass, it sees far. Farther than you can possibly imagine. Like the spyglass up close, however, things can become distorted and disorientated.' Archaon was bewitched by the gem. Drawn to its unnatural power like a man to the spectral hopes and dreams for his future. Under Sheerian's control the gem dimmed further and the sorcerer knocked the tip of the staff – nestled jewel and all – against the Chaos warrior's head. Archaon blinked.

'Who are you?' Archaon demanded savagely. Sheerian shook his head and began mumbling curses in a language the dark templar did not understand. He walked away, leaning on the staff and dragging his bird's leg through the grit on the ground. He picked up some rags from the floor of the cave and threw them at the Chaos warrior.

'Cover yourself,' the ancient said, 'for the Great Changer's sake and the sake of his servants.'

'I mean,' Archaon said, anger at himself growing behind his fumbled words. '*Who* are you? What are you doing here? What am I doing here? What is happening?'

Sheerian silenced the dark templar's questions with a scowl and a flap of his bony fingers.

'I have watched you, chosen one,' Sheerian said. 'From afar. The Eye showed me both your victories and your failures. You would be Everchosen – champion of the Daemon Lords of the Great Northern Darkness. You would be herald of the apocalypse. Master of the End Times of both man and god.'

Archaon stared at the ancient as he hobbled about the cave. He tied the rags about his waist like some Darklands barbarian.

'I am he,' Archaon said.

'Did you not think you would face others who would covet such a prize?' Sheerian put to him.

'I have put a bloody end to many who harboured such false hopes,' the Chaos warrior uttered with pride.

'On the battlefield, yes?' the ancient sorcerer said. 'You are a mighty warrior – the Infernals would not doubt it, Archaon of the Western Empire, but there are many mighty warriors from which the Dark Gods of the world may choose their champion. You think that they were all going to come at you head on? Head on, the way you would face them in return. On the field of battle, you look for weaknesses to explore in your enemies' approach, no? Unprotected flanks? Breaks in formation? Overconfidence in the attack? Did you ever think that the most dangerous of your foes – your competitors for the Ruinous blessings of eternity – might come at you sideways, eh? That they might drop on you from the sky? That they might rise from the deeps?'

'Speak plainly,' Archaon warned. 'My patience wears thin with your convolutions.'

'Always rushing on ahead,' Sheerian said. 'Eager to be part of a future you are creating for yourself. Never spending the time to take stock. To consolidate your position before pushing on into the dangers ahead. It is why you have not seen this coming. It is why you are betrayed by those you would trust to prosecute your will. Why the army you have worked so hard to build will tear itself apart above us.'

'You speak lunacy, sorcerer,' Archaon said, but his voice lacked its usual booming assuredness.

Sheerian squinted at the gem, moving the headpiece of the staff about him and the chamber like some kind of precious crystalline lens.

'The Eye shows only the truth as it comes to pass,' the sorcerer said. 'If its distant reach shows lunacy then the world must be afflicted with such.'

'Enough of this,' Archaon spat and turned to walk away.

'There you go again,' said Sheerian. 'Into an unknown that will end you and bury your path to greatness. Wait!' As the ancient's screeching syllables bounced about the environs of the cave, Archaon slowed to a stop. 'This feverish need of yours to forge on has its uses but sometimes we need to be calm. We need to be patient. Even the servants of the Dark Gods can achieve a kind of peace. It is a peace you have never known, Archaon. It is why,' Sheerian went on, 'your treasures elude you.'

Archaon turned.

'What know you of the treasures of Chaos?' he said. He walked back towards the sorcerer. 'Have you seen them? Can this Eye of yours show the way?'

The Chaos warrior went to grab the bone staff but the sorcerer clutched it back. 'Do you see a land undiscovered?' Archaon demanded.

'An island, yes,' the Chaos sorcerer said. 'A great island of daemon savagery, reaching out across the blood-dark seas for you, chosen one.'

Archaon fell to his knees, blooding them on the cave floor. 'I have searched. In the name of the Dark Gods I have searched. Tell me...' he begged. He had searched so hard and for so long that it hurt to know that another possessed information perversely denied to him. 'Tell me, Sheerian, tell me.'

The sorcerer scowled at him. 'Like your enemies, this land you seek is everywhere and nowhere. Like your enemies, you will find this island where you least expect to.'

'Where?' Archaon boomed.

'Beneath…'

'Beneath what?' Archaon asked, his mind both murk and maelstrom. 'The water?'

'It has been beneath the water but also beneath the land,' the Tzeentchian sorcerer told him. 'Now it sits only beneath the heavens.'

'Curse your riddles, daemon,' Archaon growled. 'I must know. No more searching. Give me a course.'

Sheerian considered the warlord's request.

'You will discover this realm on a Black Meridian,' the daemon sorcerer told him. 'That is your course. My lord will grant you no more at this time. He is of most help to those who help themselves. Besides, you do not stop to ask the way as an earthquake steals the ground from beneath your feet,' Sheerian told him. 'Your enemies have moved and continue to move against you.'

'What know you of my enemies?' Archaon said, getting off his knees. 'All the world is my enemy.'

'You are more right than you know, Archaon the Chosen,' Sheerian said.

'I swear, sorcerer,' Archaon told the ancient, 'that if you afflict me with one more riddle, you shall pay for it with your miserable existence.'

'You have been betrayed, Chaos warrior.'

'By whom?'

'By friends old and new,' Sheerian told him. 'By your dark lieutenants, Archaon. By those closest to your damned pursuits, who in turn pursue damnation for their own ends. By those who would have you fail so that their own prospects be furthered in the eyes of the Dark Gods.'

'I am favoured,' Archaon told the ancient. 'I bear the Mark of the Ruinous Powers that burns like a star eternal in my flesh. I earned the allegiance of the dark god's servants. Does their betrayal not anger their daemon patrons?'

'Allegiance… betrayal,' the sorcerer said. 'These terms don't apply to the Infernals and their wretched servants. How often have you given some miserable minion your word that you would spare him before striking him down at your second thought?'

Archaon gave Sheerian a glower.

'Have you not – Archaon, Chosen of the Chaos gods – plotted the end of such Powers and those they would sponsor? Is your quest not the destruction of us all and the end of the entire world? Mortals? Daemons? Gods?' Sheerian cackled his excitement. Archaon burned into the sorcerer with his gaze. For a moment the Chaos warrior considered ending Sheerian right where the ancient stood.

'If you know I have,' Archaon said, 'then why ask me, you game-playing fool?'

'My Lord Tzeentch revels in such games,' Sheerian told him. 'He is their patron. Even of yours, ender of worlds.'

'You talk of friends and enemies, sorcerer,' Archaon said, tiring of the games Sheerian spoke of and those of his lord. 'What are you? How do you come to be here? I have never admitted you into the ranks of my host.'

'Are you sure, Chaos warrior?' the ancient cackled. 'You have not been yourself of late.'

'I think I'd remember you, Sheerian.'

'I am memorable,' Sheerian admitted. 'Those already shackled to your doomed quest have freed themselves. The shrine that showed you favour now favours others also. It corrupts hearts of men as it does the very stone of the citadels and towers under which it sits. Your champions have made their pilgrimage to the darkness and the Ruinous masters of that darkness have shown them their own ways – their own paths to greatness.'

'I fight for these false gods, these inconstant things of shadow...'

'Then you fight for false gods,' Sheerian agreed, 'and inconstant things of shadow. Accept that such Powers cannot be trusted – any more than you or I.'

'How many of my men have betrayed me?'

'Many.'

'Who amongst my champions and warlords?' Archaon demanded, 'must now die for their lack of vision?'

'At this very moment,' the sorcerer told him, squinting horribly through his sorcerous Eye, 'your army is at war with itself.' Sheerian gestured to the bloody mound of flesh that Archaon had crawled through earlier, the gore and scraps of flesh still dripping from the rocky ceiling. 'Your arch sorcerers petitioned their lord and mine for ways to destroy you.'

'The Brothers Spasskov...'

'You harnessed their sorcerous rivalry, Archaon,' Sheerian said, 'but then claimed their victories for your own. Gorath the Ravager. The warrior titans of the Red Mountain. The island of the enchantress

Thusula and her daemon daughters. Was it your blade that secured such achievements or the talents of your slave sorcerers? You think in the face of both your ignorance and success that the pair would not set aside their rivalries and remember their shared blood? The blood of brothers? Being of my lord's following, they were amongst the most capable of your lieutenants and you equipped them with the tools they required to overthrow you – wounded pride and the selfish ambition that infects such a wound. You gave them that. The rest was potential they already had.'

'Vladimir... Vladislav,' Archaon murmured, looking at the pile of ruined flesh. Then to the ancient, Archaon said, 'I have not been all that I could be.'

'No,' Sheerian agreed. 'You have not. You are a warrior, as brave and untrue as any that have already held the title Everchosen of the gods. But you are not ready to command the legions of darkness.' The sorcerer shook his brown-spotted head. 'No. Those daemons, those fiends would tear your soul to shreds.'

Archaon nodded slowly. The Chaos sorcerer's cackling accusations were an annoyance but a true one. The dark templar had fallen far and was paying for his shortcomings as a leader of darkness in the world.

'But I will be ready. One day. One day soon, sorcerer. These pretenders to my title will pay for their betrayal,' Archaon growled. 'As will the Dark Gods that sponsored them.'

Sheerian gibbered to himself. 'Yes, yes...'

'How were the brothers to usurp me?' Archaon asked, looking back to the mound of shredded flesh that was Vladimir and Vladislav Spasskov.

'Rituals and summonings,' the sorcerer said. 'They called upon my Lord Tzeentch to reveal to them the secrets of releasing the serpent spirit of the *Yien-Ya-Long* – a mighty beast of antiquity that once laid waste to Grand Cathay, riding the winds of change and visiting the fires of transfiguration on the simple people of the provinces. They asked my lord for the incantations to give such a monster form.'

'The *Yien-Ya*...'

'Don't hurt yourself, boy,' the sorcerer told him. 'The *Yien-Ya-Long* or "Flamefang" in your bullock-tongue.'

'Flamefang,' Archaon repeated, 'is a dragon?'

'Oh yes,' Sheerian confirmed. 'And not some young drake or winged serpent. Flamefang is a monstrous creature. Warped and ancient. Your sorcerer-twins were to summon the beast back from the beyond.'

'They failed?' Archaon put to the sorcerer.

'They succeeded in their petition,' Sheerian admitted. 'My Lord Tzeentch sent me with the incantations but my summoning... was not without difficulty.' The daemon sorcerer jabbed his staff at the remains of the Brothers Spasskov and the mountain of fused and writhing bodies that was their conjoined army of spawn. 'Your sorcerers had prepared one of these wretches for my flesh transference. Alas, my Lord is fickle – and the summoners' own form was chosen for my emergence.'

'Then I have your Lord Tzeentch to thank,' Archaon said, 'or right now I would be facing the spirit of some great beast.'

'My patron Power has taken a great interest in you, Archaon the Chosen,' Sheerian said. 'There are not many who would use the gifts of the Dark Gods to destroy them. Such bottomless aspiration is to be admired. Rewarded, even. As the pantheon turns its back to you, Archaon, my Lord would take pity on your plight. He would see you survive your present doom, overthrow your enemies and find new friends amongst the ranks of his daemon followers.' The ancient gave him a horrid smile that almost cracked his face.

'Your Lord Tzeentch empowers a pair of his sorcerous acolytes to kill me,' Archaon marvelled, 'while sending another one to save me?'

'He is the Changer of the Ways,' Sheerian said. 'Only he knows the truth of all things, while the rest of us drown in an ocean of confusion and contradiction.'

'You spoke of reward,' Archaon pushed.

'For my Lord Tzeentch,' the ancient went on, 'the greatest weapon he can bequeath is knowledge. He sent me here not for your paltry sorcerers but for you. There are great beasts to be unleashed, Archaon, and you are one of them. Unleashed on your true path. But, like you, I digress and there isn't much time. First, your enemies.'

'Tell me.'

'While the Brothers Spasskov visited the Altar of Ultimate Darkness and prayed to my master for the means to destroy you,' the sorcerer Sheerian told him, 'others were in attendance. You know the shrine. In such darkness it can be many things to many people. That barbarian hulk you dangerously keep in the dungeons...'

'The Great Spleen?'

'Did you and the druchii really think that you could control such a creature,' Sheerian continued, 'a monstrous manifestation of the Blood God's own wrath, and hold it captive in slumber? It visits the Altar of Ultimate Darkness in its savage dreams. Your friend Vayne...'

Archaon's hand went instinctively to his throat. He could still feel the slice of the corsair-captain's dagger through his flesh. But there was no gaping wound or even the suggestion of a scar to be found.

'Dravik Vayne is no friend of mine,' Archaon snarled.

'He and his druchii witch,' the ancient said, 'while trading in the potions, poisons and concoctions that laid you low, have been negligent in their attentions to other matters. With the fires of its rage stoked from within, and without the soporifics that would keep the drugged creature so, the Blood God's monster wakes, hungry and furious.'

'What of Vayne?' Archaon said, his words searing with hatred.

'He serves the Hag Queen of Naggaroth and the Prince of Pleasure,' Sheerian said. 'He and his sorceress always have. A course has already been set for the Land of Chill where they will deliver to their queen the Altar of Ultimate Darkness as they were originally charged to do. They have their orders from the altar. Take back the *Spite*. Have the corsair crew enslave your mighty army. Kill the chosen of the Dark Gods, the bearer of the Mark eternal – Archaon of the Western Empire.' The dark templar reached once more for his throat.

'Was I lost to a dream also?'

'Yes,' the sorcerer hissed. 'You chose well in Dravik Vayne. He is as devious and deceiving a druchii as any that have existed. You chose perhaps too well. He had his witch poison your own blade, which then you used to infect those you butchered – breathing back in the poison originally intended for you, little by little. Ingenious really. Almost worthy of my own lord. With every life you took, you were in fact taking your own. Your mind enslaved. Your throat vulnerable to the druchii's own blade. The *Spite* is back under Vayne's captaincy. The quiet and steady enslavement of your crew has been going on for months, with many of your loyalists imprisoned in the sanctum dungeons. And...'

'I was slain by Dravik Vayne,' Archaon said.

'You were,' Sheerian confirmed. The sorcerer bit at his gnarled lip. 'A soul as old as yours has known death many times.'

'I'm not interested in your celestial philosophies, sorcerer.'

'But not like this,' Sheerian said. 'Emboldened by the infernal influence of the Altar of Ultimate Darkness – with the lies and whispers of their patron Powers in their ears – your enemies moved against you. All at once. Unknown to you and unknown to each other. You were slain. This is true. By the Prince of Pleasure's druchii servants. But you were not you at the time of your slaying.'

'More riddles?' Archaon snarled.

'You have been replaced, warlord,' Sheerian told him. 'Many times. The Lord of Flies – sworn god-foe of my own daemon lord – blessed the womb of his witch with a plague of men.'

'Mother Fecundus?'

'While you put the witch's army of maggot-men to your own uses, she had uses for you. Sapping your soul like a disease or some thing that lays its eggs beneath the skin, she birthed mindless monstrosities in your semblance. Into one she implanted what she had drained of your being. It is this thing that has commanded your army for past months, was subject to the druchii's treacheries and had its throat slit by Dravik Vayne.'

'Then how did I come to be down here, in the lair of the Brothers Spasskov and their monstrosities?'

'The body is but a sack of flesh without the soul. What remained of you was secreted down here, under the *Citadel*, where the Brothers Spasskov kept their spawn. While the witch's maggot took your place in degenerate impersonation, your body was here, amongst this abomination of bodies. The witch is devious but I suspect that my Lord Tzeentch had a hand in it. There is something of his tangled elegance in the idea that his sorcerers toiled here – right here – in the arts of your destruction, mere footsteps from where your body lay defenceless.' Sheerian gestured to the Fleshstorm with his bone staff. 'Here, in this spawn, like the rockpool fish that sits in the anemone unstung.'

Archaon's fists were clenched at his side. His face was a mask of stone cold fury. His army was riddled with dissemblers, assassins and usurpers. The scale and beauty of the betrayal was breathtaking. His warmongering lieutenants had used him and cast him aside. His gods had abandoned him. Failure ran like lead through his veins. His heart thumped for vengeance, hammering inside his chest as though it were fit to burst.

'I am whole again?' the Chaos warrior asked, his words like the clearing of steel from the scabbard.

'As much as you ever were,' the sorcerer said. A smile began to spread across the ancient's shrivelled face.

'I will be the end of the gods,' Archaon told Sheerian. 'I will be the death of all the world. I will slay everything that walks or crawls – but it starts here with those that have failed me and tricked me into failing myself. They shall all die for this.'

'Yes, yes…' Sheerian hissed.

Archaon turned away, the blue light of the Eye washing across his scarred back as he strode into the shadows. The dark templar's bones ached for blood. He stretched his neck from side to side and crunched the knuckles of both fists. There was killing to be done. It was time to go to war with his own army. He had made them. The scourge of the Shadowlands. Warlords of the Northern Wastes. They had ridden disaster through the chill lands of Naggaroth. They had brought destruction to the shores of the Great Eastern Ocean, encapsulating the lands, waters and tempests in a ring of Ruinous fire. Indeed, Archaon had made them. Now he would break them.

'You are Archaon,' Sheerian announced to the gloom. 'Warlord of darkness, risen out of the west like the Ruinous Star. You have gathered about you the warriors and champions of doom. Men and beasts who themselves receive the blessings of their patrons for dark service in your name. How will you, one man – one great man, but one man alone – destroy an army of destroyers? Men and beasts who have already laid you low with steel and cunning? Do not dive head first into the waters of your doom. Think. Consider. Be at dark peace. How might such decimation be achieved?'

Archaon closed his eye. He breathed. His heart slowed to the stabbing rhythm of hate. He became one with the darkness. Then it came to him. The warlord smiled.

'Your master offers reward?' Archaon asked. He did not bother to turn to address the daemon sorcerer.

'Perhaps,' Sheerian said. Then thoughtfully, 'Archaon, give him something worthy of a reward. Some offering or suggestion that his interest in your fate is justified.'

'You were sent with secrets, sorcerer,' Archaon said, his voice bouncing ominously about the cave. 'Incantations. This Flamefang…'

'The savage spirit of a serpent ancient and long passed,' the sorcerer told him. 'A monster of fang and flame that no wall or great bastion would resist. The terror of Grand Cathay has afflicted the eastern empires for the best part of a thousand years. Know what you ask, Chaos warrior. You would have me visit Lord Tzeentch's storm of change upon the world once more?'

'I would,' Archaon told him with serene certainty before striding into the shadows.

'Yes,' Khezula Sheerian, Daemon sorcerer of Tzeentch hissed, both to the departing Archaon and himself. 'Yesssss…'

CHAPTER XV

'The spawn of the north, ancient, from the clouds impending,
A thunderbolt in flesh from angry skies, like death descending,
Detested of claw, of jaw, of scale, of flame – it is nature's bane,
Hunting the lesser races, across ocean and waste, ever at change,
It is the very form of our darkest fears –
And like a nightmarish vision in the heavens – it appears...'

– Khezula Sheerian, *Visions of the Fifth Tier, Scaling the Impossible Fortress* and *Netherhell Bound*

The Black Meridian
The Great Eastern Ocean
The Festival of Ghosts – Year of the Jackal

Archaon could hear cannon fire. It had started. News of his apparent death had spread like a disease, infecting the minds of champions and madmen with fantasies of brief bloodshed and taking Archaon's place at the head of the Ruinous horde. Cut off from the influence of other champions, the warrior-captains of vessels making up Archaon's raiding flotilla were first to declare their explosive intentions for their patrons and for themselves. Months of uneasy peace and fearful unity went up like a barrel of gunpowder. War junks, marauders, pirate xebecs and slaveships were all firing upon one another in pre-emptive strikes, boarding and slaughtering crews that fought for enemy gods.

For Archaon, standing in Dravik Vayne's cabin, aboard the corsair-captain's elegant raider, nothing said coup d'état better than looking down on his own corpse. The maggot-man that Nurgle's witch had replaced him with was a ghoulish match. It filled the dark templar with disgust to know that there were others aboard the *Spite* that enjoyed muscle and reflexes tempered by decades of battle and their warlord's fearful features. The doppelganger wore a death mask now: a face from which the worries of command had been removed, from which the horror of an unexpected end had fallen. Vayne had opened his throat from ear to ear with his wicked blade and allowed gore to cascade down his victim's breastplate. The warrior's face was calm and untroubled. In death, Archaon seemed to know a peace he had never known in life. Even before renouncing his weakling God-King and accepting as his masters the capricious Chaos Powers.

He looted his own corpse. His infested plate and mail. His helmet. His boots and gauntlets. His shield. The polluted blade, *Terminus*. Tearing the Fleshstorm's shredded cast-offs from his hips, he slipped into his gore-stained arming doublet and armour sticky with blood. He shouldered the shield with a grunt. With darkness writhing and weaving about him and the weight of plate once more on his body, the Chaos warrior felt complete. Sliding his greatsword into a scabbard across his back, Archaon snatched druchii lanterns from the cabin and smashed them down on his deathly semblance. Within moments the maggot-man was a raging inferno of oil-fed flame that rapidly began spreading through the cabin.

He stared at his own funeral pyre. It was an end but also a beginning. He would start again. He would learn from his mistakes and be the herald the apocalypse truly deserved. The lieutenants, the beastmen and marauders that had betrayed him would pay with their lives. The wretches that had failed him did not deserve to live. There were only two of the hundreds and hundreds on board the floating fortress that he needed. That he wanted. That he cared to take on with him. The girl Giselle, who had once tried to save him from himself, and Father Dagobert, whose knowledge of both his past and unfolding prospect of his future made the priest indispensable. Besides, *The Liber Caelestior* was with them. Archaon would need the secret of his tomorrows, contained within the damned tome.

Taking a pair of crossed corsair cutlasses from where Vayne had them displayed on his wall, Archaon kicked open the door. He dispensed with the stealth he had used when entering the raider's cabin from the gothic maw of the rear window.

The sun had set on the Great Eastern Ocean. Morrslieb was yet to rise but great Mannslieb was low and heavy on the horizon, casting its bloody double on the dark waters that rolled beneath it. Archaon's breath clouded before him. It was cold. His search for the treasures of Chaos had taken the *Spite* to the farthest reaches of the southern seas. Beyond the Lost Isles. Beyond the continental capes of Lustria and Khuresh. Beyond the shipping lanes of the elder races and the reach of map and chart. The skies were crystal clear and the waters stabbing cold.

The druchii raider's sails were furled on their lateen gaffs. Above, dwarfing the tiny ship, was the mountainous silhouette of the *Citadel of Spite*, its crooked towers like a midnight claw reaching greedily for the heavens. The confusion of the corsairs on the raider's deck was mercilessly exploited by the Chaos warrior, who put the spiked knuckle guards of his cutlasses through the gaunt faces of the first two dark elves he met. The face-smashing cries of anguish drew corsairs and slave-crew to Archaon, who opened them up with brutal sweeps of his curved blades. One of Dravik Vayne's corsair-commanders got a cutlass straight through him and then became a shield of scale and black leather as Archaon ran at an assembling line of druchii dreadshards that punched a hail of willowy bolts from their repeater crossbows into the officer's cadaver. Throwing the bolt-mangled body at them, the dark templar slipped through their number, clipping off limbs, skewering helmed heads and carving through druchii flesh.

Leaving his cutlasses through a pair of staggering dreadshards, Archaon took their repeating crossbows from their agony-open fingers, one in each arm. As hastily armed slaves poured from their forecastle enclosures, screamed on by druchii officers, Archaon unleashed the crossbows at them. As bolts buried themselves in faces, throats and bare chests, the stream of slaves started to form a shrieking mound over which following thralls had to climb – straight into the path of Archaon's final quarrels. With both crossbows spent, the Chaos warrior allowed them to crash to the deck and snatched his cutlasses from the impaled dark elves staggering behind him. As their guts rained down on their boots, the druchii collapsed and Archaon continued his wolfish advance up the length of the vessel.

As he sliced through slaves and gutted their dark elf overlords, the Chaos warrior fired off loaded bolt throwers as he passed. Criss-crossing the raider's black deck as well as oncoming corsairs with his wicked blades, Archaon released the ballistas as he went. The corsairs called them *reapers* and their name was well-earned. As their ratchet-claws released the taut sinew of the bowstrings, the heavy trident-headed bolts shot away, smashing through the hull, rigging and druchii crew of a vessel sailing alongside Vayne's docked raider. Slamming individual reapers facing the *Spite* to maximum elevation before releasing their stone-spearing bolts, Archaon fooled the Chaos warriors crewing the floating fortress's mighty bolt throwers into thinking that they were under attack. As the dark templar took heads from Vayne's Slaaneshi elves and butchered the raider's slave-stock, he heard the buck of the colossal war machines in furious reply. Bolt shafts the size of tree trunks smashed down through the deck and screaming slaves. Archaon felt a quake pass through the ship as a third colossal bolt followed the second down through the ruin of the top decks and slammed through the bottom of the raider's hull. Skewered and in the throes of a savage fire sweeping up the ship, the druchii vessel began to take on water. Without the support of the surrounding deck, the foremast began to topple, taking the rigging, wreckage and topsails over the side with it.

Deciding that his work aboard the raider was done, Archaon ran at a throng of screeching corsairs. Skidding down onto the deck and between their boots, Archaon cleaved through the backs of their knees. A druchii officer was suddenly upon the prone templar with a pair of curved knives, but placing the soles of his boots against the leather of the corsair's chest, Archaon launched the officer back across the deck. Throwing one of his cutlasses at an oncoming druchii, the blade slamming into the middle of the dark elf's chest, Archaon plunged his other weapon into the gut of another corsair before the officer – with cat-like reflexes – was back on him. Archaon slapped the corsair back before smashing one knife from his enemy's hand with an armoured gauntlet. Again the officer came at him with the single knife. Allowing its tip to pass under his arm, Archaon grasped the druchii's slender hand in both of his own. Holding the knife in an iron grip, Archaon tore back the fingers of the corsair officer, breaking bones and ripping digits from their sockets. The Chaos warrior heard the dark elf squeal but silenced him with an armoured elbow to the face. Both knife and officer hit the deck.

Archaon heard agonised lines give and felt rigging whip over his head as the foremast started to drag the mainmast down. Scooping up the dark elf's knives from the ruined deck with their finger rings, Archaon ran at the officer, who buried both his helm and head beneath cowering arms. Springing off the corsair's back, Archaon's other boot found the ship's rail, from which he launched himself at the rope dragged upwards by the excruciating descent of the mainmast. Riding the momentum of the rope, Archaon allowed himself to be propelled upwards at the *Citadel*'s side. When the rope had nothing left to give him, the Chaos warrior stabbed out with the talon-tips of his knives, the wicked tips of the blades scoring down through the salt-dusted stone of the floating fortress's side. Scrabbling with his boots and hooking into the crooks and ridges of the black druchii stonework, Archaon's slide down the side of the floating fortress slowed to a gruelling stop. With the raider flooding and aflame in equal measure below, the dark templar had little intention of clinging to the wall like a bat above the devastation. Sticking the stone of the wall with alternate blade tips, Archaon made the muscle-roasting climb required to reach the lowest of the *Citadel of Spite*'s contorted battlements. Hauling himself over the serrated crenellations, Archaon took a moment to catch his breath before climbing on board his twisted flagship.

Beneath his boots Archaon felt the great vessel rock. Over the side he could hear furious agitation in the icy waters, an eruption of bubbles and turbulence that thrashed the surface of the sea to a white maelstrom. Peering over the fanged bulwark of the *Spite* and down its stone side, the dark templar could see light in the depths: pinks, blues and purples. Beneath the black waters Archaon fancied that he could see impossible flame and the crash of titanic bodies. Beasts were rising from the ocean. As they broke the surface, Archaon could see some of the floating fortress's monstrosities – creatures that the warlord had ordered set upon enemy hulks and flotillas – wrapped around some greater beast. Something Archaon hadn't seen before. Sea serpents and the tentacles of a giant-beaked kraken were coiled about the monster's form. The great beast rolled like a crocodile, tangling itself further in lengths of tendril and serpentine body. Archaon saw huge claws rend huge chunks of blubber and scale from its attackers. Jaws flashed and crunched serpents in two, while wings struggled to unfurl and beat through the water like monstrous fins. The kraken wanted to drag the beast down into the depths and drown it, but as the creature turned its colossal maw on the squid and its flesh-shearing beak, the kraken released it. Streams of purpurescent flame followed it into the darkness before the beast wriggled free of the last of the strangling serpents and beat its wings for the surface. Breaking through the bubbling foam rising from its own fiery breath, the gargantuan creature latched onto the side of the floating fortress with its massive claws. Once again, Archaon felt the *Spite* list to one side as the floating fortress took the extra weight of the beast on its starboard side.

There was something spellbinding about the thing. It was huge. It was obscenely ugly. It was climbing up the *Citadel of Spite* towards Archaon. The dark templar looked down on the beast. Flamefang. The curse Archaon had ordered Sheerian to unleash upon the *Spite*, upon his mutinous Chaos host, upon the world once more. All to be caught in the degenerate god Tzeentch's unfolding storm of change. The terror of Grand Cathay was flesh and doom once again – and what a horror it had become. It was a dragon – that was for sure. Its lithe body was long and serpentine, like some colossal serpent of the sky, simultaneously sinewy and powerful. Its spindly limbs supported scythe-like claws that could cut through the trunks of trees, while the beast's wings were colossal, sun-blacking shelters of gnarled bone and stretched flesh. The thick, whipping coils of its tail, which seemed simply a continuation of its snaking body, balanced the length of a slithering neck, in turn supporting a gargantuan head: an armoured skull of twisted horn, gavial jaws and twisted teeth.

The Chaos warrior had encountered nothing like it before, even in his wanderings through the Wastes. He had only seen its kind in pictorial form. Oriental dragons stitched into the flags of Cathayan vessels or carved into the lacquered breastplates of the Dreaded Wo. Its predacious size and presence was heart-stopping enough but as Archaon stared down at the ascending monstrosity he had unleashed, it somehow managed to exude a dread that was more than the threat of its savage power. At his command, Khezula Sheerian had brought into existence an otherworldly thing. A slinking beast of world-eating spirit, encased in the devastating form of its ancient terror. The creature's flesh was not its own, however. Like the daemon sorcerer who had summoned it, Flamefang had been forced to make do with the materials available. The dragon's ancient scale and primordial flesh was long gone. The small mountain of bodies that had been the Fleshstorm had found new form and purpose, stretched horrifically about the dragon's monstrous spirit. Archaon could see eyes, mouths and faces staring out from the melded beastflesh. Its skin was pale and flesh-pink, thick with muscle and tendon, threaded with rib and bone. It was a creature crafted of the living. A howling, screaming, begging nightmare of borrowed flesh and suffering – stomach-churning to behold.

As he became entranced with the dragon, the dragon in turn became entranced with its prey. The marauders and beastmen on board the *Spite* and the surrounding flotilla were all damnation's children. They all had the whiff of destined greatness about them. The Dark Gods were fickle in the choosing of their champions. To the Chaos dragon, Archaon was a blinding light amongst a constellation of lesser stars. His power and potential burned to behold and the beast knew it must have him. Like a wild thing of impulse and darkness it would swallow the swarms of souls about it like an ocean behemoth might clouds of shrimp. It knew that Archaon was special, even if it couldn't possibly conceive how or why. It had his stink in its ghastly nostrils – the stench of destiny – and knew it must have him.

It saw him with the hundreds of eyes peering in horror from its form. Its twisted cage of dagger-teeth parted and from the bottomless blackness of its throat a glorious fountain of purple flame vomited forth. Throwing himself back behind the knife-edge of the bulwark, Archaon dived for the deck, allowing the unnatural inferno to roar past and reach for the skies. Scrabbling to his feet, Archaon lurched for the nearest cover. Flamefang was suddenly there, its serpentine neck carrying the Chaos dragon's monstrous head up to the stone deck. Again the jaws parted. The dark templar clambered awkwardly over a balustrade and dropped down onto the stone steps of a stairwell leading down onto a mezzanine deck. The sky disappeared beneath a blanket of flame. Archaon expected to hit the black stone of the steps. His fall was broken, however, by Gorghas Hornsqualor and a throng of his shaggy white warriors. The beastmen roared their fury at the Chaos warrior as they tumbled together down the stairs. In a brute rage the beastmen grabbed the warrior with their brawny arms and proceeded to kick dents into his plate with their hooves.

Archaon wasn't worried about Hornsqualor's troops. He felt the deck shift as Flamefang pulled its monstrous length up onto the *Citadel*'s deck. The beastmen were so involved in defeating the Chaos warrior that had fallen on them that they hadn't noticed the colossal beast that was now snaking its way through the *Spite*'s towers and architecture. Inbetween the hairy, white fists and the bloody hooves, Archaon caught glimpses of Flamefang's horrific body passing overhead. He could hear shrieks and screams as the monster cut marauders in half with the mindless snap of its jaws and buried entire warbands, crowded tents and warriors of the Ruinous Powers in flame. Archaon got his gauntlet to his brawny restrainer's single horn. With his arm around the beastman, he twisted and snapped the creature's neck with a horrible, bleating screech. He didn't have time to deal with Gorghas Hornsqualor and his bully gors and found himself crawling away. The beastmen chuckled their harsh derision, watching the Chaos warrior scramble behind the corner.

Their mirth was lost in the purple firestorm that enveloped the stone stairwell as the dragon slipped its long neck and open, elongated jaws down through the cruel druchii architecture and blasted them to fiery oblivion. Some monstrous, primordial urge to serve its Dark Master drove it on. It wanted forms to change and the souls that fled such abomination. It wanted Archaon. The blazing light of his significance drove the monster mad, flashing briefly and temptingly before becoming lost once more in the miasma of dark souls that lit up the floating fortress.

After the heat washed away and Archaon heard Flamefang slither monstrously away to create havoc towards the stern, Archaon turned to see what remained of the beastmen. Instead of a huddle of cremated beastmen, the Chaos warrior found that the dragon's breath had actually turned the brutes into small, fleshy mounds that were erupting in change. Like anemones turning themselves inside out, the creatures had been transformed into blossoming spawn by the form-altering power of the Tzeentchian monster's fire. Instead of a fiery death, Flamefang visited upon its victims the blessings of its infernal master, Lord Tzeentch.

'What you think?' came a voice. Archaon turned to find the sorcerer Sheerian hobbling around the corner, his bone staff tapping its way along the black stone. The ancient leant on the staff and Archaon was bathed in the azure glow of its gem headpiece. The jewel seemed to blink. 'What do you think of Lord Tzeentch's gift?' Archaon didn't give an answer and Sheerian didn't wait for one. 'Change is coming, Archaon. For you, for me, for the poor mongrels hereabouts,' the sorcerer said, gesturing to the chaos and confusion that swarmed the *Citadel*'s decks. 'For the world.' The ancient smacked the base of the staff down on the stone. 'Go then, chosen one. Ring the changes with your blade, with your vengeance. Bring my lord the souls of your enemies, Archaon. Sacrifice them on the altar of your ambition.'

Archaon got to his feet. He found the sorcerer intensely annoying and didn't relish the opportunity to serve his warped god as some kind of puppet executioner.

'That means you too, sorcerer,' Archaon told him with dark certainty. Khezula Sheerian smiled his ghastly smile. He rattled the jewel of the Eye in the setting of its bone staff.

'I die,' the daemon sorcerer told him, 'but not by your hand, you insatiable cur.'

Archaon grunted and turned. The great flesh-smeared belly of the Chaos dragon snaked its way above them. It was getting bigger. With every swallowed victim, the monstrosity grew in size and horror. Its victims became part of its slithering bulk. In its warped form Archaon could see faces staring down on him. He recognised them as members of his own army. Their mouths open and screaming. Flamefang was claiming his army for its own. It was harnessing the power of their flesh. The Chaos warrior wondered if he had done the right thing in having Sheerian unleash the creature once again on the world. Indeed, it was an exquisite punishment for his enemies and the followers that had failed him. It thwarted the designs of men and gods but Archaon had to wonder whether he too would be its victim. Whether he would find himself in the colossal creature's belly and swiftly assimilated into its dreadful form or bathed in its transformative flame. Archaon knew that he possessed no blade, no shield and no armour that would turn such a weapon aside.

He had no intention of fighting the beast, however. Like all of the servants of the Dark Gods, the dragon itself was a weapon to be wielded. A punishment to be delivered. That was all that mattered. The daemons, the princes and the Dark Gods would know that he was not their plaything – a slave to infernal destiny. His choices were his own, no matter how insane they seemed to others and indeed himself. He would feed Tzeentch's monstrous pet his unworthy army. In horrible death, the warriors and marauders that had failed to unify under his banner would be joined in their shared failure. There were a few amongst their number who deserved his special attention and walking away from the cackling sorcerer Sheerian, Archaon made good on the distracting carnage that Flamefang was creating at his flagship's stern and returned to the *Citadel*'s main deck.

Even before the arrival of the horrific dragon, the *Spite* had been in chaos. News of Archaon's death, brought by Dravik Vayne and his sorceress, had initiated a full-blown mutiny. Chaos warriors who coveted command of the army for themselves went on murderous rampages, assassinating champions they considered to be their greatest competition. Weak-minded marauders and beasts flocked to the banners of such mad men, spreading the carnage, mindlessly changing allegiances as the dark warriors behind which they had thrown their brutal support were brained and butchered. Petty rivalries and long-standing hatreds – formerly kept in check by Archaon and his lieutenants through the threat of retribution – exploded in wanton murder and massacre. The case for every Chaos god was argued with the blade. Each champion and marauder fought for the prospects of his own patron or power in the bloody belief that the Blood God, the Lord of All, the Changer of Ways or the Prince of Chaos was worthy of the host's destructive potential.

Archaon drank deep in the havoc of it all. His hands trembled in expectation. His gauntlets rattled about them. He walked through the death and the destruction. Bolt throwers had been turned inwards and their spear-storms unleashed on the crowds of marauders fighting for control of the stone expanse of the *Citadel*'s blood-slick decks and wards. Punching through the bodies of five, six, sometimes seven Chaos warriors at a time, the wicked shafts tore men from their death dealing and skewered them like meat on a giant's spit. Other artillery pieces had been man-handled around in the chaos and fired into the riotous carnage. Druchii bolt throwers adorned the razor crenellations of the *Citadel of Spite*'s port and starboard sides at intervals, ready to slash through the sails of escaping enemy vessels or ensnaring them in barbed line-trailing grapnels. As well as these nightmares being turned on the Chaos host, the fevered hordes had to contend with the motley collection of other artillery pieces that the army had pilfered from captured vessels before scuttling or re-appropriating them – great cannons, mortars and carronades. Archaon blinked as the Hung marauders fighting amongst themselves before him turned to a thunderous drizzle of red. His armour was showered in their gore as the great muzzle of an ancient bronze carronade belched canister shot into the crowds, cutting a murderous swathe through the madness. A cannonball trailing some kind of enchanted fire whizzed over the warlord's head, while a corsair's crossbow bolt twanged, snapped and glanced off his armoured shoulder.

The stone deck was awash with blood and body parts, while barbarians, buccaneers and slave-warriors slaughtered each other before him. It was pure insanity. There was little room for manoeuvres amongst the throngs on the slippery deck, just grabbing and killing. The hands of the fallen grasped for Archaon's boots as he walked through the sweet butchery. Druchii corsairs, spike-furred Norsemen, clansmen and retainers of the Dreaded Wo. None of them recognised Archaon as he moved through the confusion and horror they had brought on themselves. Shaggy beastmen roared challenges at him as he moved through the mutinous massacre before being axed down by bearded berserkers of the dawi-zharr. Some madman had opened the stables and released rhinoxen and horses out onto the confusion of the deck. The animals ran about in panic, slipping in the blood and scrabbling their way through the carnage. Marauders were trampled and gored, while others saw the animals no differently to the other murderous shapes coming at them out of the pandemonium, slashing at them as they cannoned by or slaughtering the steeds and beasts of burden with pikes and spears.

Archaon saw several warriors of Chaos attempt to mount passing horses: Hrodgar Deathchosen and Orchan Varg, one of the Bloodsworn clockwork knights. They rose above the rabble and the death to ride and kill but their ascendency was short lived. The horses could not keep their footing on the rolling, blood-greased deck and swiftly both the steeds and the warriors were dragged back down into the butchery. Hands and claws grasped for them. Spearpoints jabbed. Axes flashed. Within moments the mounted warriors were part of the mess on the deck.

Archaon came to a stop. He could smell the coppery sting of death on the air. He licked his lips. He could taste annihilation. He had spent so long attracting dark souls to his destiny like moths to a flame. So many years of his life building a horde of Chaos warriors, slayers and madmen. An army of such skill and number that could end a world and be worthy of the Ruinous Star. He had failed. Even as they hacked each other to pieces about him, he could not see in them the warriors, beastmen and daemons of his doom. They were a wretched assemblage. A rag-tag union of the lost and the damned. Slaves to darkness, blundering through their existence, savagely striking out like blinded animals. They had not been worthy of his apocalyptic fate but worse, he had not been worthy of them. The loyalties of maniacs, marauder tribesmen and altereds were held together with little more than the skein of a spider's web. They were a liars' alliance, lying to each other and themselves about their intentions. They were a monster of the deep, horribly devouring itself.

Standing on the stone deck, with the crooked mast-towers and sinister citadels stretching for the skies about him, Archaon took some comfort in the likelihood that this was the way it was meant to be. He was being tested. How could he lead these legions if he couldn't hold together an army of beastmen and Shadowland marauders? Archaon nodded to himself. His worthiness was to be found in the way he had achieved so much with so little. With a malingering horde of spawn, savages and back-stabbing lieutenants he had achieved much. A place in history, at least. He had swept across the Northern Wastes, besting with sword, stratagem or number all challengers who had stood in his irresistible path. He had smashed his way through icy Naggaroth before making the Great Eastern Ocean his own. They would not be the ones to accompany him into eternity. At his side they had indeed earned their squalid place in history – but Archaon was destined to destroy the world, a world without a future and in no need of a history.

The gods were cruel. They persecuted even those that realised their prophecies and prosecuted their will. The Altar of Ultimate Darkness had been their gift. It had bequeathed on Archaon their Mark. The eight points of the Chaos Star – a Ruinous union of blood and treachery. The Chaos gods were monsters. Their gifts were invariably curses also. Like the spawn whose horrific form bequeaths strength and murderous abilities that the trapped soul within could barely have dreamed of in its former existence. Every favour of the Dark Gods was also a test or some sly part of a greater doom. Archaon only needed to look upon his flagship to know that. The *Spite* – whose banner-trailing, cloudscraping towers were a sight to strike distant captains and port governors stone dead with dread, whose flotilla trailing darkness had been the terror of an entire ocean – had been a lens through which the darklight of evil had been concentrated. The conflicting influence of the Ruinous Powers, reaching out from the Altar of Ultimate Darkness and into the souls of every great warrior, every witch and every wretched thing that fought in Archaon's name. It had promised them their heart's desire – whatever that had been – and perversely destroyed the beautiful confederacy that had united behind their chosen champion.

Dravik Vayne's *Citadel of Spite* had already been a devastating study in dark genius. The enchantments of its black stone, the lines of its serrations and crenellations, the crooked cruelty of its towering architecture. The *Spite* had indeed been a wonder. The Altar of Ultimate Darkness had sat within its depths, corrupting the simple evil of its black heart. The *Spite* had brought it to the floating fortress from which Archaon terrorised the high seas. Spreading its corruption like veins and arteries through the dark stone, it pumped its poison into the souls that called the *Spite* home. It almost became a living thing. Its catacombs were haunted by much more than nesting sea monsters. Its archways became toothed gateways to whispering oblivion. The tents and camps that sprawled across its stone decks and plazas sat upon glyphs and symbols that had wormed their way through the stone to demand sacrifice. The towers and citadels became secret temples to individual Powers, channelling the altar's dread influence. He could see that now. The warping stone and midnight metal of the *Citadel*'s architecture was not twisting into agonising new forms to honour the warlord Archaon and his victories. It was contorting with its hate for his endeavours. It was laughing at him. It was spitting in the face of his failures.

No more. No more.

Archaon looked up at the *Citadel* tower. The warlord knew where Dravik Vayne and his witch would be. Father Dagobert and Giselle would be with them, up in what had been Archaon's cabin chambers. He could feel the floating fortress turning in the water beneath his feet. The corsair would take the *Spite* back to Naggaroth. He would be changing course without delay. He would be setting that course atop the bulbous keep, crowning the main mast-tower, the tallest of the *Spite*'s towers. That was where Archaon would find him.

Between him and the tower, however, was a horde of his Dreaded Wo, arch-marauders that had terrorised Northern Cathay for as long as anyone could remember. Archaon passed through throngs of Dreaded Wo like shadow. In their lacquered armoured and horned helmets they came at their attacker. Archaon slipped their curved blades from their scabbards and drew their single edges across marauder throats. Turning his wrist and bringing the oriental blade back for the strike, the Chaos warlord cut through the Hundun sword clans with their own cursed weapons, burying steel in one warrior only to snatch a pike from another's retainer and hurl it into the chest of another. As they came at him with blade, boot and back of hand, their movements dark and graceful, Archaon broke them. He ducked beneath the discipline of their fists, scooped aside their dancing blades and killed with a messy efficiency the Hung marauders did not have within them. He turned and spun. He broke necks and twirled the vicious attacks of lesser warriors into one another, impaling tribal princes and their peasant servants on each other's weapons. Archaon stabbed and cut with the superior blades of the Dreaded Wo, slicing limbs and heads from marauder bodies, working his way across the madness of the stone deck.

The easterners became an archway of steel. Archaon worked his marauder sword, the dull glint of the wretched skies flashing off its arcs and crescents. Blood sprayed his way as throats were opened and wrists were slit. The grating hiss of razor-edges clashing filled the air, punctuated by the plunging of Archaon's blade through marauder torsos. Stabbing the weapon through the side of one unfortunate sword clansman's helm, the sword went straight through the skull and out the other side. Snatching a retainer's pike from his trembling hands, Archaon rested his boot on the marauder's lacquered breast plate and kicked the warrior away. Swinging the pike around by the tip of its shaft, the Chaos warrior opened up a throng of closing Dreaded Wo, the point of the pike blade tearing through the arms and chests of the marauders.

As the black-armoured warriors crumbled to the deck about him, Archaon heard it. The unmistakable roar of one of the Blood God's foetid servants. An unreasoning bellow of rage that shook the stone of the deck and made the littering corpses jig and dance. The Great Spleen had awoken. Dazed. Furious. Eager to appease its dread deity with sacrifices, the ogre was enraged. Like a gore-dipped statue it rose above the Hundun warriors, each bare footfall a stone-pulverising quake. Archaon saw its beady eyes – black with rage – peering over the tusk-snarled mess of its maw. He heard the rumble of the great metal links of an anchor and realised that the Great Spleen had one of the *Spite*'s colossal anchors in its possession. Throwing the cruel weight of the black, barbed thing into the air, the Great Spleen turned on its blood-slimy heel, swinging the anchor around on its length of chain. There was little Archaon could do to defend against such a weapon. Unlike the Dreaded Wo attempting to skewer him on their beautiful, curved blades, he could see the weapon coming. Dipping down into the gore, helmet pressed to the deck, the Chaos warrior heard the dreadful path of the anchor as it ploughed through the armoured bodies of the Hung marauders, dragging their smashed corpses along with it.

Archaon was up, pike ready in hand like a javelin, but the ogre heaved and the anchor hummed through the air, orbiting the corpulent mass of the Great Spleen and searing around for another pass. The anchor bounced and sparked off the deck, showering Archaon with shattered stone. Archaon went down again, allowing the deadly weight of the thing to pass over his helmet. Kneeling, Archaon launched the pike at the ogre, burying it between the slabs of pectoral fat that wobbled from its chest. The anchor came crashing down to the deck, smashing through the legs of Hung marauders and some of the Great Spleen's own blood-barbarians. The ogre snorted two streams of snot from its flat nose in fury before snatching the pike from its steaming flesh. Archaon was already up and on the run, stepping swiftly through the demolished corpses the Great Spleen's anchor had left behind, scooping up the pikes of retainers and the curved blades of Hundun sword clansmen. These came at the Blood God's champion like a shower of steel. Pikes sailed through the air, swords whirled hilt over blade at the monster. The Great Spleen roared as it feverishly removed the weapons from its belly. With all of his might, Archaon launched a pike at the ogre's head. The monster turned, just in time, allowing the pike to sink into its globed shoulder, the Great Spleen's muscle and fat soaking up the entire head of the weapon. The creature bawled its pain. Archaon had not killed the ogre – as he had hoped to – but he had reminded the Blood God's champion how to bleed and how to feel the agony of the flesh.

Archaon closed on the beast. Snatching a pair of bone axes from the deck, the Chaos warrior took the Great Spleen barbarians to task. The savages were beside themselves. They had never seen their god-monster bleed. It was impossible. It was blasphemy. Like Archaon's own, their weapons were roughly hewn from the bones of great beasts and sharpened to lethality. He hacked through the cultist barbarians, turning aside the savagery of their mindless attacks while ripping open bellies and the backs of skulls. While surrounded by the painted wildmen, Archaon heard the sound of hooves on the deck behind him. He expected to find beastmen attacking from the rear. Instead he found a recently recruited Chaos warrior called Horakrux Hearteater, mounted on a steed liberated from the deck-stables and riding down on his new master. Archaon could feel the champion's hunger for his end. Tearing a bone axe from a blood barbarian, Archaon hurled it at the rider but it glanced off the warrior's shield. The warlord need not have bothered. The Great Spleen's anchor passed straight through its own barbaric acolytes and smashed both horse and rider aside.

Before Archaon knew what was happening, the anchor had come around again. He jumped and the horrific inevitability of the thing passed beneath his boots. Again the Great Spleen swung the anchor around. Archaon tried to jump again but the anchor hooked the dark templar by the heel and sent him tumbling across the deck. Archaon felt his plate buckle and crack as he bounced off the stone deck and through the flesh-canvas tents adorning it. He hammered through a warherd of beastmen like a cannonball before smashing into the horde of foetid warriors the beasts were fighting. He came to a sudden stop.

Archaon's landing was cushioned by the throng of warriors about him. He tried to shake the confusion from his head. He slipped his helmet off and to his surprise found a hand offered to him. Not an axe coming for his head or a dagger in the gut but a hand. He took it and found himself pulled to his feet amongst a group of armoured warriors. As he blinked the daze from his eye, Archaon came to realise that they looked very much like him. Their armour was rough and chitinous but similar in style and colouring. It was not unusual for warriors to honour champions and warlords so, but the figures were eerie in their similarity, to each other and to Archaon. As several turned he saw their cold and clammy faces. A face he had seen before. And not just in a looking glass or mirror. He was amongst Mother Fecundus's maggot-men. Her birthed horrors. Her brood. The fruits of her sorcerous reproduction.

Archaon stood amongst the brood as they huddled, soaking up the bleating threats and abuse of the beastmen. Above him, on a stinking palanquin, raised upon the shoulders of ten mock-Archaons, the Chaos warrior saw Mother Fecundus, ordering her creations on. Drawing *Terminus* slowly from his scabbard and shrugging his shield from his shoulder, Archaon prepared himself. He was ready to face himself. Plunging the greatsword straight through the back of one of his doppelgangers, Archaon pulled the blade free to take the heads from two more. Mother Fecundus shrieked in maternal horror, directing her progeny to destroy the betraying son. Within moments the maggot-men had turned on Archaon. They didn't just look like him. They moved like him. They fought like him. After his initial element of surprise, the warlord suddenly found himself hard pushed, desperately trying to predict his own movements as great swords and shields clashed.

Suddenly the Great Spleen was there. The anchor came around on its colossal chain, smashing through maggot-men and the beasts fighting them. Archaon watched his own face crumple in horror as the anchor punched through bodies and dragged them away in a swirl of red. There would be little stopping the Blood God's maniac. Of that, Archaon was sure. The best the Chaos warrior could do was make the monster work for him. Stabbing the maggot-man behind him through the neck, Archaon ran up the mound of building corpses before the palanquin. He discovered Mother Fecundus in her birthing throne. Nurgle's witch gurgled her horror at Archaon. The Chaos warrior snarled up at the mountain of putrid flesh.

'You'll get no mercy from me, hag,' Archaon told her. He turned to show the Great Spleen that it was him but found the monster confused at the appearance of so many similar faces. 'Here!' Archaon called at the thing, immediately drawing the champion's attention. Archaon leapt. The anchor sailed around on its chain, the furious force of the improvised weapon smashing straight through the palanquin and birthing throne, turning Mother Fecundus into an amniotic explosion of rancid gore and fluids.

Landing and rolling across his shield, Archaon regained his footing. There was death and violence everywhere. The air was thick with the howls of vengeance and the stench of lives lost. The dragon's flames ran rampant across the decks and through the dark sanctums of the floating fortress's interior. The dragon itself had launched its slithering bulk from the *Citadel* and into the heavens. Rippling like a serpent of the skies, Flamefang weaved and banked on its great fleshy wings trying to acquire several winged warriors in flight. Nodding with admiration and approval, Archaon watched his Swords go head to head with the beast, on their own infernal wings. Diving and spinning, the Swords slashed at the monster's sides as they passed, but the creature would not be denied. Opening its narrow jaws wide, the dragon turned sharply and swallowed two of Archaon's bodyguards whole. Another landed on its back and proceeded to open the dragon up at the spine with one of his bone swords. The monster brought its wings in close and turned into a dizzying roll that threw the Sword from its flesh and sent him into a tumbling descent of his own. Before the Chaos warrior could regain control, the Chaos dragon had whipped its serpentine body around and blasted the falling warrior out of the sky with a stream of purple flame. Archaon watched the flailing spawn tumble from the heavens before thudding horribly against the stone deck of the *Spite*. It looked like it might have been Vier.

With a growing snarl on his face and his head held low, Archaon made for the main mast-tower. He could feel the pounding steps of the ogre behind him, crushing beasts and maggot-men underfoot. Cutting through Kurgan warriors on the deck as he ran, he smashed their weapons aside with *Terminus*. He left the marauders to the Great Spleen's wrath that unfolded about the monster like an unholy storm. Shouldering his shield and slipping the greatsword into his back-scabbard, Archaon weaved through the mutinous crowds. He ducked, weaved and slid out of the path of marauder blades, Norse axes and druchii crossbow bolts. As the Blood God's monster closed on him, dragging the chain and anchor across the stone deck behind him, the hordes parted ahead of Archaon. The ogre snatched up the champions of enemy gods with a colossal fist and chewed their heads clean off before tossing the armoured bodies aside and sweeping the deck for another victim.

On the final approach to the *Citadel* tower, Archaon had to rely on his bare hands alone. He turned blades around in the hands of others, popping shoulders, tearing tendons and breaking bones. He wrenched at limbs, prompting the most excruciating crunches from his passing enemies. Enemies who had been former allies. Marauders and warriors screamed as he hurt them with impunity. Several were swept by Archaon's leg but such movements were restricted by the dark templar's armour. He dallied long enough to kill two. One received a gauntleted fist in the throat while another had his neck broken in an elegant twisting motion that the warlord risked as he passed.

Leaping up at the mast-tower's willowy architecture, Archaon climbed for his life. Every wicked spur and toothed ledge was a blessing. Hauling his armoured form up the black stone of the *Citadel*, the Chaos warrior heard the Great Spleen thunder up behind. As his armoured digits clawed their way to handholds and Archaon began to climb the tower foundations he heard the whoosh of air through the thick chain and the sound of the wicked anchor cutting through the air. Archaon found that his face split with a smirk as the thing smashed through the stone beneath his dangling boot. The anchor came around. This time the Chaos warrior had to lift his knees to escape the Great Spleen's whirlwind attack. He felt the mast-tower shudder as the anchor went to work on the black stone foundations like a massive pick axe. Again and again the ogre swung its huge chain around, smashing through the stone, each time narrowly missing the dark templar.

'Come on, you beast!' Archaon called, enraging the monster further. 'Can't you hit me?' The warlord felt the *Citadel* tower foundations crumble under the ogre's relentless assault. Not that Archaon would want him to. The stone gave an ear-splitting crack from within. Like a lumberjack, the Great Spleen was felling the tower, with the temptation of Archaon's anchor-skewered body directing every swing. 'Harder, you mindless thing,' Archaon roared as he climbed. 'For the hate in your veins and your abominable god...'

Suddenly the anchor appeared beside him. The black metal of the thing was buried in the stone like a grapnel and the Great Spleen was attempting to heave its colossal blood-stained bulk up the tower after him. Archaon felt the *Citadel* quake. As the ogre hauled on the chain with its savage strength, something shattered in the stone foundations. Scrambling across the side of the tower, desperate for handholds, Archaon felt the tower go. The sound was excruciating. At first the mast-tower rocked. Then it started to lean and waver. Then it fell. Like an ancient tree it toppled, its foundations pulverising under its own weight. Rigging and the *Citadel*'s colossal sails began to fall.

Archaon dropped to the deck and scrabbled away. There was an almighty splash as the bulbous towertop struck the water. The air was thick with black dust and a teeth-grinding sound. Through the deck Archaon felt the *Spite* begin to lean to one side. Pushing himself to his feet and with the silhouettes of battling marauders all about him, Archaon climbed up onto the side of the tower. Beneath his feet he could feel the floating fortress listing. The colossal weight of the *Citadel* tower was dragging the *Spite* over onto her side, flooding her upper catacombs and lower decks. Archaon's flagship was going down. Beneath the tower base, the Chaos warrior saw what was left of the Great Spleen. The blood-mad ogre had heaved the tower over onto itself in its blind rage. The monster-champion's bulk had been crushed by the weight of the stone, so that now only a brawny arm and gore-stained fist was visible. The beast's barbarians stood before their fallen god, weeping tears of blood.

Archaon squinted through the dust along the length of the tower. The bulbous keep that crowned it was already in the water and flooding but the druchii and the degenerates that had made the tower their home were crawling out from windows and loop holes. Sliding *Terminus* from his back-scabbard and his shield from his shoulder, Archaon began to jog along the wall of the tower. As he met Chaos warriors and champions extricating themselves from the flooding tower he ended them. He briefly fought Kallidon the Dark before opening up the Kurgan warrior from the navel to the jaw. He butchered without a thought men and monsters who would formerly have given their miserable lives in his service. Archaon pushed on behind his shield as the bolts of corsair crossbows hammered into its surface. As he met them they drew their wicked cutlasses. He slammed them back, turning and cutting them down with blade-shattering sweeps of his own sword.

Beyond the corsair's cleaved corpses, Archaon found the druchii who led them: Sularii, Dravik Vayne's witch lover. *Terminus* came up to claim her but there was something in the dark elf's eyes... a gaze Archaon felt difficult to break. As she made her alluring way up the tower towards him, her dark eyes and coquettish smile becoming his world, Archaon found that he had sheathed his sword and shouldered his shield. The witch reached out for him and touched his face. She licked her lips with a forked tongue. A new blessing.

'Sularii!' Archaon heard the stabbing words of Dravik Vayne. 'Stop playing. Just kill him.'

The dark templar blinked the sorceress's bewitchments away. She was there, in front of him, but it was a curved dagger of black metal that caressed his cheek rather than the druchii's fingertips. Archaon looked down its length. The blade glistened with the witch's poisons. Further up the toppled tower Archaon could see Dravik Vayne, the corsair commander, seething with hatred. His pair of cutlasses dripped with deadliness also and their tapering points sat nestled in the back of his prisoners' skulls. Gorst and Fitch clutched each other nearby while before his blades, the servant of Slaanesh was walking Father Dagobert and Giselle down towards him.

'I'm sorry, master,' Dagobert said through his curtains of long, grey hair. The priest held the precious *Liber Caelestior* in his clawed grasp. Vayne not only had the priest prisoner but the ancient tome also. Giselle said nothing. She simply gave the Chaos warrior a stabbing glare. He watched as she slipped a stiletto knife from her sleeve, a knife she had used in attempts on his own life. Now she intended to use it on Vayne. Archaon gave the slightest shake of his head. He grabbed Sularii's wrist and brutally twisted it in his grasp, turning the poisonous blade between them and spinning the witch into his embrace. Holding the dark elf to him, Archaon put the blade in her hand to her own throat. Dravik Vayne's contorted face slackened to a smile.

'You're dead,' the druchii said, staring at the warlord.

'I'm many things,' Archaon said, 'but dead isn't one of them. You will not be able to say the same soon, you treacherous worm.'

'You have no army…'

'It wasn't worthy of my name,' Archaon told him. 'And its lieutenants were not worthy of it.' Dravik Vayne gave him a snide smile. Out of the corner of his eye, Archaon noticed movement.

'And you were not worthy of us,' the champion of Slaanesh told him.

'Perhaps,' Archaon agreed.

'You are not worthy of your gods,' Vayne continued. 'You are not worthy of your destiny.'

Like a dark thunderbolt, Eins dropped down beside him, the black stone of the tower pulverising beneath its boots. Fünf landed beyond the dark elf corsair, on the sinking tower keep. The pair drew their bone swords from their wings and prepared to engage the druchii, prompting Vayne to turn and point his poisonous blades both ways. The Slaaneshi's face screwed up with hate.

'Back,' he warned Archaon's remaining Swords.

'I am worthy of a destiny of my own,' Archaon told him. The weaving movements drew closer. 'A fate of my choosing. Not some snaking, labyrinthine path that gods, daemons and traitors choose for me.'

'Then go,' Vayne seethed, moving his poisonous blade tips between Archaon's people. 'Seek out such a fate, if it exists. Leave me to my god and his desires. Leave me to my *Spite*.'

'Your floating fortress no longer floats, druchii,' Archaon told him. 'It's going to the depths. And it's taking you with it, you treacherous scum. The captain goes down with his vessel.'

'Kill her,' came a voice from behind. It was Khezula Sheerian. The ancient was hobbling up the tower behind the Chaos warrior, his bone staff tapping its way up the black stone. 'The priest, the girl,' Sheerian said, 'they're dead. Kill the witch.'

'What are you talking about?' Archaon demanded of the sorcerer.

'Do it,' Sheerian said. 'Do what you do best, Archaon. End her.'

'You'll doom us all,' the corsair-captain snarled.

Archaon nodded slowly to himself. 'I'm known for that.'

And it was decided. Sularii managed a half-scream as he cut the witch's head from her shoulders with her own blade. Tossing the dark elf's head into the ocean, Archaon felt the stone beneath his boots suddenly judder. The charms and incantations that kept the *Citadel* afloat were losing their battle with the depths. Water about the colossal vessel began to thrash and foam as the black stone and rocky foundations of the vessel started taking it down below the waves. Vayne watched with a lover's horror as Archaon allowed Sularii's body to fall into the white water. It was all there in the druchii's screwed-up face: his love for Sularii, his love for the *Spite*.

'You idiot,' Vayne spat, his dark charm and venomous smile gone. 'You'll put the Altar of Ultimate Darkness on the bottom of the ocean.'

'Where it belongs,' Archaon told him.

'It was a gift from the gods,' Vayne said, considering his own anger at his failure to reclaim the altar for his witch-queen.

'They give,' Archaon said, 'and they take away.'

'They do...' Vayne seethed. The corsair-commander turned and rolled back up the tower at the two Swords blocking his escape. He passed under the bone blades of Fünf and slashed the Chaos warrior with the poisoned metal of his own cutlass. The Sword shrieked as Archaon had never heard and fell to his armoured knees. The warlord couldn't tell whether it was a cry of pain or pleasure, enslavement or release. The poison's effects were swift and devastating. Fünf simply withered to nothing before Archaon's eyes.

'He's mine,' Archaon called as Eins went in to attack. Vayne turned and assumed a druchii fighting stance. Something dark, exotic and designed to catch Archaon off-guard. He only need nick or slice the Chaos warrior with his blades. He sneered his madness at Archaon who advanced without drawing his blade. The black stone of the tower cracked and shattered underneath them. Water foamed and fountained about as the *Spite* began its torturous descent into the depths. Beyond, Archaon's army of darkness tore itself to pieces, the gods delighting in the butchery and spectacle.

'Master!' Giselle screamed.

'We've got to get off this ship,' Father Dagobert called.

Archaon didn't have time to dance with Dravik Vayne. Dagobert was right. The *Spite* was going down fast. Without druchii magic to keep it afloat, the unimaginable weight of the black stone fortress and the bedrock it sat upon was pulling it swiftly down. Archaon had seconds before they would all be in the freezing water being dragged down with the *Citadel of Spite*. As Dravik Vayne closed on him, his blades oozing their deadly poison, Archaon stopped and tore a piece of shattered black stone from the crumbling tower wall. Vayne ran at the Chaos warrior, eager for the advantage. Archaon hefted the small, jagged boulder up onto his armoured chest and then above his head. Throwing it down on his enemy with all his hate-fuelled might, Archaon's rock smashed through Vayne's offered blades and put the corsair's skull in. Dropping the cutlasses, the Slaaneshi's largely headless corpse stumbled about for a moment before dropping to its knees and slipping down into the foaming waters. Archaon spat after the corsair-captain and traitor.

He turned to Dagobert and Giselle, with Eins standing with them. 'Now we go–'

Sickening shock stole the words from the end of his sentence. The beast was there. Flamefang. The Chaos dragon, tearing up the water as it swooped in low and fast. It was flying for the toppled tower, intent on claiming the winged warrior that had evaded its sky-snapping pursuit.

'Down!' Archaon roared. But it was too late. It was natural for them to turn. To set their own eyes on the danger before they tried to evade it. Such split-second curiosity cost them, however. The lengths of the beast's fang-filled jaws were open. Its neck, its tail and its body were straight. Carried on a gargantuan flap of its wings, the horror came at them like a bolt from one of the druchii throwers. Gorst pushed Father Dagobert down through a tower window and into the flooded chamber within. Eins grabbed Giselle and tried to take off from the tower. Fitch stood in honest horror and soiled himself.

'No!' Archaon bawled as Giselle and Eins disappeared into the gaping trap of the dragon's maw, swiftly followed by Gorst and Fitch. 'No!' he roared again, but there was nothing to be done but save himself. He turned and ran back up the length of the tower. He found Khezula Sheerian standing there. The daemon sorcerer was clutching his bone staff, leaning against it with his misty eyes closed. The sorcerous gemstone that crowned the staff blazed blue. Sheerian had seen with his Eye his Lord Tzeentch's perversity. He had seen that as he had claimed the Brothers Spasskov in his summoning that the Chaos dragon would claim him as part of its own. Archaon leapt from the sinking, black stone of the tower. The great jaws of Flamefang missed him but took the daemon sorcerer a moment later.

Archaon felt it immediately. His armour and mail burned his skin with the deep cold of the water. The shock almost knocked the wind out of the dark templar. Within moments he had something else to worry about – the weight of his plate was dragging him down like an anchor. He clawed at the foaming water. Bubbles raged about him as the colossal *Spite* started its descent below the waves. The evacuating air and thrashing waters were about the only thing keeping the Chaos warrior from sinking. As his head broke the surface he heard the shouts and screams, the drowning boom of the sinking fortress. He saw Father Dagobert. The priest was still clutching *The Liber Caelestior* to his belly to protect it from the water. He was on his knees, precariously reaching out his pudgy hand for the struggling Archaon. The Chaos warrior went under again. Bubbles rushed past his sinking form and it took a clawing, thrashing effort to reach the surface again.

Dagobert was still there. He was shouting something to Archaon, his long, grey hair framing a face lined deeply with his concerns and fears. Dagobert never saw the Chaos dragon return for a second pass. This time flying up the length of the sinking tower, Flamefang streamed purple flame before it. Archaon looked at Dagobert. The priest looked back at him. He didn't even turn around. He knew what was coming. Archaon watched Dagobert disappear in a wall of unnatural flame. Archaon would have called out but he was already half drowning. All he could do was stare up through the shallows as Hieronymous Dagobert – his priest, his father, his friend and his conscience – was lost to the transformative horror of the dragon flame. In that one moment Archaon lost both his past and his future.

The Celestine Book of Divination, Necrodomo's predictions and the destined path he had seen for Archaon the Everchosen of Chaos was now gone. Burned. Warped to oblivion with its faithful translator. Mulched ink and parchment, sinking slowly to the bottom of the Great Eastern Ocean.

At the realisation, Archaon stopped struggling. The deadweight of his armour dragged him down towards the depths. He cared nothing for the men, beasts and daemons that had joined his ranks. To them in turn he personally was nothing. Merely a path to greatness. Hieronymous Dagobert had raised him like a son. Giselle had been ardent in both her love and hate for him. Like the girl and the priest, even Gorst had been with him at the beginning of his dark journey. In turn, the damned tome whose secrets had become both Dagobert's life and his own future was now lost. Forever. Like the Altar of Ultimate Darkness, it was on its way to the darkest depths where no champion of Chaos, no Everchosen of the Dark Gods might acquire it. He was lost and everything was lost to him. The Ruinous Powers had played their sick game. They had tricked him into thinking, feeling and believing that he was the one. They had tricked others into following such a doomed pursuit. They had done this for their own infernal entertainment. They had made Archaon a beacon of darkness. A living deathtrap – so that he might draw mighty souls to his cause before slaughtering them in the Dark Gods' names.

The *Citadel* thundered through the stormy depths. Archaon felt the weight of his armour and the irresistible pull of the sinking fortress take him down. Above, the light of the world was fading. Below there was only the cold invitation of darkness. Archaon allowed it to drag him down. He was done. He was finished with the world of men and gods. They had finished him. The remaining air in his lungs scorched his way through his chest. He wanted to let it go. He wanted the ice-stabbing cold of the blackness below to take him.

Then he saw it. Death from above. Framed in the dwindling twilight of the sea's surface, he saw the thing he had unleashed on the world. The serpentine outline of the monstrous Flamefang. The Chaos dragon had plunged below the waves, drawn down on the sinking doom that was Archaon. Its spindly claws and massive wings pushed it down through the raging bubbles, down through the crumbling masonry of the *Citadel* and down through a sea of bodies. Down to feast on the blinding darklight of the Chaos warrior's soul.

Archaon felt his body tense. The desire to breathe, to live and to fight shot through his frozen body like a lightning strike through a mountain top. *Terminus* came up in his grasp, the water and the deep cold a sluggish drag on his movements. He watched the growing silhouette slither through the water like a snake, its colossal jaws moving from side to side, the horror of its long serpent body cutting through the depths with an undulating ripple. Archaon tensed the remaining warmth in his body through his right arm, preparing for the strike. The Chaos warrior was ready. *Terminus* was ready.

Then he heard a single word echo about the addled, air-deprived rawness of his mind. That word was 'No…'

A 'No' of defiance? A 'No' of defeat?

The Chaos dragon's narrow jaws opened. The dagger-trap of its maw and the bottomless reaches of its throat beckoned. Archaon would never know. As *Terminus* slipped from his grasp and dropped quietly into the depths, Flamefang snapped its colossal jaws closed and plunged Archaon into a darkness he had never known.

'No…' was all he could hear.

'No…' said Archaon, though his lips spoke not. His tortured spirit ached for release.

'No,' said the Dark Master, his words echoing though eternity. 'You are a slave to shadow. You are the prince of calamity. You are the future, my son. You are my future.'

'I am an end to all futures,' Archaon roared at the reasoning darkness.

'Yes, you are…'

'*All* futures, thing of dread that stalks my soul,' Archaon told it. 'My will is my own. My destiny cannot be held in the pages of a damned tome. My soul will not be crushed in the claw of some daemon or dark god.'

'Whatever you need to tell yourself…'

'This flesh will never be yours,' Archaon told the darkness. 'This soul will rail against your bidding. You will come to regret the day you chose me, horror.'

'You were not chosen, Archaon,' the Dark Master raged, scorching him with every word. 'You were never chosen. You were sired on the world so that I might end it. And end it I shall, Archaon. End it I shall. Return to embrace your destiny.'

CHAPTER XV

'I am settled, and throw all that I am,
Every corporeal desire and spiritual agent at
this hopeless feat.'

– Dantalion Altieri, *From the Abyss*

The Black Meridian – The Cliff of Beasts
The Southern Wastes
The Blazes – Dies Irae dies Illa

'No...'

Just a word.

Archaon felt the scalding touch of plate against his skin. The weight of *Terminus* in his frozen fist. The darkness all about him. From the shimmering twilight above he saw the black shape of dread itself descending. The Chaos dragon, its narrow jaws stretched wide, its great talons and wings carrying its serpentine bulk down through the waters. 'No...' Archaon said, bubbles raging from his blue lips.

Instead of kicking away through the water or clawing himself to the side and out of the path of the dagger-trap maw, Archaon surged straight at it. He felt the colossal jaw envelop him like a cave, with rows of twisted stalactites and stalagmites ready to stab straight through him. The dragon's mouth began to close but the Chaos warrior had some stabbing left to do of his own. Kicking up and away from the beast's eye-pimpled tongue and its mangled lower jaw, Archaon thrust upwards with his greatsword. Up at the grotesque roof of the dragon's mouth. Up through faces that stared back down at him from the soft, wet flesh in unspeakable horror. *Terminus* slipped straight through the assimilated patchwork of victims. Archaon put everything he had behind the blade, despite resistance from the icy water. The crusader blade passed through flesh, gristle and slammed through the bone of the monster's malformed skull. Archaon slammed the weapon all the way up to its jewelled crossguard, in the hope that the blade would pierce the abomination's warped brain and once again end Flamefang's reign of transformative terror.

The jaws suddenly spasmed open. The tongue assumed a choked rigidity and the water about Archaon clouded with regurgitated blood. The jaws closed and then jerked opened again. Archaon's gauntlet slipped from the sword's grip and the Chaos warrior found himself tumbling through the dark water as the creature's neck retracted the colossal set of jaws. *Terminus* had not sliced deep enough to kill the monstrous thing. With the length of crafted steel embedded in the back of its throat, the monster was finding it difficult to swallow. Archaon watched the snaking shape of the monstrosity beat its wings for the surface. Fading… fading until finally it broke the ocean surface and disappeared.

Archaon yearned for the weight of *Terminus* in his grip but the greatsword had gone with the dragon. The Chaos warrior had bigger problems. The air trapped in his lungs was roasting him from the inside out. The pressure was unbearable. It threatened to rip its way out of him. He instinctively tried to breathe deeper but there was nothing left of the desperate gasp he had taken on the surface and only the murk of salt water about him. He was deep. Deeper than he had thought possible and between the dragging force of the descending *Spite* and the deadweight of his own plate he was sinking further. With feverish hands he began to tear the mangled plate and shredded mail from his body. Armour sank from his thrashing form and with every piece the dark templar felt the grip the depths had on him loosen. As he tore the final few pieces away from his blood-sticky body he kicked for the surface. The Chaos dragon was gone from his thoughts. As was the loss of his blade. Armies and the destinies that went with them were unreachable in his thoughts. He had only one feeling. One desire. A need so overwhelming that all else fizzled to oblivion. Air. Archaon needed air. He felt his limbs weaken. He felt his mind slip. The Old World had not claimed him and neither had the New. He had survived the insanity of the Northern Wastes. He would be thrice-damned before he allowed the Great Eastern Ocean to claim him. He kicked. He clawed. He roared himself free of the freezing water's seductive grasp.

The sound echoed through the clear, chill skies above. There was splashing. There was coughing and spluttering. There was the sweet ecstasy of lungs filled to bursting with urgent air. Archaon kicked in the water to keep his head above the surface. For a moment he just breathed. He blinked the stinging salt water from his eye. He was there, in the frozen seas of the south. The unexplored seas near the bottom of the world – which no northerner had known – skirted even by the traders of the elder races. Into waters only the damned would dare to venture. Archaon was not alone, however. The *Citadel of Spite* had gone down, taking the Altar of Ultimate Darkness with it to the bottom of the cursed ocean. Wreckage floated about the site of the *Spite*'s sinking: canvas and cordage mostly. Vessels from Archaon's flotilla that had not blown each other to pieces had been flame-savaged by the Chaos dragon and were now making their escape. The water was crowded with bodies. Some had been dead before they hit the water, victims of the mutinous insanity that had swept through the *Spite*. Others had succumbed to the deep cold, as Archaon would if he couldn't find a way to get out of the water.

Marauders and Chaos warriors were screaming for help. With their last frosted breaths they called for compatriots and enemies to return in the fleeing vessels, but the ships were leaving. Archaon could tell by the angle of their masts that many were listing and wouldn't make it far anyway. Those that could make their escape did, on a northerly heading. They weren't coming back. Not for the scum of the world or the Chaos warrior that had led them. They were wise to do so. If they had returned, Archaon would have butchered them for their betrayal.

Archaon swam. It was the only thing he could do to retain what little warmth remained in his body. He felt the icy tendrils of doom creep through his body and stab through his mind. It was becoming difficult to think. Men and beasts died about him in the water, their fur frosting, their armour dragging them down. The dark templar sensed creatures in the water – monstrosities newly liberated from the caverns beneath the *Citadel* had surfaced to feed on the calamitous bounty. Warriors screamed for their lives as serpents and great-gulleted beasts took them. As an undulating monstrosity closed on Archaon, the Chaos warrior smacked his fist at the freezing waters. Sensing that the dark templar might be more trouble than he was worth, the sea monster followed its instincts and slithered at a nearby Hundun tribesman who let loose a gargling scream before being chomped below the waves.

Archaon knew he had little time. As he rolled with the motion of the waves he stared up at the empty sky. If the cold or sea creatures didn't get him then the returning Flamefang would. He could only hope that it had sought out havoc elsewhere. Spotting a tangled piece of floating wreckage, Archaon swam arm over exhausted arm across to it. It appeared to be some mangled spars and cordage from a sunken war-junk. Upon reaching the debris, Archaon discovered that the wreckage had already been claimed by three Kurgan warriors, huddled together and shivering. Archaon hauled himself up onto the bobbing spars, drawing from the marauders a storm of curses and warnings in their tribal tongue. Archaon – bare-chested and white with rime – climbed out of the water. The Kurgans drew their cruel weapons. Archaon gave them the slit of one eye. His mouth curled to a frozen snarl. For the first time the marauders saw the patch on his eye and the eternally burning Mark of Chaos that smouldered like a crown about his bare head.

'Leave,' Archaon growled. The Kurgan looked to one another for reassurance but there wasn't any. They looked to their weapons. 'Go on, get out of here,' the unarmed templar snapped as he moved towards them, prompting the marauders to jump into the deadly waters.

After the *Spite,* the collection of ropes and spars was a miserable command. That didn't stop rabid Chaos warriors from trying to climb aboard – like Archaon attempting to save themselves from the frozen waters. Taking a length of spar, the dark templar bludgeoned his former allies, caving in their helmets and heads before lashing their bodies to the wreckage for extra buoyancy. Stripped bodies of wet floating debris and mounds of corpses floated about him. What full-bellied sea monsters could not swallow, Archaon claimed for his raft. Some were almost frozen solid by the time he got to them, while others – in death – had started to rot and balloon with unnatural speed. As he rolled corpses in the water to get them into position, Archaon discovered that one of the ragged cadavers was a winged warrior of Chaos. It was one of his Swords. Vier. There was movement beneath the Sword's armour that Archaon took for breathing and the dark templar hauled the warrior up onto the raft.

Incredibly, Vier was alive. He had not only survived the dragon's flame but also the fall and brutal landing. Archaon swiftly discovered, however, that the movement wasn't breathing. Vier was suffering under the influence of the Chaos dragon's breath. His form was undergoing grotesque changes that simply through force of will alone Vier was attempting to resist.

Archaon dragged Vier's mangled body into an upright position. Beyond having bone-shattered injuries, his back was hunched. At least one of his wings and an arm had been horribly fused to his body. Things writhed about within him wanting to be free, wanting to blossom into new forms, but the Chaos warrior groaned his way through them. The two of them sat and they shivered as the raft bobbed away from the floating collection of bodies and debris.

Without means to steer the raft, Archaon was at the perverse mercy of the currents that seemed to be dragging his macabre jury-rigged vessel further south into the darkness and temperatures that plunged further than Archaon could imagine.

Frosted in his scraps of armour and decorated in a motley collection of mismatched weaponry, Archaon appeared more like one of his miserable marauders or tribesmen than the warlord who had led them. Survival was his prime concern. Water. Food. Warmth. He licked the frost and rime routinely formed on the wood of the spars. He cut frozen meat from the mound of corpses that made up the raft. He established a small fire in a cooking pot, burning scalps and the fat cut from the better-fed of the cadavers. Enough to dry his furs and armour – scrap by painstaking scrap – and warm hands that felt as if they had already fallen off. Vier took nothing. The Sword just sat and suffered through his attempted transformations. Archaon found himself watching the Chaos warrior for signs of treachery, signs that he might have become something else. He was loath to dump his Sword of Chaos, however, and secretly welcomed the distraction.

It was a miserable existence but as the days turned to weeks, it was an existence – and to Archaon that was all that mattered. He spent his time searching both the seas and sky. Flamefang would make short work of the raft with its narrow jaws and streams of warping flame. He saw nothing of the dragon, however, and assumed that it had headed inland in search of more populous prey. The bleak horizon was equally empty. The waters were dark, the air cutting and the seas empty of sail. Mainly Archaon slept. Boredom, exhaustion and futility combined to drag him into wretched dreams. In some he was still a warlord, commanding champions and the legions of Chaos. In others he was haunted by a daemon darkness. The thing that watched him from the shadows and even now, in the stark emptiness of the polar seas, seemed to be with him. Murmuring the insanities of fevered sleep, Archaon wished it gone. Sometimes it stayed. Sometimes it seemed to leave. Sometimes it left others in its stead. Corpses that rose from the lashed cadavers to point, to accuse and berate with droning insistence. Father Dagobert, Giselle, Sheerian. Giselle in particular would scream at him, spit at him, slap him. Her furious strikes were too feeble to leave an impression on the Chaos warrior but were sometimes enough to snap him from his nightmares.

Shuddering to wakefulness, Archaon found that he was shaking. It was cold. Colder than before. The fire in the pot was out. Vier was groaning his agonies. The raft was rocking and the dark templar could hear a slushy creak. He had been asleep for some time. Rubbing some life back into the frozen mask of his face, Archaon got to his feet. The horizon had changed. It was not the mind-bending flat line stretching into eternity that it had been. It was angular and shattered. He had reached the seasonal ice of some southern land. Great bergs bobbed about him. The dark waters were gone. Ice lay before the raft and the skies were the broiling black of pitch. Far beyond, in the distance, Archaon could see the distant pinnacle glow of eruptions, betraying the presence of volcanoes dotted about the horizon.

It seemed that the raft had been drifting for some time through the outer extent of the ice. Its passage was demonstrated in the narrow channel of black water and slush it had cut south as it had drifted. Before the raft the ice had also cracked. The fracture extended south, as far as Archaon could see, funnelling the ramshackle raft on. It was like a long, black line extending into the distance.

Archaon's mind ached back through the slaughter, the devastation and the cold. Back to what Sheerian had told him. That the next treasure of Chaos to be discovered lay on a Black Meridian. The Chaos warrior's eyes followed the fracture south. A black line of water through the whiteness of the ice. A Black Meridian. A nasty chuckle escaped the dark templar's burning lips.

As the raft bounced and slushed its way through the fracture, the blackening skies plunged the frozen wilderness into darkness. With the volcanic brume churning above, lanced by strange lightning it became clear that these southern lands had never seen sun, moon or the blessing of a clear sky. There was something supernatural and potent about the place. The freezing air could not only graze the skin and stop the heart, it burned with the presence of the Dark Gods and their daemons. Far, far across the great oceans – at the bottom of the world – Archaon had discovered the Southern Wastes. A frozen hell like the one he had traversed in the north. As the cursed heavens raged and the darkness became absolute, drowning the meridian and turning the ice to a frosted obsidian, Archaon came to realise that these Southern Wastes were much, much worse.

The land seemed as if it was surrounded by the chill seas. It shared no border with the realms of men. There was no eternal battle to fight. No champions vying for the favour of Ruinous gods. This was a darker place – of abyssal soul and purpose. It was primordial. A land of chaos and havoc. A place of degenerate malevolence. As he drifted further into the savage lands, the temperature plummeted and the winds picked up. The darkness beyond the raft became a blurred stream of snow and howling elemental ferocity. The mountains of fire and fury drew closer. They stormed the explosive brilliance of magma into the inky skies above, raining ash into the maelstrom and trailing bifurcating rivers of lava that cut through the unnatural ice, giving the land what little light it enjoyed – the infernal glow of a dungeon or underworld.

In the light of the lava, the denizens of this desperate land were revealed to Archaon. Even in the blackness of the storm, Archaon could make out shapes in the darkness. The movement of beings. Hundreds of them. Thousands. He was in an undiscovered realm. The darklight of his own doom didn't extend very far in such a place. In the radiance of the crawling rivers of magma, however, Archaon saw that the bleak realm was overrun with monsters. In the depths of the darkness, in the shrieking swirl and the infernal cold, Archaon saw beastmen without number. These were not the weakling corruptions of man and beast he had encountered in the forests of the Empire, nor the savage tribes of animal fury he had yoked to his warmongering in the Shadowlands. These were daemonbreeds.

Diabolical fusions of fiend, beast and god knows what else. These shaggy beasts were sculptures in midnight muscle, cloven of hoof and crowned with extravagant tangles of daemon horn. In the ember twilight, their gore-smeared snouts and bestial fang-faces were contorted with the base desires that ruled their monstrous kingdom. On those faces Archaon found his Dark Gods – rage and the barbaric tribal ambitions it served, the hang-dog suffering of such a wretched existence and the animal indulgences that were to alleviate the afflictions of both mind and the flesh. The ruinous drives of all living things were to be found in the swarming hordes of beasts that plagued the storm-scathed wilderness.

When a throng of monstrosities were drawn in on the thawing flesh of his corpse-raft, Archaon and Vier were forced to abandon the craft. Sinking into his scraps of fur and leather and tightening a belt heavy with recovered weapons, the dark templar set off on foot with the horribly transformed Vier limping behind. Despite a broken leg, hunched back and malformed limbs, the Sword of Chaos simply would not give up and die. Drawing a bone sword from his remaining wing he hobbled behind his master like a wretched sentinel, moaning his exertions.

The beastfiends about the raft had no weapons of their own – no blades to cut flesh or hack bone. Instead they just set upon the dead marauders with their clawed hands, tearing flesh and organs out of the cadavers with animal abandon. Archaon left them to sink their muzzles into the spoiling meat but as he crept away he could hear the creatures' fangs tearing and the pegs of their chisel-teeth working their way through the carcasses. Nothing would be wasted – of that Archaon was sure. The Chaos warrior didn't plan on being there when the meat ran out.

His footsteps in borrowed boots took him through the howling storm. For six days and six nights Archaon stumbled along the benighted path – although without sun or moon to tell one from the other it was almost impossible to tell. All Archaon knew was that his belly burned with hunger and his lips cracked for want of water. His legs fell to numbness with the torment of steps never-ending and his senses ached with the demands of constant vigilance. Beyond, Archaon could hear the infernal roaring of beastmen at war. Tribes of fiendbreeds fought for the miserable featureless territory about the meltwater darkness of their birthing pools on the obsidian ice. They snorted, wrangled and butchered each other without end, burdening the icy gales with the perpetual bellows of death and savage celebration. Those closest sniffed with suspicion at the advancing Chaos warrior. Their milky eyes saw little but opportunity and death but their sense of smell was daemonically acute. If Archaon had been anyone else, he was sure that he would have been torn to pieces in moments. He wasn't just anyone else. He was Archaon. Chosen of the Ruinous Powers and Herald of the End Times. None of the creatures would know his name or have heard of his deeds but the Chaos warrior had the stink of dark destiny on him. He was an evil they had never known and they were cautious of it. Occasionally beasts would charge from the darkness and rage at Archaon, prompting the dark templar's frost-scalded hands to slip down to the jangling nest of blades and axes that sat snug in his belt. They would not attack him and as soon as he had trudged out of the barren slush of their territory, they left him alone to pursue aggressions elsewhere.

As the black fissure in the ice turned to a river of inky meltwater and the channel in turn became a road of solidifying volcanic stone, Archaon saw other things in the storm-flashed hordes. The landscape was a colossal graveyard. The bleak, howling wilderness was littered with the monstrous bones and skeletons of legendary creatures. Things giant, warped and long dead. Like outposts or tribal hubs, the great bones and vaulted ribcages of these beasts formed shelters for the swarming beastfiends of the wilderness. There were daemons here – in profusion. The storms begat the infernal things – monsters springing forth from the momentary blindness of lightning strikes and billowing blizzards of ice and ash. The creatures of nightmare stalked Archaon and each other through the crowded forest of shaggy beastmen. Their outlandish forms and the horror of their fiendflesh and faces were pure terror to behold. They were the diabolical servants of the Dark Gods, crafted in their image and just about everything else. They knew Archaon not by his scent but the potency of his presence. The Chaos warrior burned with the darklight of fate. It drew them down on him and Archaon had to be constantly alert to their predations.

Every time a horror leapt from the storm or tore through a roaring sea of beasts at him, another suddenly emerged from its hiding place in the infernal gloom and horribly destroyed its devilkin. The daemons and fiend-princes of different Chaos gods played at the game of death and destruction about the dark templar's implacable advance, ripping each other apart in contestation for the Chaos warrior's soul. With the maelstrom swirling above his head, Archaon could almost imagine the Ruinous Powers looking down on him. Their eyes could be hungry for glory or full of disappointment and disapproval. Archaon could not know and he did not care. He had found the undiscovered realm and was on the Black Meridian. A mighty treasure of Chaos waited for him and nothing would put the warrior from his path.

Then he heard it. Not the roar of a beastman or a daemon shriek. It was the heaven-shattering thunder of dragoncall. Tzeentch's monstrous calamity. The *Yien-Ya-Long.* Flamefang. The terror of Grand Cathay and now the terror of the Southern Wastes. Denied its prize and still hungry for the warlord's soul, the creature was hunting him through the maelstrom. Archaon peered into the raging tempest about him and up into the spewing murk above. For a moment he thought he saw the winged monstrosity, beating its wings through the raging turmoil of the skies, but he couldn't be sure. The purple inferno that erupted some way distant into the hordes was unmistakable, however. Bathed in the violaceous glow of its own transformative flame, Archaon saw the thing. He dropped into a crouch, desperate not to be spotted by one of the many eyes that writhed in the smeared flesh of its supernatural hide. It was huge. Much bigger than when Sheerian had given the monster's spirit form on board the *Citadel of Spite* or when Archaon had fought it below the waves. As the Chaos dragon carpeted the bestial hordes with Lord Tzeentch's blessing, turning the beastfiend and the daemon, the torched and thrashing to spawn, Archaon could see why. Turning its head to one side and opening the colossal length of its narrow jaws wide, Flamefang funnelled the changelings down its gaping throat – their precious flesh to be assimilated into its own. With such an appetite, the Chaos dragon had decimated the east. Now, fuelled by fiendflesh and daemon souls, the gargantuan beast intended to make the Southern Wastes its own.

Archaon pushed on. Flamefang had been unleashed at his command. It had feasted on his failure but it would not claim him. The Chaos warrior nodded to himself. Greater things waited for him than a dragon's gullet. Keeping low, Archaon hurried on along his damned path. His Black Meridian. As the endless road of black volcanic rock approached one of the many black peaks that blighted the swarming ice, the Chaos warrior felt the soles of his boots warm. The stone was shot through with glowing cracks, betraying the melted rock beneath. The road was leading him right up to the volcano and had in fact been created by a channel of magma that had cascaded down the mountainside and slowly slurped its way impossibly straight and impossibly north towards the coast. Unusually, the volcano's summit was dark and dormant but for the slightest suggestion of a cooling glow. A crown of lesser cones reached out of the black scree-side of the central tor, each summit a furious pinnacle of dribbling ash and sky-scorching lava.

Stepping from the burning stone, Archaon trekked alongside the road, his path turning from black crust to the murky red of bubbling magma to the furious splashing yellow of liquid rock. The sputtering lava glowed with the diabolical heat of a daemon furnace and Archaon was forced further and further from its flaming shores as the channel grew wider. As he neared the volcano, with Vier hobbling behind, it became clear that a series of structures had been carved into the igneous rock. A small, craggy city of black stone, dusted with ash. The architecture was colossal and ancient. Massive pillars. Standing stone archways. Dark temples. Rough amphitheatres.

As Archaon and Vier moved through the damned structures on the rising slope of the volcano, it became clear that the city had been long abandoned. Beastfiends swarmed the ruins, assuming structures for themselves with territorial ferocity. They fought between themselves. They gorged themselves. They cannibalised their own. They slept. All the while, hunted through the ancient derelicts by predacious daemons.

Archaon and Vier moved up through the city-slope as quietly as they could. Progress was agonisingly slow, moving from building to shattered building. They hid behind fallen pillars and crumbling ruins. They moved through the darkness of collapsed temples and across the ash of forgotten arenas. They waited while hordes of beasts fought each other in the streets. They held still and silent while the victors crunched the bones of the fallen. They moved on only when the hordes passed on. Still, the Chaos warriors were forced to butcher many of the beastfiends. Grabbing the monsters. Strangling. Slitting throats. Stabbing through muscle and into hearts. Their murderous progress through the city was silent and bloody. They could not afford to bring a city of bestial monstrosities down on them.

As the ruins began to thin on the lower slopes of the volcano peak and the ascent became harsh, Archaon picked out standing stones at intervals about the mountainside. The stones bore a selection of runes and symbols, obviously infernal in nature but many the Chaos warrior didn't recognise. Even the storm seemed to grow to a respectful stillness about the mountain. Assuming the dark peak to have some corrupt spiritual significance, like a shrine or burial ground, the Chaos warrior strode on unmolested. Beastfiends and daemons seemed not to congregate in the craggy upper reaches, where the lava channels raged and the standing stones communicated silent significance.

Step by step Archaon began to loosen the rags, furs and shreds of armour that had provided feeble protection from the murderous cold and freezing temperatures of the Southern Wastes. As the rigid rags began to thaw, Archaon felt drenched to the marrow but a few minutes walking alongside the roasting river of molten stone dried and warmed the warrior's frozen bones. Holding a hand out against the glare and the intense heat, Archaon ascended the slope, jumping from burning boulder to igneous crag. The climb was harsh but welcome after the monotonous road leading to it through the dark wilderness and the slow progress through the ruined city. Above, Archaon could see that the channel was oozing its way from a ragged cave entrance in the side of the main tor. An entrance shaped like an eight-pointed star. The realisation put a crooked smile on the dark templar's lips and a surge in his step. He was close.

The first indication that there was anything wrong was the coolness on the back of his head. For a while now, Archaon had been baked in the unrelenting heat of the lava channel. Beads of sweat had rolled from his brow and down his bare head. The sensation of the breeze dancing across his skin was immediately pleasant and horrifying. Spinning around, Archaon caught the final moments of Flamefang's descent. Spotting him alone on the scree slope, the Chaos dragon had thundered from the black, billowing heavens, flapping its wings at the last moment to effect a landing on the volcano's side. Smashing into the mountainside, its talons sinking into the hot rock like anchors, the sheer size of the beast shook the ground beneath Archaon's boots.

Behind the creature, stone archways toppled and columns crumbled to the ground. The dragon's mighty arrival had sent a quake through the ruined city, sending the fragility of its structures into a succession of collapses that swallowed the city in a cloud of black dust. From below Archaon could hear the furious bellow of disturbed beastfiends and the howl of daemons. As Flamefang clawed its thunderous way up the side of the volcano, its tail whipped this way and that, cleaving through the structures behind it and laying fiend-swarming temples to waste. With every colossal movement, the Chaos dragon shook the ground.

Archaon lost his footing and began to skid down towards the monster. Boulders bounced down the slope, dislodged from above, and tumbled down at both Archaon and the dragon. Moving from side to side, the dark templar allowed the larger pieces of rock to plunge past him and shatter on the assimilated bulk of the Chaos dragon.

Flamefang too was struggling with its footing, its great claws tearing through the loose rock and scree of the slope. Sweeping its neck around, the monster reached up, snapping at Archaon with its gargantuan jaws. Archaon leapt from his purchase, sending the boulder he was standing on down towards the beast where it was pulverised in the trapjaw tip of the dragon's maw instead of the Chaos warrior.

Flame washed up the mountainside, forcing Archaon to take cover behind a rocky outcrop, where he found the Sword Vier similarly taking cover. Looking back up at the cave entrance, Archaon snarled. He would never make the climb up there with the Chaos dragon at his back.

Vier seemed to know exactly what his master was thinking. What his master needed. Painfully drawing his bone sword from one warped wing, the warrior bumped his mangled fist off Archaon's shoulder before moving out from the outcrop. Archaon nodded, peering out after the Sword of Chaos. He skidded down the scree-side at Flamefang, who was simultaneously distracted by the beastfiends swarming at it from the demolished section of ruinscape. As it snapped and streamed purple flame at the gathering hordes, Vier made his wretched approach, his vengeance intended to buy his master the time he needed to reach his prize.

Clawing with bloody fingers at the shattered rock, Archaon pulled himself up towards the cave entrance. His only chance was to get inside and put the mountainside between himself and the dragon. As the agony of the climb took hold, Archaon could hear the screeches of daemons and the savage futility of beastfiends snapped up in Flamefang's monstrous jaws. Soon Vier was lost to him, as was the crumbling city and its fell denizens as the demolishing of structures sent great clouds of ash and black dust skyward. The volcanic miasma was lit up by the purple flash of flame, as the Chaos dragon visited the transformative wrath of Tzeentch on the Infernals.

It was a gruelling climb. The ledges and handholds cut like glass and most of what Archaon placed his boots on came away from the cliff face. Below, the carnage had ended. Flamefang erupted out of the cloud of dust and destruction the undisputed victor, clawing its colossal way up the steep incline after Archaon. The beast of Tzeentch surged up the slope, several beats of its wings carrying it to its prey – the blazing soulfire of the Chaos warrior's irrepressible spirit leading it on. Once more the jaws opened. With nowhere to jump to, the dark templar was forced to allow his boot to skid down the slope. The dragon chomped at the side of the mountain, its twisted teeth dislodging chunks of black rock and a shower of gravel.

Climbing around the side of the volcano, Archaon attempted to take shelter behind one of the razor-sharp ridges running down the side of the mountain. He heard a horrible thunder build up within the creature's gigantic form and knew it was about to breathe its purple flame. The inferno torched the mountainside, blasting grit and loose rock from the volcano. Archaon managed to haul himself around the razor-sharp ridge in time, the black rock soaking up the worst of Flamefang's warpflame. With horror the dark templar realised that the purple flame had washed across the furs covering the back of his shoulder and two fingers of his left hand. The little finger and ring finger seared, as if they had been dipped in boiling oil. Archaon snarled through a cry of pain and tried to secure his purchase.

Suddenly he felt the burning furs draping one of his shoulders move. The warpflame had given them a new and horrible life. Feeling a morphing set of jaws sink into his shoulder, Archaon tore the rippling fur from his flesh and cast the mutating thing down the mountainside. Through the scalding sensation of his two fingers, Archaon felt his flesh rebel. Skin stretched. Flesh changed. Bone began to grow. Disgust washed through him. He thought of the unfortunate Vier and the horror he had both resisted and become. The fingers began to change and Archaon didn't want to know what they were to become. He certainly didn't want the flesh-warping effect to spread. Slipping a marauder's axe from his belt and placing his left hand against the warm rock of the mountainside, the Chaos warrior cleaved down with the axe and struck them off. As the two digits fell with the sparks from the stone, Archaon clutched the injured hand to him. He felt his own blood soak through the material to his chest.

Again, Flamefang's great gavial jaws came at him and with pain-fuelled fury, Archaon flung the axe at the beast. The weapon's rough blade buried itself in the creature's nostril-flaring snout, doing little to persuade the beast to leave him alone. With one bloody fist clutched to his chest, Archaon climbed for his life. With the monster's jaws chewing through the scenery behind him, the Chaos warrior scrabbled his way up the scree slope, punching handholds into the igneous rubble. With the dragon's jaws just torso-sheering moments behind him, Archaon hauled himself up through the ragged star-shaped opening to the cave. The light. The heat. The radiance of the river of lava slowly coursing through the rough, black passage beyond was almost unbearable. Everything was bathed in a blinding infernal glow and flame danced from the shreds of clothing and armour that Archaon was wearing, just by being close to the channel of bubbling magma. Slapping out the flames and dragging himself along the course with one arm, the Chaos warrior kicked back through the gravel to safety.

Or so the dark templar thought. Suddenly the Chaos dragon's jaws were there. It had hauled itself up to the cave entrance and pushed the colossal length of its narrow jaws down into its depths. Archaon heard the tortured screams of the assimilated unfortunates whose stolen flesh charred and burned at such proximity to the molten rock.

'Burn, you monstrosity,' Archaon hissed back at the creature as the mournful roar of Flamefang itself joined the flesh-stolen of its form. The thing struggled with its purchase, the dragon tearing its claw-holds away and dashing itself with spatters of hide-scorching lava. Its jaws suddenly plunged down the length of the cave, the writhing dimensions of its head turning the star-shaped opening to rubble. Archaon kicked back through the grit. The blaze of the liquid rock roasted him from one side while Flamefang's mangled fangs attempted to snap up a scrabbling foot or leg and drag its soul-prey back into the open.

Archaon watched as the dragon's jaws opened. Bathed in the effulgence of the passage, the horror of the monster's maw was revealed. Within its depths Archaon saw another head – a blind, obscene set of jaws set within the first. The huge head shot out at the Chaos warrior, all malformed flesh and twisted fang. Archaon kicked back from the thing that seemed to extend on a horrid neck of its own. The jaws parted to reveal a third set of jaws within the second. Like a telescope the horrid appendage extended, snapping at Archaon with a savage, rhythmic abandon. The beast wanted his flesh and his soul so badly that Archaon could feel it in the feverish snap of the inset jaw. Archaon kicked back at the monster's reach, his right boot snagging on the monstrous fang-trap. The jaws retracted and dragged the dark templar a little way back through the grit before his boot came free. With nothing but a scavenged marauder boot for its agony and trouble, the furious Flamefang withdrew its narrow jaws from the cave entrance and took its lava-scorched screeches into the sky.

Archaon tried to spit after the beast but the chamber was too hot and his mouth was too dry. He had to get away from the infernal intensity of the lava flow. Limping with one boot through the razor-sharp volcanic shale, Archaon made his way up the searing passage. As it snaked through the blackness of the mountain's interior, the molten glow lighting his way, Archaon looked down to his bloodied hand, to his missing fingers. He had to do something about the injury. Crouching and reaching for the bubbling lava as close as he dared, he felt the searing agony flare up once again as the heat cauterised the wound. Retracting the hand and working his remaining fingers and thumb, he found them to be burned but serviceable. Tearing a scrap of clothing from his body he fashioned and tied off a swift bandage before lurching on through the brilliance of the cave.

The draining potency seemed to go on forever. The passage wormed its way through the roasting mountain, with Archaon stumbling along it, the half of his face and head turned towards the molten river scorched to redness. The Chaos warrior finally found some brief relief as the passage opened out and the channel widened. He rested for a moment against a crag of jagged black rock, cowering before the intense heat before drawing his gaze upwards. Only then did he realise that he had reached the end of the cursed Black Meridian. The journey was over. He had arrived.

CHAPTER XVI

'Unconquered.'

– Epitaph – The tomb of Morkar 'The Uniter',
First Everchosen of Chaos

Mount Ceno
The Southern Wastes
Horns Harrowing: The Season of Fire

Pulling his rags across his mouth, Archaon found it difficult to breathe. The opening chamber was a pit of heat and noxious gases. He found himself within the colossal cone of the volcano tor. The interior seemed dormant but for the bubbling lake of lava that dominated the chamber floor and lit the walls of the cone with a dungeon glow. Limping towards it, Archaon discovered that a series of stones – like stepping stones – led from the seething shore to an island of black rock that occupied the middle of the lake. Looking about him, Archaon found that the walls all about the cone interior were decorated with stone caskets. Resting on crags and spurs, equal in distance from one another and reaching up the dormant volcano interior, Archaon beheld thousands of sarcophagi, rough and carved of igneous rock. Hobbling over to the nearest, resting on jagged spurs in the rockface nearby, the dark templar saw that it bore the Ruinous Star of the Chaos Powers united. Putting his ear to the casket top, the Chaos warrior heard the strangest sound. Archaon would recognise it anywhere. It was the sound of battle. It was the sound of blades clashing, bawling war cries and men dying. The sound was distant. Like an echo of eternity. Archaon drew one of several short blades he was carrying – a Kurgan falchion. Using the flared tip of the poor blade, Archaon prised the lid off the sarcophagus and pushed it aside. Within, the sound of battle eternal died. The coffin was bare of bones. It contained only the rusted remnants of a Chaos blade. Listening through the lids of the next and the next, Archaon found the same. The distant cacophony of war. Different battles. Different voices calling out in triumph or death. In each Archaon found a mouldering weapon, some still bearing the stains of ancient slaughter.

The dark templar nodded to himself. He was standing in a tomb. Here, in the wickedness of the Southern Wastes, the exalted warriors of Chaos had been laid to rest – their bones recovered to wither in the noxious heart of this mountain, their souls to fight on for the glory of their deranged gods.

Tearing a rag from his torso, Archaon tied the material about his foot and strode on towards the molten lake. Once again the intense heat threatened to overwhelm him. Stepping out onto the first stone, Archaon felt assailed from all sides by the blinding fury of the lake. As he stepped from one stone to another, his will weakening and his knees faltering, the poisonous gases of the chamber filled his lungs and the heat scorched his skin. Everything sizzled, slurped and crackled. As he reached the final stone, the craggy footfall cracked and sheared away into the lava. Falling to a crouch, his hands clutching the small rock and his foot held over the searing surface of the lake, Archaon jumped. He landed on the island's shale shore and rolled through the shattered rock, cutting his back to ribbons. Pulling shards of stone from his flesh, the dark templar walked up the shore. Above him, the volcano opened out onto the broiling blackness of a doom-laden sky.

The island seemed to support a roughly hewn architecture. It was scorch-shattered and dusted with ash. The structure lay in ruins but Archaon recognised certain elements of its construction. There seemed to be a hearth and a firepot of molten rock. Hollows contained the solidified dregs of molten metal. Shapes and moulds that had been carved into the stone. Archaon even saw what was left of a hammer, buried in the dust. The Chaos warrior was fairly sure that he was standing in some infernal smithy or daemon forge. As he passed through the crumbling ruins and reached the heart of the forge tomb, his suspicions were confirmed.

Archaon fell down to his knees in the volcanic grit. He lowered his head in reverence and relief. Before him stood a stone dais bearing the assembled pieces of a suit of infernal armour. Archaon stared up at the ancient plate. Its design had a simple monstrosity to it. The work of the insane genius of some daemon craftsman. Both the metal plates and the mail upon which they were set were fashioned of some outlandish metal. The suit's bold cuirass and pauldrons suggested both fortitude and elegance, while the plates that covered both arms and legs appeared to overlap for extra protection, like the hull planks of a clinker-built vessel. Sturdy armoured boots and the intricate workings of plate gauntlets sat abandoned in the dust, while the reinforced expanse of a body shield bearing the riveted glory of an eight-pointed star and a central spike rested nearby. Bronzed skulls had been crafted seamlessly into the suit's fearful breastplate. They appeared to complement the leering, brazen skull that was the suit's fearful helmet. Extravagant eruptions of daemon horn adorned the sides of the helm while the sculpted eye sockets allowed the infernal light of the forge to probe its inner darkness.

Archaon rose before the ancient armour. He approached the daemon design with the flutter of excitement and expectation in his chest. This was truly a treasure of Chaos. He took the skull-crafted breastplate from the stone dais and held it up for inspection. The metal was thick but unexpectedly light. Unlike the weapons within the caskets, the unusual metal of the suit's forging seemed untouched by the ravages of time or the decimating attentions of the environment. Turning the breastplate around, Archaon noticed that there was a bronze plate on the gorget interior bearing an inscription. It was an epitaph, like one might find on an ancient tomb. It simply said *'Unconquered'* and bore the name Morkar beneath.

Morkar. *Morkar*. Archaon knew the name. How could he not? It echoed about the Northern Wastes, carried on the curses of champions and the boasts of murderous marauders. Morkar was legend. Morkar – the Uniter. The beacon of Chaos whose dark light eclipsed the dawn of civilisation. The First Everchosen of the Ruinous Powers.

Morkar – Ravager of the fledgling Empire of man. Slain by a false god two and a half thousand years before Archaon had been born. Archaon stared about the volcano interior at the thousands of sarcophagi lining the black walls. Morkar's United. The honoured warriors of Chaos who had fought at Morkar's side. Archaon nodded to himself with dark glee. The fabled armour of Morkar was his. How it came to be here so long after the Everchosen's defeat, Archaon could not tell. All he knew was that the Dark Gods had tested him. They had sent Archaon by way of insanity, betrayal and death but finally the path to damnation had led him to victory – to this infernal mountain and a Ruinous treasure of the Chaos Powers. The armour of Morkar was his reward. The second treasure by which the Everchosen and Lord of the End Times would be known.

A smile bled through the dark templar's cracked lips. He began tearing the rags and scraps of leather from his body. The armour was his and plate by damned plate, Archaon dressed his bruised and broken body with both its physical and infernal protections. Despite the heat of the surroundings, the armour felt cool on the Chaos warrior's skin. Volcanic dust showered from the ancient plate revealing the strange lustre of the metal beneath. Hefting the body shield onto his left arm, he snatched up the skull-helm by one great horn. He went to slip the helmet over his bare head – to plunge face first into the darkness within – but something caught his eye. Turning the helmet around and staring down at the leering skull Archaon noticed that between the horns and set in the brow between the crafted eye sockets, there was a depression. This the Chaos warrior found odd since the armour bore no other examples of damage. Scraping the depression with the finger of one gauntlet, the dust that caked it fell away, revealing its true shape and dimension. A shape and dimension that the dark templar had seen before and instantly recognised.

Crafted in the forehead of the helm was a distinctive socket – an eye-shaped socket – set to receive a decorative jewel of some kind. And Archaon knew which jewel. It was just the right size and shape to ensconce the Eye of Sheerian. The prophetic gem of Khezula Sheerian, the daemon sorcerer of Tzeentch.

Archaon looked up from the helm. Up the black rock of the mountain interior and up out of the caldera top. He stared up at the tumultuous black skies with wretched scorn and a face full of hate.

'You faithless gods,' he roared up at them. 'You monsters of the perverse. You givers and takers... Why?'

Archaon angled the helmet to see inside. The helm had been crafted to allow its owner to wear a band or crown. Morkar's armour was that of Ruinous royalty. The front of both the missing crown and the helm allowed the setting of the sorcerous jewel which had to be a further treasure of the Chaos Powers. A treasure both Archaon and the Dark Gods had conspired to put in the belly of the monstrous dragon, Flamefang. Both cold fury and futility flooded the Chaos warrior. Then, as he thought on such a treasure being so close to his feverish grasp, Archaon's god-cursing snarl dropped to a savage smile. As the Dark Gods had set Ruinous champion against Ruinous champion, Archaon would do the same with their hallowed treasures. With the enchanted armour of Morkar, perhaps Archaon could defeat the colossal Chaos dragon that hunted him like soul-prey across ocean and Southern Wastes. His fate decided, Archaon slipped the helm over his head and became one with the darkness within.

Staring about the inside of the helmet, Archaon knew only the deepest darkness. The slits of the skull-helm eye sockets admitted none of the evil glare of the lava lake. Holding his gauntlets out in front of him, Archaon could not see them. When he tried to take the helmet off, he discovered that it refused to be separated from the gorget and cuirass upon which it sat.

Then he heard a noise in the darkness. Distant. An ancient echo of slaughter long past. Building to a cacophonous crescendo. In the blackness of the helm he heard the sounds of battle. Blades. Shouts. Screams. Just like he had heard within the sarcophagi of Morkar's long dead warriors of Chaos.

'Worm…' a blistering voice ventured from the black oblivion. It sounded as old as time itself, like an antique blade honed on the events of a dark history to come. 'Scavenger… Robber of graves. This is blasphemy. That the pantheon would send such a miserable beggar to fall before their warlord, their prince. To fail so completely and to have his screams echo for always about the darkness of my tomb.'

As the potent presence spoke, Archaon felt the darkness within the armour wash over his skin. Like a man drowning in a lightless void, Archaon felt the darkness enter his ears, his nose and his roaring mouth. It gushed down his throat and soaked through his skin. It granted him oblivion. He was completely alone. Not even he was there. There was only the voice.

'You thought you could steal from me, worm?' the words proceeded, powerful and primordial. 'I wore this armour on the precipice of dark providence. It was baptised in the blood of a king who would become a god. It carried me to my doom. *My* doom – as it carries you to your own, pretender to the crown. This armour is mine.'

Morkar...

The impact was like nothing Archaon had ever felt. The Chaos warrior was not accustomed to being hit but occasionally it happened. When it did it felt nothing like the colossal blow that had just knocked him from his feet. He felt himself skid through the volcanic dust before coming to a stop. He was blind. He was trapped on an island of black stone at the heart of a molten lake. He was being attacked. Archaon tried to get up. The dreadful force had hammered him from the right. He instinctively brought up his shield. The same force suddenly smashed into him from the left. The Chaos warrior flew to the side, smashing straight through the igneous rock of the forge before rolling to a stop in the dust and shattered stone. Archaon tried to get up but he couldn't even find his way to the thought. The impact had smashed his mind into a stunned ache.

Pushing up out of the grit, another blow found him beneath the chin of his helm. Archaon flew backwards through the air before coming back down with a heart-stopping crash. Archaon clawed at the shale beneath his armoured fingertips. Volcanic shale. The Chaos warrior tried to find his way to a single thought. Shale. The shore. Archaon was locked in an abyssal darkness. The blows smashing him about the island were daemonic in their intensity, supernatural in their precisely applied force. Incredibly, these were not his biggest problem. His biggest problem was the likelihood that the next blow would send him flying off the shale shoreline and into the lake of molten rock. When the impact came, it was soul-shattering.

Suddenly, light. The blinding radiance of the day. A sun Archaon had not seen in what seemed like forever. Colours. Shapes. Trees. He was there. Back in the forests of the Empire. Smoke stung his nostrils. The smoke of destruction, utter and merciless. He could taste blood on his lips. His own and that of barbarian tribesmen whose slaughter hung on the air like a bloody mist. There was a barbarian before him. A Reiklander. A small mountain of muscle, decked in forest furs, trailing the long, unkempt mane of a savage. He was not alone. He introduced Archaon to his companion. A dwarf hammer. A warhammer of haft, rune and gold. A warhammer whose enchanted and unstoppable head trailed blood and destiny. *Ghal Maraz*. Skull-splitter. And then Sigmar hit him.

Something broke deep within Archaon. His body smashed through the trees before bouncing off and around the thick trunks of Empire oaks and Reikland heartwoods. His armoured form spun like a discarded doll before coming to a stop in the leaves and the dirt. Archaon brought up his weapon, a sword that smoked with daemonic fury… but again Sigmar was there. The Unberogen had stormed through the forest at Archaon like a force of nature. *Ghal Maraz* smashed though the blade and it shattered like silver glass. The barbarian turned on his heel and brought the terrible weapon around and down.

When it hit Archaon it felt like an earthquake. The Chaos warrior was smashed down through the black forest earth, the stone and roots and into a hollow of his own making. Sigmar leapt into the pit, landing like a great cat. Like a wild lion, his face was contorted with noble savagery. Eyes narrow and teeth bared. He had confronted a thing of evil and now he was to destroy it. It was the end for Archaon. His God-King would destroy him.

His God-King. Archaon reached back. Back through the blood and treachery – back to a time of simple falsehoods. A God-King and the tales that were told about him. Tales that false priests and templars promoted as belief, venerated and worshipped. Archaon knew this tale. He knew how it ended.

Morkar the Uniter. Favoured of darkness. Everchosen of the Chaos gods – smashed and defeated – pushed his helm up off his head and looked up at Sigmar Heldenhammer. The man who would be a god. *Ghal Maraz* came up, for it was his destiny to end the evil that had ridden out of the north on a deluge of Ruinous warrior-savages.

'Brinnan utva lioht,' Sigmar spat – a curse of his barbarian ancestors. An Unberogen curse Archaon had come to know in his former calling. Not only as his God-King's holy words but also a Sigmarite templar's way of life. *Brinnan utva lioht. Burn by the light.*

'Brinnan utva lioht,' Archaon spat and brought the great hammer down on Morkar's head with such righteous force that rather than split the Everchosen's skull, he obliterated it, hammering blood and bone into the forest bedrock.

Archaon rose from the molten rock of the lake. Lava spilled down his glowing plate. Magma dribbled from his backplate and pauldrons. Through the socket-slits of his skull-helm and the haze of heat, Archaon could see. Liquid rock bubbled and spat about him like an infernal sea. He had been knocked into the lake of lava but the daemon runes and dark enchantments of Morkar's armour had saved him. Striding out of the magma and up the shale shore, Archaon shook the igneous globs of cooling stone from his shield. Within the plate it was as dark, cool and empty of vengeance as Archaon could wish it. Outside, the outlandish metal of the armour steamed and cooled.

Snatching up furs for his shoulders and the ragged cloak that had failed miserably to keep him warm out in the frozen wilderness of the Southern Wastes, Archaon moved with power and purpose across the stepping stones of the raging lake. Like the twin-tailed comet that heralded the Heldenhammer's coming – he would not be stopped. Like the world's wretched end – he would not be stopped. When he reached the wall of rugged, black stone that was the hollow interior of the volcano, Archaon started to climb. He hauled himself up the stone sarcophagi of Morkar's marauders and the razor-sharp jags and ledges. He climbed. Like a rising star of the Ruinous Powers he ascended. The mountain's height was nothing. The weight of his armour was nothing. The dark templar hauled himself up over the lip of the caldera, the lake of lava raging beneath him.

Hubris had put him from his path. It had made him blind to treachery. It had sent the army with which he was going to conquer the world to the bottom of the ocean. But he had come back from calamity. Another treasure of Chaos was his. And another would be also, if he could only find a way into the belly of the daemon-dragon that had swallowed it.

He did not have to wait long.

CHAPTER XVII

'So two titans of darkness met,
In sight of daemonlands undreamt.
One shook the world with titan's deeds,
The other to death was condemn…'

– Necrodomo the Insane, *'The Liber Caelestior'*

The Hinterdark – The Obliviate Plain
The Southern Wastes
Horns Harrowing: Season of Fire

Out of the storm-swirling skies it came. The *Yien-Ya-Long*. Flamefang. Chaos dragon and terror of Grand Cathay. A thing crafted of stolen flesh. A great serpent slithering through the heavens, the beast beat its stretched skin and clawed its way into a banking turn. Mouths screamed in its sides, eyeballs writhed in the sockets set in its warped form – ever on the lookout for soul-prey. Within moments of emerging from the cavernous crater, Archaon knew it had him. It wheeled. It turned. It surged. It cut down through the howling gales and swooped in on the lone figure standing atop the glowering summit of the volcano. In the maelstrom, in the darkness, against the black rock of the mountain, Archaon would have been all but invisible – but to Tzeentch's monster, he was a beacon of soulfire calling the beast down on him.

'Come on,' Archaon grizzled, his boots crunching through the grit. 'Come on you ugly brute.'

And then it was there, a plume of purple flame raging before its mangled jaws. Archaon's instinct was to run, to take cover behind the boulders and crags of the mountaintop. The disgusting sensation of the warpflame's effects still remained with him. Through the searing agony that was his left hand, he fancied he could still feel his missing digits and their rebellion in flesh. The inferno washed across the peak, feeling its way about the rocks and ridges before it found its victim. Archaon stood like a statue, with the purple blaze raging about him. It filled his socket-slits with its blaze of change that danced across the surface of his plate. As the firestream abated, Archaon felt no scorching warmth through the armour. He felt no rebellion of the flesh as spawndom claimed him. Morkar's armour was impervious to the dragon's wrath. Slipping an axe from his belt the Chaos warrior threw the weapon at the passing beast, burying the blade in its morphing flesh.

Again the dragon came at him. And again. Each time its warped jaws were preceded by the fury of its transformative flame but again and again the dark templar emerged from the inferno unscathed and ready with a sword or axe to toss at the beast. Then suddenly the colossal creature was gone. It had vanished into the broiling, black heavens.

'No!' Archaon roared. 'I'm here you aberration. I'm here!'

He glared up at the firmament as it boiled like molten pitch above him. He peered through the swirling maelstrom that howled across the Southern Wastes. He stared at the darkness beyond the infernal glow of the volcano, at the savage hordes of beastfiends and daemons that were tearing each other to pieces in the madness of the storm.

He heard Flamefang before he saw it. He never actually saw it at all. As he turned, the great jaws of the Chaos dragon were already there, beckoning like the entrance of a cave. Archaon was knocked from his feet by the snapping force of the maw as it snatched him from the mountaintop. Then the dragon's mangled mouth clamped shut, trapping the Chaos warrior in a prison of fang and twisted tooth.

Archaon had seen Flamefang claim its victims before. Like a hungry hound it gorged itself, wolfing down its prey, sometimes using the length of its jaws like a trough to scoop screaming crowds of unfortunates into its gullet in eagerness to assimilate their flesh and forms. And with each victim the beast had grown. Not Archaon. The Chaos dragon reserved extra suffering for him. Crunching down on the dark templar, the monster intended to masticate him first. Crush him within its titanic jaw. Skewer him with fang. Shear him to miserable pieces within its mangled maw. The armour of Morkar would not allow such desecration. Ordinarily the victim would be blind to the gnashing horror within the beast's mouth but Lord Tzeentch's beast flooded its mouth with warping flame that lit up its maw and bathed Archaon in a purple blaze. To the dragon, Archaon mused, his armoured form must have felt like chewing on a musket ball.

Then, through the fires of change he saw it. The Imperial cross of the pommel. The modest twinkle of gems set in the crossguard. *Terminus*. The greatsword still sat in its scabbard of morphing flesh, buried in an outbreak of faces that peered down from the roof of the Chaos dragon's mouth like blisters. Archaon reached for the blade, but as he did the mouth was suddenly awash with a burning liquid that exuded from his monstrous surroundings. The stinking deluge preceded a swallowing action, and the telescopic jaws of its inner mouth and the one within that shot forward to snap shut about the Chaos warrior like a toothed cage of smeared flesh and bone. Pressing himself against the inside of the inner maw and reaching between the bars of its stabbing fangs, Archaon stretched. He reached. He snatched at the sword with his armoured fingertips. As he reached it, clamping the pommel between two fingers, the Chaos dragon ingurgitated. Dragging the sword free of its fleshy prison, Archaon held on to the blade as his armoured form was hauled to the back of the dragon's throat where he was swallowed again and began a horrible journey down through the beast's undulating gullet.

Archaon was filled with pure disgust. His plate was awash with the creature's assimilating slime. The stench inside the monster was an overwhelming, oblivion-inviting air the dark templar was forced to breathe. The creature was living horror. Archaon could feel the morphing, muscular movements in the flesh about him, taking him down the beast's snaking throat and into the cavernous lairs of its monstrous body. Spat and slinked through a series of gullet sphincters, Archaon found himself sliding further through a slurping passage in which the mouths of victims set in the walls bit at his armour and hands tore at the difficult to digest plate. The assimilated unfortunates did not succeed and within several horrid moments Archaon slid down into a larger chamber – some kind of pre-stomach or gizzard – and came to a stop in the digestive shallows of a small lake.

Clawing his way back up through the slime and the fleshly shoreline, Archaon turned to take in his surroundings. The walls had a flesh-smeared architecture – a horror all of their own. Within their trembling, ooze-exuding structure were bones, ribs and scraps of armour. It was here, in the prison of its own flesh that it kept its captured treasure. In amongst the gristle and sinew Archaon could see coin, precious stones and Ruinous artefacts. Assimilated victims reached out for him with arms that extended from the walls. Others screamed in perpetual agony, all merged mouths and torment. The pool from which he had hauled himself was alight with isolated tongues of transformative flame. The waters shifted from side to side, splashing up one side of the chamber and then the other as the great dragon banked and flew. The pool itself was drowning in part-assimilated bodies. From there, it seemed, the poor wretches would find themselves part of Flamefang. One with its flesh. Trapped in gibbets of twisted bone. Draped behind the stretching transparency of its skin. Doomed – until finally their horror would be complete as limbs and organs parted ways to serve the Chaos dragon's warped form. Archaon had never known such rancid disgust. He knew only that the colossal beast had to die.

Stomping through moaning shallows, with *Terminus* clamped in the vice-like grip of his gauntlet, Archaon advanced through the beast. Pushing through fleshy slits and serrated valves, Archaon traversed bloody, rippling chambers lined with shredding teeth. He pushed through forests of embedded limbs that clawed for his mercy. He marched through masticating orifices that threatened to smother and absorb him. Everywhere he searched for the sapphire glow of the daemon sorcerer's gem. The prophetic Eye of Sheerian. A Tzeentchian treasure that had blessed the endeavours of Morkar the Uniter and belonged in the setting of his mighty helm. As it had fostered the decimations of the first Everchosen of Chaos, it would do the same for the last. It did not deserve to furnish the fantasies of a senile sorcerer or slosh around the digestive pool of a damned abomination like Flamefang. It was destined for greater service. Without *The Celestine Book of Divination*, Archaon would need the enchanted jewel to show him the path ahead. To show him the Ruinous treasures that once reclaimed would mark him as the herald of Armageddon and Lord of the End Times.

As the Eye beheld Archaon, Archaon beheld the eye. Through the womb-like darkness of the dragon's warped innards, the Chaos warrior saw the slightest suggestion of the gemstone's ethereal glow. Hefting *Terminus*, the dark templar stabbed his way through the writhing flesh of the stomach wall and sawed his way to systems new. As he cut his way to an adjacent set of chambers, Archaon felt the dragon twist and contort about him. He was up to his knees in blood as the beast bled internally. It could feel the agonies its last meal was inflicting on it from within and was forced to land on the black ice of a midnight plain. Even from within, Archaon could hear the war cries of beastfiends attacking in number. He heard daemons leaping from the storm to sink their defiant talons into dragon flesh. They would tear it apart, Archaon knew, but as the stomach walls stiffened and bucked, Archaon knew that Flamefang was visiting the wrath of its transformative flame on the dark monstrosities of the Southern Wastes. Small lakes of assimilate slime erupted in purple flame as the Chaos dragon scorched the hordes about it to spawn.

Archaon stepped back. Swinging *Terminus* about him, Archaon hacked at the tendon and sinew that blocked his progress. It was butcher's work but as mouths in the flesh about him screamed and the Chaos dragon coughed and spluttered its torment, a mad grin spread across Archaon's face.

'Hurt, you abominable thing,' Archaon roared. 'I want you to feel this,' he spat, doused in blood and hacking through the thick flesh. 'I want you to feel it all.'

Tearing his way through its last sinewy resistance, Archaon stepped through into a different chamber. It was tighter. Darker. It even smelled differently. There were riches here. As well as the horror of flesh-smeared unfortunates embedded in the walls of the chamber there was coin, jewels and objects of precious metal. Archaon had entered some kind of inner lair, within the Chaos dragon itself, encrusted with swallowed wealth. The dark templar felt suddenly on edge. Something wasn't right. Moving around the twisting corners of a fleshy canal, Archaon saw it. A bright blue radiance that seemed to call out to him. His armoured boots slapped through the chamber's blood-threaded slime and he quickened his step.

There was a sudden cracking sound. Something the Chaos warrior hadn't heard before. He froze. The glowing gemstone shone. It twinkled. It blinked at the dark templar. Archaon almost had it in his grasp. But he was not alone in the canal chamber. He was being stalked by something from within the Chaos dragon's warped body. Archaon turned his head. He could hear more cracking. Peering through the gloom he saw movement. There were other riches here. The most precious of the lair's treasures. There were eggs set within the fleshy walls of the chamber. The lair was some kind of birthing canal. Archaon had no idea whether the Chaos dragon was male or female, some combination of the two or neither, but deep within its grotesque carcass it was harbouring the next generation of monstrous calamity, ready to inflict on the world.

Archaon's lip formed a snarl. He watched the shell of the egg before him fracture and crack. The internal agonies he had visited upon Flamefang had awoken the infant dragons. The stink of Archaon's fresh flesh and the prospect of a first meal now drew them from their shells. Archaon revolved his armoured wrist, turning *Terminus* around in the grip of his gauntlet.

'All right,' the dark templar announced to the chamber. 'Let's go.'

The dragon exploded from its shell. A sinewy gargoyle of half-formed flesh and fang. Flapping its slime-coated wings and tearing its way from one wall of the birthing canal to the other, the infant monstrosity came at him. Before the beast even leapt for the Chaos warrior, a second was on his back and a third hammered into his shield from the side. Archaon fell through the fleshy curtains of the chamber, his ears full of the metal-scraping cacophony of dragonclaw. The monsters were supernaturally strong. They were ravenous and prised at his infernal armour for the succulent flesh within. They snaggled his armoured limbs and one had the back of his skull-helm in the flesh-stripping fangs of its maw. Archaon rolled and the infant dragons rolled with him – grotesque sculptures crafted of misbegotten flesh. They tumbled and ploughed through the shell of a fourth egg, liberating another beast, the commotion drawing a fifth – some kind of malformed runt – from the sphincter of some side chamber.

Archaon was buried in dragonflesh, the beasts slithering about him like a nest of strangling serpents. With the chamber moving about him with Flamefang's own movements, it was difficult for the Chaos warrior to find his bearings. He felt their plate-wrenching claws, the lengths of their gnashing jaws and the muscular constriction of their bodies test his armour. He had no idea how long it would take the supernatural spawn of the Chaos dragon to find a weakness and exploit it, burrowing into his torso with their twisted, narrow jaws. As their tumble came to a stop at the canal wall, the Chaos warrior found himself on top of one of the monsters. Bucking and landing on his shield with the full weight of his armour and all the force he could muster, Archaon slammed the shield's spike straight through the trapped beast, bursting what passed for its malformed heart. Pressing his advantage, Archaon worked his arm free and smashed the infant dragon that had him clamped in its maw across the snout with his greatsword's crossguard. Drawing *Terminus* back immediately, Archaon sliced the head of the dazed dragon from its warped shoulders.

As the infant dragons died, the faces set in the wall of the birthing canal screeched Flamefang's horror. The beasts' siblings hissed and hackled with reptilian hate. Two retreated momentarily to the walls, the monster that had come straight at him and its sibling runt, leaping from fleshy surface to surface, their savage senses driving them to find a weakness and exploit an opportunity. Archaon tried to get to his feet again but the dragon snaggling the back of his helm, his neck and his furs was anchored to his back. Tripping across an embedded ribcage and the grasping attentions of limbs snatching at his from the chamber floor, *Terminus* tumbled from Archaon's grasp and the Chaos warrior once more fell to the floor. With the birthling snapping and clawing at him, the dark templar took the ragged length of his slime-drenched cloak and wrapped it about the monster. It had him but now he had it. He felt the muscles in his arms burn as he heaved at the cloak-fashioned noose, watching it tighten about the creature's sinewy neck. Its larger sibling hissed at the Chaos warrior and leapt for his back but Archaon gave its surging snout an answer with his armoured elbow, batting the thing aside. With a roar, Archaon returned to the beast before him, heaving and strangling until finally he heard the bones within the monstrosity's neck break and a final breath rattle from its choking maw.

Shaking the impact from its warped skull, the larger sibling came back at Archaon but the Chaos warrior was done with the abomination. As he rolled over to meet it, he hammered the creature in the face with the unrelenting force of one armoured fist, sending it coiling and hissing back at the wall. As he got to his feet, picking up his shield, the runt leapt at Archaon through a leathery curtain of flesh. Smashing the creature aside with the shield, Archaon batted it back, again and again until it lay senseless before him. Holding the edge of the shield above the trembling monstrosity's head, Archaon watched it experience some kind of brain-dazed fit before bringing the shield down on the beast's skull and ending the horror.

Turning, Archaon beheld the final monster before him, holding itself low to the fleshy floor, snaking this way and that. Snatching *Terminus* up from where it had tumbled from his hand and buried its tip in the chamber floor, Archaon came for the creature. The beast retreated, no longer feeling the advantage. No longer on the attack. When he had backed it up to the wall, with nowhere left to go and no option other than to attack, Archaon waited. He waited for the beast to give him everything it had. It did not disappoint. With the savagery of its parent abomination, the dragon sprang forth. With wings held close and neck extended, the monster shot forward with its fang-filled maw. Side-stepping and lifting his shield, Archaon allowed it in under his arm. Grabbing the back of its ferocious skull with one gauntlet he swept *Terminus* down with the other. The gore-smeared blade cleaved the dragon's head from its shoulders, like a woodcutter's axe to a branch.

With the dark metal of his chestplate and pauldrons rising and falling with the exertion of battle, Archaon took a moment before marching on through the birthing canal, towards the searing glow of the Eye of Sheerian. Around the next fleshy corner he found his treasure. The sorcerous jewel was embedded in the chamber wall, the burning inner darkness of its eye inviting Archaon to prise the artefact free. Bathed in its sapphire radiance, Archaon could feel the prophetic power of the artefact. He saw himself dig the gem from the wall of flesh and clean it with his cloak. Before the Chaos warrior knew what was happening, it was done. He saw himself slot the Ruinous treasure into the socket of his helm, feeling the potency of its predictive power close to his mind. And it was so. The Eye of Sheerian flooded him with possibility. He lived in the searing immediacy of the moment but also in the moments of others. As the dark eye of the jewel blinked, Archaon had other sights, other perspectives flash through his mind. With the eyes of so many victims embedded throughout the Chaos dragon's body, the experience was a sickening whirl of disorientation. Like the fear of a fall from tree or cliff, the visions that preceded each blink of the jewel filled Archaon with a heart-sinking rush. He was privy to the darkest recesses of the daemon-dragon's form: the suffering of half-assimilated unfortunates, the rage-tinged sights of slaughter-fuelled beastfiends and the preysight of daemons hunting Flamefang's wounded progress through the bestial hordes of the ice-wept plain. He even saw through the Chaos dragon's own eyes as it snapped up the monstrosities of the Southern Wastes in its mighty jaws and blasted the Dark God's predacious daemonkin to oblivion with terrible streams of its warpflame.

Finally his wandering gaze came to settle on himself. Archaon, dressed in the dark armour of the Everchosen of Chaos, the Ruinous Star of Chaos on his shield and the greatsword *Terminus* in his hand. The Eye of Sheerian blazing back at him from its resting place in the leering skull of his horned helm. Willing the potent jewel closed, the sapphire radiance that lit up the chamber with its ghoulish glow died, returning the birthing canal to a womb-like gloom. Stepping forward, the Chaos warrior saw the eyes through which he had seen himself. A face in the flesh-sculpted wall of the chamber that he recognised. The naked suggestion of limb and curve that he had known. That he had touched and felt for.

'Archaon…'

It stung to hear his name spoken by Giselle. Giselle Dantziger, the Sister of the Imperial Cross. Giselle Dantziger, who had shared his bed, had tried to save his soul, had failed. Archaon moved to her and knelt before her assimilated form. 'Archaon,' she begged. The Chaos warrior laid his gauntlet against the soft skin of her cheek. She begged him to perform the service she had failed to perform for him. She begged him to do what he did best. 'Archaon… kill me.'

Archaon stared at Giselle. The wretched hordes of Chaos, the beastmen, the murderous marauders, the treacherous champions of the Dark Gods. All who had betrayed him, as was their nature. They had deserved no fate better than the monstrous Flamefang had offered. The Swords. Hieronymous Dagobert. Gorst. Giselle. They had just been victims of the calamity Archaon had ordered the daemon sorcerer Sheerian to inflict on the world once more. He shook his head. Feelings, raw and unpleasant exploded in the Chaos warrior's chest. He didn't want to kill Giselle. He didn't want her to live like this either. All he really knew was that he wanted the Chaos dragon dead. Archaon quaked in the Everchosen's damned plate. He wanted to send its monstrous spirit howling back to its twisted master. He brought up *Terminus*. He would kill the beast of Tzeentch. He would kill it from the inside. Archaon plunged the greatsword into the ceiling of the fleshy lair. Tendons contorted and a ripple of agony passed down the length of the canal.

'Yes...' the warrior of Chaos hissed. He pulled the blade free and stabbed it through a nearby wall and into the organs beyond. He went mad, like a frenzied animal, skewering, gutting and stabbing any horrific thing inside the beast that looked important. Blood flooded the chamber and those beyond like a tide washing into a coastal cave. He buried *Terminus* in the assimilated wretches of lair walls and organs, releasing those that had betrayed him from their suffering. He sliced the dragon open, rending gashes in the beast's belly and sides, cutting his way through from the inside out. As the great Flamefang flew, it roared its torment, funnelling flame through the labyrinthine butchery of its insides. The Chaos dragon was attempting to repair itself as fast as Archaon was taking it apart. About him the great caverns of the monster's innards shook, as though the wounded beast had landed.

'No,' Archaon roared above the dragon's furies. He plunged *Terminus* as deep as the blade would go into the creature. Then he forced it further and further, piercing his way through the monster. The greatsword sliced through organs and sinewy flesh. Archaon climbed in after the weapon – almost swimming through the dragon's insides. He squirmed the blade onwards. About him he could hear the thunder of Flamefang's heart and the rhythmic pulse of its beating in the raw horror about him. 'You... have... to...' Archaon snarled as his exertions pushed the blade on. He suddenly felt it hit the tough resistance of muscle. He could feel the dragon's lifeforce quaking through the length of the blade. 'Die...'

Archaon thrust the templar blade ahead of him. He felt it pierce deep into the thunder of muscle. He felt the great organ burst and shred itself in the futility of beating. He felt the Chaos dragon spasm about the failing organ in the serpentine death throes of a legendary beast. The *Yien-Ya-Long* – Flamefang – the terror of Grand Cathay, had been felled by the Chaos warrior. As he waded through the blood and back to Giselle, he felt its flesh quiver horribly about him as the monster began to die. Mouths in the walls and muffled deep within the flesh began to scream. Giselle was out of her mind. Flamefang was dying and as part of the horrific fusion, she too felt the approaching end.

'I'll get you out of here,' he promised her. He meant it. But she was no sorcerer's jewel. She would not be plucked from the dragon's flesh. It was impossible to tell where her flesh began and that of other unfortunates emerged. He brought the gore-dripping *Terminus* up, producing from the girl a miserable sob. The sword dropped. He would kill her just trying to cut her out. The Chaos warrior looked about the chamber, powerless to act. Taking a life was simple. Saving one – one already taken by the Dark Gods for their entertainment and the feasting of souls – altogether impossible. Archaon thought on Father Dagobert, who had saved him more times than he cared to remember. Father Dagobert, who Archaon had been powerless to save. Archaon quaked with frustration. With rage. Then it came to him. A name.

'Sheerian!' Archaon roared, his fury echoing through the cavernous confines of the daemon-dragon. In the silence that followed, Archaon heard a grunt from the other side of the chamber. Cutting a leathery curtain out of his path, the dark templar found the sorcerer embedded in the flesh of the opposite wall. His age-mottled skull protruded from the slime-streaming wall of sinew, as well as the hobbling bird's foot blessing of his master Lord Tzeentch. His withered arms and bone staff were lost to the dragon's flesh and his mouth was covered by a film of stretched skin across his yellowing teeth. The daemon sorcerer watched him with his milky eyes. He couldn't take his gaze from the Eye that sat in Archaon's helm. The prophetic jewel that had been his.

'Sheerian,' Archaon said. 'You snake. You devil. Save me from the dagger in my back, would you? While having me sharpening one of your own.' Archaon gestured about him. 'Only a sorcerer of the Lord Tzeentch would make the instrument of my salvation the very instrument of my destruction. It seems that your thrice-duplicitous lord had a surprise for you also, daemon. Didn't expect to find yourself in the belly of the beast you unleashed, eh?' Archaon rested the blade tip of *Terminus* under the ancient's squirming chin. 'You work for me now, do you understand, daemon? I am Archaon, Everchosen of Chaos and Lord of the End Times. Your soul – like all others – belongs to me.'

Archaon watched the sorcerer blink his milky eyes slowly in acceptance.

'Your treacherous god gave you the incantations to give this monstrosity life and form,' Archaon spat. 'Can you take away what you have given it, sorcerer?' From behind his sinewy mask, Khezula Sheerian – sorcerer of Tzeentch – nodded from his prison of flesh. Drawing the blade tip of *Terminus* through the skin stretched across his mouth, Archaon tore away the obstruction. The sorcerer worked his ancient jaw and licked his cracked lips.

'Archaon…'

The dark templar was in no mood for the daemon sorcerer's cackling lies and entreaties.

'Incantations,' the Chaos warrior ordered. 'Now!'

Sheerian went to work mumbling the enchantments, invocations and bindings that had harnessed the raging soul of the mighty *Yien-Ya-Long* in the flesh of men. As the powerful magic, learned from the lips of Lord Tzeentch himself, began to take hold, Archaon waded back over to Giselle. He sheathed the mighty *Terminus* and shouldered his shield. The dark templar took hold of two fingers of one hand that protruded from the wall of smeared flesh. 'Hold on,' he told his lover. His saviour. 'Just hold on.'

The dying Flamefang instantly knew something was wrong. An agony that could not be felt nor described began to tear at its soul. It was a torment not known by man nor beast. It wasn't like the freezing maelstrom of the Southern Wastes or the scorching embrace of molten rock. It was nothing like the raging of beastfiend hordes or the sinking of daemonclaw into its inconstant flesh. It wasn't even the hot torture of armoured and indomitable souls upon which it had feasted, felt deep within. It was deeper even than that. Tzeentch was calling back its abomination. Archaon heard the Chaos dragon rage against its master. It roared across the icy plains, through the maelstrom and up into the black, boiling skies. The dragon's flesh began to melt. To fall away. To disintegrate. The thousands of unfortunates that made up the great beast's horrific form fell upon the creature, tearing it to pieces. Archaon looked about the chamber. The walls were alive, thrashing in their traumatic fury. Flesh dribbled from the ceiling and down the walls. Limbs emerged. Naked bodies. Howling victims, bereft of sanity. Men, women and beasts that had been through misery and back.

The floor of the birthing chamber began to give way. Archaon held onto Giselle, pulling the girl free of the shredding sinew and to him. As the dragon returned all that it had eaten, all it had consumed, Archaon stood atop a writhing mountain of bodies. There were screams of joy. Of pain. Of minds lost and never to return. Wrapping Giselle in the ragged length of his cloak, Archaon carried the girl in his arms. He stepped down through the bodies, out onto the icy expanse of the bestial swarming plain. As beastfiends set upon the victim mound, sinking their muzzles into fresh flesh, Archaon became aware of a commotion behind him. Turning to face the threat he discovered that throngs of beastmen were being slaughtered. The Chaos warrior saw the flash of bone swords and fountains of black blood erupt from the decapitated and limbless. From the brief butchery, Archaon watched his knights, his Ruinous honour guard, his Swords of Chaos emerge. Bereft of their armour, Eins, Zwei and Drei were a trio of dark angels. They were ashen of flesh, with gargoyle's wings. Limping up behind them was the misshapen Vier. Archaon was glad to see him, despite the horrors the dragon's flame had wrought on his form. Archaon nodded to himself as he came to realise that the bronzed bone that had grown about the heads of the Swords like helms matched his own helmet. Morkar's helmet. The helm of the Everchosen. As he moved on, the winged warriors cut down the few beastfiends drawn to members of Archaon's departing party rather than the feast-mound of defenceless victims before them. In silent subservience and with their wings enclosed about them against the bitter cold of the Southern Wastes, the Swords of Chaos followed their master.

As he passed Sheerian, the sorcerer was recovering his bone staff and rolling the corpse of a butchered beastfiend chieftain out of furs that had been skinned from its tribal foes. As the ancient hobbled with his bird's foot and staff towards Archaon, his cloak of furs trailing through the ice and gore behind him, his milky eyes were downcast. He was no longer the daemon emissary of Lord Tzeentch. No longer the guardian of the Eye and surveyor of a thousand glorious sights. Like Archaon he had been betrayed by his gods. He was now slave-sorcerer to the Everchosen of Chaos, Lord of the End Times. The sorcerer usually had a lot to say for himself. But not today. He gestured to the mountain of tumbling bodies with his bone staff, the living, screaming corpse of the Chaos dragon.

'Master…'

'It will serve, sorcerer,' Archaon said simply and walked on. The warlord would no longer play at politics. Lieutenants were not to be flattered and promoted to positions of trust and authority. Archaon would rather be feared than respected for his powers of leadership. Those that followed the herald of the apocalypse would please him with their service or they would die – it was as simple as that.

As he led the Swords and his slave-sorcerer out into the stormy maelstrom of the Southern Wastes with the girl Giselle in his arms, Archaon found his progress unimpeded. The savage beast-fiends through which he would have had to hack were swarming the bounty the warrior had left behind. He heard the crunch of bone on the wind, the slurp and flesh tearing of muzzles buried in bodies. He heard the screams of men and beasts being eaten alive. Archaon could think of no fate better for the champions of Chaos and marauder tribesmen that had failed him. In the swirling havoc ahead, Archaon sensed the predacious stalking of daemons in the furious darkness. He slowed to a stop.

'Don't,' he warned them, calling into the storm. 'Just don't.'

As Archaon walked on he could not know it, but the daemons of the Southern Wastes were parting. Parting to clear the Chaos warlord's dark path.

EPILOGUE

'Who-e'er thou art these lines now reading,
Think not this world your gaze receding
I wander on, my doom to lead
Through daemontide and deserts drear
With dry eye and heart bereft of bleeding
I commit myself to damnation's deeds
For them alone hath brought us here.'

– Fliessbach, *Tales Untold*

The Obliviate Plain – Skelter Delta
The Southern Wastes
Horns Harrowing: Season of Fire

Archaon lay Giselle down on the warm volcanic rock. The Chaos warrior had made for an infernal glow on the horizon. It was the only light in the benighted place and drew Archaon and his miserable band of followers on like moths to a lonely candle. Skies of broiling pitch and storm-smeared gales of ash and ice closed in on them. The temperature plummeted to a brutal freeze and the depths of darkness hid things that lived fantasies of killing them. The light turned out to be a delta of crackling lava, a creeping channel of molten rock from a distant volcano denied to them by the storm. The river of glowing, red death had bifurcated into a delta on the approach to an abyssal escarpment. The separated lava flows dribbled down the cliff face, into a chasm the depths of which allowed no light to escape.

It was as good a place as any to make their miserable camp, Archaon had decided. With the bottomless chasm at their backs and the channels of slurping magma on all other sides of their position within the delta, they were unlikely to be rushed by the hordes of beastfiends they could hear beyond, in perpetual preoccupation of tribal slaughter. The glow of the molten rock would also show the daemons stalking them through the wilderness before they got too close. Most importantly, the delta had what they needed more than shelter, food or water. Warmth. The Southern Wastes didn't need its daemon denizens to kill them. The murderous drop in temperature alone would see to that.

Posting the silent Swords on the three corners of their wretched triangle of land to ensure nothing tried to leap the lava channels or climb up the abyssal cliff face at their backs, Archaon cut a length of Sheerian's foetid fur cloak and covered Giselle with it. He had the misshapen Vier stand over the girl as a personal sentry. Despite the improvised blanket and the lava-warmed rock upon which she lay, the girl was still shivering. Archaon suspected that it would take time to recover from the dreadful experience of being one with the daemon-dragon. Perhaps she never would. The Swords, the sorcerer Sheerian: they were already part of the infernal insanity that was the raw power of Chaos. The girl had no such expectations or defences. She had been dragged into damnation kicking and screaming. For that the warlord knew he would have to answer. The servants of Dark Gods volunteered for their sufferings. The pig-subjects of Sigmar and the worshippers of weakling gods everywhere had it coming. There were few who were truly innocent and undeserving of their doom but Archaon suspected that Giselle might be such a soul. It was what had compelled him to save her. He was simultaneously drawn to and repelled by her. No doubt, the Chaos warrior decided, this was some other perversity of the Dark Gods. They enjoyed their games and for now Archaon was saddled with his conflicted feelings for the girl. It was about the only other thing he felt beyond seething hatred for the Ruinous Powers he served and the bottomless need he had to bring an end to the world of their enemies.

Archaon joined Khezula Sheerian by the searing radiance of the lava channel, where the ancient was warming his bones. Sheerian leant against his staff and peered into the swirling storm beyond.

'One of yours?' the sorcerer asked, gesturing towards a figure working his way towards them. Archaon's gauntlet strayed for his greatsword but narrowing his eye he recognised the miserable wastrel approaching. With frosted rags and chains pulled about him and his head trapped in a cage, Archaon recognised Gorst. Somehow the flagellant had tracked them from the site of his soul-scarring liberation and followed them through the storm. Archaon grunted. Yet again, the flagellant had followed his master. Even here in the impossible lethality of the Wastes, Gorst had found them. It was like old times with the madman following him across all creation.

'One of mine,' Archaon admitted, indicating to the winged Eins that he should bring Gorst across the scorching channel. There were few to truly call themselves such and Gorst had more than earned it. Archaon had led and Gorst had, continued to follow. To where the warlord did not know.

'Where are we?' Archaon asked the daemon sorcerer.

'A dark realm of nowheres,' Sheerian told him.

'No riddles,' Archaon warned.

'There are no riddles to be had here, master,' the ancient said. 'We are in the Southern Wastes, a place of primordial evil. Where the Dark Gods are free to craft their servants from the storm. Where daemons rule and no men exist to bring sense to the dread pantheon's insanities. We are about as far from salvation as any mortal man has been, my lord. Where are we? All frequented have names but I have no idea what this blasted place is called. I cannot tell you where we have been or where we are – and only the Eye can show you where we are going.'

The sorcerer licked his thin lips. The skeletal fingers about his staff began to shake. He stared up at the jewel set in Archaon's skull-helm in the hope that the warlord might use the potent artefact before him so that the sorcerer might once again experience some suggestion of its power and radiance. The Eye opened. It blazed to life, blinking as Archaon cast his gaze across the horizon – its inner darkness seeing all.

Archaon stared into the Southern Wastes. The glorious, Byzantine brutality of it all. The thunder of beastfiend herds clashing in the darkness. Soul-starved daemons feasting on the wretched existence of such creatures. The abyssal cold. The deep darkness. The raging mountaintops that banished both in their volcanic brilliance. The god-furious approach of some decimating superstorm. Sheerian waited. Archaon said nothing for what seemed like an eternity. The wandering gaze of the Eye moved between the dread perspectives of the Waste's wicked denizens. Then, 'I see an infernal palace, distant and huge,' Archaon told the sorcerer. 'No. Many palaces. All colossal. Ever changing. Indescribable.'

'And, and?' the sorcerer feverishly prompted.

'Beyond them, the dark heart of the entire world,' Archaon told him.

'Yes?'

'Like the fallen sun,' Archaon said, 'as black as it was bright. Impossible. Irresistible. Blazing its darkness but drawing all into the depths of its brilliance.'

'As it draws your gaze, Archaon,' the sorcerer told him, 'and that of the all-powerful Eye.'

'What draws it?' Archaon demanded. 'I must know.'

'You fought your way across the Shadowlands of the north, yes?'

'Yes,' the Chaos warlord confirmed.

'But never the pole,' Sheerian pushed. 'Never the very top of the world. The Realm of Chaos itself.'

'No...'

'Where reality gives way and men may walk the path of the gods,' the sorcerer cackled in excitement.

'Then what is this oblivion into which I stare?' Archaon put to him.

'No man can guess,' Sheerian said. It was not the answer Archaon was looking for.

'But if a man,' Archaon said, 'in fear for his very existence had to guess?'

The daemonic glee on the sorcerer's face died a little.

'Some say the darkness at the top of the world is a gateway through which the dread of destiny pours. A broken gateway, ever open to an unknowable realm beyond. It infects all with its rank possibility.'

'And of this southern darkness?'

'A polar gateway the same, my lord,' Sheerian said. 'Bleeding the unknown into the world we know.'

'And a man who would walk the path of the gods would need to pass through such a gateway,' Archaon said. He was no longer asking.

The daemon sorcerer nodded his agreement. 'And might enter one gateway only to leave through another…'

'Yes, master, yes!' the ancient cackled.

'Yes… Yes…' Archaon heard. The words burned to hear and echoed about the confines of his mortal mind. A voice. From the storm.

'Did you hear that?' Archaon asked.

'Hear what, my lord?' the venerable sorcerer asked, still living their previous glee.

There was something out there with them. Of that Archaon was sure. Unlike the monstrous creatures of the maelstrom, it was a familiar darkness. Something that had been with Archaon his whole life. Always in the shadows. A lord of such burning obscurity. Using the searing power of the Eye, Archaon searched the blackness of the furious oblivion. His gaze settled on a monstrous form, hidden in the approaching tempest. An ancient evil. Dreadful… Potent…

'Do not see meeee…'

Gone.

'It will not be seen,' Archaon said. The ancient stared out into the maelstrom.

'The Eye sees all, master.'

'Well it does not see this,' Archaon rumbled.

'What was it, my lord?'

Archaon struggled for the words.

'Some daemon,' Archaon said. 'Some dark prince of oblivion. A beast eternal that wishes to stay in the shadows – as it always has. It stalks us. It stalks me and the doom that is my fate. What being could do such a thing? Hide itself from the Eye's gaze? Shield itself from a gift of the gods?'

It was the ancient's turn to struggle for words.

'Well…'

'Speak, sorcerer!' Archaon boomed. He drew the blade *Terminus* with sudden savagery. 'You counsel me in such matters of the damned. Without counsel, what use are you to me, daemon?'

Sheerian searched for an answer to please the Chaos lord.

'There is one,' the sorcerer croaked as Archaon's blade came up. 'A beast that led the legions at the dawn of time.'

'Speak on,' Archaon hissed, bringing *Terminus* down.

'He plunged the world into darkness but lit the abyss with his daemon arrogance,' Sheerian told the Chaos warrior. 'For that my master, the dark god Tzeentch – the Great Changer of Ways – punished him.'

'How?' Archaon demanded.

'He cursed the prince of daemons,' the sorcerer said, 'forcing him into infernal subservience, stripping him of absolute power and denying him permanent form.'

Archaon nodded slowly. 'He might escape the Eye's almighty gaze,' Sheerian assured him, 'for if set on his daemon form there would be nothing for the Eye to see.'

Archaon stared at the nearing tempest, as it raged its unfolding darkness through the maelstrom towards them.

'I feel it near.'

'The daemon dooms of men are rarely far away,' Sheerian told him. 'They like to remain close. Observing first hand the havoc they have wrought. This thing has no form, which means he is free to assume any.'

Archaon looked hard at Sheerian and then cast his gaze across to the sleeping Giselle, his Swords of Chaos and finally Gorst, the miserable wretch who had followed him across the face of the world, without doubt and without question.

'This beast hides both in the shadows and plain sight. If this daemon prince is invested in you, my master,' Sheerian said, 'he could be any of us… at any time.'

'Does this thing of the abyss have a name?' Archaon asked.

'He has many names,' the daemon sorcerer told him, seeming not to want to call the daemon by its given name. 'The Harbinger, the Herald, the Bearer. In the frozen north, he is the Shadowlord. In the east and the west, the Dark Master.'

'And to your master?' Archaon snarled.

'To my Lord Tzeentch and the dread pantheon he is… Be'lakor.'

'Be'lakor.'

It was as though Archaon had known the name his whole life. Always on the tongue's tip or just beyond the reaches of recollection. No more. Archaon would drag this monstrous force of darkness into the light. He would know its dealings in his destiny. The daemon prince Be'lakor would answer to the Lord of the End Times or would share in the world's fate. Archaon would extinguish the darklight of this Be'lakor's existence and claim its dark dominion as his own.

For a while, the Chaos lord and the sorcerer said nothing. Sheerian settled into his furs. Even without the Eye, he could see the furious tempest sweeping in.

'There is a storm approaching.'

Archaon thought on all that had come to pass and the doom he had pledged on his very soul to the waiting world.

'I am already here.'

ABOUT THE AUTHOR

Rob Sanders is the author of *The Serpent Beneath,* a novella that appeared in the *New York Times* bestselling Horus Heresy anthology *The Primarchs.* His other Black Library credits include the Warhammer novels *Archaon: Everchosen* and *Archaon: Lord of Chaos,* the Warhammer 40,000 books *Redemption Corps, Atlas Infernal, Legion of the Damned* and various shorter tales for the Horus Heresy. He lives in the small city of Lincoln, UK.

WARHAMMER
ROB SANDERS
ARCHAON
LORD OF CHAOS

An extract from Archaon: Lord of Chaos
by Rob Sanders

Taking the weight of his shield, Archaon drew *Terminus*. The templar blade smouldered in the gloom of the palace. The Sigmarite sword had travelled with its wielder to hell and back. It had sparked blade to blade with daemon swords and been buried in the corruption of the doubly-damned. Its metal and the carved iconography of the God-King had been stained by the slaying of thousands in the name of the Ruinous Powers... and still a little of its nobility remained. In the deep strength of the blade, the trueness of its cleaving edge and the ring of its metal off enemy steel, it still carried some of the calibre of its former calling. Despite this, and in some ways because of it, there was no blade Archaon would rather have between him and a foe. Indeed, to the daemon and the damned, the sword still stank of faith and burned the flesh with its cold virtue.

Leading the way with the faintly glowing blade, Archaon moved through the rib-lined chambers and rachidian passageways of the palace. He was focused. He was ready. Should any daemon servant proceed from the darkness or rush him from the strange architecture, the dark templar would cleave them in two. There was nothing, however. No horrors haunted the palace. No things waited for him in the shadow. The Forsaken Fortress seemed empty. Yet Archaon felt like he was being watched. The darkness that afflicted the lengths of bone-lined corridors was a mirror through which he could not see but could be seen.

You are far from home...

The voice was everywhere. The boom was bottomless, like the abyss, and the words seethed like hellish flame. It was a voice he had known his whole life yet had never heard... until now.

The Chaos warrior moved across a large chamber, looking about him. He slowly turned and swished *Terminus* about him. He peered into the dark recesses of alcoves. He crooked his neck to look back the way he had come, the path now lost to shadow. As he moved through the nightmarish interior of the palace, the murk receded to reveal a large figure in the centre of the chamber. Like the Forsaken Fortress, it was horned, cloven-clawed and broad of wing. To Archaon, it appeared to be a replica of the fortress in miniature.

At first, he took it for the daemon overlord of the palace itself, but as his shuffled steps and defensive turns took him closer, he saw the infernal figure for what it was. A throne. Crafted from the same rough stone as the palace in which it sat. The daemon prince's crouching legs formed the seat, its star-scarred chest the back and its clasped talons the arms. The horned horror that was the daemon's grotesque head formed a kind of crafted crown, while the leathery, outstretched wings, hewn from volcanic rock, gave the throne a hellish grandness. For all its imposing abomination, the throne was empty, like the palace.

'I am where I need to be, daemon,' Archaon answered back finally. His words returned to him with a strange quality, echoing through the torturous skeletal structure of the daemon palace.

That is more true than you can ever know. Though not many who have sought out the Forsaken Fortress have found it.

'I am Archaon,' the Chaos warrior spat, angling his helm about the dark entrances to the chamber. 'I am the chosen of the Dark Gods and the end to the entire world. Nothing is beyond me.'

I am beyond you, chosen one.

'And yet here I stand, *Be'lakor*,'

Archaon spat. 'I have your name, daemon. I have all your names. Shadowlord. Dark Master. Cursed of the Ruinous Gods. You, who have watched me from oblivion, like the craven being you are. I stare back, abyssal thing. I see you now, daemon prince, though there be little or nothing to see. And here I stand, before your cursed throne within your cursed castle.' Archaon waved *Terminus* at the darkness in invitation. The blade smouldered with expectation. 'Time for us both to take a closer look, don't you think? If I'm lucky, like your palace, I might get to see inside.'

As Archaon turned, his weapon ready, his good eye and the dark-sight of his ruined socket everywhere, he set his afflicted gaze once more on the mighty throne. In it sat the insanity that was the daemon Be'lakor, crafted in his own image, within a rocky palace that was the same.

'Daemon,' Archaon told it. 'You have an undue fascination with yourself.'

The beast laughed. It was horrible to hear. Like the deep torment of rock and earth, as the land quakes and continents heave.

And with you...

As the creature spoke, the blue inferno burning within him escaped his ugly maw.

'I'm here to put an end to that, creature,' the dark templar told it, moving slowly and steadily in on the thing in the throne. A great infernal blade of jagged black steel stood upright before the throne, held in place by the loosely clasped talon of the stone arm. The daemon prince's own claw rested on the pommel spike of the weapon.

Oh, you are, are you?

'But first you will give me the satisfaction of all that is unknown to me, but known to you,' the Chaos warrior threatened.

You want secrets...

'I want truths,' he told it. 'And I'll have them, even if I have to cut them out of you, dread thing.'

The living truth that is Archaon, chosen of the Chaos gods.

'Aye.'

Archaon moved in. The daemon prince reared from his throne of stone, dragging his colossal blade with him. The beast's wings spread and he thrust his ferocious daemon head forward, shaking the crown of horns as he spoke.

Well you can't have it, mortal, Be'lakor roared at him, his words searing with hellfire. *You impudent worm – bold of word but feeble of flesh.*

'I thought you might say that,' Archaon returned. As Be'lakor dragged the tip of his infernal blade across the floor of the throne room and turned it upright in his claws, the Chaos warrior did the opposite. Turning *Terminus* about in his gauntlets, he aimed the point of the crusader blade at the floor. 'See, you can't give what you don't have, daemon.'

Archaon stabbed his Sigmarite sword straight down into the floor of the throne room. Instead of turning the blade tip aside like the smooth rock it appeared to be, the material admitted its length with a shower of sparks. The blade steamed with the honour of its past deeds in the name of the God-King. The stone about it began to bubble and churn. Be'lakor let out a roar that descended into a hideous shriek. The palace trembled about Archaon and the daemon. It shuddered. It quaked. The daemon prince clutched his chest and crashed to his knees. The Ruinous Star scarred into his flesh steamed also. The infernal blade tumbled from his grip, falling straight through the floor with a splatter of stone, as though it had been dropped into a lake.

Archaon turned his greatsword in the broiling stone of the wound. Be'lakor screeched. His wings flapped and his spine arched. His knees sank into the floor and his claws trailed stringy stone where he had splashed the morphing material in his infernal agonies.

'Now we're talking,' Archaon told the daemon. 'This is a language that both of us can understand.'

Be'lakor's claws tore at his daemon form. He was becoming one with his surroundings. In the throes of white-hot pain and the purity that still afflicted the crusader sword's steel, he was changing. The palace was also losing its consistency. Liquid rock glooped and streamed from the ceiling while the ribs and bones contorted within the structure. Be'lakor and palace were as one. Except neither were Be'lakor.